dark
deception

BOOK ONE

VAMPIRE ROYALS OF NEW YORK

CHAPTER ONE

Dorian Redthorne stepped out of the limousine onto Central Park West and buttoned his suit jacket, cursing his father from here to hell.

The wretched cunt couldn't have chosen a *less* convenient time to die.

"I'm so sorry, Mr. Redthorne." His driver, who'd remained silent behind the privacy window the entire two-hour trip, shut the car door and lowered his head. "For your... For the loss."

The loss.

Dorian glanced at his watch. Ash clung to his jacket sleeve, a stark smudge against the fine black wool. He stared at it, unblinking, figuring he ought to feel some way about it—the ash, the condolences, the fact that he'd spent the last two days presiding over the interment of a man who'd dominated his life for two and a half centuries.

But when he prodded his heart, he found only an iron gate, eternally locked.

No, the death of his father wasn't a loss.

It was a fucking complication. One Dorian and his brothers had just inherited, along with a sizable estate and a list of adversaries that stretched round the globe, every last one of them doubtlessly celebrating the demise of the Redthorne vampire king.

Among the cursed and the damned, good news always traveled fast.

He erased the ash with his thumb. "Thank you, Jameson. I'll phone you after the auction."

With a curt nod, Jameson returned to his post in the driver's seat, leaving Dorian in the company of thoughts so black they threatened to swallow the setting sun.

It was the city itself that saved him, soothing him with its autumn heartbeat as he walked alongside the park. Two sleek, chocolate-brown horses trotted by, pulling carriages full of gaping tourists, and Dorian gave them wide berth. Unlike humans, horses instinctively distrusted vampires, which was unfortunate. He'd always loved the creatures as a boy, and he missed riding them. Now, their sharp, pungent odor mingled with the sweet smell of honey-roasted peanuts from a nearby cart, reminding him of simpler times.

But as much as the English countryside remained in his blood, New York had been his home for more than two hundred years. And now, with his father gone, the city was his to rule, his to command.

It should've thrilled him. But the feeling burning through his veins wasn't power or freedom.

It was dread.

Crossing Central Park West, he made his way toward the Salvatore, the exclusive apartments where tonight's auction would take place. He'd just reached Seventy-Third when the hairs on his arms lifted, the air around him thickening. He scented it immediately—a putrid mix of sweat, sulfur, and desperation that could only mean one thing.

Sodding fucking demons.

Dorian's hands tightened into fists. A hundred miles north in Annendale-on-Hudson, smoldering in the crypts beneath Ravenswood Manor, the remnants of his father's corpse had just begun to cool. Yet here in the city, the immortal enemies of House Redthorne were already pressing their advantage.

His gut rolled once more at the stench—a final warning before a pair of lesser demons slithered out from a bus idling several paces ahead. Their presence in Manhattan was a direct violation of the Shadow Accords, but the demons were about to commit a crime even more egregious than trespassing.

A human male trailed them like a puppy.

Again, Dorian checked his watch. If he arrived at the auction after the bidding began, they'd refuse him entry. But he couldn't let demons poach a human soul in his father's territory—*his* territory. Not unless he wanted the whole of New York's supernatural underworld staging a coup.

The demons were so drunk on their impending victory they paid Dorian no mind as he followed them down Seventy-Fourth and into a dark, narrow alley wedged between a parking garage and an abandoned construction zone.

"Where are we going?" the human asked his new friends. Poor bastard couldn't have been more than twenty, fresh-faced in his dark purple NYU T-shirt, all too eager for whatever the demons were offering. Dorian pegged his accent as American Midwest. Indiana, perhaps. Briefly, he wondered if there were parents back home. A girlfriend waiting on a goodnight text.

One of the demons—a guy with a face full of metal hoops—grinned. "Down here."

"Will... will it hurt?" the human asked.

Dorian wanted to smack him.

No, selling your soul is a real pleasure. Bloody idiot.

Most humans didn't know about the supernatural races that walked among them, and the few that did either made peace with it and kept their heads down, tried to hunt them to extinction, or convinced themselves they could use a supernatural being's power to short-cut their way to riches and glory.

In Dorian's experience, the latter camp never read the fine print.

"Hurt?" The other demon laughed, his long, white-blond hair floating over his shoulders like a ghost. He tossed an arm around the human as if they were best mates. "Not for a good ten years."

Blondie led the guy deeper into the alley, leaving Metalhead to stand guard near the construction site's dumpster.

Dorian waited for cover from the sound of a passing ambulance, then approached Metalhead with a friendly smile.

"Pardon me, could I trouble you for a—" He slammed his fist into the demon's jaw, then hauled him close, sinking his fangs into his neck before the bastard could conjure his deadly demonic hellfire.

Demon blood slid down his throat, saccharine and terrible, like burned sugar poured over hot rubbish. The rancid taste made Dorian's eyes water, everything in him begging him to retreat, but his hunger made it impossible. Like a living, breathing entity, it took over, stripping Dorian of all humanity, of memory, of understanding. In these brief but bloody seconds, he was nothing but a predator devouring his meal, the demon twitching helplessly in his arms.

The only thing that prevented Dorian from killing him outright—from killing *any* demon—was the threat of possession. Demonic entities could be banished to hell, but only by a skilled witch. If a demon's physical body died, the entity itself would slide into the closest available human host—a fate to which Dorian wouldn't condemn his worst human enemy, let alone an innocent moron in an NYU shirt.

When Dorian sensed the demon's heartbeat slow to an acceptably near-death rhythm, he unlatched from the artery and turned the limp body around, holding it face-out like a shield as he moved down the alley. Tucked away in the shadows, Blondie muttered his ancient incantations, ready to slice the human's hand and finalize the blood deal. The smell of brimstone hung heavy in the air. The ritual was nearly complete.

"I believe you dropped something," Dorian announced, then shoved Metalhead into the surprised arms of his mate. In a blur of speed no demon could match, he rushed forward and slammed them both against the bricks, biting into Blondie's artery and draining him with an efficiency born of centuries of practice.

Thoroughly weakened and teetering on the precipice of death, the demons slid to the ground in a quivering, moaning heap.

The quick pattering of another heartbeat caught Dorian's attention, and he turned to find the human gaping at him, pale and shocked. In the frenzy of the feed, he'd almost forgotten about the little twat.

"Well? Anything to say for yourself?" Dorian wiped the blood from his lips, scowling at the taste.

"I... I needed tuition money, and..." He swallowed hard, fingers trembling as he fished out his wallet and handed it over. "Take it. Just don't hurt me."

If Dorian hadn't just fed, his predatory instincts would've kicked in, and this sniveling man-child would be an easy dinner—much more flavorful than the demons. As it was, he looked about thirty seconds from pissing himself.

"Oh, for fuck's sake." Dorian snatched the wallet, sparing a brief glance at the driver's license inside.

Jonathan Braynard of Tipton, Indiana. He'd just turned eighteen.

Old enough to consent, young enough to give up his best years as a slave of hell.

Dorian retrieved his platinum money clip and stuffed it into the wallet, handing it back to the kid with a deadly glare.

"Return home, Johnny," he said smoothly, the kid's pupils dilating as the vampire compulsion took hold. "Forget this happened. Whatever darkness led you to bargain with demons, that path is closed. You've got a new lease on life." Dorian dismissed him with a wave of his hand. "Run along."

Still shaking, the guy turned and vomited, narrowly missing Dorian's shoes. Then he took off, stumbling into the sunlit street and out of sight.

"You're welcome," Dorian grumbled.

"Dumpster diving, brother?" a voice taunted from behind, achingly familiar, supremely irritating. "What *will* the neighbors think?"

Malcolm.

Dorian cursed under his breath. "How long have you been standing there?"

"Long enough to hear the speech. Nice touch, that bit about a new lease on life."

"I've been working on the pitch." Dorian tried to hold fast to his annoyance, but his heart betrayed him, and a genuine smile spread across his face as he turned to take stock of the man before him—a man he hadn't seen in five decades, who now stood tall and confident, with piercing golden eyes and smooth, tanned skin that made him look even younger than Dorian remembered. "New Orleans favors you, brother."

They'd all come to America together, but unlike Dorian, Malcolm preferred the languid pace of the South to the rapid-fire beat of New York.

Yet news of Father's demise had brought him home, as Dorian knew it would.

Malcolm returned the smile and stepped closer, but the brothers didn't embrace. Too much time had passed; too many old wounds lingered for either to allow such easy affections.

"You needn't have made the trip," Dorian said. "Father's attorneys will ensure the assets are transferred equitably."

"So it's true. He's dead."

It wasn't a question, and the minuscule twitch of an eyelid—an old tell—was all the emotion Malcolm revealed.

"I'd prefer to keep Ravenswood," Dorian continued, sparing them both the trouble of sorting out their feelings. "I'm prepared to buy it outright. But if you've got your heart set on any of Father's artwork or antiques, we can discuss—"

"An alliance."

Dorian raised an eyebrow. *Straight to the point, then.*

"Now that Father's gone," Malcolm continued, "the covens will expect us to consolidate power with one of the other greater vampire families. Have you considered our options?"

Our options?

Dorian nearly laughed. Malcolm hadn't set foot in this city in fifty years. Hadn't spoken with him or their father in just as long. But here he was, picking up the endless game of political maneuvering as if he'd never left Ravenswood.

Rather than dig *that* dead horse out of the ground for another beating, Dorian said simply, "I've got everything under control."

"Yes, I can see that." Malcolm toed the twitching blond body sprawled on the ground between them. "How long until these sods are back on their feet, looking to set your cock on fire?"

"Fifteen minutes, maybe twenty." Dorian scanned the alley again, hoping the human had truly fled. "Though it's not my cock I'm worried about."

Hellfire was one of the few methods guaranteed to kill vampires, and demons were especially fond of burning them alive from the inside out. It was a brutal way to go, no respite from the flames as they consumed every ounce of flesh, blood, and bone inside. Without a witch to perform a banishment, a vampire's only advantage against a demon was speed. Most low-level demons couldn't conjure the fire fast enough to outpace a charging vampire.

But *some* could.

And those odds, however minuscule, were enough to earn demons the title of immortal enemy.

Malcolm crouched down to inspect the bodies, tugging

down their shirt collars to reveal the tell-tale brands on their sternums—marks that bonded all demons to a particular crew.

"Cortelli?" Dorian guessed, trying to recall the names of the lesser demon crime families, most of whom occupied territory in Brooklyn and Queens. "Adamson? Surely Denton's underlings know better than to test a vampire king so soon after a family tragedy."

The unmitigated string of curses that escaped Malcolm's lips sent a bolt of ice to Dorian's gut. None of his guesses had been right. Which left only one option.

The worst one.

They weren't low-level demons looking to make a name for themselves. These pricks swore allegiance to Nikolai Chernikov, the most powerful, most ruthless demon in the city. One whose organization had been growing like a cancer, kept in check only by a mysterious, centuries-old agreement with a vampire who—as of this morning—was no more than a pile of dust and memory.

Augustus Redthorne. Their father.

Malcolm stood, brushing the filth from his hands. "Remind me again how you've got things under control?"

"I spared a human soul from eternal damnation. I got a hot meal out of the arrangement. And no one had to die." Forcing a smile, Dorian kicked Metalhead's boot, unleashing a watery moan. "I'm calling that a win."

"There are other ways, brother." Malcolm reached over to swipe an errant streak of blood from Dorian's cheek. "Legal, consensual ways that don't involve provoking enemies." He licked the blood from his thumb, then grimaced. "Ways that don't taste like utter shite."

Dorian turned away from the unwanted touch as well as the unwanted lecture. "Not for me, there aren't."

It may have taken him a few centuries and more nightmares than he could count to learn the lesson, but now it was as firmly embedded in his psyche as his own name.

He didn't feed on fresh humans for the same reason he didn't fall in love—dalliances with both had made him weak and stupid. Mistakes he *wouldn't* make again. Foul as it was, fresh demon blood offered the same nourishment as its human counterpart without the nasty side effects: arousal, euphoria, complete and utter obsession...

Just thinking about it sent Dorian's mind into a dangerous spin.

He closed his eyes and took a deep breath. Eventually, word would reach Chernikov, and—Shadow Accords violation be damned—this incident would come back to bite Dorian in the ass.

But that was a problem for another night.

Tonight, he had an annoying brother to ditch, a rare painting to acquire, and an equally rare bottle of single malt scotch to crawl into before he jerked himself off to sleep, putting the last twenty-four hours swiftly behind him.

"My apologies," Dorian said, already making his way out of the alley. "I'm nearly late for an appointment. Are you staying at Ravenswood? Perhaps we might catch up another night."

"An alliance makes sense, Dorian," Malcolm said, jogging to keep up.

Stopping at a newsstand, he bought a bottle of sparkling water and a pack of mints, downing them both in quick succession. Neither relieved the sharp tang of demon blood from his senses.

Unsurprising. In Dorian's experience, there was only *one* sure-fire cure for that. But it'd been far too long since he'd had the pleasure of burying his face between a woman's thighs, and he doubted tonight would end any differently.

"With Father gone," Malcolm continued, "and no witch bound to our line—"

"Careful, brother. In this city, even the gargoyles have ears."

In truth, Dorian was less concerned about spies than he was about entertaining his brother's endless quest for power. Dorian was the eldest; these decisions were his to command or ignore as he saw fit.

Malcolm had always struggled to remember it. Which was a fine oversight while he built his empire in the bayou, but *less* fine when he brought his aspirations north.

They walked in tense silence for the last two blocks, then Dorian spotted the blood-red awning marking the entrance to the Salvatore, a massive double-tower, thirty-story apartment building on Central Park West. The auction would take place in the penthouse, with the bidding set to begin in half an hour, and he definitely needed a drink first —a *real* drink. It left precious little time for chit-chat with Malcolm.

Thank the devil's cock for small favors.

He stepped through the opulent glass-front entry, hoping Malcolm would fuck off back to Ravenswood and spare him the headache of further spectacle. But even that was too much to ask, and his younger brother followed him into the lobby, footfalls echoing on the gleaming marble floor.

A doorman inquired about their business, but Dorian sent a wave of compulsion his way, and the man returned to his station, content to let the vampires pass.

"There are but four of us left," Malcolm said, trailing him to the elevator bay. "Four royal vampires standing against an entire city of demons, witches, and lesser blood-suckers who'd sell us to the highest bidder without a second thought."

"Let them try." Dorian hit the button for the penthouse elevator. "The last vampire who crossed—"

Movement at the lobby doors silenced him, and Dorian turned to assess the newcomer.

Everything about the moment changed, the darkness and dread that surrounded him parting like a heavy curtain to reveal the light.

The woman stepped into an alcove at the front of the lobby, her smile bright, her laughter floating to his ears like a symphony.

"...evoking veto power," she was saying into her cell phone. "Those are *terrible* choices." A pause, then she laughed again. "No, I said you can pick any movie as long as it's *not* about vampires." Another pause. "Because I want to watch *normal* people fall in love and mash their faces together! God, you're obsessed!"

Dorian smiled, wondering what she'd say if she knew the vampires of this century's bubble-gum books and movies were *nothing* like the real thing, especially when it came to, quote, mashing their faces together.

"I'll be home as soon as I can ditch this work thing," she said. "Nine o'clock, ten tops."

Not if I have anything to say about it, love...

She put the phone away, and Dorian watched in abject fascination as she removed a mirror from her purse and checked her makeup and hair, brow furrowed as she smoothed back an errant auburn lock. Her movements stirred the air, carrying her scent.

Citrus and vanilla, with a hint of something all her own.

After two and a half centuries walking the earth, Dorian had enjoyed his share of beautiful women. But something about this one captivated him in ways he'd never before experienced and couldn't begin to explain.

"Dorian, we need to discuss—"

He cut his brother off with a raised hand, attention still fixated on the woman. Her sweet summer scent intoxicated him, the soft beat of her heart pulling him into a deep trance.

As she walked across the lobby to the elevators, ignoring the now-docile doorman, their gazes met and locked for a beat... two... three...

Dorian inhaled sharply. Behind her coppery eyes, beneath the sunshine and light, darkness gathered like a storm on the horizon, stirring a terrible, ancient longing inside him.

Mine.

After what felt like an eternity, the woman averted her eyes and headed into the waiting elevator, tapping the button for her floor. But not before granting him the faintest, rose-colored smile and a shiver she tried desperately—unsuccessfully—to suppress.

Dorian's lips curved in response, his mouth watering, predatory instincts flaring as thoughts of the woman's soft skin invaded his consciousness. The taste of demon blood lingered in his throat, but perhaps he'd get to sample some of that sure-fire remedy tonight after all.

His cock stirred at the thought.

He took a step toward her, but a solid grip on his shoulder stopped him in his tracks, and the elevator doors closed, ferrying her away.

Dorian wheeled on his brother, fully intending to hit him with the same right hook he'd given the overly-pierced demon. But the look in Malcolm's eyes stayed his hand, and he lowered it to his side, letting out a deep sigh instead.

"Bloody hell, Mac," he said. "You show up after fifty years... What did you think would happen? We'd pop over to the nearest pub, grab a few pints, and reminisce about the good times?"

Malcolm's face reddened. "I'm here to see to Father's affairs. To ensure our longevity."

"That is not your responsibility."

"Whose, then? Yours?" He practically sneered. "We're

alone, Dorian. Father is dead. Without him, the few allies who remained loyal to House Redthorne will turn, if they haven't already. Our power is waning. How long until we can no longer walk in the daylight? Until we can no longer pass as human? Without a witch or an alliance..." Malcolm shook his head, frustration and disappointment warring in his eyes. "If you see an alternate ending to this fairytale, I'm all ears."

"What I see is a washed-up vampire prince attempting to manipulate his eldest brother with guilt and melodrama. I assure you, I'm moved by neither." The elevator returned, and he stepped inside, hitting the button for the penthouse.

"Dorian. This isn't—"

"Don't wait up," he said, smiling at his brother as the elevator doors began to close.

"Colin and Gabriel," Malcolm blurted out. "They've already arrived at Ravenswood. They're expecting us to return together."

Dorian held his smile despite the fresh pit opening up in his stomach. "Tell *them* not to wait up either."

"Your family needs you, Dorian."

Silence.

It wasn't until the elevator doors closed and the lift began its silent ascent that Dorian dropped his grin.

Reality hit him then, a wrecking ball straight to the chest.

It wasn't the hush of his father's final breaths. It wasn't the scrape of the match against the flint, the blaze of the fire as it consumed the corpse, the fetid stench of it all. It wasn't preparing paperwork for the attorney, or receiving the condolences from his driver, or wiping his father's ashes from the sleeve of his bespoke Italian suit.

It was *this* moment, right now, when Dorian finally understood. *This* moment, when the brother he'd taught to read and write and shoe a horse looked into his eyes with the pain of a thousand regrets and spoke the words that had plagued Dorian's nightmares for centuries.

Your family needs you...

Malcolm. Colin. Gabriel. All that remained of his once expansive family. Bound to him first by blood, second by love, and lastly by the brutal legacy none of them—no matter how far they'd scattered, no matter how many years had passed—could ever outrun.

The king is dead, long live the king.

The vampire royals of New York have returned.

Dorian's chest squeezed tight, forcing out a ragged breath and a single utterance that encapsulated the entirety of his thoughts.

"Well, *fuck*."

CHAPTER TWO

Get in. Get the intel. Get out. And above all, don't get noticed.

Repeating the mantra in her head, Charley D'Amico sipped her Sapphire and tonic, steeling her nerves for tonight's assignment.

Thirteen years on the job, and she'd never broken the rules. Never left a shred of evidence behind. That was her *thing*—no trace. The whole reason *she* handled the public-facing gigs. She was, as her father had declared after her first big win all those years ago, a phantom.

So how the hell did a phantom manage to screw up before she'd even stepped into the elevator?

The man in the lobby had *definitely* noticed her. And in the span of four seconds, the sinfully hot stranger had burrowed so deeply under her skin, he was practically all she could think about. The sensual curve of his lips, the fire in his eyes, the commanding presence that made it impossible to look away...

Hell on hotcakes, *that* kind of distraction was enough to put her life at risk.

As if she needed another reminder, her phone buzzed with a text.

Status?

Charley rolled her eyes, thumbing a quick reply. *Waiting for the right opportunity. More soon.*

Don't wait too long, kiddo, he replied, but there was nothing sweet in his message.

Even through texts, Uncle Rudy's voice chilled her to the core. It was like he was standing on her shoulder, waiting for her to fuck up.

Salivating for it.

No matter how many successful missions she'd accomplished, no matter how much lucrative intel she'd delivered, no matter the fact that her late father had built the entire D'Amico empire, good ol' Uncle Rudy never let her forget who was *really* in charge.

And though she spent the majority of every day rehearsing all the different languages in which she could tell him to go fuck himself, one thought of her nineteen-year-old sister was enough to put her bravado on ice.

Sasha had a real shot at a decent life. She'd just started at Hunter College, and she was already kicking ass, even while holding down a job at a nearby coffee shop. She would *not* be part of this screwed-up, bullshit con game. Not as long as Charley had the ability to keep her out of it. To keep her ignorant and safe. To keep her alive.

Get your head in the game, girl.

With an epic sigh and one more glance toward the elevator—one more pang of disappointment that the stranger from downstairs hadn't magically appeared—she shut down her half-starved libido and snapped into work mode.

Get in. Get the intel. Get out. And above all, don't get noticed... again.

The penthouse at the Salvatore was enormous by New York standards—a prewar stunner with breathtaking views of Central Park and the glittering buildings that surrounded it. The monthly maintenance fees alone were in the five-figure range, but word on the street said the current owners were tapped out, teetering on the edge of bankruptcy. All their valuables would be auctioned off, the apartment sold, the family expatriating to Greece.

Charley hated kicking people when they were down, but in the words of the old family motto they'd probably carve on her tombstone...

"If you're not an asset, you're a liability," she muttered.

Charley already knew the floor plan—she'd memorized the documents Rudy had obtained from the city planning office—but now she scanned the scene, taking in the relevant details:

About forty guests, plus the host. Two people working the bar just past the foyer, two more serving hors d'oeuvres. One security guard making the rounds, beefy but unarmed. Huge, open-plan living area set up with chairs and a small platform for the auction, artwork already on display. Private hallway roped off with theater stanchions, leading to four bedrooms and a study. No visible cameras.

The auction was set to begin soon, but for now, most of the guests mingled at the bar, blathering on about the cutthroat admissions process for Manhattan preschools and exclusive spa vacations for pets.

Reining in an eye-roll, Charley sipped her drink, projecting the cool detachment of the one-percenters surrounding her. Despite her working-class, Jersey-girl roots, it wasn't hard to look the part, especially with her off-the-books expense account keeping her salon-polished and stylish. Tonight, she wore her auburn hair in a loose twist at the base of her neck, light on the makeup, and a strapless midnight blue cocktail dress tied with a simple sash around the waist.

If anyone were questioned about her later, they'd remember only a classy woman in a dark dress, a splash of tasteful yet unremarkable jewelry. Calm and unconcerned, totally in control.

The exact opposite of her reality.

The security guard headed into the living area, leaving the hallway unguarded.

Go-time.

Charley downed the last of her drink, set the glass on the bar, and slipped past the ropes undetected. She'd just ducked into the master suite when her phone buzzed with four rapid-fire texts.

What's happening in there?

I don't like it when you go radio silent.

Charlotte?

?????

The question marks at the end were the worst, the threat behind them evident.

Passive-aggressive asshole.

Her thumb hovered over the screen, a quick reassurance at the ready, but screw it. She was tired of jumping at Rudy's every command, cowering before him as if she was still a little girl.

Busy, she texted.

Charley didn't bother waiting for his reply. She silenced the phone, donned her gloves, and got to work.

With clinical efficiency, she searched the suite's massive oak dressers, vanity, night tables, bookcases, closets, master bathroom drawers, and medicine cabinets, looking for any information that might help. She found a few pieces of jewelry, some antique knickknacks, plenty of prescription drugs, and—*bingo*—a printout of the family's travel itinerary. They'd be apartment-hunting in Greece for two weeks at the end of the month.

The opportunity was there, just as Rudy had hoped.

But the score? That wasn't looking too promising.

The other three bedrooms were sparsely appointed, and Rudy wasn't interested in a handful of jewels and some dusty figurines. Too late, Charley realized their initial intel must've been bad. Tonight wasn't the first auction—it couldn't have been. The massive trove of art and antiquities the crew had traced to this family were long gone, likely auctioned off in pieces over the last several weeks. All that remained was the small, somewhat odd collection in the living area.

A flood of conflicting feelings washed through Charley's heart: relief for the family, that they wouldn't have to endure a robbery. Disgust at herself, at her crew, for doing what they did. And of course, the dread that always preceded having to face Rudy empty-handed—a situation that was quickly becoming her norm.

Rudy wouldn't tolerate it. Not for long.

Tears of frustration pricked her eyes, but Charley blinked them away. There was still one more room to search —the potential goldmine otherwise known as the study. Rich people kept all kinds of important shit in there, like it was some kind of private Fort Knox no thief would ever penetrate.

For her sake, Charley hoped that was the case tonight.

"Saving the best for last," she whispered hopefully, turning to exit the smallest bedroom.

But she couldn't. Towering in the doorway, a huge beast of a man blocked her path.

It wasn't the security guard, but a guest she'd spotted at the bar earlier. Now, he was grinning at Charley like she was a prized piece of art he'd won.

"Oh, hi!" she said brightly, pressing a hand to her chest to keep her heart from bursting out. "I didn't see you."

Tall and imposing, with dark, malicious eyes that matched his expensive charcoal-gray suit, he folded his arms over his chest and grinned. "Lost, little one?"

"No, I... I'm looking for—"

"Yes," the man said, taking a few steps toward her. "*Do* tell me what you're looking for, here in the *private* bedrooms of our hosts."

The icy tone in his voice sent chills down her spine. Beyond the fact that he'd busted her, there was something off about the guy.

The word *unnatural* popped into her head. He was too still, even when he moved. Too calm.

And now he had her cornered.

"Tampons," Charley blurted out, forcing an embarrassed giggle as she reached inside her purse and gripped Beyoncé, her trusty taser. "I was looking for tampons. Don't suppose you've got any?"

The man didn't flinch, and he sure wasn't buying her ditzy female act, either. He took another step forward, forcing her back into the bedroom. The chill in his eyes shifted to solid ice, a look of deadly determination Charley knew all too well.

Shit. She really, really didn't want to tase the guy. Tasing meant causing a scene. It meant people asking questions and calling the cops. It meant getting noticed.

But she wasn't about to let this guy fuck with her, either.

"Back off, asshole," she warned, her Jersey-girl soul breaking through the refined exterior as she pointed Beyoncé at his crotch. "Or I'll send you home with a stutter and a smoking dick."

He grinned and raised his hands in surrender, and for a second Charley thought it was done. But then he lunged for her, knocking her purse and weapon to the ground, crushing her upper arms in a bruising grip.

Without hesitation, she slammed her knee into his exposed crotch.

But he didn't go down. Didn't even grunt. Just kept grinning at her, his teeth long and sharp and…

Are those fangs?

Charley didn't waste time second-guessing. She threw herself forward, the unexpected move buying her a momentary reprieve from his clutches, but then he was right back in her face again, hauling her against the brick wall of his chest as he kicked the door shut behind them.

The door didn't slam, though.

Someone caught it.

"Is everything all right in here?" A smooth, deep-voiced English accent wrapped around her like a hot bath, and when the man it belonged to stepped inside, Charley gasped.

It was him. Her fantasy man from the lobby.

Perfect timing, hot stuff.

He took one look at the scene—giant asshole manhandling her like a rag doll, her belongings scattered on the floor—and his body went rigid.

"Renault Duchanes," he said, his tone so dark, Charley's skin erupted in goosebumps.

But that was all it took. One word, one look, and the asshole released her.

"You two are… acquainted?" The creep—Duchanes—stepped away from Charley like she was radioactive.

Ignoring the question, her man turned to her and held out his arm. "They're almost ready to start the bidding, love. Shall we?"

Love? God, the sweet seduction in his voice made her ache.

She took the offered arm, surprised at how firm his forearm muscle was, thick and taut beneath a soft wool suit jacket.

Duchanes narrowed his eyes, but Charley wouldn't give him the satisfaction of calling them out. Flashing a smug smile, she said to her man, "You were right, honey. These auctions *do* bring out the douchebags."

"I warned you." He winked at her, but when he turned back to the other guy, it felt like someone sucked all the air out of the room.

Tension simmered between them. Clearly, they knew each other. Clearly, they weren't friends. They seemed to be having an entire conversation with nothing more than dirty looks and threatening scowls.

Finally, Duchanes backed off, exiting the room with a grunt of annoyance.

Charley blew out a breath, her heart rate slowing back to normal.

"Are you hurt?" the man asked, crouching down to pick up her things.

"I'll survive. That asshole a friend of yours?"

"He won't bother you again."

"Better fucking not." She reached out to collect her purse and the taser, the slightest brush of his fingertips sending a zing of pleasure up her arm. "Prick was *this* close to getting fifty thousand volts up the ass."

She kept the taser in hand, just in case.

The man chuckled and shook his head, and Charley snapped her mouth shut, stashing the Jersey girl back inside. She was supposed to be a wealthy art collector, and art collectors didn't go around tasing random creeps at auctions or cursing like scrappy bitches in front of polite company.

Shit, shit, shit.

Tonight was *not* going according to plan.

"Thanks for the save," she said, searching for a way to break free of his heated gaze. "I should... check my messages. My boss is... messaging me."

Smooth, Charley. Real smooth.

Cringing, she traded her weapon for the phone, turning it back on vibrate. A dozen notifications flooded in from Rudy, but there was a text from her sister too—no note, just a picture of a huge cucumber strategically positioned between two shriveled avocados.

"Your boss sends you pictures of erotic vegetable art?" the man asked, a hint of playfulness in his tone.

Damn. She hadn't realized he was standing so close.

"That one's from my sister," she said.

His eyes sparkled with mischief and intrigue, a combination that was quickly unraveling her. "Which begs the question... Your *sister* sends you pictures of erotic vegetable art?"

"It's... kind of a thing with us. Last night I sent her one

27

with two bananas with whipped cream on the tips, and…"
Charley caught herself and shook her head, dropping the
phone back into her purse. "Why am I telling you this?"

"Maybe I'm easy to talk to."

You're easy to look at, that's for sure…

He held her gaze another beat, his smile making her
heart sputter, then placed his hand on the small of her back.
"Follow me."

I follow no *man*, Charley thought. The words were poised
on the tip of her tongue, but instead of voicing them, she
inexplicably gave in to the light pressure of his touch,
heading back out into the hallway and wondering why the
hell his presence made her so damn lightheaded.

CHAPTER THREE

The walk from the bedroom was a blur, but when the fog finally cleared from her head, Charley found herself seated at the bar, furiously studying a cocktail napkin while her mystery man ordered drinks.

Shock. That's all it was. And now that the last of it was fading, it was time to escort herself right on out of there. One drink was usually her on-the-clock max, and she wasn't a big fan of accepting gifts from strangers, either—they always wanted something in return.

But she also sensed he wasn't the kind of guy who took no for an answer.

Not a stellar quality in a man, but in certain situations? It drove her wild.

This was one of those situations.

Besides, she was feeling rebellious now. Rudy had her working auctions and charity events nearly every night this month, each one demanding a new identity—private collector, curator, estate lawyer, art student. The whole arrangement was giving her whiplash. And that wasn't even accounting for the rich assholes she ran into on the regular. Granted, they hadn't *all* tried to corner her in a bedroom like Duchanes, but you never knew. Sometimes, words and threats could do just as much damage as hands and teeth.

A shiver rolled through her body as she remembered the ice in that awful man's eyes, the bruising grip of his fingers. She didn't see him among the guests now, but he had to be around somewhere. Charley was good with gut feelings, and right now, she could feel the asshole's eyes on her, crawling over her skin.

As if he could sense her nerves, her man shifted his barstool closer, their arms brushing as he settled in.

His presence calmed her, even as it riled her up inside. As he spoke with the bartender, she stared at his lush mouth, imagining what it would feel like running over her lips, down her neck, down to her—

"You seem to be having quite a think," he mused, turning to look at her full on.

Fucking hell, he was gorgeous. Something about his eyes… Golden-brown, threaded with rich undertones she could've sworn kept changing color. And that mouth…

Charley cleared her throat, blinking away the images of his red-hot kisses. "Maybe I was. Thinking about things, I mean."

He leaned in close, warm breath stirring the fine hairs on her neck. "*Wicked* things, I hope."

Damn him. She held back a shiver. That deep, liquid

voice and sexy accent were enough to drive any woman wild, but his gorgeous honey-brown eyes, tousled black hair, and the confident, masculine way he carried himself sealed the deal. Even sitting down, he projected the kind of energy that could command a room.

Or a bedroom...

Charley's thighs clenched in a weak attempt to staunch her throbbing desire.

"Wicked thoughts," she replied, "are the only ones that make these events bearable."

He laughed, loosening his tie and releasing a button at the top of his white dress shirt. His smile was dazzling—equally rakish and warm, the kind of smile that warned of dangerous, delicious things to come. "So it isn't the pleasant company?"

"Tonight? Not so much."

He didn't respond, just pinned her with his fiery gaze until the arrival of their drinks broke the heated connection.

She had no idea how he'd guessed her favorite drink, but he passed her the Sapphire and tonic, raising his scotch in a toast. "To better company."

"Mine or yours?" she teased.

"That, love, remains to be seen."

They clinked glasses and drank, their eyes locked in an unspoken dare.

Here's a man who can dish it out and take it too. Yum.

A dim warning rang in Charley's head, but she shut it down. She was a professional, God dammit. She didn't need warnings. Her eyes were *firmly* fixed on the prize.

31

Right now, flirting with the hot stranger who'd come to her rescue was just part of the persona. And what harm could it do? It was just a drink and a few laughs. She deserved to indulge in a little fun with a smart, sexy guy.

Rudy would never know about it.

Rudy. The thought of him soured the sweet bite of gin on her tongue, and she let out a soft sigh, knowing she'd have to respond to his messages before he came looking for her.

Owned. That's how she felt. A familiar rage burned beneath her skin, but again, she thought of her sister. Of the life she wanted to build for them both. A legitimate job, a cute little house, maybe an art collection of their own, no strings attached.

It was her "someday" vision, and Charley held onto it like a lifeline.

But the only way to get to *someday* was to go through *now*. So after some harmless flirting, she'd sit in on the auction, make a few fake bids, then slip away to finish the job she'd started in the bedrooms.

"I never did catch your name." The man held out his hand for a proper introduction. "I'm—"

"Don't tell me. You'll ruin my fantasy about a torrid affair with a mysterious stranger."

"Torrid affair?" He cleared his throat, further loosening his tie. "Our relationship is progressing rather urgently."

Charley tapped her temple. "Wicked thoughts, remember?"

"How many of these auctions have you been to?"

"Enough to know how to thoroughly entertain myself."

And enough to know not to give out her name, fake or otherwise. Her carefully chosen identity served two purposes—getting in the door and making fake bids on the art. Nowhere on the list was making new friends.

Even extremely sexy British friends with the kind of body built for pinning her down on the bed and a mouth she'd already imagined melting between her thighs.

"So you're a regular," he said, eyeing her up. "Let's see. A curator, collector, or just another member of the idle rich?"

Charley laughed. "Depends on your definition of collector."

"How so?"

Charley gestured behind them, where the beautiful elite sipped champagne and laughed agreeably at one another's polite conversation. Serious collectors occasionally attended, but private auctions were more often populated by eccentric billionaires who treated rare art acquisition like hunting safaris, and bored socialites looking to one-up the neighbors.

As a girl hanging on her father's arm, Charley had attended these same events, watching in awe as he worked the room. Not much had changed since then.

"Out of the dozens of people here," she said, "how many know anything about the pieces they're bidding on?"

"Perhaps they just know what they want when they see it." He held her gaze, those eyes entrancing her as he inched closer. Heat radiated between them where their thighs touched. "Some things are quite pleasurable in their own right, aren't they."

He wasn't asking her. He was telling her.

A thrill shot through her veins.

Charley looked away, unable to take the intensity building between them. She didn't know if she was imagining it, or if the alcohol had lowered her guard, or if her fantasies were finally overtaking the last bit of logical resistance in her head, but everything about this man—his words, his sultry voice, the way he'd come to her aid in the bedroom—was making her embarrassingly, undeniably wet.

She shifted on the barstool, still not meeting his eyes. "Just because something looks pretty doesn't mean it's art."

"What *is* art, if not beauty? Art stirs our deepest passions, regardless of its origins. Is knowledge of its history a prerequisite to our pleasure?"

"Of course not, but that definition is too broad. Bordain's *Garden of the Divine* is art, but then, so are the flowers that inspired it. Is a building art? A sunset? A child's painting?"

"The curve of a lover's mouth?" he asked.

She sipped her drink, eyes fixed on the glass. "Depends on the lover, doesn't it?"

"Indeed, it does."

Charley finally met his gaze, electricity crackling between them. A lock of her hair slipped from its knot, falling over her cheek, and he reached up to brush it aside.

Despite their flirting, the gesture felt shockingly intimate, sending a hot rush of desire between her thighs.

She'd never had such a strong, visceral reaction to a man before, and the idea left her both terrified and excited.

"We're talking about what makes a serious collector," she continued, forcing herself to stay in character. Besides, this was the easy part. Charley adored art. If she'd been born to a different family, a different life, she might've been a *real* collector, or an art history professor, or any one of the roles she played for Rudy. It was the one bright spot her career afforded—a chance to indulge in her true passion.

Maybe that made her a fraud, but it was the truth.

"Collectors know the history because they care enough to find out." Charley turned to face him fully, her bare knees brushing against his thigh. "How much more pleasurable is a painting when you know what inspired it? When you know what kind of struggles or pain served as the artist's muse?"

"Pain as a muse?" He lifted his eyebrows. "And here I thought you were the rainbows-and-sunshine type."

Charley touched his knee, her manicured fingertips resting lightly against the cool fabric of his suit pants. "Precisely what happens when you judge without knowing what lies beneath."

She kept her hand there, unable—or maybe just unwilling—to remove it. It was a dangerous tease, and one she couldn't indulge in for long.

But damn, it was fun.

"To pain, then." He touched his glass to hers again. "And beauty."

"And the wisdom to know the difference," she added confidently.

He frowned in mock disappointment.

"Too far?" she asked.

"Sorry, love. Now you sound like a motivational speaker. A bad one, at that."

Charley laughed, relishing in his warm gaze, in the way he called her "love." By the time he signaled the bartender for another round, she was feeling so good, so carefree, she almost forgot she was on the clock.

Almost.

CHAPTER FOUR

Dorian had come to the Salvatore to acquire one new possession—the Hans Whitfield painting.

Now, he wanted a second.

Needed it, actually. The siren call of her scent stirred him to a frenzy that muted all else—his father's death, the unfortunate incident in the alley with Chernikov's demons, the convergence of his estranged brothers on his home.

Not to mention Renault *fucking* Duchanes, doubtlessly angling for a way to parlay his father's death into a power grab. The bastard had been trying to break into the Redthorne family for a century; Dorian guessed he'd shown up here tonight hoping for a meeting.

How and why he'd tangled with the woman, Dorian could only guess. But that was over now. Dorian was the new king, and he'd all but claimed her; further harassment from Duchanes could only be treated as an act of aggression, responded to in kind.

That was a war not even a bloodthirsty, power-hungry vamp like Duchanes would bring upon his house.

So for now, Dorian set aside the politics of his father's demise and focused his attention on his fiery, auburn-haired beauty, determined to end the evening on a better note than how it'd begun.

The hosts called for everyone to take a seat in the main room, and Dorian held out his arm. With a soft smile, she reached for him, but then hesitated, a silent war waging in her eyes.

"It's all right, love," he teased. "I don't bite—not until the second date."

Whatever her reservations, they vanished in an instant. She flashed him a look so fierce and wanton, it left no doubt about their common interests.

"In that case, we're counting drinks as our first." She wrapped her hand around his arm and leaned in close. "Let's hope you're a man of your word."

With her firm breasts pressed against him, it was all Dorian could do to keep his cock in check.

If I didn't want that painting so badly, I'd drag her into the nearest coat closet, tie her up, and—

"Come on," she said, leading him into the auction room without another word.

Leading *him*. Dorian Redthorne. Like a damn puppy.

Bloody hell, how had she managed to turn the tables so quickly? In her captivating presence, Dorian was powerless to resist—a state that agitated him greatly. The last time he allowed a woman to get the upper hand, he'd lost complete control, and a hundred and forty-nine people died in the aftermath—a bloodbath Dorian was still paying for and not keen to repeat.

Despite the warning echoes of the past, there was something about her—a physical magnetism he couldn't ignore. She'd intrigued him from the moment she stepped into the lobby downstairs, and every moment he spent in her presence drew him in deeper.

Entranced. It was the only word for it.

Stupid was another one, perhaps, but he pushed that thought aside.

As they settled into adjacent seats, he rested his arm around the back of her chair, inhaling another breath of her intoxicating scent, wondering at her strange contradictions. Despite her passion for art, her intelligence, the way her eyes danced with laughter, the darkness he'd noticed downstairs was still lurking, roiling beneath the surface like a tempest she could barely contain.

What secrets are you harboring, love?

If she felt his intense gaze, she didn't show it. The woman kept her eyes on the artwork at the front of the room, her jaw set, looking determined as hell.

He wondered what piece she was after today. Hopefully not the Whitfield. If Dorian was going to do battle with her, he'd much rather have it unfold in his bedroom.

The very thought of her creamy flesh against his dark silk sheets made his cock stir, and he pulled his jacket closed to hide the evidence, affixing a polite smile to his face as the rest of the guests filed in.

Duchanes strolled in dead last, taking a seat directly in front of them, acknowledging them both with a curt nod.

His woman stiffened, and Dorian moved closer, protective instincts kicking into overdrive. Despite her bravery, the relief in her eyes when he'd barged into that bedroom... It was a look Dorian wouldn't soon forget.

Duchanes wasn't the only vampire in attendance tonight, either. Two women from House Connelly sat a few rows away, and he'd noticed a man from House Pritchard at the bar earlier. He also counted two wolf shifters in the crowd, along with a witch from Darkmoon coven whose services he'd occasionally employed.

The presence of supernaturals at private human auctions wasn't unheard of, but it *was* unusual. Mostly, his kind preferred to avoid the company of humans in large groups—less chance of violence, less chance of discovery. To see this many gathered at the same auction—so soon after his father's death, no less—left him uneasy at best.

At worst? Well, Dorian preferred not to think about that, choosing instead to glare at the back of Duchanes' head, imagining it popping right off his neck and rolling along the floor like a bloody bowling ball.

With everyone finally seated, the auctioneer got down to business, starting with a small but richly colored painting of a Parisian sidewalk scene—*A Moment's Pause*, the last known work of Johan Saccari. Dorian didn't recognize it.

"What do you think it's worth?" he whispered to his companion. "Fifty thousand?"

"Not even close." The woman leaned in, a conspiratorial grin lighting her face. "Can you keep a secret?"

"Of course."

"After Saccari's death, his apprentice sold a dozen of his own paintings under his master's name. When he was finally caught, he admitted that *A Moment's Pause* was Saccari's final painting, and its value skyrocketed. It was stolen from the Louvre in the thirties, returned in the forties, and stolen again in the fifties. After they recovered it the second time, it was sold to a private collector for three million dollars."

"No kidding?" Dorian was impressed by her knowledge. The bidding had already gone up to $80,000, and it was climbing steadily. "Think it'll go for six figures?"

"Probably. But here's the real secret: it's worthless."

"You said it was Saccari's last—"

"This one's a fake. You can tell by the flat texture. Saccari was known for mixing foreign matter into his paints —sand, glass, stones, even hair. The real *Moment's Pause* is hanging over a fireplace in Spain, still with the family who purchased it from the Louvre."

"Sold!" the auctioneer said. "Four hundred thousand dollars from bidder seven."

"Wow," Dorian said. "Poor bastard."

"You know what they say about suckers, right?"

Dorian grinned. "Bet bidder seven wishes he was sitting next to you."

"Bidder seven wouldn't stand a chance with me. *He* probably doesn't bite until the *fourth* date."

Heat flared in her eyes, sending another bolt of desire to his cock. But with a frightening realization, Dorian's blood went cold.

"The Whitfield painting," he said urgently. "Do you know it?"

"Of course. Are you interested?"

"I am if it's really the Whitfield."

"Oh, that one's totally authentic. I was relieved to see it, actually. For years it's been... unaccounted for." Her face clouded, a tiny wrinkle appearing between her eyebrows, her heart rate spiking ever so slightly. It looked as though she had more to say on the matter, but when Dorian pressed, she waved it off.

"Now *that's* an interesting piece," she said instead, drawing his attention to an ancient alabaster bust that just went up for bid. "Also authentic. It's King Darius the First, carved in the late period Egyptian style. Egypt was part of the Achaemenid Empire by then. The piece was probably commissioned by one of the king's local wives."

The auctioneer opened the bidding at $8,000. "Eight, to the gentleman in front. Do I hear eight five?"

"Nine," his woman called out. She was all business now, the playfulness gone from her voice.

A third and fourth bidder entered the game, his woman keeping pace through a volley of bids. The price climbed to $55,000 before she finally dropped out. In the end, it sold for $72,000 to the Darkmoon witch.

Dorian wasn't surprised. Witches often collected antiquities, using them to tap into ancient magic. And at the rates they charged for their services, they could certainly afford the bids.

"I'm sorry, love. I hope you aren't too disappointed."

"Nah. It's a great piece, but not a *stellar* example of late period Egyptian art by any means. Certainly not worth seventy grand."

"Someone disagrees with you."

"What did I tell you about suckers?"

"After all your talk of pretense," Dorian said, nudging her knee with his, "could it be you're an art snob?"

She pressed a hand to her chest, feigning offense.

"It's all right," he whispered. "I'm a bit of an art snob too."

"You don't say?" She fingered the cuff of his suit jacket, stroking the fine Italian wool where not too long ago the evidence of his father's demise glowed white in the setting sun. "Here I thought you were the type to have a trophy room full of dead-animal heads."

"To be fair, the live ones are a bit harder to mount."

Her unabashed laughter attracted more than a few impatient glares, but Dorian couldn't get enough of it. She was even more beautiful when she laughed; her entire body glowed with it.

The curve of her bare shoulder glimmered—a temptation Dorian could no longer resist. With his arm still resting on the back of her chair, he reached out and risked a delicate caress. Her skin rippled with goosebumps, and she sucked in a sharp breath, her heart rate kicking up.

Dorian traced a soft path from her shoulder to her neck,

fingers dancing over the pulse point near her throat. Beneath her satin-smooth skin, warm blood stirred at his touch, calling to that dark, ancient beast inside him, drawing his cock to painfully abrupt attention.

All this, from a mere shoulder and neck. He could only imagine what the rest of her body felt like, what it looked like under that dress, what it tasted like.

He drew his hand back, unleashing a sigh from her lips, a gentle shiver trembling across her shoulders like a wave kissing the shoreline.

Dorian's mouth quirked into a smile. With nothing more than a touch, he'd commanded such a response. It was as if her body had already foreseen its destiny, already resigned itself to a future pinned beneath his hungry, insatiable mouth.

The dizzying scent of her desire washed over him anew.

And in that moment, he knew with utter certainty—despite his vows, despite his responsibilities, despite *everything*—tonight could only end in one of two ways.

He was going to fuck her.

Or he was going to feed on her.

"...Desolate Rains by Hans Whitfield."

The announcement cut into his carnal thoughts, bringing the auction room back into sharp focus. His painting was up for bid—a moment he'd been working on for years. He couldn't turn his back on it now—not even for her.

The woman glanced up at him, her eyes dark with

unfulfilled need. But she quickly blinked it away, forcing a smile and wishing him luck on the bidding.

Clinging to the last vestiges of his control, he returned her smile and whispered a quick retort. "I don't need luck, gorgeous. I've got money."

Sliding the bid card from his suit jacket, he quickly scanned the room, assessing the competition. A handful of people leaned forward in their chairs, but to Dorian it looked more like curiosity than commitment.

He hoped that wasn't the case. He needed the adrenaline rush of a good fight to take his mind off the throbbing ache below his belt.

"We'll start the bidding at ten thousand dollars," the auctioneer said. It was an insulting opener for such a priceless piece, and several bid cards floated lazily into the air. He waited until the bidding reached $50,000 before making his first move.

"Fifty-five," he said calmly. He was prepared to go as high as a million, but from the looks of things, it wouldn't get close to that.

"Sixty," Duchanes said, turning to offer a smug smile.

Irritation burned in his chest, but Dorian nodded politely, holding off on raising the asshole's bid. Another woman went to $70,000, volleying with a few others until it reached $100,000.

Dorian raised it by ten.

"Do we have one twenty?" the auctioneer asked. "One twenty for Hans Whitfield's *Desolate Rains, Series Two*?"

For a moment it seemed no one else had any interest.

Disappointment settled into Dorian's stomach—the painting had to be worth more than a paltry $110,000.

"One ten, going once," the auctioneer said. "Going twice—"

"One fifty," Duchanes said.

Before Dorian could respond, another bidder jumped in at one seventy-five.

The woman.

He glared at her, unable to hide his surprise.

She raised her eyebrows, offering Dorian her best innocent-looking smile, the kind that was clearly anything but. "I couldn't let him get away with that."

Heat raced through Dorian's veins. "You're after my painting, love?"

"I'm after a lot of things. Care to raise the stakes?"

"One seventy-five," the auctioneer said. "Do we have one eighty?"

"Two hundred," Dorian said.

His woman squared her shoulders. "Two fifty."

"Two seventy-five," Dorian said.

"Three."

So she likes to play hardball too.

He grinned, filing away the information for later. "Three fifty."

Duchanes jumped in at $360,000, and then another bidder offered $400,000. Dorian's pulse kicked up with each new bid.

This is more like it.

He leaned forward, eager to keep his head in the game.

His mystery woman might feel differently about what made these events bearable, but Dorian loved this part—the hunt, the strategy, figuring out when to jump in and when to ease up, knowing exactly when to deliver the final blow.

But by the time the bidding reached $600,000, the other bidders bowed out, leaving only Dorian, Duchanes, and his woman.

"Six fifty," she said.

Dorian narrowed his eyes, trying to figure out her game. This wasn't a tag sale. You didn't show up at an exclusive art auction to browse the shelves, pick up a bit of this-and-that for the summer cottage.

What are you playing at, darling?

"Do I hear six seventy-five?" the auctioneer asked.

"Seven," Dorian said.

"Eight," the woman countered.

"Nine."

"Nine fifty," Duchanes said.

Dorian's heart banged in his chest. He didn't know what the woman was after, but Duchanes was clearly antagonizing him.

"One million dollars," Dorian said.

The woman held her bid card against her chest, nibbling her lower lip, contemplating her next move.

Dorian leaned in close, whispering hotly in her ear. "Is that all you've got for me, love?"

Her eyes blazed. She waved her card with renewed vigor. "A million five."

"Two million," Duchanes said, sucking the last of the fun out of the game.

Dorian was already well past his intended max, but he couldn't quit now. Not while Duchanes held the winning bid.

"Three million dollars," he said firmly.

Everyone held a breath as they awaited another volley.

"Three million dollars for the Hans Whitfield," the auctioneer said. "Do I hear three million five? Three four?" She scanned the room, waiting for another bid that never came. "Going once. Going twice. Sold, to bidder twelve for three million dollars."

The room erupted in applause, and Dorian closed his eyes, momentarily lost in the rush of victory such conquests always brought him... and a wave of relief they usually didn't.

By the time he regained his senses and turned to face her again, his mystery woman was gone.

"Ah, but they fly the nest so quickly." Duchanes flashed a smarmy grin Dorian wanted to carve from his face. Then, with a slight bow of his head, "Mr. Redthorne, I'd like to request an audience."

Dorian didn't bother hiding his displeasure, but Duchanes kept right on grinning.

Since he'd issued the request on neutral ground, honor and tradition prevented Dorian from refusing—especially in the presence of other vampires.

But he didn't have to like it.

"What do you *want*, Duchanes?"

"It's not so much what I want, as what I can offer." The twat's eyes darkened with his unchecked lust for power, and Dorian knew before the words even graced his lips what was coming next. "In your time of need, House Duchanes extends the invitation of an alliance."

CHAPTER FIVE

"An alliance. With House Duchanes." Dorian paced before the bar, the thin veneer of his patience finally shattering. His woman was still on the premises—her scent was all around him now, driving him to the very brink of sanity— but rather than hunting her down and devouring every silky, forbidden inch of her body, Dorian was here, listening to a bloodsucking opportunist he'd been swatting away like a gnat since Prohibition.

Duchanes swirled his bourbon, his gold signet ring glittering on a fat finger. "Consider your predicament, Redthorne. Your father's gone. You've no sired heirs in your line. Your family's power is waning. And last I heard," he said, lowering his voice as if he actually gave a damn about decorum, "there isn't a witch in all five boroughs willing to bind herself to the Redthorne royals."

Dorian seethed. He didn't need Renault Duchanes to

articulate his *predicament*; he could feel his very cells dying with each passing heartbeat. Tonight's curbside meal, which should've been enough to sate him for a week, had done little to ease the burn of hunger in his gut. Even in low light, his eyes constantly ached. And every day the sun rose, the fog in his head lingered a bit longer, dulling his senses by degrees.

Such was the nature of creatures of the night—a nature that could only be mitigated by a skilled witch, and only by vampires that could afford one.

Through spells and enchantments that enhanced their powers and muted their limitations, witches allowed vampires to live as humans in all the ways that mattered most, sparing them the agony of an immortal life in a dank cave or tunnel, hunting one another like so many of the wraith-like creatures Dorian had encountered when he'd first been turned. Such creatures could never venture into the light, never taste human food, never love.

In return, a family of witches who bound themselves to a vampire line received protection, housing, more money than they could spend in a lifetime, and unlimited access to one of the most magical ingredients in the known world—vampire blood.

But as much as it burned Dorian's balls to admit it, Duchanes was right. Aside from selling him the occasional one-off spell or hex, there wasn't a witch on the entire eastern seaboard suicidal enough to align herself with House Redthorne.

Dorian couldn't blame them. The last Redthorne witch hadn't survived past her twenty-third birthday.

Memories of his brutal failures wrapped their cold fingers around his heart, but he wouldn't give Duchanes the satisfaction of showing a shred of vulnerability.

"I appreciate your concern," Dorian said evenly. "But we're not seeking an alliance at this time. Now if you'll excuse me, I—"

"But I thought... Well, this is awkward. Malcolm assured me you'd be on board. Did he not speak with you?" He furrowed his brow in confusion, but the smug satisfaction dripping from his tone said it all.

He knew damn well Malcolm hadn't discussed this with Dorian. Knew damn well the revelation would drive another nail into the coffin of the brothers' already fraught relationship.

Next time aim for the heart, Mac. You'll kill me faster that way.

Dorian gripped his drink so tightly, his fingertips turned white. No wonder Malcolm was so keen on pushing an alliance earlier; from the sound of it, he'd all but signed on the dotted line.

"Malcolm has neither the experience nor the authority to make deals for House Redthorne," Dorian said, fighting to keep the bitterness from his tone. Then, with a smile that belied his anger, "But I'll bring your proposition to my family for proper consideration."

And prompt dismissal, you arrogant dick.

Before another calculated response could slip from Duchanes' greasy lips, Dorian set his glass on the bar, turned his back on the bloodsucker, and stalked off in search of the only thing that could salvage an otherwise dreadful night.

CHAPTER SIX

Safely out of view, Charley leaned against the door inside the study, blinking back tears of relief. Adrenaline coursed through her veins, her limbs trembling and hot.

Holy. Shit.

She couldn't believe she'd taken it so far.

A million five? What was she *thinking*? Christ, Rudy would've had her executed if she called for a wire transfer like that. Her bids were primarily for show—all part of blending in, except on the rare occasion when Rudy wanted a piece for his personal collection. Sure, she would've loved to nab the Egyptian piece for Sasha—her sister was as obsessed with ancient art as she was with vampires—but even *that* was a fantasy.

A million dollars, fifty-five thousand… For Charley, it was all the same.

Completely unreachable.

But something had overtaken her tonight, breaking

through all the rules and boundaries that were supposed to keep her safe and on point.

It was that damned *man*. She couldn't keep her head straight around him. Each time she told herself to walk away, something about him lured her right back in again—a dark magnetism she couldn't escape.

From that first sighting in the lobby, he'd ignited something dangerous inside her.

Something that made her want to play with fire.

Fitting, since Rudy would burn me at the stake if he found out about this.

Thankfully, the stranger was a fighter. Charley had to admire his grit. She'd only intended to tease him, to up the stakes in a game he obviously enjoyed—okay, and maybe screw with that Duchanes asshole in the process—but her competitive streak took over, driving her to keep pushing, pushing, pushing.

In the end, the man was on the hook for three million for a piece that was probably worth a third of that on the private market, tonight's auction notwithstanding. He must've *really* wanted it.

Or maybe he just enjoyed sparring with me…

Charley closed her eyes as a shiver gripped her spine, imagining for the hundredth time what that man could do to her with a few hours and a pair of handcuffs…

God, this job was *killing* her sex life. D-O-motherfuck-ing-A.

The sound of the security guard's clunky footsteps in the hallway yanked her thoughts out of the sex morgue and back to the task at hand. Instinctively she dropped to the floor, scooting beneath a massive oak desk just before the door swung open.

From her vantage point, she could only see the man's scuffed black shoes. He stepped into the room, shifting his weight from one foot to the other. Charley held her breath, hoping like hell he couldn't smell her perfume or hear the tell-tale thump of her heart.

In the auction room, another round of applause erupted, and the guard finally retreated, closing the door behind him.

Charley released her breath, the tension and leftover adrenaline making her stiff and achy.

Still under the desk, she pulled on her gloves, then felt along the underside for the mechanism that would unlatch the drawers. After a quick bit of maneuvering, she popped it, releasing the flimsy locks.

Every drawer held more of the same—old receipts, computer manuals, junk mail, random family photos, recipe cards, office supplies. Totally worthless.

Fuck.

It'd been months since her intel had netted anything worthwhile, and after ignoring Rudy's texts all night, she was already setting herself up for a fight. She needed a win, and she needed it now.

Safe. There had to be a safe. Something with documents or bills of sale or keys to offsite storage rooms where the rest of the artwork might be stashed.

She got to her feet and paced the perimeter, scanning the

straight-out-of-a-bourbon-commercial decor and peacock-green walls for anything that might be hiding a safe. Bookcases full of dusty but worthless tomes, a couple of plain oak lamp stands, a small walk-in closet stuffed with winter coats and boots...

Pointless.

Frustration set her blood to simmer. She was about to head back to the bar and drown her sorrows with another Sapphire and tonic before bailing on the whole thing when she caught sight of something that made her heart skip.

There, in the far corner of the room, a piece of art hung over a small fireplace—a painting she knew well.

Adrift by Heinrich von Hausen, a ship tossed about on a black and stormy sea, destined to smash against the rocks, a hopeless and heartbreaking scene but for one ray of sunshine beaming down on the deck.

The last time she'd seen it, it was hanging in the Smithsonian in Washington.

The last time she'd seen it, she was eight years old.

Again, Charley thought of her father. How could she not? Despite his mistakes, despite all the rotten parts of his legacy, his true passion for fine art was like the sunshine in the painting, the one sliver of goodness Charley had always held close. On that trip to D.C., he'd taken her to a dozen museums, teaching her all about the vanitas works of the sixteenth and seventeenth centuries—paintings that reflected the transient nature of life, the futility of earthly pleasures. *Adrift* was a treasure, a stunning example that had hung in the museum for decades.

And now it was here, nailed to the wall in some soon-to-be-foreclosed-upon Upper West Side penthouse. Unobserved, unappreciated, utterly forgotten.

Charley swallowed the knot in her throat. People like this—like this family, like the others here tonight, like all the wealthy clients her father had fenced for—thought nothing of exchanging their millions for the pleasure of possessing something beautiful, something they could hang over the mantel to impress their guests.

But unlike the bidders out there, Charley couldn't feign ignorance about where the art had come from. There was a reason these auctions were held at private penthouses and VIP clubs rather than at Christy's or Sotheby's. A reason why the artifacts—no matter how precious—weren't in a museum, even if they'd started out there. Charley wondered if her mystery man had any idea that his precious Whitfield was pilfered from a Polish museum during the Second World War—first by the Nazis, second by American soldiers.

And after that, by people like Charley's father. People like her.

She thought back to the night of her first score—the night of her nineteenth birthday.

You're a phantom, Charley, her father had said. *They didn't even know you were there.*

It was only a few grand in jewelry from a political fundraiser in Sleepy Hollow, nothing like the multi-million-dollar art scenes she worked today. But it meant something back then; after years of being treated like the cute team mascot by her father's crew, she'd finally impressed them.

At nineteen, it'd made her feel like a superhero, like she'd grow up to be this unstoppable badass in black leather and red lipstick—a woman who could crack a safe, defuse an alarm, and seduce a man into revealing his deepest secrets, all without breaking a sweat.

Now, her father dead five years and counting, it made her feel empty.

Glancing back at the ship in the painting, Charley shook her head. Guilt gnawed her insides. It was a familiar on-the-job companion, but now it was edged with anger, a red-hot blaze seething beneath her skin. The anger swelled, and for a second she considered moving her *someday* to right *now*—taking Sasha and hitting the road, finding a real job, turning her back on Rudy and her past for good.

No trace.

But as she studied the painting, the near-ruined ship, the jagged rocks, the sunshine, Charley knew she wasn't allowed to live by other people's rules. Society's rules. Legal rules. She'd been raised for this, apprenticed by a master thief and his best men. Aside from the mother who'd left when Charley was a kid, she'd grown up wanting for nothing, doted on and groomed by a loving, larger-than-life father who'd promised her the world and tried his best to deliver, right up until the day he died.

By the time Charley was old enough to realize she didn't want her father's world, it was too late. She'd seen too much, gotten her hands too dirty. And now, with the last of her legal inheritance dwindling and Rudy in charge of the crew she'd once thought of as family, she was trapped.

Fuck you, Uncle Rudy.

Turning away from the painting, Charley shoved the guilt and anger back inside, locking them in a box where they belonged.

She took a deep breath, trying to think through her next move. The study was her last shot; the Salvatore penthouse was a total bust.

Which meant she was heading home empty-handed. Again.

One thing was certain. Her next assignment—assuming Rudy didn't relegate her to cleaning his toilets—was going to suck.

With a sigh, she pulled out her phone, tugged off one of her gloves, and sent the dreaded text.

Nada.

It was the only word needed.

The three dots came quickly, and she waited for the undoubtedly furious reply, her stomach in knots, heart slamming against her ribs. But then the dots vanished, and her phone lit up with a call instead, his image filling the screen.

"Are you going to answer that, love?"

"Shit!" Charley dropped her phone and whipped around, trembling at the sight of her mystery man. He stood right in front of her, eyes glittering, mouth stretched into a deadly grin.

She felt like a mouse standing in the shadow of a wolf.

She hadn't heard his footsteps in the hall. Hadn't heard the door. Hadn't heard so much as a single breath.

Yet there he was, right in her fucking space. Lurking. Looming. Intimidating.

Tempting.

"My, my," he said, his voice as smooth as the expensive scotch he drank. "*Someone's* been a bad kitty."

You have no fucking idea...

On the floor, the phone blinked up at her, but Charley ignored it, reaching into her purse instead.

"Don't come any closer." She pointed Beyoncé at his chest. "Or I'll fry your ass with—"

"Fifty thousand volts. I'm aware." Ignoring the threat, he bent down and grabbed her phone from the floor, glancing at the screen. "Shall I tell this... *Rudy*... you're otherwise occupied trying to fry the ass of an innocent man?"

"I wouldn't. Not unless you want a side order of Jimmy Choo to the nuts." Charley lifted her foot to show him the spiked heel, then held out her free hand, gesturing for the phone.

The man obliged, but that damn smirk wasn't going anywhere.

"Twice in one night I find you sneaking around where you shouldn't be. What are the chances?" His gaze trailed down her body, then back up, his eyes narrowing at the sight of her still-gloved hand. "And what in the devil's name are you doing?"

Panic rose in her chest, but she quickly tamped it down. Her little rebellion had made her careless tonight—drinking, flirting, not covering her tracks. She'd gotten herself noticed—*more* than noticed.

But that didn't mean she was exposed. Not yet.

"Not that it's any of *your* business..." Lowering the taser, she peeled the satin glove from her hand and stuffed it into her purse. "I needed some privacy. For the phone call."

"The one you still haven't answered."

"I was *going* to, but then you interrupted."

"By all means." He nodded toward the phone, still blinking in her hand like a bomb about to go off.

Right. Because getting reamed out in front of the hot stranger who'd busted her sneaking into the study at a fancy-ass auction sounded like the *perfect* way to wrap up her night.

She sent the call to voicemail and shoved the phone and Beyoncé back into her purse.

"Does this mean my ass is safe?" he asked.

"For now."

"Perfect." His grin fell, his gaze turning cold and calculating. "Now tell me what you're *really* doing in here."

"I... I needed..." Charley shook her head, thoughts and words crashing together in her brain, her heart hammering.

"No alibi, love?" He took a step closer, his crisp, delicious scent invading her senses. "You'd better think of *something*. Security is right down the hall." He cocked his head as he pretended to listen for the guard's footsteps.

"Getting close, I'll bet. Maybe I should let him know we're—"

"Wait! I can explain."

The man took another step closer. Lowering his voice to a raspy whisper, he said, "I'm on pins and needles."

Charley forced herself to stand strong, but inside, she was quaking like a prom-night virgin. Hundreds of jobs, hundreds of scenes, and she'd *never* been so damn reckless, never come so close to blowing her cover. Yet something about his intensity, his persistence, his very *existence* made her want to push past every boundary, to unlatch every safety mechanism, to risk it all.

What the hell is wrong with me?

"I don't like to be kept waiting," the man said.

Charley wondered how much longer he'd play along—how much longer she could string him along until he finally turned her over to the security guard.

Or worse—the police.

God, she hated herself in this moment, but if she didn't make a move—the only move she had left—this could become a bona fide, five-alarm emergency worse than any punishment Rudy could ever dish out.

She cringed to think what Sasha's feminist theory text-books would say about this scenario—about her whole life, really—but fuck it, survival instinct was a hell of a drug. And right now, Charley was hooked.

Use what you've got, girl.

Hoping she'd read his earlier signals right, Charley placed her hand against his broad, firm chest, letting her fingertips brush the exposed skin beneath his collarbone, grateful he'd left the top button undone.

His breath hitched, pupils dilating a fraction.

They were tiny tells, almost imperceptible behind the facade of his teasing, but all the confirmation she needed.

This man was *totally* turned on.

A seductive smile slid across her face, and she stretched up on her toes, bringing her lips close to his ear. "Can you keep another secret?"

CHAPTER SEVEN

"I'll keep *all* your secrets, love." Dorian covered the woman's delicate fingers, holding her hand firmly against his chest. "Though I strongly caution you against deceiving me."

She gazed up at him through dark, feathery lashes and bit her lower lip, likely buying more time to invent her excuse. The woman was no louse in the fine art of seduction, and she was clearly up to no good. But what *kind* of no good, Dorian could only speculate. Robbery was top of mind, but if that were the case, she had very few options for hiding her treasure; that hot little dress was definitely *not* made for smuggling.

"I have reason to believe the family is on the verge of bankruptcy," she finally said. "I heard they might consider offers for pieces not officially on the block."

Dorian laughed. "Considering what I paid for that painting, it's likely they're back in the black."

"Three million dollars? Doubtful. That's a drop in the bucket for these people."

"*These* people?" He raised an eyebrow, gaze sweeping up from her designer shoes to the tasteful but nevertheless authentic diamonds studding her earlobes. The woman even *smelled* rich—a combination of scents so firmly embedded in his mind it would follow him through eternity.

Who did she think she was fooling?

"I just meant..." She closed her mouth and pulled away from his grasp, doing her best to mask her irritation. When she spoke again, her voice had softened considerably. "It's a terrible situation. They have a lot of debt. The penthouse is in foreclosure. They're actually moving overseas."

Trading gossip about other people's misfortunes was beneath him, but he suspected her theory was true. He'd been gouged on the painting, but they would've settled for a lot less if she and Duchanes hadn't run up the bidding.

"I fail to see what their financial situation has to do with your sneaking around."

"It has everything to do with it," she snapped, her cheeks blushing with frustration and more than a little arousal. "But nothing to do with *you*. So if you don't mind, please show yourself out."

"You expect me to turn my back on a potential crime in progress?"

"I expect you to... Look, I totally appreciate the earlier save. Who knows what that creep would've done if you hadn't ridden in on your white horse? And thanks for the drinks, and the fun conversation, and…" She closed her eyes and blew out a breath, shaking her head as if she were having an argument with her own mind.

Dorian wasn't sure who won, but when she looked at him again, her eyes blazed with fresh anger.

"But seriously," she said. "It doesn't concern you."

"I see." Dorian offered a wry smile. Trouble or not, her feistiness turned him on beyond reason. The attitude, the taser, the spark of disobedience in her eyes…

You need to be tied up and spanked, little prowler.

Blood and power hummed through his veins, the image of his handprint on her bare flesh igniting a different sort of hunger inside.

This long into an immortal life, there were few things Dorian still enjoyed. The company of a beautiful woman was, on occasion, one of them.

But nothing—*nothing*—made him harder than a woman with fire. A woman who could hold her own, even as she begged to be dominated.

Soon enough, he'd have her doing both.

He took a step toward her, the soft thud of her pulse an erotic drumbeat that damn near hypnotized him.

For a moment, her anger faded, and she held his gaze in silence, tension crackling between them, her breath shallow, mouth slightly parted. She bit her bottom lip again, and he stared eagerly, already imagining the sweet taste of her kiss, the dangerous tease of her blood as his fangs grazed the plump flesh…

"The painting," she said suddenly, breaking the trance.

She turned toward the fireplace, gesturing at the art displayed over the mantle. "Heinrich von Hausen's *Adrift*. One of his lesser known works, but still a masterpiece by any measure."

"You'll have to try harder than that," he said. "You've already impressed me with your knowledge of art."

"I'm not trying to impress you. I'm trying to tell you that *this* painting is one of my favorites. My father took me to see it at the Smithsonian when I was a kid. How it ended up here, I can only imagine. But as soon as I saw it, I knew I wanted to ask the owners about it. Maybe arrange for a private bid, or... I don't know. Something."

An echo of sadness lingered in her voice, as raw and authentic as the painting itself, chased by a wave of the same darkness he'd seen earlier, rising anew in her eyes.

If he'd met her a hundred years ago—fifty, even—maybe he would've asked her about it. Offered comfort. Promises. Hell, maybe he'd have marched right back into the auction room, tracked down the host, and bought the damn painting for her on the spot, just to make her smile.

But these days, there was no room in his heart for sentimentality.

Only hunger.

Only desire.

In a flash, he closed the last of the distance between them, forcing her to take a step back, then another. Her shoulders hit the door of a small closet, and she dropped her purse and gasped, looking up at him with a mix of fear and lust, a combination that all but sealed her fate.

"Touching story." He trailed a finger across her exposed collarbone. Not far below, the curve of her breasts peaked out over the top of her dress, full and inviting. It was another of her many contradictions—hot and hard on the inside, soft and elegant on the outside—and Dorian couldn't wait to make her unravel. To expose every last one of her secrets—mind, body, and soul. "Forgive me if I don't quite buy it."

"What... what are you doing?" she whispered, heart fluttering like a hummingbird, the swell of her breasts rising and falling with every frightened breath.

But the scent of her desire didn't lie.

Dorian reached up and cupped her face, dragging his thumb across those plump lips, already imagining what they'd feel like wrapped around his cock. What she'd look like on her knees, wrists bound behind her back, *begging* him for it.

But when it came to pleasure, he was a master of... Well, some might call it patience. He preferred a more accurate descriptor.

Restraint.

It was an exquisite torture, the administration of which brought him as much pleasure as the ultimate surrender.

As badly as he wanted to fuck her hot mouth, to unleash every bit of pent-up yearning her presence had stirred to life inside him, he was even more desperate to taste her. To drive her to the knife's edge between pleasure and pain, and watch her fall over the precipice, her body submitting to his every command.

He lowered his hand again, fingers skimming the top edge of her dress, the heat of her skin weakening his resolve.

A soft moan escaped her lips, despite her best efforts to contain it. Her eyelids fluttered closed.

"Ah, there's nothing quite like a bad girl in a beautiful dress," he murmured, and she arched her back, bringing her breast to his palm. Beneath his touch, her taut nipple rose against the fabric. "I suppose you think that's enough to make me fall at your feet, lapping up your lies like a starved kitten at the milk bowl."

"I didn't... I was trying to... I'm..." She tripped over her words, her breathing turning more erratic with every gentle stroke. "It's not a lie. I—"

"Shh." Dorian ran his hand down to her rib cage, thumb teasing her nipple, his other hand sliding into the hair gathered at the base of her neck. The silky knot came loose from its binds, long auburn locks tumbling over her shoulders and unleashing more of the citrus-and-vanilla scent that made his head spin.

"If I were a decent man," he said, "I'd haul you out to security and pat myself on the back for saving the poor bastard who owns this place from whatever schemes you're undoubtedly planning."

Dorian released her neck, and she opened her eyes, irises nearly swallowed by the dark pupils.

He pressed a finger to her lips to silence another excuse. The soft heat of her breath ghosted across his fingertip, the promise of her wet mouth making his cock throb.

"But since I'm *not* a decent man," he said, "I'm going to make you an offer instead. Two choices. Think very, very carefully about your response—I'm only going to ask once. Understand?"

She nodded, blood pulsing visibly beneath the pale skin of her throat, every heartbeat a seductive whisper, a promise, a warning.

Don't do this, Redthorne. You know what happens...

Ignoring the voice of reason, he gazed into her beautiful, devious eyes, his cock so hard it fucking *ached*.

"Option one," he said. "You walk out that door right now, take the elevator to the ground floor, and disappear. Don't return to this building. Don't return to this neighborhood. Forget we ever crossed paths."

"What's... what's option two?"

"Option two." Dorian lowered his mouth to hers, so close he could taste the gin on her tongue, and fisted her dress, hiking it up to reveal her bare, toned thighs. He slid a hand between them, wet heat radiating through the thin black lace of her panties. With the softest brush of his lips against hers, he whispered, "I'm tearing off this *pathetic* scrap of lace, dropping to my knees, and fucking you with my mouth until I'm absolutely *convinced* you'll never look at another painting again without recalling the time a stranger cornered you in the study at the Salvatore penthouse and forced you to come for him, again... and again... and again."

She drew a sharp breath, and he increased the pressure between her thighs, dragging his knuckles back and forth.

"So what's it going to be, little prowler? Will you go, or will you..." He arched his hand up, pushing hard against the damp fabric. "...come?"

"*Fuck.*" The whisper fell against his lips, her hips rocking as Dorian restarted the slow, teasing strokes.

"What's that, gorgeous? I didn't quite catch your answer."

"Fuck off," she said, feisty until the very end. Then, with new heat blazing in her eyes, "God, I want option two. Fucking give me option two."

"Good answer, love. Because here's *my* secret." He hooked his fingers into the panties, and with a swift jerk of his wrist, tore them from her body like tissue paper. "You never really had a choice."

CHAPTER EIGHT

Charley didn't give a flying fuck *what* he said about choices.

For her, there was only one way this ended. It was hot, dirty as hell, and screw it—she was *more* than okay with it. She was a hot-blooded, consenting adult who'd gone without the touch of a man for far too long, and she *wanted* this. No, she *deserved* this—a quick indulgence to fuel her imagination for all the lonely nights to come.

"Trust me." She flashed him a sexy smile. "There's nowhere I'd rather be than right here, fucking a hot stranger in the study."

"Ah, but you won't *be* fucking a hot stranger." The man stuffed her ruined underwear into his pocket, then flashed his wolf's grin, ready to devour her. "The stranger will be fucking *you*."

He spun her around and lifted her dress again, fisting the fabric in one hand while his other slipped between her thighs from behind. She leaned against the closet door for leverage as his strong, demanding fingers drove into her aching pussy, stroking her with a masterful touch that threatened to send her over the edge in thirty seconds flat.

"It seems I've put you in quite a state," he rasped, breath hot in her ear. Then, leaning in close, he dragged his hand out and lifted it to his mouth. With a soft, reverent moan he slid his fingers into his mouth, sucking on the evidence of her desire, his eyes dark and foreboding. "My, but you're exquisite."

Holy fuck, this guy is off the rails...

And God, he knew *exactly* how to tease her, how to whisper all the forbidden things that left her wet and throbbing. His deep voice, the accent, his commanding touch... Charley's skin was covered in goosebumps, her legs already trembling, and she had the distinct impression he was just getting started.

"But as lovely and delicious as you may be," he said. "I *don't* trust you. You're a bad girl, sneaking past the ropes, touching things that don't belong to you. Running off after bidding on my painting."

She felt a tug at her waist as he freed the satin sash and unzipped the dress, letting it fall to the floor.

A shiver worked through her body, but Charley wasn't cold. She was on fire, her skin blazing, her body wound tight as she stood before him, naked but for her strapless black bra, more aroused than she'd ever been in her entire life.

"Give me your hands. Now." His voice was firm and

severe, taking on an authoritative tone that made her nipples ache.

He was still holding the sash from her dress, and Charley knew in an instant what he planned to do with it.

Just as she knew what it would mean to obey him.

It was one thing to consent to the demands of his sexy power games. It was another to allow him to strip her nearly bare in a stranger's penthouse.

She'd agreed to both, without hesitation.

But tying her up? That was something else entirely. A whole new level of risk.

Don't be stupid. The minute you give him what he wants, he'll blow your cover, expose you to the guard, and leave you to the damn wolves.

That was her brain's warning, and it sounded totally reasonable.

But her instincts said otherwise, and they'd never misled her. After years of putting herself in harm's way on the job, Charley had learned to listen to her body before listening to her head, and right now, with this man's hot mouth a tantalizing tease behind her ear, his filthy promises melting her from the inside out, Charley's body was *screaming* for his touch.

Butterflies flooded her insides. She'd never been so bold, so daring with a man before.

Her lifestyle didn't exactly lend itself to long-term relationships with decent men, and her ex—a documents forger Rudy sometimes contracted—had tried his damnedest to make her feel selfish for acting on her desires. For even *having* desires in the first place.

But tonight, stripped down by her enigmatic stranger in the study of the penthouse her crew was planning to rob, her nipples aching, core dripping with desire, Charley felt her deepest yearnings blooming inside, desperate to be unleashed, aching to be tamed.

By him.

Yeah, he was a total stranger. But *no* man had ever made her feel so powerful, so wanted before. However far he planned to take this game tonight, Charley was willing to follow him.

All the fucking way.

Closing her eyes, she crossed her arms behind her.

He bound her wrists, pulling the sash so tight her hands ached.

Hell yes.

She was so wet for this guy, so ready to submit to him. When he'd first surprised her in the study, her mind was on one thing—saving her cover. She'd flirted with him to distract him, to buy herself a few extra minutes until she could figure things out. But the moment he backed her against the closet door and dished out his ultimatum, everything changed.

And she knew, despite his obvious need for control, that she'd had a similar effect on him. Her every word, every movement seemed to unlock something primal in the man —a raw, dominant power that had lain dormant beneath the surface, waiting to be unleashed by the right woman.

The heat between them was off the charts. Suddenly distraction wasn't enough—Charley needed him to take her. To totally fucking possess her.

A moan escaped her lips, unbidden as he tugged harder on her restraints. Everything about this man was turning into a thrill ride, a dark fantasy in which she couldn't wait to lose herself.

"Fucking gorgeous." He ran his hands down her arms, her hips, the curve of her ass, setting her nerves ablaze. After taking his sweet time admiring the view from behind, he finally grabbed her shoulders and turned her around, his gaze trailing a searing-hot path from head to toe, then back up again.

Her heart beat in wild anticipation as he ran his thumb along her lower lip, staring at her mouth as if he wanted to bite her. The wait was pure torture, but she'd be lying if she said she didn't love it.

He glanced up into her eyes one last time, his gaze a feral warning. Then, with no more than a wicked quirk of his lips, he descended, kissing her hungrily, nipping and sucking before delving in deeper, his breath hot in her mouth, the faint tang of scotch lingering on his tongue.

She moaned in pleasure, imagining the ecstasy his deft, eager tongue could unleash on the rest of her body.

"Shh," he whispered, pulling back to admonish her. "We don't want our friend from security coming to investigate."

They both listened intently as the tell-tale footsteps clomped down the hall. For a moment Charley tensed, but the thought of getting caught in such a severely compromised state sent a new thrill coursing through her veins.

"Maybe he'd like the show," she teased.

The man slid his hands behind her, grabbing her ass and pulling her close. Charley's knees weakened at the press of his rock-hard cock against her belly, thrilled that she'd driven him to the same state of desire as he'd driven her.

Reaching past her, he pulled open the closet door and slowly backed her inside, then shut the door behind them, enveloping them in darkness. The air was warm and thick, heavy with the delicious, clean scent of his skin and the leather from the coats hanging beside them. Charley had never been blindfolded, but she imagined it felt a lot like being in the dark closet, all her other senses on high alert.

He still hadn't released her from his touch, and now he kissed her again, blazing a red-hot path along her jaw to her ear. In a possessive tone that flooded her core with molten heat, he said, "If you think for one minute I'd share you with another man, love, you're *sorely* mistaken."

And then, finally making good on his threat, her insane, commanding, rock-hard stranger dropped to his knees.

CHAPTER NINE

Dorian didn't know how much time they had before someone discovered them, but for now, tucked away in a forgotten closet, she *belonged* to him—a beautiful, auburn-haired package gift-wrapped in secrets and satin.

His.

It was that simple.

Kneeling before her, Dorian pressed his face to the apex of her thighs. Her scent invaded every part of him, threatening to eradicate the very last of his control. He felt the familiar burn of fangs descending, but he knew that if he gave in now—if he tasted even one drop of her blood—he wouldn't be able to stop.

And he couldn't hurt her. *Wouldn't*, no matter how desperately her blood called to him.

Turning his face, he pressed his stubbled cheek to the bare, silky-soft skin between her legs, forcing the dark hunger inside him to settle. Certain his fangs had finally receded, he turned his attention back to his gift, glad he'd ruined those sexy black panties. Now, there was nothing standing in the way of devouring her hot, needy flesh.

But first, he'd make her writhe—a delicious punishment for the state she'd left him in.

His tongue darted out from between his lips, stealing an all-too-brief taste. As if she could escape his teasing, she backed up against the closet's inner wall, knocking a few coats and hangers to the ground.

"Be still, little prowler," he warned, pressing his lips to the hollow below her hipbone. "Or I'll have to spank you."

She let out a soft moan, but did as he asked, holding absolutely still as he traced a light path along her inner thigh with his tongue. The taste of her skin was even more addicting than he'd imagined—soft and creamy and entirely too decadent for mere mortals to enjoy.

Gripping her thighs, he drew one long, toned leg over his shoulder and blew a soft breath across her clit. She trembled in his hands, her flesh erupting in goosebumps.

It was a powerful feeling—one he'd be fantasizing about for years to come.

She was so wet, so ready for him, so earnestly desperate for more, his resolve soon crumbled. As much as he'd wanted to teach her the fine art of restraint, he couldn't deny her for another moment.

Couldn't deny *himself*.

On a deep inhale, he buried his face between her thighs, licking and sucking, exploring every red-hot inch with his tongue. It wasn't long before the taste of his earlier meal was forgotten, along with all the things conspiring to ruin him tonight. Right now, there was only his mouth upon her flesh, the breathy sounds escaping her lips, the ripple of pleasure pulsing beneath her skin as he slaked another hunger.

Even with her back against the wall, the woman was growing weaker, her body slipping into a state of pure ecstasy as the inevitable climax simmered. Dorian felt the quickening of her heartbeat, the hot rush of blood in her veins.

He sucked her clit between his lips, gently grazing it with his teeth.

"Right there," she whispered frantically. "God, that's so... *yes*!"

He pulled back, blowing another soft breath between her thighs. She squirmed and struggled with the sash around her wrists, but here in the forbidden closet, hands bound, one leg draped over his shoulder, there was nothing for her to do but submit, relinquishing control of her pleasure to a man who could—in less time than it took her heart to pump another course of blood through her body—sink his fangs into her femoral artery and suck her dry.

"Don't tease me," she begged, the sweet seduction of her voice bringing him back from that dangerous edge. "I'm so close."

"Your mouth says one thing, but..." Dorian slipped his fingers inside her with a long, deep stroke. "I think you like being teased, don't you?"

"*Yes*," she breathed.

"But if you want me to stop..." He pulled his fingers out, hovering near her entrance.

"Don't stop. Please don't stop. You're making me fucking crazy, but I love it."

"Good girl." He plunged into her again, stroking her with his fingers while he licked the hot, swollen nub of her clit, pulling back each time she got too close to ecstasy.

When he finally sensed she couldn't endure another moment of his torture, he stopped his teasing and kissed her madly, fucking her with his mouth, harder, faster, deeper as he pushed her to the very edge.

And then, right over it.

"Fucking *hell!*" she breathed, her voice a desperate whisper, making Dorian regret not telling her his name. What he wouldn't give to hear it now, rushing out with her last, gasping breaths as her hips bucked wildly against his face, her whole body humming with euphoria.

Dorian had given her the ultimatum in hopes of maintaining the tenuous hold on his control, but now he was absolutely drunk on the woman, quickly falling under whatever spell she'd intended on casting when he caught her in the study. Maybe all she wanted was his wallet, his passport, the keys to Ravenswood—hell, maybe she was a hunter, stake at the ready, but Dorian didn't care. Right now, all that mattered was the taste. The feel. The promise of what came next.

The clock was ticking on their last secluded moments—Dorian knew they didn't have much time. But he wasn't ready to let her go. How could he say goodbye without knowing how it felt to be inside her, to drive her over the edge again as he fell right along with her? He'd gotten his taste, but now his cock was more than ready, desperate to ruin her for anyone else.

She was still buzzing from the orgasm when he rose from the floor, kissing his way from her thighs to her hips, her belly, her breasts. Through the lace of her bra, he scraped his teeth against her nipple, and then bit gently, unleashing another moan of pleasure.

"Untie me," she said. "Please. I need to touch you."

He unbound her wrists, and she pressed a hand to the front of his suit pants, palming his cock. Dorian's breath caught, his own heart banging as wildly as hers. As she fumbled with his belt buckle, he reached behind her and unhooked her bra, freeing her firm, perfect breasts and sucking a nipple into his mouth. Her skin was so smooth and soft, like warm velvet beneath his stubbled jaw, and *bloody hell* he needed to be inside her—right fucking now.

"I should probably warn you." He slid his hand between her thighs, stroking her slick heat. "I'm going to fuck you now."

"Then I should probably warn *you*." The woman reached inside his boxers and gripped him hard, then leaned in close, her words a hot rush in his ear. "I like it rough. Don't you *dare* disappoint me."

Dorian sputtered out a laugh. Who *was* this woman? Every time he thought he'd regained the upper hand, she swept in with another feisty remark, another touch, another dare that knocked him off-balance and made it more unlikely that he'd let her go.

He was about to assure her he'd be glad to accommodate, when a noise beyond the closet door cut him off, and suddenly the world went stark white, their dark hideaway flooded with harsh, accusatory light.

"You gotta be *kidding* me." The security guard stood in the doorway, one hand on the doorknob, the other on his cell. Shooting them a look that could cut glass, he spoke brusquely into the phone. "False alarm, sir. We're good."

Dorian shifted to block his woman's nakedness from view.

"You wanna tell me what the hell you're doin' in here?" The guard spoke with a thick Brooklyn-Italian accent, and Dorian couldn't decipher whether he was angry, shocked, or seriously entertained—maybe a bit of all three. "You didn't see them big-ass ropes? This room is off-limits."

"My apologies," Dorian said, hoping he wouldn't have to compel the man in front of his guest. "If you'll allow me to explain—"

"Pretty sure I don't need a diagram, sir."

"We were just working through some differences," the woman said, peeking her head out from behind Dorian's shoulder. "About the Whitfield painting? I don't know if you saw the big showdown, but things got pretty heated."

He barked out a laugh. "Lady, I've seen some freaky shit at this job, but you two are a real piece."

"I suppose we got a bit carried away," Dorian said. "My

wife can be quite…" He inhaled deeply, taking in her heady scent as he sought the right word. "…*insatiable.*"

"I don't care if she's dying and the only thing that can save her is regular injections of your gold-plated dick." He bent down to pick up the woman's purse and the dress Dorian had unceremoniously dropped outside the door, then handed them over. "You can't come past the ropes, *capisce?*"

"Of course." Dorian bit back a grin at the image of his so-called gold-plated dick. "From now on, I'll make sure she knows *exactly* where she can come."

Behind him, the woman snickered softly, but the guard was less than amused.

"Get dressed and hang up those coats. Now." He slammed the door shut, giving them a few final moments of privacy.

Bathed again in darkness, Dorian and his woman could only laugh.

"I *knew* you'd get me into trouble," he whispered, holding out an arm to steady her as she stepped into the dress.

"Me? You're the one who dragged me into the closet and—"

"And *what?*" He zipped her up and pulled her close again, his hand dipping up under the dress, right between her thighs.

It was his new favorite place, and he wasn't quite ready to leave it.

"And touched me," she whispered.

"Did I?" He ran a feather-light finger along her clit, then slipped inside. She was still so wet for him, so eager. "If this was *my* penthouse, I'd have you tied up and spread out on my bed by now. No interruptions. No company." He ran his nose along the elegant slope of her neck, nipping her shoulder. "No escape."

The woman gasped, her legs quaking again as he pumped her with slow, deliberate thrusts. The guard was certainly standing right outside the door, but Dorian suspected his woman didn't care, and for the moment, neither did he.

"We've got fifteen seconds, maybe thirty before he opens that door again," he whispered. "Can you come for me that quickly?"

He thrust in deeper, thumb rubbing her clit. She opened her mouth to moan, to scream, to let it all out, but he silenced her with a kiss, stealing her breath as he coaxed a final, epic wave from her beautiful body, holding her through the very last tremor.

When they finally opened the closet door, they were the very picture of composure.

"Christ, mister." The guard eyed them warily as they stepped into the study. "You drop three *large* on a painting of wet fuckin' grass, and you can't afford to take your wife somewhere nice?"

"Maybe for our next date." Dorian slipped his arm around the woman's waist, guiding her out of the study and into the hallway.

The guard followed. "A hotel? There's lots of 'em in this city. Real fancy ones too."

"Good call," he said.

"Maybe a cruise? Ladies love that shit."

"Thank you for your input."

"Anytime," the guard said. They'd reached the foyer, and he punched the button to call up the elevator, then turned to them with a threatening smile. "Now get the fuck outta here. And have a lovely evening."

CHAPTER TEN

Reeling. That was the only word for it.

Charley's head was as hot and floaty as a helium balloon, the rest of her body still vibrating from all the things he'd done to her with that sexy, filthy mouth.

Good *lord*, that man had a gift.

She was weak, she was wet, but even as the elevator doors closed, cutting them off from the guard's punishing glare, Charley couldn't stop laughing.

"Did that just happen?" she asked. "Did we seriously get kicked out of a private auction like a couple of kids caught stealing booze?"

"Fughettaboutit, lady. This ain't a hotel." Her man scowled, doing a terrible job impersonating the security guard's Brooklyn accent, sending Charley into another laughing fit.

They cracked up the entire ride to the ground level, all the way through the lobby, and out onto the sidewalk, where they nearly collided with a hot-dog cart.

"Could this night get any more perfect?" The man spread his hands like he was receiving a blessing, some divine intervention raining down upon them from the cart's red-and-yellow umbrellas. "Tell me you're hungry, and tell me you like hot dogs."

Charley hesitated, but the auction wasn't set to end for another hour at least; she still had some breathing room before Rudy returned to pick her up.

With a wide smile, she said, "Starving, and I love them, *obviously*."

"Then allow me to buy you dinner."

"Dinner? Sounds an awful lot like a real date."

"Surely the security guard would approve."

"Well, it's not a cruise by *any* stretch, but I do love a good hot dog."

"Somehow, I knew that about you." The man turned to the vendor and ordered sodas and two jumbo dogs, hold the onions, just how Charley liked them.

Dinner in hand, they crossed Central Park West and headed into the park, leaving the incessant hum of traffic for the calming whispers of stately trees and the murmurs of pedestrian traffic buzzing through the park. At the Strawberry Fields memorial, they found a bench across from a young musician working on a Led Zeppelin cover.

"Tell me," she said to her companion as he wolfed down his hot dog, "how *does* a proper English fellow like yourself go from dropping three million dollars on a painting of wet fuckin' grass to eating a dirty-water dog on a bird-shit covered bench with me?"

"Charmed life, I guess." He blotted his mouth with a napkin, then flashed his panty-melting grin. "But you left out the whole middle part of your story, love."

"Oh? Which part was that?" She took a bite of her dog, wrapping her lips around the end of it.

"Yes, exactly that part," he whispered.

"You're the one that left something out. Of *me.*"

"And they say it's gold-plated, besides."

"Alas, I'll never know."

He leaned in close, lips buzzing her ear. "I can fix that right now."

Charley shivered, a new hum settling into her core. Everything felt so much more intense without her underwear, and between her thighs was a pool of liquid heat, her body still aching for his final undelivered promise.

I'm going to fuck you now...

"Not at the dinner table." She shoved in another bite of hot dog to avoid saying something she shouldn't. Something like, *What was that you said about taking me home to your penthouse and tying me to the bed?*

After dinner, she dropped a few bills into the singer's guitar case, then they wandered further along the paved path, snaking deep into the park. A gentle breeze stirred the leaves overhead, the night air cool and refreshing on Charley's bare shoulders. It was late September, when the sweltering city nights transitioned to damn near perfect, and the park was full of people—couples on dates, bike riders, street performers. At eight o'clock in New York, the evening was still young, and she was grateful to get a glimpse of it.

But as much as she'd enjoyed the spontaneous turn of events, it wasn't long before Charley had exhausted the safe topics of conversation. She still wouldn't reveal her name or allow him to reveal his. And she certainly wasn't going to invent some intricate story about her family or the perfect, big-city childhood she'd never had.

In her experience, it was better to keep quiet then to lie.

Eventually, silence fell between them, and her *someday* life whispered in her ear, reminding her of everything she was missing out on. Charley closed her eyes, and images of what this moment *could've* been like flickered across her lids. Ridiculous as it was to project these feelings onto a total stranger, she couldn't help them; suddenly, she wished she belonged to him. That they already knew each other's stories, that their histories were intertwined long ago. That they always shared hot dogs and listened to musicians in the park on Sundays, and then they went home together, fed the dog, put on their favorite jazz playlist, and had deliciously naughty sex all night long.

No interruptions. No secrets. No lies.

But that fantasy was even crazier than the one that had started this thing.

There's nowhere I'd rather be than right here, fucking a hot stranger in the study…

The breeze picked up, and Charley opened her eyes, rubbing a new chill from her arms.

She hadn't seen him slipping out of his suit jacket, but suddenly he draped it over her shoulders, the soft wool wrapping her in a comforting hug, his delicious, masculine scent swirling around her head, setting the butterflies loose in her stomach again. He slid his hand beneath her hair, gently squeezing the back of her neck, and *God* what Charley wouldn't have given to linger in this fantasy all night long.

But even with his tender touches, Charley felt the distance growing between them, the walls rising up around her heart. Her body still longed for his touch, and whenever she glanced his way, she found the same look in his eyes— dark and sensual, wondering if they might pick up where they left off in the closet. But she never should've let it go that far in the first place. It was a bad idea, and bad ideas usually lead to worse ones.

Deadly ones.

She hated cutting the evening short when it still had so much potential, but for now, with no foreseeable way out of the life she'd inherited, she didn't have a choice. People could get hurt. *Sasha* could get hurt.

They'd wandered into a secluded area of the park, and now Charley stopped beside a massive red oak tree and turned to face him, sliding her hands over his broad shoulders. He looked at her curiously, a playful question lingering in his eyes.

Where do we go from here?

In that moment, a new weight settled on her heart.

Regret.

"Thank you for... for an *interesting* evening," she finally said, breaking the spell. She gazed into those honey-brown eyes, unable to look away. Even more than the things he'd done to her in the study, she wanted to remember those eyes, remember him gazing at her with smoldering, unchecked desire even as he must've sensed their inevitable end. "You were right—I won't be able to look at a painting again without remembering tonight. Not even in an art history book."

He gave a slight bow. "In all things, I'm a man of my word."

"I do believe you've changed my mind about these events, Stranger."

"Likewise, my troublesome, insatiable wife." His golden eyes sparkled, and he took her face between his palms and kissed her deeply, both of them savoring the sweet intensity.

God, they'd been so good together...

No.

Charley wasn't one for long goodbyes—she didn't even like the word. Instead, she broke their kiss, offered one last smile, and turned away from him, intending to find her way back to the penthouse to look for Rudy. But before she could take another step, he grabbed her wrist and hauled her close again, pinning her against his broad chest.

The look in his eyes was no longer sparkling and playful, but dominant and possessive, setting her insides ablaze.

"Come home with me tonight," he demanded. And

that's exactly what it was. Not a request or an invitation, but a demand.

Charley's thighs clenched.

"I promise I'll be a very, very good boy," the man said, pressing his lips to her neck.

"That doesn't sound like fun at all."

"I was being a gentleman." He moved up to her ear, leaving a trail of fiery kisses on her skin. "I don't think you're ready to see my bad side."

Fuck. Charley was *so* ready to see his bad side—especially after he'd so expertly tapped into hers. With every kiss, every hot swirl of breath, her resolve was cracking...

The image of a shipwreck flashed through her mind, and she remembered the von Hausen hanging above the fireplace—a cold, harsh reminder that she wasn't allowed to give in. To let her guard down. To turn a momentary lapse in judgment into an epic disaster.

"Enticing as your offer sounds," she said, pulling back, "I really can't. I'm sorry."

And she was, too. More than he'd ever know.

He held her gaze for an eternity, the wheels spinning behind his eyes. "No."

"No?"

Cupping her face, he dragged a thumb across her lower lip, his eyelids weighted with desire. "I'm sorry, love. But I'm *far* from finished with you."

Her knees weakened, her lungs struggling to take in enough air. Never before had she felt such a palpable battle between the angel and the devil on her shoulders, each one making its own extremely compelling case.

The man ran his other hand down her back, pulling her even closer, the hard steel at her belly confirming his words.

He was far from finished with her.

He opened his mouth to speak again, and Charley knew that whatever he said next, she'd accept. Go home with him, strip off her clothes and take their chances right there in the park, anything. He was a drug to which she'd quickly become addicted, and despite the warnings blasting alarm bells in her head, she couldn't walk away now.

It was too late.

The man took a breath and leaned in close. But before he could utter the words that would finally sway her, three assholes stepped out of the shadows, surrounding them.

In a flash, he turned to face the trio and pushed Charley behind him, positioning her between the oak at her back and his rigid body, spring-loaded and ready to fight.

One of them glared hard at her man, his facial piercings shining in the moonlight, eyes lighting up with an insane, inhuman hunger that had Charley immediately reaching for Beyoncé.

"Been looking for you, bloodsucker," the pierced guy said. "Nice night for a little payback, ain't it?"

CHAPTER ELEVEN

Brimstone soured the air, followed by a wave of heat that sent Dorian into a coughing fit. As the first spark took root inside his chest, he felt his tender pink lung tissue turning black, and in that moment, he knew two things.

One, he would die before he'd let any harm come to his woman.

And two, he had approximately three seconds before he was completely incinerated.

Without another thought, he rushed forward in a blur, colliding with Metalhead just as Blondie mysteriously dropped to the ground in a fit of spasms. For the second time in a handful of hours, Dorian sank his fangs into Metalhead's artery, the putrid taste filling his mouth, temporarily easing his cough. He'd just noticed the stun-gun wires protruding from Blondie's chest when another vampire blurred into view, smashing into the third attacker a mere instant before the demon got to his woman.

The new vamp tore into the demon's throat with his bare hands, his signet ring flashing in a river of dark blood.

Fucking Duchanes.

"Jesus fucking Christ!" the woman cried out. "What the fuck are you doing?"

Dorian didn't know who she was asking—him, Duchanes, the rotten demons themselves—but there was no time to answer. He needed to grab her, blur her someplace safe, and wipe her memories.

Now.

He dropped Metalhead on top of the still-trembling blond demon, glancing once more at Duchanes.

"Go," Duchanes said. "I'll take care of them."

"You can't kill them," Dorian warned. "They'll—"

"I'm not a newborn, Redthorne. You'd do well to remember it." Duchanes finally released his prey, dropping him onto the pile with the others, the demon's heartbeat faint but present.

Dorian shook his head. As much as he appreciated the assist—odds were, he would've been a pile of ash if the vampire hadn't shown up—Duchanes wasn't known for his altruism. And why the hell had he followed Dorian and the woman into the park in the first place?

"I said I'd take care of it." Duchanes removed a white handkerchief from his pocket and wiped the blood from his hands, paying special attention to his ring. "Get the woman out of here before the poor thing has a heart attack."

Dorian turned toward the woman, who continued to stare at the scene before her, her eyes wide with horror, mouth opening and closing as if she couldn't remember how to breathe.

He offered Duchanes a nod of thanks. The interrogation would have to wait.

"Come on, love. Let's go." He reached out for her, but she flinched away.

"Don't touch me. Don't you dare fucking touch me!"

Her words stung, but Dorian couldn't blame her.

He couldn't honor her request, either. The longer they stayed, the more likely trouble would find them.

Ignoring her protests, he wrapped his arms around the woman and blurred her back to the street, safe in a sea of strangers once again. She wobbled on her feet, her body instinctively reacting to the unnatural speed as her brain tried to process everything she'd seen.

Dorian hated what came next, but there was no way he'd leave her in this state. The demon attack, the brutal vampire counter-attack, the blurring… Such nightmares were *his* curse to bear; he wouldn't allow them to darken her memories. Not now. Not ever.

Taking her face between his hands, he held her gaze and spoke softly, willing the compulsion to do its work. "You and I enjoyed a lovely, uneventful stroll through the park. We saw nothing out of the ordinary—just shared a few laughs and a lovely goodnight kiss."

He'd be lying if he said he wasn't tempted to compel her to accept his invitation home, but that was a line he wouldn't cross, no matter how desperately he wanted her in his bed.

The woman blinked rapidly, then finally nodded, the color returning to her cheeks, her breathing soft and even once again.

"Holy shit." She gazed up at him, then at the street, confusion creasing the skin between her eyebrows. "What... what's going on?"

"Are you all right?" Dorian didn't have to feign the concern in his tone, though she'd never know his true reasons. "You nearly fainted."

"What? I've never fainted in my life. I... Wait..." She pulled out of his embrace, then spun around, scanning the park behind them. "Those dickheads in the park... I thought... What the hell happened?"

Dorian bit back a curse. In his efforts to keep his mental meddling to a minimum, he hadn't taken the compulsion far enough.

"What do you remember?" he asked cautiously.

"I'm not sure." She pinched her forehead and let out a soft sigh. "We were kissing under the tree, and those guys came out of nowhere. One of them said something about payback? After that it's... Everything's kind of a blur. Did someone help us? I feel like... No, that can't be right."

He smiled, tucking a lock of hair behind her ear. "Just a couple of punks trying to score some quick cash. And you're right—a jogger came by and helped chase them off."

"Really? And I didn't fight back?" She opened her purse, frantically digging through it. "Damn it. Where's Beyoncé?"

"The situation unfolded rather quickly," he said, closing

his hands over hers. "You must've dropped it in the confusion."

She bit her lip, likely trying to reconcile his version of events with her own. Despite his best efforts at a convincing tone, Dorian knew it sounded like bullshit, and he waited for her to make the obvious suggestion about calling the police and filing a report.

But she said nothing more about it, accepting his explanation with little more than a long, shaky exhale. "I guess I'm a little overwhelmed. Still processing, you know? That was fucking *weird*."

Dorian nodded. He still hadn't processed it himself. He'd been a mere heartbeat away from oblivion. He'd smelled the brimstone, felt the heat in his lungs. They were going to unleash hellfire, certainly killing him.

As for the woman...

A shudder wracked his body. Dorian didn't even want to think about what they would've done to her in his absence.

Yesterday, the very idea of demons even setting foot in Manhattan would've been preposterous—the Accords prohibited it, and for decades, the creatures had obeyed, just as vampires avoided the demonic-held territories of Brooklyn and Queens. Violations could lead to war or widespread discovery—twin threats that, save for the occasional skirmish, had kept the supernatural communities in a peaceful state of suspension.

Yet tonight, Chernikov demons had not only set foot in

vampire territory, but attempted to claim a human soul, unleashed an attack in front of another human, and damn near assassinated the Redthorne vampire king.

If war was what they were after, Dorian could deliver their dreams on a silver fucking platter.

"Oh, great," the woman said suddenly. "Another ambush."

He followed her gaze to a black SUV that had pulled up to the curb. From the backseat, a man emerged—late fifties, maybe, with thinning gray hair slicked back off a high forehead and a mediocre suit trying its damnedest to look expensive. He glared at the woman with such contempt, Dorian wanted to tear out his heart and feed his soul to the demons—a peace offering for his enemies.

Instinctively, he reached for the woman's hand, but she ignored his touch, folding her arms over her chest instead. Everything inside her tensed, her pulse racing with new urgency.

"Do you know him?" Dorian asked.

Through clenched teeth, she whispered her reply. "That's my... boss."

The man barely spared a glance for Dorian, his cold gaze fixated on the woman. "I've been looking for you everywhere, Charlotte. Where have you been?"

Charlotte. Dorian let the name rest on his tongue, melting like rich, dark chocolate. It suited her—a sweet sonnet tinged with a hint of spice.

"Yeah, sorry about that," she replied. Disappointment

and frustration warred for dominance in her tone, but she offered the man a smile anyway. "I decided to stretch my legs in the park."

Her smile was nothing like the radiant looks she'd shared with Dorian, but that fact was little comfort; he may have earned her genuine expressions, but in the end, it seemed she'd still be going home with another man.

Now, that man opened the SUV's back door. "Get in. We have things to discuss."

"Just give me a sec," she said, not bothering to hide her annoyance. Then, turning to Dorian, she offered one last smile. The real one.

Dorian tried not to gloat.

In a soft, wistful tone, she said, "I have to go now."

"You really don't."

"Thanks again for the company."

"Charlotte," he said, savoring the taste of it, the way her eyes softened when he said it. "This isn't necessary. I can have my driver here in a matter of minutes. We'll take you anywhere you'd like."

As long as it's not anywhere near this man and his ice-cold eyes.

"I appreciate the offer." Charlotte lowered her gaze, cheeks blushing, and Dorian wanted to freeze the moment right there, to stop the inevitable goodbye poised on her lips.

But he could no more stop time than he could reverse it.

"Technically I'm still on the clock," she continued. "I don't have a choice."

He wanted to kiss her. To memorize the feel of those soft, plump lips, to welcome the warmth of her sigh against his ear one more time. But with the other man standing so close, Charlotte's discomfort was obvious.

"It was lovely to meet you," Dorian said instead, cursing himself, cursing the demons, cursing the man in the SUV, cursing the very witch who'd created the first vampires eons ago.

For all the blood and fury, *this* was the true bane of an immortal life.

Regret, heavy and inescapable, destined to haunt him for eternity.

"Goodnight, Charlotte," he said, resisting the urge to touch her face.

"Goodnight, Stranger."

And then she was gone, climbing into the SUV without a backward glance.

Dorian took a deep breath, her scent lingering on his skin, despite the second dose of demon blood.

They may have said their goodnights, but it wasn't a *goodbye*.

Not for him. Not by a long shot.

Dorian felt the burn of a dark gaze on his skin, and he glanced up to find the man watching him, a puzzled expression on his face. He schooled it quickly, rearranging his features into a mask of neutral disinterest.

"Mr. Redthorne." The man offered a curt nod, then climbed into the backseat with Charlotte, shutting the door behind him.

It was only after the SUV vanished into a sea of taillights that Dorian realized he'd never actually introduced himself.

CHAPTER TWELVE

As much as she hated to admit it, Rudy's ill-timed arrival was just the bucket of ice water to the crotch Charley needed. Tonight was a crazy fantasy, and she'd enjoyed every mouthwatering second of it, right up until the part where they nearly got mugged.

Even *that* felt like a fantasy—a blurry smudge of a story she could barely remember, no matter how hard she tried.

What was the point, anyway? Story time was over. Her clock had struck midnight, her stagecoach turned back into a pumpkin, and now Charley would return to reality, the man no more than a delicious memory of a life she could never have.

Resting her head against the tinted window, she closed her eyes and let the hum of the road vibrate through her skull, enjoying the last few minutes of silence before Rudy started up the inevitable third degree.

What do you mean, nada?

You didn't find a single thing of value in that entire penthouse?

What's wrong with you, Charlotte?

Are you sure you're committed to this?

"What were you doing with Dorian Redthorne?"

The last question hadn't come from inside her head, and Charley sat up, blinking away her thoughts. From the adjacent seat, Rudy stared at her, impatient and annoyed—his default setting.

"Who the fuck's Dorian Redthorne?" she asked, but as soon as the name passed through her lips, she *knew.*

Her man. The formality in his mannerisms, the obvious money, the sheer power emanating from his every word and movement. Only a man like that would have a name like Dorian Redthorne.

She repeated it in her mind, the memory of his accent making her stomach lurch.

He still had her underwear, she realized suddenly. Stuffed into his pants pocket.

Biting back a smile at the image of him discovering them later, she turned back to the window, hoping her disinterest would send Rudy sniffing up another tree.

But he wouldn't let it go.

"You're telling me you spent the night with a man and never bothered asking his name?"

"I didn't spend the night with *anyone*, Rudy. I'm here. With you. As usual." Then, tempering her tone, she waved her hand in front of her face like she was shooing a fly. "I didn't get his name because he's nobody—just some rich guy from the auction. We left at the same time, and he offered to walk me to the park."

Rudy glanced at his watch, a gold monstrosity that had probably cost more than a year's worth of Sasha's schoolbooks. "I may be old, kiddo, but I'm not blind."

"How do *you* know him?"

He turned away from her and stared out his window, rubbing his thumb along his watchband. "He's the CEO of FierceConnect, among other things."

"FierceConnect? Never heard of it."

He turned and leveled her with another icy glare. "You two clearly had a connection."

"Sure. Keep dreaming, Uncle Rudy."

"You're wearing his clothes."

Charley glanced down, shocked to find herself clutching the suit jacket around her shoulders. In the chaos of the near-mugging and the rushed goodbye that followed, she'd all but forgotten about it.

She released the soft fabric, folding her hands in her lap.

"You wasted precious time on a job you claim yielded no results," Rudy said. "You ignored my calls and texts. You ducked out early, forcing me to waste even more time driving around the block looking for you. And this isn't the first time you've turned up empty-handed lately. Not by a long shot."

"I know," she said softly, shame heating her cheeks.

"So I'll ask you again. What were you doing with Dorian Redthorne?"

"Nothing—I swear. He… he bought the Whitfield," she

blurted out.

Rudy cocked his head, looking at her with renewed interest.

Shit. Why had she said that? God, she hated the way Rudy got under her skin. He'd been like that ever since she was a kid, needling her until she finally gave up whatever secrets he was after—what her parents had been fighting about, where her mother kept the stash of tips from her waitressing gig, where her father had hidden the whiskey.

Looking at him now, she wondered how he'd managed to survive the game these last five years without her father around to clean up his messes. Sure, he played the part— tailored suit, that blingy-ass watch, the formal tone he'd adopted in recent years to impress wealthier clients. To anyone else, he probably looked like a successful business- man. But whenever Charley looked at him, she saw the same old Uncle Rudy from the trailer park, dressed in worn jeans and a beer-stained Bon Jovi T-shirt with holes in the armpits, a cheap gold chain around his neck, banging on the door and asking her father for a loan, for help with another one of his schemes, for a place to crash for the night or the week or the month.

Despite the money they'd earned since, the high-class art scenes they'd worked, and their lavish Manhattan addresses, most of the time, Charley felt as if they'd never left that run-down double-wide in Jersey.

And sometimes, in her darkest moments, part of her wished they *hadn't* left.

"I asked you a question, Charlotte."

His cold voice brought her back to the present, and she blinked away the memories.

"Sorry. I didn't hear you."

A deep sigh rushed out through his nose. "How much did Redthorne pay for the Whitfield?"

Charley thought about lying, but Rudy would find out soon enough anyway. Charley didn't know all their methods, but somehow, when it came to the amount of cash trading hands in the world of fine art, the D'Amico crew always had their finger on the pulse.

"Three million," she admitted.

Rudy's eyebrows shot up, but then he turned away again. He was silent for a long time. *Too* fucking long, which meant one of two things.

He was plotting.

Or he was gearing up for an explosion—one Charley would catch, right in the face.

Not for the first time, she wished the damn SUV didn't have a privacy screen separating them from the driver. Then again, the types of guys Rudy hired—the same types her father had hired—were paid not to notice. Not to interfere. Not to help, even when someone begged for it.

Charley did her best to remain still, to take up as little space as possible.

…and above all, don't get noticed…

Even more than the threat of violence, this was the part she hated. Biting her tongue. Holding her breath. Shrinking, shrinking, shrinking, a little more each time.

One day, she might disappear entirely.

Fifteen minutes passed. Thirty. They were taking the long way home, a route undoubtedly planned to keep her in a state of constant unease. Charley longed to reach for her phone, to send a text to Sasha, but she didn't dare move.

She closed her eyes and tried to relax, tried to remind herself that this was all part of Rudy's game. She'd just started to nod off when the bastard finally decided to speak, his voice so loud and abrupt she nearly yelped.

"Well," Rudy said sharply. "I guess the outing wasn't a total loss after all."

A slow smile crept across his face, bringing with it a cold dread that lodged itself right in her belly.

"How do you figure?" she asked. "The place was a dead end. I searched the whole thing."

"Sometimes, what looks like a dead end is actually a well-hidden doorway to something *much* more prosperous."

He reached over and patted her thigh, holding her gaze another beat before leaning back against the headrest and closing his eyes.

The conversation was over.

Charley didn't need to ask what he'd meant.

The doorway to prosperity was Dorian Redthorne.

And the powerful, sexy, panty-melting gazillionaire who'd given her the most intense orgasms of her life, bought her a jumbo hot dog, and set her whole world on fire had no idea what kind of trouble he'd just invited in for tea.

CHAPTER THIRTEEN

In Dorian's mind, there ought to have been a sacredness to the tables around which families gathered to share their meals. He'd never understood how people could so readily dine in the same spaces where they'd played out all their domestic tragedies—news of deaths and divorces, neighborhood gossip, a call from the doctor about an abnormal test result. Arguments about money and religion and sex—too much, not enough. Punishments meted out to errant children—extra chores, a grounding, a beating. Threats.

For Dorian, the blackest, most brutal night of his life had unfolded in the dining room at the manor in West Sussex over an otherwise perfectly pleasant meal of roasted quail. Though the battered remains of the Redthorne family had later emigrated to New York for a fresh start, his father had painstakingly recreated their original family home here in Annandale-on-Hudson, right down to the embossed ceilings and oak wainscoting. And while his brothers had scattered across the country and his father traveled the world in service to his own crown, hardly ever stepping foot in the manor he'd erected, Dorian had made Ravenswood his home, ensuring it was updated as modern advances allowed—plumbing, electricity, everything he needed to live in total comfort.

There were only two areas he avoided—his father's private quarters, and the dining room.

The few times he'd caught sight of it through the ornately carved pocket doors, all he saw was the blood splatter. All he heard were the screams.

So tonight, while his three brothers shared a late meal at the massive oak dining table, the king himself remained sequestered in his study before a roaring fire, nursing a glass of scotch in one hand, a scrap of black lace in the other, wondering if there was enough alcohol or pussy in the world to dull the sharp blade of the past.

He sipped his scotch, then pressed the lace to his mouth and closed his eyes, chasing much more pleasant memories.

Ah, Charlotte. I never should've let you go...

A knock on the study door tore him from his thoughts, and he tucked the panties back into his pocket, calling for the intruder to enter.

Intruders, he realized. All three of them glided into the room, the sight of his brothers standing side by side for the first time in five decades twisting the blade a little deeper.

The twins were missing, of course—dead at sixteen years old.

Murdered at sixteen years old.

They hadn't survived the change.

Emotion welled in the back of his throat. He tipped back his glass, drowning it.

Then, leveling his brothers with a gaze as neutral as he could manage, he said evenly, "Welcome to Ravenswood, brothers. You're all looking... well."

It was true, Dorian realized, cataloging each in turn.

Malcolm, golden-eyed and tanned from his time in New Orleans. Turned at thirty-two, he was three years younger than Dorian, but had always acted as if he were the only adult in the room. Now, he carried himself like a man far beyond his years.

Colin, next in line at thirty, with dark, shoulder-length hair and a dimpled smile that had solved more family conflicts than Dorian could count, effortlessly melting their mother's heart and sparing him the brunt of Father's ill temper. He'd inherited the man's interest in medicine, and last Dorian knew, he'd been working as a doctor in a small town in the Rocky Mountains.

Lastly, Gabriel. Turned at twenty-eight, the youngest remaining Redthorne had always been their ticking time bomb. He was a rebellious child and an angry adolescent, his untamable wildness only intensifying with the change. He'd built his empire in Sin City, earning a terrifying reputation Dorian preferred not to think about.

Now, his baby brother looked upon him with eyes as cold and calculating as their father's. It chilled Dorian to the marrow.

"Witches aren't hard to come by in New Orleans,"

Malcolm said, breaking the tense silence. He placed another log on the fire, the flames popping. "I'd assumed that was the case here as well, but it seems you've let yourself go a bit, brother."

He'd meant it as a joke, but only Colin laughed.

Dorian's very veins itched. "I've managed."

"And Father?" Gabriel asked, his voice like a steel sword. "He managed as well?"

Ignoring the dig, Dorian raised his glass and grinned. "Until the very end."

Without further encouragement, his brothers made themselves at home in the study, occupying the leather chairs around the fireplace, pouring another round of bourbon from the bottle Colin brought.

"To Father," Colin said, raising his glass.

"May his eternal rest be as terrible as the torments he inflicted upon us," Malcolm said.

Now *that* was something Dorian could drink to. He nodded and took another swig.

Gabriel remained silent, seething in the farthest chair, but he lifted his glass to his lips anyway.

None of them asked how Father had died, which was just as well. Dorian had started the rumor of a foreign demon attack—an old enemy come to repay an old slight—but that was simply to assuage the supernatural grapevine. He wasn't prepared to discuss the true cause—not until he figured out how to prevent it from happening to the rest of them.

Not until he figured out how it'd even happened in the first place.

The warmth of the fire lulled them into silence, each lost in his own thoughts. It was a long while before anyone spoke again.

"Dorian," Malcolm finally said, his tone careful, "we've all discussed this, and we're in agreement. Perhaps I could've handled our earlier conversation with a bit more diplomacy, but I stand by my position. Given the circumstances, an alliance is our best option." He sipped his bourbon, then shrugged. "House Duchanes is prepared to make an offer. I think we should take them up on it."

"Yes," Dorian said, keeping his anger on simmer. "I ran into your friend Renault at the auction tonight."

"So he approached you, then."

"Oh, he more than approached me. He made quite a show of assuring me you'd already agreed." Dorian glared at him, waiting for him to deny it. Hoping, against the odds, that he would.

But Malcolm's silence spoke volumes.

"Renault *Duchanes*?" Dorian slammed his glass on the end table. "You can't *possibly* be serious, Mac."

"Alliances are rarely perfect," Malcolm said. "Simply a means to an end."

"What you're proposing is a means to *our* end—one Duchanes would gladly usher in."

"His is the only greater house willing to work with us."

"And why do you suppose that is? Because they've

taken pity on us in our time of need? Because Renault is just an all-around decent fellow?"

"Father's legacy—"

"You're so concerned about father's legacy, you're willing to destroy what's left of it by playing high-stakes Monopoly with blood slavers and sex traffickers?" Dorian rose from his chair and turned toward the hearth, wishing he could dive right into the flames, let them consume him as readily as hellfire. "If that's all we've got to offer, maybe it's time to let our legacy die."

"And do what?" Malcolm snapped. "Crawl into the crypt with Father? Is that what you wish?"

Dorian ran his fingers along the mahogany mantle, remembering all the times he and his brothers had stolen into Father's study in West Sussex, giggling as they snuck forbidden glimpses at his illustrated anatomy books. "Perhaps it's where we belong."

Colin, ever the peacemaker, stood and placed a hand on Dorian's shoulder. Dorian forced himself not to recoil, despite the burn of shame in his gut.

"Don't speak of such things, brother," Colin said. "We'll find the answers."

He closed his eyes, wishing he already *had* the answers.

More than anything, he wanted to make this right for them, whether they planned to return to New York permanently, or they walked out of his life tomorrow without a backward glance.

But how could he?

Since the turning, Dorian had been taught to believe

vampires held all the power. They were at the top of the supernatural food chain, stronger and deadlier than the other races, their blood coveted for its magical and healing properties by witches and lesser beings alike. They outnumbered demons and shifters by threefold and could much more easily grow their ranks—with or without human consent.

But what experience and pain had shown him was that *alliances* held the power. It just so happened that vampires —particularly the oldest, wealthiest families like his—had no shortage of eager allies.

Until the great cock-up of 1972—*Dorian's* great cock-up —when he'd failed to protect their bonded witch from an attack and, in the bloody aftermath, the witches cut ties, nearly all the prominent families turned their backs on House Redthorne, and his brothers vanished from his life.

Now, by a chance order of birth and the twist of fate that had killed his immortal father, Dorian was the rightful vampire king. His family had money—more than they could spend in a hundred lifetimes. They had stocks and art collections valued in the billions. Luxury automobiles that filled the wet dreams of lesser men. Property in more than a dozen countries, and businesses in twice as many.

But when it came to trusted friendships, to partners, to those precious allies that secured true power, they had nothing. At a time when the greater families were vying for power, the lesser vampires were growing restless, and demons were quickly encroaching on their territory, Dorian and his brothers stood virtually alone.

He thought again of Chernikov's demons, the attack in the park. His own dulled instincts, the ache behind his eyes, the mental fog. All the ailments he'd once been magically spelled against—something he'd taken for granted when he had access to a bonded witch.

And if any of their enemies discovered his father's weakness? The same weakness that likely ran through the entire Redthorne line?

The royal family was in deep shit—more than their father had admitted to Dorian. More than Dorian would admit to his brothers now.

But aligning with Duchanes was not the answer.

"So you'd rather do nothing?" Gabriel shook his head. "How utterly predictable of you."

Dorian curled his hand into a fist on the mantle, then released it, letting out a sigh. He hadn't planned to reveal his strategy to his brothers, but without it, they'd surely stage a coup.

More importantly—a fact Dorian was loath to admit—they'd shown up. They remained in his home even now, despite the tension and bickering. For how long, he couldn't say. But tonight, the surviving Redthorne Royals were present and accounted for. His brothers were home, looking to him for guidance, whether they'd readily acknowledge it or not.

He owed them.

"Nothing could be farther from the truth." Dorian finally turned to face them again. "I'm in the process of acquiring Armitage Holdings."

"As in... Lucien Armitage?" Colin asked. "The old mage?"

Dorian reclaimed his chair and poured himself a fresh glass of scotch. "Lucien and Father became quite close in recent years. Now, he's retiring, and he doesn't want his company disbanded and sold to vultures. FierceConnect is a good fit."

Armitage Holdings was a mage-owned company that specialized in illusion magic used in all sorts of human visual technologies, from apps to artificial intelligence to virtual reality. Dorian's company—a social gaming platform with 500 million worldwide users—was most interested in the latter. It really was the perfect marriage.

"What of his children?" Malcolm asked.

"Neither of his sons is interested in running the company," Dorian said.

"And his daughter?" This, from Gabriel, who'd never trusted witches and always resented that vampires were so dependent upon them.

Dorian glanced at the thin magical tattoos snaking up Gabriel's forearms, without which he'd be confined to the darkness, unable to enjoy even the simplest human pleasure of a meal or a stiff drink. He thought Gabriel ought to be a bit less judgmental of witches, but kept the opinion to himself, waiting instead for his brothers to put the pieces together.

"I see," Malcolm said, first to figure it out. "And you think Isabelle Armitage will simply throw herself into the desperately waiting arms of the very vampire family accused of murdering their last—"

"Lucien and Isabelle are *both* eager for her to be placed with a prominent family," Dorian said.

"And you think that family is ours?" Malcolm asked. "Has this been promised?"

"Not in so many words. But with our business interests closely aligned, it's only a matter of time before our personal interests align as well."

"And once we have a Redthorne-bonded witch," Colin said, his dimples flashing, "we've no need of alliances."

"Not from the likes of House Duchanes, anyways," Dorian said. With their own witch, they'd have unlimited access to all the spells and enchantments that kept vampires strong and, for the most part, human. Alliances—proper, mutually beneficial alliances—would certainly follow.

"You're assuming our enemies are going to nod and smile and let you continue to play king," Gabriel said. "That they're not already plotting against us. That your witch and her father will blindly overlook your past indiscretions and—"

"Armitage is no fool," Dorian said. "He's well aware of my history, and the history of this *entire* family." He sipped his scotch, letting that comment simmer a bit. His brothers' hands were covered in as much blood as Dorian's, and he was tired of pretending otherwise.

"He's got a consulting firm conducting all the requisite investigations of my company," Dorian continued. "And I assure you, our dealings are completely aboveboard."

"And your personal life?" Malcolm asked, abandoning his efforts at diplomacy. "Is he looking into that as well?"

"Indeed, he is."

Colin's eyebrows lifted. "An investigation?"

"Not... exactly." Dorian's insides twisted. It was bad enough he'd let his business partner convince him to host the fundraiser in the first place—a show for Armitage and his executives to prove how generous, gregarious, and stable Dorian really was. The proceeds would benefit one of Armitage's pet projects—a children's art museum in the Bronx.

Inviting his estranged family to attend was the last thing he wanted. But they were staying here now, for the foreseeable future. He couldn't very well ask them to vacate the premises while he held the soiree of the century on their sprawling estate.

Malcolm narrowed his eyes at Dorian. "What are you on about?"

"Gentleman, I hope you're still in possession of your most exquisite formalwear." Dorian tipped back the last of his scotch and rose from his chair, then grabbed the bottle and stalked toward the exit, tossing a wry smile over his shoulder. "Chins up, brothers. The Redthorne Royals are throwing a party."

CHAPTER FOURTEEN

When Charley was a kid, her father and Rudy used to take her to Cape May on the Jersey Shore in the off-season. There were fewer tourists, parking wasn't a problem, and everything on the promenade was cheap enough that even the D'Amicos could feel like royalty for a few days.

Charley didn't care about the fried food or the beach-town trinkets, though. For her, the big draw was always the ocean. It fascinated and terrified her, possessing a dark allure she couldn't resist. On every trip, while her father and Rudy parked themselves in the sand with a cooler full of beer and a deck of cards, she'd wade out into the sea alone, daring herself to go deeper, one baby step at a time. First up to her ankles, then her knees, then her hips, palms skimming over the surface as sunlight glinted like diamonds, so bright it hurt her eyes.

But for all its beauty, the Atlantic Ocean harbored a dark secret—a cold and deadly undercurrent lurking beneath its diamond-bright sheen. Resisting was pointless; the harder she fought against it, the stronger the current pulled, tugging her so far out that her father and uncle became nothing but pink dots on a distant shore.

Sometimes, the ocean would tire of playing with her, spitting her back onto the sand in a watery tumble of seaweed and driftwood.

Other times, her father would have to swim out after her, tossing her over his shoulder and dragging her back to safety, laughing as if she'd never been in any danger at all.

My little mermaid, he'd say, gently patting her bottom as the tears spilled from her eyes. *How 'bout we get some ice cream and call it a day?*

She *had* been in danger, though—that was the thing. Charley knew she'd brushed against death on those trips, and every time, she swore she'd never return to Cape May, never give the sea another chance to steal her soul.

It was only back in the trailer after the long drive home, snugly tucked into the princess bed she'd outgrown years earlier, that the *other* feeling took root.

Survival.

It warmed her, knowing she'd outsmarted a force as terrible and ancient as the sea. It made her feel like a fighter. And as the months passed, the fear receded, leaving only the feeling of triumph—a hot blaze in her chest that fueled her through the long northeast winters, driving her right back to the shores the following year, waves nipping her toes, her nemesis whispering an invitation she could never refuse.

Charley hadn't thought about those trips, about that feeling, in more than a decade.

But when she woke up in her late father's Park Avenue penthouse the morning after the auction, her body still aching with desire, the memories rushed back in a blink.

Because that feeling—the undertow, the danger, the pure exhilaration of touching the edge of death and living to tell the tale—was exactly how it'd felt to be in the stranger's arms.

In Dorian Redthorne's arms.

And just like all those trips to the Cape, Charley found herself wanting to go back to him, forgetting the danger, remembering only the survival. The wicked rush. The desperate need to feel the blaze of heat in her chest, again and again...

In a fit of frustration, she threw off her duvet and hit the remote for the blinds, flooding her bedroom with light.

But even as the bright morning sun burned away the last of her erotic dreams, darkness crept in along the edges.

Charley glanced at the suit jacket draped over her reading chair. Rudy hadn't said another word about Dorian last night, but her uncle was like a dog with a bone. There was no way he'd let it go—not after hearing about the Whitfield.

She had no idea what he was planning—only that he *was* planning. All Charley could do now was brace for the storm... and hope like hell she survived.

~

"*Someone* had a good night." Sasha breezed into the kitchen with a grin that lit up the room, her blond ponytail swishing across her shoulders. "And that someone needs to spill it, especially since she stood me up for vampire movie night."

Charley's cheeks burned, but she recovered quickly, forcing a playful eye-roll. "If you call schmoozing with a bunch of art stiffs a good night, I feel sorry for your future boyfriends. Sorry I didn't text—that auction dragged on forever."

"Are your pants hot? Like, on fire?"

"Excuse me?"

"Because you're such a liar!" Sasha poured herself a coffee, dumping in about half the sugar bowl and enough almond creamer to turn it beige. In a singsong voice, she said, "I know your faces, Chuck. And that…" She swirled her finger in front of Charley's eyes. "…is *not* the face of a woman who spent the night schmoozing."

"You're a regular private eye, aren't you?" Charley stuck out her tongue.

"Was he cute, at least? What'd y'all do?" At the granite-topped breakfast bar, she took the seat next to Charley, stirring her coffee with trademark Sasha exuberance, spoon clinking against the mug like a bell. "I'm not leaving this room until I get the scoop—starting with the dude's name."

God, I need more caffeine for this conversation…

Unlike her big sister, Sasha was an open book. She talked in her sleep, sang in the shower, thought and daydreamed out loud. She did *everything* out loud, full blast, no holding back. Charley admired that about her, but it also made her feel like a total fraud. There was a lot Sasha didn't know about Charley's life, and as much as Charley loved her, she needed to keep it that way.

The girls had different fathers, and since Charley's mother had split and moved to Florida when she was six, searching for a man with, quote, *potential*, Charley didn't even know Sasha existed—not until Mom called up one day with some sob story, trying to extort them. Charley's father told her about the call afterward—broke the news that Charley had a baby sister.

Charley was unfazed. She was twelve years old by then, and her father and the crew he'd put together over the years—Uncle Rudy, Trick, Welshman, and Bones—were the only family she needed. As far as Charley was concerned, Mom could take her new family and jump off the closest pier.

But five years ago—about a week after her father's death—a young girl showed up unannounced at Charley's building, shivering and hungry, eyes wild with the kind of desperate, bone-deep fear no fourteen-year-old should ever know.

Charley didn't recognize her, but in her backpack—shoved in with a bunch of tattered clothes and a dog-eared romance novel the girl had found on the bus—was an envelope with Charley's name and address. The letter inside was from their mother.

It was full of bullshit about wanting a better life for Sasha, about how wrong she'd been to keep the sisters apart, but the truth Sasha shared later was much more sinister. Mom was using again—a habit she'd nursed long before she left Charley and her dad—and her dickbag, drug-dealing, boyfriend-of-the-month had driven Sasha to the Greyhound station in Jacksonville that morning, getting her a one-way ticket to New York.

Don't come back, the boyfriend warned. *You've upset your mother enough. Nothing left for you here.*

I understand if you don't want me, Sasha had said to Charley. *But maybe I could have a sandwich? Then I'll figure something else out. Please—I just need to eat.*

Charley's life may have been fucked up, but she'd never been hungry. In that moment, it didn't matter that Charley was raised in a life of crime, that Sasha was a stranger, that her own mother could be so cruel. She vowed, right then and there, her sister would never know that kind of hunger or helpless fear again.

Five years on, she was still doing her best to keep Sasha safe, to give her a good life.

Unfortunately, that required a few little white lies. And a few major ones, too. About Charley's job. Her boss. Where the money had come from.

Where it was *still* coming from.

"The dude's name," Charley said now, "is already forgotten."

"So you *did* have a date! I knew it!" Sasha cocked an eyebrow, a cute trick she'd recently mastered. "Did you get any?"

"Nope." Charley forged on, feigning defeat. "It sucked. Everything about the guy sucked."

In more ways than one...

"Bummer. Maybe you should update your dating profile? No offense, but 'museum consultant' doesn't exactly scream 'I'm hot and spontaneous and totally down to fuck.'"

Charley laughed. She'd deleted that "profile" about fifteen minutes after Sasha set it up for her last year. Her sister's heart was in the right place—she'd been worried about Charley after things crashed and burned with the documents forger, a man Sasha believed was an insurance salesman. But come *on*. Online dating? Even if Charley *was* a legitimate museum consultant—a girl with a normal job and a regular life—how could she find the kind of man she wanted through an app? The kind of man who could take her to the edge, test her limits, talk dirty to her all night long, and wake her up with soft cuddles and kisses and breakfast in bed? Danger wrapped in silk—that's what she wanted.

Did that kind of man even exist?

Charley loved the idea of trusting her pleasure to a strong, dominant man, but she'd learned the hard way that those men—*real* men, the ones who'd know how to take care of her—were few and far between. Her ex talked a good game, but when it came down to it, he preferred to demean rather than dominate. For him, it was all about ego, and whenever Charley tried to express her needs, he shut her down—sometimes by withholding sex, other times with a cruel joke, often with humiliation. The last time she'd tried to talk dirty, to push the boundaries a bit, he'd called her a filthy whore and accused her of cheating. Slapped her hard on the mouth, drawing blood and leaving one hell of a bruise.

That was nearly a year ago. She hadn't shared his bed since.

Charley's mind drifted back to last night's forbidden rendezvous. *God*, she would've loved to dish about it with her sister, but when it came to her "work" events, Charley had a strict need-to-know policy, and Sasha didn't need to know. As far as Sasha was concerned, her big sister was a consultant who spent a lot of time looking at old paintings and helping people buy and sell family heirlooms. There were more than a few shades of gray in that definition, but for now, Charley needed to keep the specifics to herself.

Specifics… like how his strong, talented fingers put my vibrator to shame…

Charley cleared her throat and blinked away the memories, locking them back in that closet where they belonged.

"Sasha," she said, "I appreciate your concern. Really. But I'm done dating. I'm perfectly capable of taking care of myself."

"In bed?" Sasha teased.

"*Anyway*, what about *your* night?"

"Well, since you stood me up, I finished my English essay."

The word "English" sent another unbidden spark through Charley's insides. Thankfully, Sasha was still talking, and Charley gave her the undivided attention she deserved.

"I heard back from the professor this morning," Sasha said. "She thinks I might be a good candidate for her advanced literature seminar in the spring. She only takes ten students—mostly seniors—and you have to be invited to even apply. If I get in, I'll be the first freshman ever admitted."

"Sasha, that's amazing!" Charley beamed. She was so proud of her sister. Sasha's education—her entire future— was the reason Charley did what she did, and nothing made her happier than hearing about her sister's hard-earned achievements. Despite a rocky childhood, Sasha had worked her ass off in high school, earning a scholarship to Hunter College in the city, which she supplemented with a coffee shop gig to cover the extras. She'd even taken two classes in the summer, trying to get some of her basic coursework done early while she figured out what she wanted to study.

Charley might not have had the opportunity to go to college, to follow a path of her own choosing, but she'd be damned if she wouldn't give that to her sister. Sasha was the best thing in her life, and she deserved the world. There was nothing Charley wouldn't do to protect her. To keep that big, live-out-loud smile on her beautiful face.

"This calls for a celebration," Charley said, already rising to rummage through the cupboards. "Chocolate chip banana pancakes?"

"But I didn't get in yet! I won't know until the end of the semester."

"You'll get in. I know it." Charley pulled out the flour, sugar, and a bag of chocolate chips.

"We should've planned this better! I'm on the lunch shift at Perk." Sasha reached for her cell. "Lemme see if I can get Darcy to switch—she owes me. We can spend the whole day together."

"Oh... I've got a lunch thing I can't get out of." Charley frowned, thoughts of Rudy souring her mood. There was no way he'd let her bail on their appointment today—especially after last night's failure.

Sasha's smile slipped. "Okay, no problem."

Charley hated that she'd put that disappointed look in her sister's eyes, but she understood all too well where it had come from. Between Sasha's classes and Charley's crazy job, the girls had barely shared a meal together all month, let alone spent any quality time together. And even though last night was totally Rudy's fault, the end result was the same. Charley had missed plans with her sister. Again.

"Hey," Charley said. "How about tonight? We'll go out —just the two of us."

Sasha brightened. "For real? You don't have to work?"

"Nope—just the lunch thing. So... we'll grab an early dinner somewhere later, maybe see a movie?"

"Let's go to Bryant Park!" Sasha bounced on her toes, her blue eyes glittering. "They're showing Sleepless in Seattle tonight. We can do a Shake Shack picnic."

"It's a date." Charley dumped the chocolate chips into a bowl, deciding to make the pancakes anyway. Her anxiety about Rudy was already melting away, the thought of a picnic and outdoor movie with her sister bolstering her mood.

Sasha hugged her from behind as she leaned in to steal a chocolate chip. "What did I do to deserve you, Chuck?"

Charley grinned, turning to press a kiss to Sasha's cheek.

You showed up, she thought. *And you stayed.*

CHAPTER FIFTEEN

That fucking closet was going to haunt him for the rest of his immortal life.

Charlotte had awoken something inside him—a hunger that had lain dormant for far too long. Now, Dorian couldn't even hang up his suit coat in the office this morning without his cock getting hard—a situation that would become problematic if he didn't do something about it.

Like track that woman down, drag her back to Ravenswood, and show her exactly *what she's been missing out on her whole life...*

Dorian sighed. *He* was the one missing out. Last night he'd sent her home with another man without a fight, and now he'd probably never see her again.

Maybe it was for the best.

Behind those seductive copper eyes, Charlotte was a deep vault of secrets. *Nothing* about her was innocent, and with everything else going on in his life right now, Dorian didn't need that kind of trouble.

At least she didn't walk away with the Whitfield.

It was a small comfort—one that didn't last long. How had she gotten so thoroughly under his skin? He couldn't remember the last time he'd felt more than a vague curiosity about a woman, let alone the borderline obsessing he was doing right now.

Sipping coffee as black and bitter as his heart, he stood before his fortieth-floor office windows and took in the view, a vast sea of skyscrapers that stretched from his building in Tribeca up to the northern edge of Manhattan. In the distance, the top of the Chrysler Building gleamed beneath a gorgeous sapphire-blue sky, making it nearly impossible for his foul mood to linger. Despite the ache behind his eyes, his mind was clear today—a sign that the second round of demon blood had nourished him.

That was something, anyway.

"Rough night, mate?" Aiden Donovan, Dorian's business partner and best friend, barged into his office with his usual lack of decorum. "You look like hell."

"And you look like someone who thinks he can show up without an appointment."

"So rude, right?" Aiden laughed, and—just as he'd been doing since they were children in West Sussex centuries ago —made himself at home.

Today, it meant kicking back in Dorian's leather executive chair. Back then, it'd meant accompanying the Redthorne boys on every trip into London for supplies for their father's medical experiments, or helping Dorian care for his horse, or partaking in the family's meals. He was the son of a local blacksmith, but his mother had died giving birth to him, and his father pretended Aiden didn't exist. He spent so much time at the Redthorne residence that eventually Dorian's mother gave him a room and instructed the staff to set a regular place for him at the table, where he dined with them for hundreds of meals throughout childhood and into adulthood, until the very last.

"Yet you never make good on those threats to fire me," Aiden said now.

Dorian scrubbed a hand over his face. "Bit of a long night, is all."

Long was an understatement. Trouble or not, Charlotte had gotten to him. Badly. No matter how many cold showers and stiff drinks later, he couldn't get her out of his system. Even a morning run around lower Manhattan before work couldn't clear his head. The feel of her velvety skin, the sounds she'd made as she writhed in his arms, the taste of her flesh still lingering on his lips, the dangerously addicting scent of her blood, rich and warm beneath her skin...

Every last memory conspired to undo him.

Drink her or fuck her, that's what he'd said. And though he'd come close to doing both, in the end, he'd walked away.

"What's her name?" Aiden asked. When Dorian didn't respond, Aiden laughed. "I've known you since your first wank, Redthorne. As a *human*. You think I don't recognize your morning-after look? Must've been one hell of a row. Vampire?"

"Stop talking," Dorian said, settling into the chair across from him. "Unless you're looking for a severance package. As in, the kind where I sever your head from your body."

Aiden laughed again. "You know I'm right."

Of course he was right. Aiden knew almost everything about him. After the massacre at West Sussex, when the dust had finally settled and Dorian's father decided they'd move to New York, Aiden's accompaniment wasn't even up for debate. As far as Aiden and Dorian were concerned, they were brothers, blood or not.

First as humans, then as vampires.

Aiden traveled with them to New York. Made a good life for himself here, learning the ropes of a new country and new customs right alongside Dorian. And later, when Dorian's actual brothers had turned their backs on him, Aiden's loyalty had never wavered.

Fifteen years ago, ready for new challenges, the pair started a new business venture together. From humble beginnings in a Chelsea storefront shoehorned between a highly questionable Indian restaurant and an even more questionable no-name drug store, they'd built FierceConnect, now a multi-billion-dollar company that had given Dorian more focus, purpose, and joy than he'd ever thought possible.

He owed the man his life. And he'd never be able to repay him—not if they had a hundred immortal lifetimes together.

"And how was your reunion with the little princelings?" Aiden asked now. "I trust they're all settled in at Ravenswood?"

Aiden had never been close with Dorian's brothers. They'd always treated him as a lowly outsider, even after he'd been turned right alongside them. It was a slight Aiden had never quite forgiven, and neither had Dorian.

He'd texted Aiden last night with a bare sketch of the situation with his brothers, including the news about Duchanes and the Chernikov demons, but now he filled him in on the rest.

"All in all, it was a right celebration," he finished up, "just as you'd expect from a family who spent the last half-century pretending one another were dead. Wait, did I say pretending? I meant wishing."

"It's good you told them about the acquisition. Perhaps they'll ease up about the alliance."

Dorian nodded, though he didn't share Aiden's optimism.

"And your father's death?" Aiden asked carefully.

"They didn't inquire."

"Dorian…"

He held up a hand, silencing Aiden's warnings. The truth would reveal itself eventually—either by Dorian's confession, or an enemy's ill-timed discovery. Dorian would do his best to ensure it was the former, but until then, he didn't wish to discuss it.

Taking his cue, Aiden switched tacks. "Sounds like quite an adventurous evening for a brooding recluse who hates socializing. Does this mean we're still not talking about the woman?"

Dorian shot him a warning glare.

"Keep your secrets, then. But here's something *else* that'll put your cock on ice." Aiden tossed a folder across the desk. "Armitage's sons are involved now, and they want more face-time and more intel."

"What? Why?" Dorian flipped through the file, a series of legal briefs outlining the types of information the Armitage mages wanted: SEC filings, P&L statements, trademark and patent filings, interviews of key staff, and the worst part—a bunch of informal meetings and get-to-know-you dinners.

Investigations were standard procedure during mergers and acquisitions for supernatural-owned and human companies alike, all to ensure the deal was aboveboard and the companies were a good match. But this felt downright invasive. Meetings? Dinners?

"Where is all this coming from?" Dorian asked. "I thought we were through the dog-and-pony phase. The fundraiser was supposed to be the last big hurrah."

Aiden passed him another sheet of paper. "Apparently they're fielding another bid, and you'll never guess who's offering."

Dorian scanned the text, his blood turning to ice. "House Duchanes? You've *got* to be shitting me. What could those overgrown fraternity boys possibly want with Armitage Holdings?"

"Leverage."

Dorian dropped the paper and massaged his temples, wishing he had something stronger than coffee. He didn't think Armitage would back out of their deal now—not with Isabelle's placement on the line, and the history of friendship he shared with Dorian's father—but how could he be certain? Who knew what sort of discontent Duchanes had been sowing? Money and power talked—in business and alliances both—but so did gossip.

"What am I supposed to do about this prick?" Dorian asked.

"Invite him to the fundraiser. Show him you're not intimidated by his antics."

"I'd rather stuff him into an iron box and drop him at the bottom of the Atlantic."

"All right, then. I'll make some calls, see what we might arrange."

Dorian sighed. The fundraiser was becoming more of a pain in his ass by the minute.

"Look, if you want Duchanes to back off," Aiden said, helping himself to a sip of Dorian's coffee, "you need to bring him into the fold. Treat him like family, maybe even offer him a position here, and perhaps he'll let his guard down a bit."

"Did you just put your filthy mouth on my favorite mug?"

Aiden raised his pinky alongside the mug, striking a posh pose. "I wouldn't be stooping to such pedestrian levels if you'd been a proper host and offered me refreshment upon arrival."

"How about a beating upon arrival?"

"That's not my kink, Mr. Redthorne," he said with a wink. "But no judgments."

Dorian shook his head. He'd never known his friend to be in a sour mood—not even when Dorian was doing his best to push his buttons. But despite Aiden's cheery disposition and the gorgeous weather outside, a deep sense of foreboding had crept into the day—one Dorian couldn't seem to shake.

"Talk to me, Dori," Aiden said, his voice softening. "Something's got your knickers in a twist."

"It's this deal." He flipped through the folder again. "Setting aside the problem of Renault Duchanes, why is Armitage dicking us around? They've seen our numbers. They know we've made every acquisition profitable, and with very little staff reduction. The old mage wants to unload his assets, and we're the best suited to facilitate that. What are they worried about?"

"Come on, mate. Armitage is old money, conservative as hell—especially for a mage. With Duchanes entering the playing field, I'm sure his sons want to make sure he's getting the best deal—for his business *and* for their sister, should it come to that."

It made sense, and Dorian finally nodded, the knot in his chest loosening a bit. "You're probably right."

"You'd think after all these centuries, you'd remember it." Aiden offered another smile, then drained the last of Dorian's coffee. "I don't suppose you've got any biscuits?"

"Bloody hell." Dorian rose from the chair to fetch the

box of cookies he kept stashed in the file cabinet and passed it over.

"Very kind of you, thanks," Aiden said. "So... free advice?"

"Remind me again what I'm paying you for, exactly?"

"Play the game, mate. Just until the acquisition goes through and you've secured the witch. Then your family will be revitalized, Armitage can retire into the sunset, and you can go back to being that reclusive billionaire vampire jackoff we all know and love."

"You're a prince, Aiden. A real fucking prince."

"My DNA spared me that particular curse." He pulled a cookie from the box and pointed it at Dorian. "But Dori, you've *got* to make an impression at the fundraiser. A *good* impression. That's why you're hosting it."

"I don't like hosting parties."

"I don't care what you like. Louse it up, and these guys will walk—straight into the arms of House Duchanes." He shoved the cookie into his mouth, powdered sugar coating his lips. "Wow, are these lemon biscuits? They're wonderful. Don't mind if I have another, do you?"

"We don't even know if Armitage's people will show." Dorian pressed the intercom for his assistant. "Veronica, do we have an update on the final head count for Friday?"

Seconds later, she poked her head into the office. "Two hundred and sixty-one confirmed tickets."

"And the Armitage people?"

"They've all RSVP'd."

Dorian took a steadying breath. "I don't suppose we've any regrets?"

"Not one."

"Fuck me." His foul mood was back with a vengeance, rapidly turning into a headache that drilled through the base of his skull. All those people, parading around Ravenswood, taking selfies in his garden, blathering on about the preschool admissions process, just as they'd done at the auction...

Sneaking into the closet for a night to remember...

"Don't they have anything better to do?" Dorian snapped.

"What did you expect, Mr. Dark and Mysterious?" Aiden asked. "They all want a look-see behind the curtain."

"I shouldn't have put in that infinity pool."

"I tried to tell you," Aiden said.

"People are drawn to money like flies on shit," Veronica said. "Rich flies. On solid gold shit. But still, I stand by the metaphor."

Dorian looked at his assistant in the doorway. Along with his driver Jameson, she was one of only a handful of humans in his employ. Ten years ago, she'd come to him as a blood donor—a human who consented to feeding vampires in exchange for money—but in the end, Dorian couldn't do it. She'd begged him for the bite, desperately in need of cash.

He'd offered her a job instead.

It was the best decision he ever made. She practically

ran the whole place, and unlike the other women in his life, she'd never betrayed his trust.

"Veronica," he said, "if you and Matthew had children, would you ever send them to a preschool that cost more than a university?"

Veronica laughed. "Oh, sweetie. If we had kids, we'd send them to your house. *You* have an infinity pool."

On the desk, Dorian's cell beeped with an appointment reminder.

"That'll be your one o'clock," Veronica said. "I'll call for your car. Make sure you're back for your two-thirty with the Armitage CFO. Oh, and you got a message from the bursar's office at NYU. Something about finalizing a tuition payment for a Jonathan Braynard?"

"Thank you, Veronica. I'll take care of it."

"Fine. Just don't forget about the two-thirty."

"You have my word."

He'd almost forgotten about the two-thirty. The CFO wanted to meet with Dorian for another walkthrough of the acquisition, an exercise in futility that would involve a lot of corporate-speak like "help me understand the narrative" and "I'm not seeing the vision, Mr. Redthorne."

Total fucking waste of time.

"Anything else?" Veronica asked.

Dorian was about to send her off, but Aiden cleared his throat, tapping impatiently on the folder on the desk.

There was no way around it. Not yet, anyway.

"Extend an invitation to House Duchanes for Friday's festivities," he said grudgingly.

If Veronica was surprised at the request, she didn't show it. "You got it."

"All right." Aiden rose from the chair and collected his files. "I'm heading out."

"Does this mean I can have my chair back? And my desk? And my bloody coffee mug?"

"Of course, your highness. I've got a lunch date—Layla, hot new vampire from marketing. Wish me luck."

"Workplace romance?" Dorian shook his head. "Now there's a right terrible idea."

"Who said anything about romance? I'd be happy with a shag in the copy room. Or maybe in the boss's office since he'll be out."

"As will you, if you make good on that threat."

"Did you know she competed on the Italian gymnastics team in the 1936 Olympics? I might need to limber up for this one."

"Don't break anything."

"No promises." Aiden leaned across the desk, scooping up the last cookie and smacking Dorian twice on the cheek. "In the meantime, I trust you'll behave yourself for our Hastings visitors?"

Dorian flashed a wolfish smile. "Mr. Donovan, when am I not a *perfect* gentleman?"

Aiden waited until he was safely out the door before he finally replied. "Would you like my response in an e-mail, a photo essay, or a spreadsheet with sortable columns?"

CHAPTER SIXTEEN

"I've been thinking about our arrangement." Rudy drained his martini and set the glass down hard on the patio table, making Charley flinch. "To say I'm disappointed is an understatement."

She shrunk down in her chair, hoping no one else in the restaurant's small outdoor seating area was listening in.

"I know. I'm... I'm sorry." She cringed at the meek and desperate sound of her own voice—a ridiculous combo, considering her résumé. She was Charlotte fucking D'Amico, for chrissake. She'd learned how to crack a safe by the time she was fifteen, could spot a fake Dutch Master at a hundred yards, and had amassed more knowledge of art history than most PhDs and museum curators twice her age. Her father's crew had watched her grow from a gangly kid into the strong, capable criminal she was today, but in Rudy's presence, Charley would always feel like a silly little girl getting underfoot while the grownups planned their next big score.

Through a cool, gentle voice that belied the anger in his eyes, Rudy said, "Your last several outings have been less than informative."

"How is that my fault? I can't control what people do with their belongings before we get there."

Rudy slammed his fist on the table, making her jump again. The people at the table behind them looked over.

Great. The last thing she wanted was another scene at Beyoglu. Just a ten-block walk from home, the Turkish café used to be one of her favorite lunch spots on the Upper East Side, but ever since Rudy had declared it their "usual" place, she hadn't been back on her own. He'd embarrassed her in front of the staff too many times for that. Now, whenever they arrived together, the hostess sat them outside.

"I'd advise you not to take that adolescent tone with me," he said, which Charley found ironic, considering he'd never stopped treating her like a kid. Still, she knew she was on dangerous ground.

Pulling off a successful heist wasn't like the movies, where everything came together seamlessly over a pack of cigarettes, a few cartons of Chinese takeout, and a music montage. It took weeks—even months—of careful, tedious preparation involving blueprints and public records searches, background checks on the property owners, surveillance, onsite intelligence gathering, payoffs of household employees and security technicians, identity theft, document forging, route planning, in-case-of-injury planning, contingency planning, and yes—lots and lots of Chinese takeout.

Lately, Rudy had been relegating Charley to mind-numbing fact-finding missions at private auctions and events, bringing her in later, cutting her out earlier, sharing fewer secrets. For months, her efforts had turned up jack shit; she figured that's why he'd been giving her the crap assignments. A punishment, a warning, call it what you want.

But lately she was starting to wonder if he believed she was involved in the infamous double-cross.

If he believed betrayal was genetic, passed down from father to daughter.

Charley sipped her water, trying to cool the rage boiling up inside her.

Rudy was pissed about her bad luck streak? Fine. But Charley was pissed too. Pissed that her parents had brought her into this world with no intention of helping her become a legitimate, tax-paying adult. Pissed that no one seemed to know what had truly happened to her father. Pissed that no one had bothered to find out.

It was her father's inside guy, Rudy had always believed. A man none of them had ever met. Her dad had vouched for him, bringing him in at the last minute on a big job in the West Village. The mark was an extensive art collector, the cache valued at $70 million on the street.

Posing as contractors, her dad and the guy went in alone, with Rudy and the others in strategic positions throughout the city. Charley was at Rudy's apartment, coordinating the whole thing through an elaborate system of coded text messages they'd worked out in advance.

The men had made it in, made it out, made it to the Holland Tunnel.

But that was the last anyone had heard from them. They never checked in again, never showed at the rally point in Jersey.

Hours turned into days. Charley and Rudy were frantic, the rest of the crew looking to them for answers they just didn't have.

A week after the heist, her dad finally turned up—murdered and left in an abandoned tire warehouse in Trenton.

The art he'd boosted—along with the inside guy—had vanished.

There was no evidence at the scene, nothing to tie him to the theft. The police said it was a gang hit—gunshot to the head, body stashed, wrong-place-wrong-time kind of thing. But that was bullshit. People like Charley's father never died from being in the wrong place at the wrong time. Everything was calculated and planned, nothing left to chance.

Rudy was out of his mind with grief over the loss of his brother, but he and the others were convinced it was an inside job—the worst kind. They believed Charley's father had double-crossed them, intending to split the proceeds with his man, only to have it all go south on him.

Charley blinked away old tears.

In his life, her father had been a lot of things. A master

thief. A violent drunk. A cheating husband. Even a murderer, at least one time that Charley knew about. But he was a loving father, and unwaveringly loyal to the crew he'd handpicked from the best guys he'd ever worked with. Unwaveringly loyal to Charley.

Yeah, he was a bad man—she'd accepted that long ago.

But he was not a traitor.

Unfortunately, Charley was alone in that opinion, and she'd learned long ago not to bring it up to Uncle Rudy. When it came to the death and apparent betrayal of his only brother, he couldn't go there.

"Tell me why we should keep investing in your professional development," Rudy said now, "when you're giving us nothing in return? The team is starting to question whether your head is in the game."

Charley clenched her jaw. *Nothing* could be further from the truth. The game, as he put it, was her pathway to a normal life, and she was *all* in.

But how much longer could she keep playing by his fucked-up rules?

"I get it," she said calmly, forcing a contrite smile. She needed to get back on his good side, and fast. "I'm sorry, Uncle Rudy. I'm frustrated too. The family from last night? They're broke. Almost everything valuable went to auction long before we heard about them. And they—"

Charley snapped her mouth shut as the waiter approached.

"Get some appetizers, kiddo," Rudy said, waving a hand over the menu. "Whatever you want."

Charley had already lost her appetite, but she ordered the hummus to make him happy, along with her favorite lunch platter and some baklava she'd take home for Sasha. Second only to making her feel like a child, Rudy's favorite hobby was picking up the check—the bigger the better.

They never talked about money, but despite the fact that her job didn't exactly offer a salary and benefits, and most of her father's liquid assets were stashed in offshore accounts she couldn't access, the $5,000 monthly mainte-nance fee on her father's penthouse always got paid, the lights stayed on, and no matter how often she charged up the credit card, Charley never once saw a bill.

Sasha may have gotten a scholarship to college, but when it came to everything else? Charley knew damn well who was taking care of them, and it wasn't some rainy-day insurance policy her father had set up.

Rudy didn't mind the elephant in the room, though, so long as it was *his* elephant. It gave him power over her, a fundamental control that guaranteed she'd never leave or betray him. Never mind what she wanted, what she thought was right. Charley didn't even know *how* to do anything else.

Worse, she didn't have the courage to try.

She'd helped plan complicated, dangerous heists, evaded the FBI... Hell, she'd even been stabbed once. But none of that mattered, because when push came to shove, Charley was a fucking coward. Afraid to look in the mirror. Afraid to live.

Without the life her father had built for her, the person

he'd molded her into, what did she have? What did she know?

The waiter returned with their appetizers and another martini for Rudy.

Now, watching him shove bread and hummus into his greasy mouth, Charley swallowed the bitter truth: without Rudy and the crew, Charlotte D'Amico didn't exist.

"Talk to me about the Whitfield," he said suddenly, a glob of hummus stuck on the corner of his mouth. "Dorian Redthorne has already made arrangements to donate it to the Jewish Historical Society."

Charley nearly choked on her water. "What? How do you know that?"

He smiled without showing his teeth, which meant he wouldn't reveal his source. After Charley and Rudy, there were three guys officially on the crew, but Rudy had an entire network of seedy freelance associates, every one of them jockeying for higher positions. Charley wasn't surprised he'd already heard about the painting. In this city, even the rats had ears.

"He must've mentioned his plans last night," he said. "You two seemed to be getting along quite famously when I saw you."

Charley's thighs clenched beneath the table as she tried in vain to stave off the memories, the ghost of Dorian's passionate touch still burning her skin.

"Charlotte." Rudy reached across the table, caging her hand in an icy grip. Then, in a tone as cold as his touch, "If this job isn't a priority for you anymore, maybe we need to have a *different* sort of conversation."

Charley tried not to squirm as shame and anger waged war in her chest.

Fuck you and your fucked-up priorities.

"It's my *only* priority, I swear." Charley's vision blurred with unshed tears, but she refused to cry in front of him. Crying wouldn't get the job done, and it certainly wouldn't win her any favors with Rudy. "It's just a run of bad luck. I'll break it—I know I will. Whatever you need from me, I'm here."

"Good." He finally released her hand, adjusting the hideous gold watch on his wrist. "I needed to hear that."

They finished their meal in silence, Charley picking at her food while Rudy shoveled it in by the forkful, pausing occasionally to leer at women passing on the sidewalk. After his third martini, Rudy finally wiped his mouth, and then tossed the blue cloth napkin over his empty plate. "I want you to head over to the JHS. Nose around, see if you can uncover anything about Redthorne's situation."

"Right now?"

"Unless you have something better to do?" Rudy narrowed his eyes, a slow smile spreading across his face. "Hey, how's Sasha? It's been so long since we've all had dinner together. Maybe I'll pay her a visit. I bet she'd like that."

Charley trembled inside. That's all it took. The barest hint of a threat, a subtle reminder that Rudy knew *exactly* what mattered most to Charley—and exactly how to leverage it.

"JHS. Thirty-Fourth Street, right? Already on my way." Charley rose from her chair and leaned in to kiss his cheek. "Thanks for lunch, Uncle Rudy. I'll call with an update later."

"Do that." He waited until she'd reached the corner before speaking again, calling out so loudly that everyone else on the sidewalk turned to look. "Charlotte?"

She spun to face him, forcing a smile despite the bile rising in her throat.

"You forgot Sasha's baklava." Rudy held up a to-go container, his smirk making her skin crawl. "Should I deliver it myself?"

CHAPTER SEVENTEEN

A hard-on was the last thing Dorian expected to get from his meeting at the JHS, but when he saw the woman standing at the information desk, all bets were off.

Impossible.

He'd been obsessing about her all day, and suddenly there she was, leaning against the desk with her beautiful ass calling to him like a beacon. She was dressed casually today—a V-neck blouse that showed off her neck and throat and dark jeans that hugged every delicious curve—but it was definitely Charlotte. The auburn hair, the delicate features, that confident, take-no-prisoners stance.

The scent.

He'd recognize his woman anywhere.

But what the bloody hell is she doing here?

Dorian never found out why she'd been snooping around the Salvatore penthouse last night, and now she was here, snooping around the museum moments after his meeting with the curator about the Whitfield.

It couldn't have been a coincidence.

Without making his presence known, Dorian crept up behind her, eavesdropping on her conversation with the desk attendant.

"Let me check," the attendant said, tabbing through files on his computer. "Desolate Rains. Okay, here it is. Acquisition is still pending, but yes, it's slated to be displayed in our permanent collection later this winter."

"Is there any other information you can give me?" Charlotte asked.

"It says here that the painting was one of a series looted during the Second World War," he said. "From—"

"Poland's National Art Institute," Charlotte said. "Yes, I'm familiar with the painting's history."

So was Dorian. The Whitfield was long thought destroyed. Since he'd heard a rumor of its reappearance in the States several years ago, Dorian had been working closely with the museum to locate it, the promise of his donation years in the making. He doubted the family he'd bought it from had any clue about its history, but the museum's curator certainly did.

To Dorian, he was the one who mattered.

"I'm afraid that's all the information I have right now," the attendant said. "But you're welcome to check back again next month. The curator should have more details about the exhibit by then."

"What about the donor? Did he say why he purchased the painting for you?"

"I'm sorry, ma'am. That's confidential. The donor has asked to remain anonymous."

"I might be able to answer your questions," Dorian said, finally revealing himself. "The donor and I have quite a history."

The smile on Charlotte's face as she turned toward him was worthy of its own painting, a work of art he tried desperately to memorize. She hid it quickly, masking her surprise, but the damage was done, and the verdict was in.

She was as happy to see him as he'd been to see her.

"Hello, Charlotte," he said warmly.

"Hi to you, too, Mr. Redthorne."

The sound of his name on her lips stirred his cock, and something inside his chest lurched sideways. The momentary confusion must have shown on his face, because Charlotte offered a smile and said, "Apparently my boss recognized you last night. I didn't know you were famous."

"Not quite. But I *am* curious."

"About?"

"Come with me." He led her into a secluded alcove behind the membership desk, desperate to get her alone. It wasn't exactly private, but Dorian didn't hesitate to pull her close, dragging his nose up the elegant slope of her neck, inhaling her scent.

"Are you following me, love?" He teased her skin with his lips, leaving a trail of light, fluttery kisses up to her ear.

She was so warm and soft, every inch of her begging for his touch.

She smells so fucking good…

"This is…" She trailed off, her eyelids fluttering closed.

"One hell of a coincidence? Also, not too terrible for a Monday."

She sighed in his arms, but the momentary excitement of their reunion was already fading. He could feel it in the tension of her muscles, see it in the determined set of her jaw as she pulled away from his kisses.

Charlotte cleared her throat and put a hand on his chest, holding him at arm's length. "This is really not a good idea."

Liar.

Dorian, who never backed down from a conquest, took a step backward to give her space.

"Why didn't you tell me you'd planned on donating the Whitfield?" she asked.

"It was supposed to be anonymous. And as I recall, you didn't even want to know my name."

"I was just surprised to hear about the donation, especially after what you paid for it. It seemed like you really wanted the painting."

"I did."

"Just to give it away?"

He shrugged. "That painting never should've ended up on the private market. It's a cultural treasure, and it needed to be returned."

She considered his words, her brow furrowed.

"You don't believe me," he said, the taste of his own lies burning his throat.

She was right to distrust him. Dorian had his reasons for doing what he did, but altruism certainly wasn't one of them. Atonement came close, but even that word couldn't encompass the true depth of his motives, nor illuminate the darkness that lived within them.

She adjusted the handbag draped over her shoulder, catching the neckline of her blouse and revealing the pink, lacy edge of her bra. "Most guys wouldn't give up a trophy like that. Especially without taking credit for it."

"Is it so hard to believe I'm a nice chap?"

Charlotte laughed—a sound Dorian wasn't ready to walk away from again. He wanted to hear it in the morning, coming from his shower. In the evening, coming from his bed. At all hours of the night, echoing off the walls of his game room and study and kitchen...

"I don't know any *chaps* that nice," she said.

He took a step toward her, closing the distance between them again. "That doesn't mean we don't exist."

"Even though you're totally staring at my tits?"

"What can I say? I'm a nice chap who happens to love your tits. Especially with that pink lace number you've got going on here." He traced a line down the center of her breast, her nipple hardening in the wake of his touch.

Charlotte smiled again, a look that felt more like an invitation than a goodbye, but then her eyes darkened, and she pulled her blouse back into place. "I... I should go. It was lovely seeing you again, Mr. Redthorne."

"Dorian. And just a moment, little prowler." He grabbed her hand, hoping it was enough to keep her here, at least for a few more seconds. "Is that really why you're here? To find out what I did with my painting?"

"I'd heard a rumor it was being donated. So yes, I came down to confirm."

"You came all the way down here," he said, running his thumb along the palm of her hand, "for something that could've been confirmed with a phone call? I don't think so."

A blush crept across the woman's exposed neck and cheeks, setting her copper eyes in sharp contrast. "Enlighten me with your theory, then."

"*I* think," he said, bringing his lips to her ear again and lowering his voice, "you were hoping to run into me."

"Why would I want to run into you?"

"Unfinished business."

When she didn't deny it, Dorian released her hand and moved to her curves, skimming the sides of her firm, beautiful breasts. She let out a soft sigh as his thumbs grazed her nipples, diamond-hard points that rose again at his touch.

Devil's balls, what he'd give for a closet right now, a stolen moment to finish what they'd started last night.

"You sure about that?" Charlotte tried to sound flirty and stern, but her voice trembled, her heartbeat turning ragged behind that thin pink bra.

"Oh, yes. I'm betting it kept you up all night," he whispered, gently nipping her ear, her neck. "Wondering what might've been. What it would've felt like with my cock sliding between your thighs, teasing you all night long, making you beg for more."

Charlotte swallowed hard, her pulse throbbing. "Is that what kept *you* up all night?"

He pressed his lips to her temple, considering the question. The same dirty, delicious thoughts *had* been on his mind all night, but it was so much more than that. Sure, he'd tried valiantly to convince himself it was just the interrupted sex—that maybe if he would've fucked her properly, he wouldn't be obsessing about her today.

But seeing her in the daylight, her bright smile, the heady way she looked at him after he'd whispered those dark, sexy promises in her ear... It was more than physical. There was something about Charlotte that had ensnared him from that first moment in the lobby of the Salvatore, and now, Dorian wanted to know her. *All* of her.

"Since I met you?" he asked. "Absolutely."

"We met less than twenty-four hours ago," she said.

"And I haven't slept a wink. You?"

She looked up at Dorian through thick lashes, eyes full of a desire so unchecked it sent an electric jolt straight to his cock.

"I... I really should go," she said, breaking their intense eye contact and reaching for her phone, as if she might be saved by the buzz or the bell. "I have to meet—"

"I'm going to ask you a question." Dorian encircled her wrist with his fingers. "Your answer will determine how the rest of this plays out."

Goosebumps rose along her arms, and when she spoke,

her voice was tentative, her gaze dreamy and faraway. "Okay."

"Do you want me to let you go?"

She stared at the fingers wrapped around her wrist, no idea what the soft pulse beneath her skin was doing to him, no idea what he could do to *her* if he let his true desires take hold.

Silence descended, the only sounds her sharp intake of breath and the steady thrum of that pulse, beckoning him closer. Teasing him. Tormenting him.

"It's a simple question, Charlotte." He released her wrist and took her face between his hands, her silky hair tickling his fingers. It was impossible not to imagine pulling on that hair while he fucked her mouth, sliding into the back of her throat as she sucked him in deep, a fantasy he'd lived out a hundred times since last night. He'd still tasted her on his skin this morning, on his lips, on his fingers, and all he could think about was stripping her bare and plundering her until they both collapsed from exhausted pleasure.

He thought he'd never see her again.

And now, standing so close to the woman of his fantasies he could almost taste her, he looked deep into her eyes, whispering one last time against those luscious, rose-colored lips. "Yes, or no?"

CHAPTER EIGHTEEN

Yes, or no?

After a picnic dinner of cheese fries and vanilla shakes, Charley lounged on a blanket in Bryant Park with Sasha, alternately watching the movie and wondering if she'd done the right thing.

In the hours since she'd run into Dorian at the museum, she'd gone from yes, to no, to *hell* no, and was currently hovering around "worst mistake of her life" territory. But the moment her phone lit up with a text from her newest contact, that "hell no" turned into a "holy orgasmic yes" in a heartbeat.

Miss me, love?

I've been keeping myself occupied, she replied.

Literally or figuratively?

Use your imagination.

I'm sitting at home doing just that. Where are you?

On a date. Go away.

You're on a date, but you're texting me?

YOU'RE texting ME.

And yet...

Charley bit back a smile. *You're impossible!*

I must've made quite a second impression if you're still ignoring your date for me.

I'm not ignoring her! But for the record, my sister would think you're a total creep.

What kind of creep buys a girl a jumbo hot dog on their first date?

Hot dogs are the creepy man's trademark. And that wasn't our first date. More like #4.

I see you've given our relationship a lot of thought.

You're the one who called me your wife.

Married within an hour of meeting. Yet, sadly, a relationship unconsummated.

Charley could practically hear the teasing sigh in his voice.

Pro tip, hot stuff, she replied. *If you want your wife to put out, take her to a hotel. Or on a cruise. I hear the ladies love that shit.*

You're dreadful!

Sooo not what you said last night.

You're lucky I couldn't find any closets in the museum. Today might've turned out differently for both of us.

The idea made her stomach flip. Charley couldn't decide whether she was relieved about the lack of closets or disappointed.

Pretty cocky for a man sitting home alone while his wife's out on a date, she replied.

At least tell me what you're wearing.

You already know. You saw me earlier, remember?

How could I forget? Seeing your ass in those tight jeans distracted me so much I missed my 2:30 meeting. So tell me again.

Charley sent him the shrugging emoji.

Well, he replied. *You're not very fun.*

Really? Even though I'm not wearing underwear? I bet the rest of the guys here think a girl who goes commando to a movie in a public park is LOTS of fun. Maybe I should take a poll?

Just so we're clear, I'll kill the first man who answers that question. Wait… does this mean you weren't wearing panties at the museum?

BRB—just got to my favorite part in the movie.

Which movie?

Sleepless in Seattle. Empire State Building scene.

I knew it! You're a hopeless romantic. A sexy-as-hell, hopeless, panty-less romantic who drives me—

"You are *so* busted!" Sasha swiped the phone from Charley's hand, her eyes lit with mischief as she scanned the screen. "Is this Mr. Already Forgotten?"

Charley reached for the phone, but Sasha wouldn't relent.

"I can't believe I'm watching this movie while you're sexting some guy like it's no big deal." Sasha glanced down at the phone, her expression souring. "You're not wearing underwear?"

An older couple on a blanket in front of them turned around to give Charley the evil eye.

"Sasha!" Charley whispered. Her cheeks burned, but Sasha only giggled.

"He thinks you're romantic," she whispered. "Obviously he doesn't know you very well. Oh, he sent a new one!" Sasha glanced again at the phone, eyes narrowing as she read the latest message. "Wait. Now he sounds like a psycho."

"Give me that." Charley swiped the phone back and checked the screen.

I need you here ASAP, Charlotte. Nonnegotiable. Find a cab —my driver is unavailable.

It wasn't her man. It was Rudy.

"It's the boss," Charley said, unable to keep the disappointment from her voice.

"Good ol' Uncle Rudy." Sasha rolled her eyes. "We already know *he's* a psycho."

Everything okay? Charley texted back.

Be here in 30 minutes. Time to talk about your future.

Charley's stomach bubbled, threatening to revolt against the milkshake. She was already on Rudy's shit list, and she'd completely forgotten to report in on her museum findings. There was no telling what he wanted now.

"You need to ditch that gig," Sasha said. "I know he's your uncle, but still. You're super smart, talented, driven. Why stay in a crappy job when you can find something awesome?"

"It pays really well, Sasha. I can't just walk away."

The movie credits were rolling, but the sisters were still drawing nasty looks from everyone around them.

"So that's the most important thing?" Sasha asked. "Money?"

"It is when you don't have any. And that's not something I want *either* of us to worry about—not ever. Okay?"

It wasn't the first time they'd had this argument, and Charley knew it wouldn't be the last. But for now Sasha dropped it, gathering up their trash and helping Charley fold the blanket.

"Guess I need to grab a cab," Charley said. Rudy lived in a massive steel-and-glass tower in the no-man's land between Chinatown and the Financial District, arguably the most inconvenient location in Manhattan. Getting there in thirty minutes was about as likely as finding that awesome new job Sasha thought she deserved, but she had to try. "You heading home?"

"Nah, I'll see if Darcy wants to meet up." Sasha linked her arm with Charley's. "Come on, I'll wait with you. Forty-Second Street?"

"Let's try Fifth," Charley said. On Fifth, she could at least wait in front of the library, one of her favorite buildings in the city.

They packed up the rest of their things and threaded their way through the post-movie crowd. Traffic on Fifth Avenue was a nightmare; every cab that passed was already occupied.

"Figures." Charley sat on the library steps, gazing up at the stately marble lions that'd guarded the entrance for more than a hundred years. In their familiar company, she relaxed.

So many people thought living in New York was exactly like a movie, where everyone was fabulous and rich, spending their evenings at A-list restaurants with doll-house-sized meal portions and rude waiters, or hopping from club to exclusive club, or—at the other end of the spectrum—getting drunk on cheap beer and stumbling through Times Square.

But for Charley—more than the restaurants, the clubs, the music scene, the tourist traps—the best places in New York were the ones that had survived the centuries. Libraries, museums, universities—the places that showcased and archived humanity's great achievements, the things that would continue to inspire awe, even when people themselves no longer could.

Charley blew out a breath. Even as her own life descended into chaos, at least she could count on her beloved lions, always here to remind her that no matter what mistakes she made, some things endured.

Maybe she would, too.

"What are you thinking about?" Sasha asked.

"Patience and Fortitude," Charley said.

"What?"

"The lions. Those are their names—Patience and Fortitude."

Sasha finally smiled. "You're a nut. Hey, an empty cab! Come on."

In a flash Sasha bolted to the street, hailing the cab as Charley ran to catch up.

"Have fun with Uncle Boss," Sasha said, opening the door for her. "Later, we're working on your résumé."

Charley climbed into the cab and blew a kiss goodbye, telling herself for the millionth time that she'd find a way out of this life eventually.

It just wasn't going to be tonight.

"Fulton and Water Street," she told the driver. "Fast as you can."

CHAPTER NINETEEN

A vampire, upon the rare occurrence of his death, swiftly turned to ash. As such, he required neither a coffin nor a crypt; the four winds would simply scatter him where he fell.

Yet Ravenswood was an exact replica of the West Sussex estate, with no detail left to chance. Not the stately manor itself. Not the lush, verdant gardens. And not the crypts that stretched out beneath the property in an endless network of stone arteries. In England, when the original home was occupied by humans, such crypts held the bones of generations of Redthornes, an honorable resting place for members of the bloodline whose prominence was rivaled only by its longevity.

Until it wasn't.

Here at Ravenswood, the crypts held no bones, no honorable men, for none were left in the Redthorne line. Instead, they housed only the ashes of Augustus

Redthorne, still lying where he'd fallen, no winds to scatter him.

Across from the vampire king's eternal resting place was a hollow tomb, a cavernous chamber for which he had—in the final months of a life that should've been immortal—found another use.

"It was his research laboratory," Dorian said now, watching his youngest brother flip through one of their father's journals.

Dorian had come down to the crypts to do the same, though he wasn't expecting company. He suspected he and his brother had very different motives.

"He never stopped." Gabriel set the book on the stone slab at the center of the tomb, then picked up another, running his fingers along the cracked spine. "So many bloody experiments, so many theories."

And no time for his children, Dorian thought. It was an old refrain; one they'd stopped speaking aloud in adolescence, but one that still rang in Dorian's ears whenever he thought of his father. Though the man had been born a noble who wouldn't have had to work a day in his life, curiosity drove him to medicine, and he'd spent the majority of his human years bent over such work.

When he wasn't treating patients in London, he was writing about them in West Sussex, candle burning low on the desk, quill scratching across the page, each illness a puzzle to be solved.

But here at Ravenswood, hundreds of years and thousands of miles away from his old life as a human doctor, he *became* those patients. An ailment with no cure. A mystery. A complex puzzle only he could solve.

And maybe he would have, if he'd had more time.

"It wasn't a demon attack, was it?" Gabriel asked.

"Father had many enemies."

"As do you. Answer the question."

Answer the question. Dorian wished he could. It was a simple word—*no*. But that one simple word would unleash *much* more complicated questions—questions Dorian had neither the knowledge nor the heart to field tonight.

He closed his eyes and leaned back against the stone wall, letting the cold seep into his bones, wondering—yet again—how the fuck it had come to this.

Dorian had been estranged from his brothers for five decades, but there was one thread that would always bind them: a mutual, all-encompassing hatred of the man who'd turned them into vampires.

Augustus Redthorne.

He'd been a difficult father as a man, a brutal bastard as an immortal, and for Dorian and his brothers, the only good thing about his royal ascendency was that he spent so much time overseas on diplomatic missions, they hardly crossed paths. Even after his brothers had relocated to other states, leaving Dorian to clean up his own messes in New York, their father rarely set foot on American soil. When he did, he was easy enough to avoid; he spent most of his time in Manhattan, meeting with the other supernatural leaders and the heads of the greater vampire houses.

Several months ago, however, Augustus turned up at

Ravenswood after cutting short a trip to France. Normally Dorian would've retreated to his penthouse in Tribeca, but something held him back.

His father seemed unwell—not a word Dorian had come to associate with *any* vampire, let alone the king.

The two barely exchanged words, and it took his father a full month to finally admit what Dorian had already suspected: he'd fallen ill, and he needed time to diagnose the problem. To find the cure.

It wasn't possible for an immortal vampire to get sick, yet he was. Clearly. Dorian wouldn't have believed it if the evidence wasn't staring him right in the face, night after night.

Dorian hated his father with a passion that rivaled the burning sun over the Sahara, but that didn't mean he wanted him to die. He tried to help, but Augustus refused the intervention of a freelance witch, refused any spells and enchantments Dorian procured. Eventually, he stopped feeding, turning away human blood donors and blood bags alike. Even demons.

Dorian had felt like a child again, peering through the gap of the door into his father's study, watching him pore over his books while his dinner turned cold and the candles burned to nubs. Augustus spent all his time in the makeshift laboratory, examining his hair and blood under the microscope, taking notes, making sketches, performing experiments. Dorian was instructed to inform the other leaders and houses that Augustus was attending to important, groundbreaking research and could not be disturbed.

If there were breakthroughs, he never shared them with Dorian.

If there were regrets, he never shared those either.

He was, in his final months, as he'd always been— completely unreachable.

Gabriel was right.

In the end, it wasn't an enemy attack that had taken Augustus.

It was an illness. A violent, human illness that had ravaged his body, thoroughly and ceaselessly, until his final labored breaths. And with those breaths, Augustus asked his eldest son for the simple courtesy of a fast end.

For centuries, Dorian had wanted his father to suffer. To live in agony for betraying his family, killing his wife and youngest sons while condemning the other four to an eternity of misery.

But for that brief moment, there wasn't two and a half centuries of anger and resentment. There was only the last wish of a dying man, and Dorian obliged, for both their sakes.

Dorian opened his eyes now, the sulfuric smell of the match lingering in his memories. Suddenly he wanted to tell Gabriel everything, to relieve himself of the great burden of these secrets. He wanted his father's death to draw them close, as his life had driven them apart. He wanted them all to know how much he loved them, how he'd never stop searching for the answers his father couldn't seem to find.

But when he looked at Gabriel now, the tension in his

muscles, the fist clenched at his side, he knew he couldn't burden him with this. He couldn't burden any of them.

Not until they were safe.

"He died by fire," Dorian finally said. That, at least, was true.

"By his own hand?"

"By mine." Dorian scrubbed a hand over his mouth. "He asked me to do it, Gabriel. To end his suffering."

"Suffering from what?"

"He wouldn't say."

"You think it really *was* an attack?"

"Frankly, I don't know what to think."

Gabriel tossed the journal onto the pile, then put his hands behind his head, tipping back to look at the rough stone ceiling. The tombs were fitted with overhead lights, and in the soft orange-yellow glow of the bulb, his skin looked eerily pale.

"Any last words?" he asked.

For a moment, Dorian wished he could ease his youngest brother's ache with a pleasant end to the otherwise gruesome tale of their father's demise.

But the man's last words were much too terrifying to share.

Stark in their utter simplicity, as cold and cutting as the scalpel he'd wielded against his own flesh, night after night as he desperately chased his cure.

Your brothers… you must find… genetic…

Then, he went up in smoke.

There were answers to the riddles, Dorian suspected,

encoded in those journals. But so far, Dorian hadn't made head nor tail of them. All he knew was that his father, the most powerful immortal vampire in an age, had suffered and died of a human illness, and that illness—that weakness—allegedly ran through the blood of the four remaining Redthorne royals. Even a *whisper* of that knowledge would be a deadly weapon in enemy hands, and down here in the crypts of Ravenswood was an entire tomb filled with such secrets.

Just because Dorian hadn't deciphered them yet didn't mean they were undecipherable.

"Nothing, right?" Gabriel asked, head still tipped back, arms spread wide as if he were looking to the heavens for answers from their dead father.

Wrong direction, brother.

Testing the iron gate around his heart, Dorian said, "If you're looking for deathbed confessions and an unburdening of regrets about what a terrible father he was, I'm sorry to disappoint you. He said nothing, Gabriel. He died empty, but for the secrets he carried with him to hell."

A bitter laugh escaped Gabriel's mouth. "You'd think I'd be used to it by now, but it never gets easier, does it?"

"Hearing of Father's abject failings?"

"No." Gabriel lowered his arms and turned to face him, his eyes as cold and black as the crypts themselves, a darkness that echoed for eternity. "Being disappointed by you."

CHAPTER TWENTY

There was a snake in Rudy's living room. A snake with dull gray eyes and spiky, over-gelled hair who leered at Charley with a mix of lust and pure hatred.

Mental note: order a new Beyoncé later.

"Charley, Charley, *Charley*," the snake said, running his tongue along his top teeth in a move he probably thought was sexy. "You're looking fine as *fuck*."

"Travis." It was all she could give him—his name. It'd been more than a year since their last night together, but the sight of her ex still made her skin crawl. It probably always would.

"So glad you could finally join us." Uncle Rudy stepped out from the kitchen and handed Charley a gin and tonic, gesturing for her to take the seat next to Travis on the couch, probably as punishment for being late. "Care to tell me about your evening?"

Charley sipped her drink—cheap gin for the guests, of

course—buying herself a minute to think. Rudy was definitely angling for something. He hadn't asked about the JHS, and none of the other crew members were here to talk shop. Only Travis, a freelancer they'd met the year after her father's death. The others didn't think much of him—in fact, Bones had never quite forgiven Charley for getting involved with such a lowlife—but Rudy still used him sometimes for fake passports and customs forms.

So what the fuck was he doing there now?

"Charlotte?" Rudy pressed. "I asked you a question."

Charley shrugged her shoulders, downing another gulp. "I was about to call you when I got your text—I went to the JHS earlier to snoop around. The Whitfield was donated, like you said. The details are confidential, but everything seemed on the up-and-up."

"Why would a man like Dorian Redthorne pay that much for a painting just to donate it?" Rudy asked, downing the last of his drink.

Charley hid the smile behind her glass, remembering what Dorian had said. "Maybe he's just a nice chap."

Rudy laughed, a machine-gun cackle that hurt her ears. "Oh, kiddo. Didn't the old man ever teach you there's no such thing?"

"Guess we didn't get around to that lesson."

"No, I suppose not." Rudy turned back toward the kitchen. "I need another drink. Why don't you two catch up?"

The moment he left the room, Travis was practically on

top of her, stroking her arm with his cold fingers, sniffing her hair. "It's good to see you, baby."

She curled in on herself, shrugging him off.

"Aw, don't be like that." Travis trailed a finger along her cheek, tongue darting out between his lips like a damn reptile. "I haven't stopped thinking about you. All those nasty things you used to say. You remember, don't you?"

"Not really." She slid as far as she could to the other end of the couch, feigning indifference. "Guess I've moved on."

"Guess you're still a stuck-up cunt."

She glared at him, new fire crackling in her belly. "*Never* doubt it, snake."

God, how the fuck had she ever fallen for this guy? The memory of his hands on her body, his crunchy hair, his sloppy tongue in her ear as he grunted over her like an ape... She nearly gagged.

"Come on, baby. I'm just playing." Travis' gaze traveled down her body, stopping to rest at her crotch. "You still want it. I can tell by those tight jeans you wore for me."

"Don't touch me, Travis. I mean it."

"Nah, I don't think you do." He shoved his hand between her thighs, pinching her crotch through the jeans. "That's a good little slut. Just like—what the *fuck*, bitch?"

Travis recoiled, his clothes soaked in Charley's gin and tonic.

"I told you not to touch me, asshole. Do it again, and I'll do something more... *permanent*." This time, she glared at *his* crotch, making sure he got the message loud and clear.

Then, calling out to Rudy, "I need another drink, Uncle Rudy. And Travis needs a towel."

Her uncle returned a few minutes later with fresh drinks and a kitchen towel. He took one look at Travis, sulking at the far end of the couch in a soaked shirt, and laughed. "I see the reunion is going well."

"Smashing. What's on the agenda tonight?" Charley asked, forcing a smile. She wasn't interested in reunions or laughs over a few drinks. She'd bailed on the rest of girls' night with Sasha, turned off her phone during a perfectly delicious text volley with Dorian on the cab ride up, and endured the filthy, unwanted advances of her sleazy ex. The *least* Rudy could do was get to the fucking point.

"A new assignment, possibly. But believe me when I say there's *no* room for error here." He sipped his martini so delicately it looked like a kiss. Over the rim, he exchanged a glance with Travis that Charley couldn't decipher. "We need to be certain you can handle it. We have... concerns."

"What about Bones and the guys?" she asked, wondering when the fuck Rudy and Travis had become a 'we.'

Where was the rest of the crew?

"This is more of a... side project." Rudy and his pet snake shared another cryptic glance. "We're counting on your discretion."

Charley nodded, forcing herself not to push. She knew better than to challenge Rudy or go behind his back to the others, but this kind of secrecy was bad news. The fresh churn in her gut went well beyond her usual attack of conscience; something about this gig was off.

"Are you interested in the details?" Rudy asked.

What I'm interested in, you son of a bitch, is dumping this drink in your face, setting you on fire, and shooting your charred corpse out of a cannon over the East River.

"Of course," she said brightly, setting her drink on the coffee table. "What's the job?"

Travis retrieved an envelope from the back of his waistband and handed it over. "Shindig upstate on Friday night. You're an attorney attending at the behest of your client."

The envelope was still warm from his body heat. Charley tried not to grimace as she thumbed through the contents: a satellite map of a sprawling estate in Annandale-on-Hudson, a ticket to the event, and a few details about her temporary identity.

"What am I bidding on?" she asked.

"No bids," Travis said. "This one's a fundraiser for some kiddie art charity. A thousand bucks a head too. You'd think they were trying to *adopt* those fucking rug rats."

"You shelled out a grand for this?" Charley raised her eyebrows at her uncle. "Must be a pretty sure thing."

Rudy sprayed her with his machine-gun laugh. "Not a cent. That ticket is Travis' handiwork."

A forgery. Great. Let's hope they're not checking these against the guest list.

"According to our sources," Rudy said, "the estate is one of only a handful of private residences in the hamlet.

It's allegedly furnished with rare artifacts and art dating back to ancient times."

"The guy also collects vintage cars," Travis said.

"Sounds like you've got this one locked down." Charley stuffed the paperwork back into the envelope and tossed it onto the coffee table, retrieving her drink. "What do you need me for?"

"An inside look," Rudy said. From a leather folio, he pulled out a stack of surveillance photos and a detailed floor plan of the house. "We've got a good handle on the external points of entry," he said, pointing out the red Xs marked around the perimeter, "but we don't know the precise security situation, or how many people have access. Preliminary surveillance suggests two groundskeepers, a cook, a driver, and at least three housekeepers on a rotating weekly schedule."

"How many residents?" she asked.

"One man, with only occasional guests, some of which may be there now."

"The alarm system was upgraded about six months ago," Travis said, pointing out a photo of a security company van parked in the driveway, a pair of contractors standing next to it. Charley wondered if the contractors were on Rudy's payroll.

With so much intel, it was clear Travis and Rudy had already done a ton of digging.

She brought the drink to her lips, covering her frustration with a long pull. It was just like Rudy not to involve her until the last minute. That's all she'd ever be to him—a pawn. If anything went south, she'd be the first to go down and the last to talk, because she had the most to lose.

Even more than the money, the penthouse, the credit card bill he paid without fail, Sasha's life would *always* be Rudy's true bargaining chip, and everyone in that room knew it.

"In addition to the security details," Rudy went on, "we need more intel about the cache itself. We've traced a lot of artwork to this location, but we can't be sure exactly what's there. When we go in—not if, but *when*—we need to be prepared for anything. We won't get another shot."

Charley spread the photos out on the table, giving everything a closer look. The property featured a 20,000-square-foot Elizabethan manor home on fifty acres of lush gardens, with stunning views of the Hudson River and the Catskill Mountains beyond. There was also a massive garage, a guesthouse, and several smaller outbuildings, everything pristine and perfect.

It was breathtaking.

Also, a ridiculous amount of property for one man.

It was situated far away from the main roads. If Charley needed to make a quick escape, it wouldn't be a simple matter of dashing out into the street and hailing a cab.

Worse, fundraisers required a lot more social interaction than auctions. With no main event to keep people occupied, everyone would want to talk and network and generally pry into one another's business—all things that could get her noticed if she didn't keep her story straight. She'd have to really be on her game, and the "attorney" cover felt too complicated, too easy to screw up.

It was a lot to consider.

But like all of Rudy's "requests," refusing wasn't really an option.

"I want a driver," she said finally. "He has to stay within a mile of the home at all times."

"Absolutely," Rudy said.

"I'm not sitting in weekend traffic on I-87, either. Get me a room in town for Thursday night."

"Consider it done."

"I'll need a new dress."

"Of course."

"Shoes and accessories too."

"You've got the credit card—go crazy." Rudy sipped his drink, eyes sparkling over the rim of his glass. "Any other demands, kiddo?"

"Just one." Charley leaned back on the couch and crossed her arms over her chest. "After this job, I want a vacation. Three weeks in Spain, all expenses paid. And that's for me *and* my sister. Nonnegotiable."

Rudy narrowed his eyes, but he was already nodding. "Do the job right, and you'll be rewarded."

He swept the surveillance photos and floor plans back into his folio, leaving Charley with the envelope containing her fundraiser ticket, map, and details about her identity. She stuffed it into her purse, glancing once more at Travis.

"I'm so glad you're getting in bed with us on this," he said, flashing another creepy grin.

Other than the forged ticket and surveillance details he'd provided, she couldn't figure out why he was still here.

"What's your involvement, exactly?" she asked.

The look in his eyes was so gleefully menacing, she half expected him to unhinge his jaw and swallow her whole.

"I'm your driver, baby." He reached over and squeezed her knee, a promise and a threat. "Just you and me, like old times."

CHAPTER TWENTY-ONE

The cool, white bedding was the best invitation Charley had gotten all night.

After following her into the elevator at Rudy's, Travis had spent the entire ride down groping and pawing, pressing her against the wall like a dog in heat. He'd stopped short of climbing into the cab with her, but that was only because she'd slammed the door in his face.

A long, hot shower helped calm her nerves, and now Charley sank into her luxurious down pillows, ready to put that part of the evening squarely in the rearview.

But the oblivion of sleep wouldn't take her. Her mind was too busy racing through the details of the fundraiser: the cover story she'd have to embellish, the risks she'd have to anticipate, the contingency plans, the backup contingency plans. With Travis as her driver, she couldn't leave anything to chance.

After an hour of tossing and turning, she finally got out

of bed, clicking the remote to open the blinds. Thirty stories below her windows, the streets of Park Avenue pulsed with nightlife, the car horns a muted symphony through the glass.

She wondered if Dorian was awake. He'd said he had a house upstate as well as a penthouse in Tribeca, a Manhattan neighborhood she couldn't see from her place on Park Avenue. As the cabs raced by below, she imagined one of them ferrying her downtown to his apartment, straight into the blissful heat of his touch.

Her cell phone taunted her from the nightstand, silent and black, nothing but pure, untarnished potential. Before she could talk herself out of it, she grabbed it and pulled up his number.

You awake? she texted.

Yes, he replied immediately. *Thinking of you, actually. What are you doing Friday night?*

Hmm. That sounds suspiciously like a lead-up to a date.

So?

We said no dating!

When she'd finally agreed to exchange numbers at the museum, she did so on one condition: that they'd keep it casual. Flirty texts were risky enough, but under no circumstances could they actually date. She thought she'd made that clear.

So why was he asking her out?

It's not a date, he replied. *It's a party. A terribly boring party. Please come.*

Why would I come to a terribly boring party?

Not come TO. Come AT.

Charley cracked up. *Assumptions, assumptions!*

We'll have access to at least a dozen closets.

Hmm... this party is sounding less boring by the minute.

So... it's a non-date?

Disappointment settled into her stomach. *Can't*, she replied. *Work thing.*

Cancel.

I wish. Rain check?

Charley froze, her fingers hot over the screen. Why did she ask for a rain check? She was the one who'd made the no-dating rule in the first place, and now she was encouraging him.

God, what is it about this guy?

Her phone buzzed with his reply. *I'll hold you to it. The hot dog cart isn't the same without you.*

I'll bet. Charley smiled, but as much as she was enjoying their texts, she knew they couldn't lead anywhere. Eventually, she and her Mr. Redthorne would hit a dead-end, and he'd become nothing more than a memory.

With a soft sigh, she texted her response. *Ok, gotta go. Time for bed.*

Alone?

Wouldn't you like to know?

Seconds later her phone vibrated with a call. *DORIAN REDTHORNE* flashed on her screen, and the angel on her shoulder shouted a firm warning.

Don't fucking answer it. Hit ignore, delete his number, block him, erase him from your mind...

But in the end, the devil won out, and Charley hit the answer button, a grin spreading on her face. "Good evening, Mr. Redthorne."

"Yes," the man said firmly.

"Yes, what?"

"Yes, I *would* like to know. I would *very* much like to know if you're in bed alone."

"I am," she admitted. "Unfortunately. And before you get your hopes up about what I'm wearing, it's just boxer shorts and an old T-shirt from—"

"Take them off. Now."

The command, so firm and delicious after all their earlier jokes, made her instantly hot. She set the phone on the bed and stripped off every last scrap of fabric. She thought about closing the blinds, but decided against it, her body basking in the glow from the neighboring towers. With her bedroom lights turned off, no one could see inside, but the thought that someone might be watching anyway sent a forbidden thrill to her core.

Charley grabbed the phone. "Okay. I'm here."

"Are you naked?"

She lay back on her bed, stretched out over the top of her soft down comforter, grateful that Sasha's room was on the other side of the penthouse. "Naked and alone on this huge king bed, and I'm very, *very* wet."

"Bloody hell," Dorian said. "Do you have any idea what I'd do to you if I were there right now?"

"I'm a little hazy on the details." Charley was playing with serious fire, but she couldn't stop. It wasn't just the museum run-in; she hadn't stopped thinking about Dorian for more than five minutes since she'd first seen him in the Salvatore lobby. After that, he'd rescued her from that Duchanes dickweed, bought her drinks, made her laugh, touched her in ways that no other man had ever dared, *and* saved her from a mugging in Central Park.

Just seeing his name light up her phone made Charley ache with a desire that pulsed hot through her veins.

Now, Charley's fantasies would never let her be free of him.

She didn't *want* to be free of him.

"Tell me," she whispered, her hand trailing over her belly, down to the smooth mound below. She stroked a finger lightly over her clit, shocked at how wet she really was. "Tell me what you'd do to me if you were here right now."

He groaned in her ear, a deep vibration that made her stomach flip.

"Are you touching yourself?" he asked.

"Yes."

"Did you touch yourself last night, all alone in that great big bed without me?"

"Yes," Charley moaned, her fingers slipping inside. "I thought of you, your face buried between my thighs, fucking me with your dirty mouth."

"I'd tie you to the bed first, though, good and tight. Then I'd lick every inch of your flesh, sucking and tasting until I had my fill, until you were writhing on the bed, *begging* me to let you come. Would you like that, Charlotte?"

"So much," Charley breathed. She stroked herself, slipping her fingers in and out of her pussy as she pictured his face, his lips, imagining him sucking her nipples, licking a hot path down her belly. "You have no idea."

"You're getting close, love. I can hear it in your voice."

Dorian moaned softly, a sound that raised goosebumps on Charley's skin as she drove her fingers inside, then pulled out, massaging her clit in slow, tantalizing circles as the sound of his deep, delicious voice made her even wetter.

She was almost there, her muscles clenching, her heart beating wildly as she stroked faster and harder...

"That's it, gorgeous," he purred. "I want you to come hard for me, come like it's my tongue between your thighs, sucking that exquisite—"

"Dorian! Oh *fuck*, yes!"

The orgasm hit her hard and fast, and Charley damn near exploded, gasping into the phone as waves of white-hot pleasure slammed through her body.

It took her a few minutes to come back down, and when she finally did, Dorian was still on the phone, waiting patiently for her return. In the neon blaze of the city lights, her skin glistened, her body warm and relaxed.

Charley let out a deep sigh, thinking again of the ocean. Dorian was the tide, pushing her past her limits, dragging her to the very edge, making her feel powerful and alive.

It was terrifying.

It was beautiful.

It was *addicting*, and now that she'd gotten another taste, Charley didn't think she'd ever be able to stop.

"I wish you were here," she whispered, an unplanned admission that felt a hell of a lot more needy than sexy, but Charley didn't care. She *did* wish he was there, lying next to her in that great big bed, whispering about all the naughty things he wanted to do to her. Kissing her. Holding her close as she drifted into a dreamless, worry-less sleep, carried away by the surging sea.

"Me too." Dorian's breath was slow and even, his voice gentle and a little sad when he finally spoke again, the last words she heard before she finally passed out. "Sweet dreams, love."

CHAPTER TWENTY-TWO

"Thank you for accommodating me on such short notice, Marlys." Dorian held open the door, ushering the Darkmoon witch into Luna del Mar, a witch-owned café in Staten Island that served as neutral territory for all supernaturals.

She flashed a radiant grin. "You know I'm always honored to serve House Redthorne, Dorian."

Yes, and he'd just paid $150,000 and a good amount of his own blood for that honor. It was extortion, plain and simple, but Dorian couldn't proceed without a high-level witch at his side.

Chernikov had finally requested an audience. Playing politics with the demon lord was the *very* last thing Dorian wanted to be doing, especially with all the preparations he still had to make for tomorrow's ridiculous fundraiser, but refusing the demon's invitation would've been taken as a slight.

For now, Dorian was eager to keep the peace.

He followed Marlys to the private room at the back of the café, where Chernikov sat alone, looking every bit the Russian mobster he fancied himself—dark, slicked-back hair, graying at the temples. Bespoke suit. No tie. The demon kept the top three buttons on his shirt open, making sure everyone could see the snake tattoo wrapped around his neck, eating its own tail.

"Ah, Mr. Redthorne. Is good to see you," Chernikov said in his thick Russian accent. He rose from his chair, gesturing for Dorian to take the seat across from him. "Or do I call you highness now? So many titles, I lose track."

"Call me Dorian. I insist." Dorian took a seat, Marlys standing right by his side, ready to smoke the demon's ass to oblivion if he made a wrong move.

"You are Dorian—fine. Then I am Nikolai. Yes?" He picked up a half-spent bottle of Russian vodka from a healthy stash beside him and gave it a swirl. "Let us drink to our newfound camaraderie."

"I would be honored. But first, precautions."

At this, Marlys stepped forward, placing her ritual case on the end of the table.

Nikolai grunted and waved a dismissive hand, but these were the rules of the Accords—rules their communities had adopted centuries ago and must continue to obey if they hoped to keep peace among the factions.

From her case, Marlys retrieved a silver athame, a small metal bowl, a bundle of dried herbs, and two large gold rings. She dropped the rings into the bowl and set it between the men, gesturing for them to hold out their hands.

Gripping the athame, she made a clean slice in Dorian's palm, then turned the blade and sliced Chernikov, gesturing for them to squeeze their blood onto the rings. Then, satisfied they'd spilled enough, she lifted the bowl above her head and began the chant, swirling the bowl until the rings were completely coated.

The scent of Chernikov's blood reminded Dorian of his recent demonic run-ins, memories that made him both hungry and nauseated.

All he wanted to do was leap across the table, wrap his hands around that awful snake tattoo, and throttle the asshole.

But until he could find the loophole in the Accords that would allow him to eradicate the demonic race from the top down, he had to play nice with men like Chernikov and the other syndicate leaders. Politics was a delicate dance—one he'd never quite mastered before his father's death dumped the responsibility upon him. And despite his family's waning power and the dark shadows that hovered over them—shadows that undermined his ultimate authority over the supernatural territories in this city and beyond— he had to at least *attempt* to fulfill his duties.

To live up to the crown his father had stolen all those centuries ago.

Chant complete, Marlys retrieved the rings from the bowl, passing one to each man, watching as they slid the bloody jewels over their fingers. The rings temporarily muted their natural powers, preventing Chernikov from setting Dorian's balls on fire and Dorian from ripping off the demon's head.

Win-win for all involved.

Rings in place, Marlys lit the herb bundle, sweeping it around the small room. Faint, purple smoke encased them in a shimmering screen—a magical soundproofing that would ensure only Dorian and Chernikov could hear their conversation, but Marlys could easily access them if the demon attempted to discard the muting ring and conjure hellfire.

The ritual was expensive and cumbersome, but when it came to drinking with one's enemies, one could never be too cautious.

Spells complete, Marlys retreated to the doorway, and Chernikov poured two glasses of vodka, sliding one across the table to Dorian. There was no need for concern about the contents; vampires couldn't be poisoned.

"To your father." Chernikov raised his glass. "May he find peace."

"In hell? Tough mission, Nikolai. Even for a king."

"Perhaps he has treasure map."

Dorian chuckled at the image of his father wandering the dark tunnels of hell with a map and a shovel, seeking his eternal chest of gold. But the smile didn't last long; they had business to discuss, and it was time to get to it.

They both took a deep pull from their drinks. When they locked eyes again, Chernikov's face turned serious.

"Apology is in order," he said, topping off their glasses from the bottle.

Dorian hadn't expected the demand to come so quickly or so bluntly, and he tried to maintain his calm demeanor. "Nikolai, I assure you. I was unaware of their allegiance when—"

He held up a hand, cutting him off. "My men were in violation of the Shadow Accords, so you bled them. Is understandable. You know, I try to run an obedient organization, yet sometimes, there are cracks. They should not have been in your territory, let alone conducting business and attacking you."

Twice, Dorian thought, but kept that to himself.

"For that," Chernikov said, "you have my apologies, and my assurance that responsible parties have been... dealt with."

Dorian offered a slight bow of thanks, then took another drink, steeling himself. As much as he appreciated Chernikov accepting responsibility, there was no way the demon had invited him all the way out here just to eat crow.

It was several full minutes of sipping vodka and playing with their figurative cocks before Chernikov finally spoke again.

"We are not so different," he said, "the blood-drinkers and the dark ones."

"No?"

"We love our city. We drink. We fuck." He laughed, then raised his glass in another toast, his face turning somber once again. "And most important, we know the value of good friends."

Dorian couldn't argue with the premise, though he wondered where the fuck this was going.

"Your father, Augustus," he continued. "He was good friend. Maybe not good man, but good friend."

The vodka churned in his gut, but Dorian remained impassive.

"I have known him many, many years," Chernikov said. "And in that time, he had many, many secrets. Some that would surprise even you, his oldest son."

Dorian refused to take the bait. Whether Chernikov had dirt on his father was irrelevant; the elder vampire was dead.

He sipped his vodka, wondering how long, precisely, his father and the demon lord had been acquainted. He vaguely remembered seeing Chernikov at Ravenswood on more than one occasion, not long after the manor had been built. In the time since, his father had probably amassed as many secrets as he'd amassed enemies, but the elder Redthorne had never deigned to share such things with his royal sons.

Now, all Dorian could say in response was, "That he did, Nikolai."

The demon lifted his glass, frowning as he gazed at the clear liquid sloshing inside. Then, in a low, menacing voice, "His secrets are *your* secrets now, Dorian Redthorne."

Fucking hell, Dorian hated dealing with demons. They were worse than the bloody fae, what with all the double talk and veiled threats. No wonder their contracts had so much fine print.

Patience, never Dorian's strong suit, was quickly ebbing. He set down his glass.

"Forgive me, Nikolai, but was there something specific you wished to discuss tonight, aside from the transgressions of your underlings?"

The demon glared at him, frustration simmering behind his dark eyes, but Dorian held his ground. He was the vampire king, for fuck's sake. He did *not* trek all the way out to Staten *fucking* Island to be bullied, intimidated, or subjected to demonic guessing games by a glorified mobster. If Chernikov wanted something from him, he needed to spell it out, and quickly.

"Very well," the demon finally said. "Before his... *untimely* death, Augustus was working on procuring something of great importance to me. For many years he searched, but never found it."

"What was this item?"

"A sculpture. It belonged to my people, long ago."

"What sort of sculpture?"

"She is called Mother of Lost Souls. Very rare, very valuable."

Cold dread pooled in his gut. Mother of Lost Souls was a fertility goddess sculpture crafted in Finland in the fourteenth century. Dorian was intimately familiar with her; in 1815, his father had stolen her from the vampire royal family in London, right after he'd slaughtered them and usurped the crown. He then smuggled the statue into

America, where she remained under lock and key until the crypts were constructed beneath Ravenswood, at which time she was unceremoniously bricked up behind a wall.

Which wall? Could be any one of hundreds, Dorian supposed. It was yet another secret his father had concealed, telling them only that the Mother of Lost Souls would be unearthed when the time was right.

She is what makes us powerful, he'd said. *One day, you will see.*

So, what was so damn important about this sculpture? And why the fuck did Chernikov want it so badly? Dorian could damn near taste the greed and desire on the demon's fetid breath.

"My father and I didn't spend much time together on his last visit," Dorian said, as close to the truth as he was willing to get. "He did not discuss this with me."

"He never told you of our arrangement?" Chernikov held Dorian's gaze, a spark of challenge in his eyes. "I find this... unusual."

"If I discover anything about the sculpture, I will inform you straightaway."

Clearly unsatisfied with the lukewarm response, Chernikov tossed back the last of his vodka, then wiped his lips with a finger and thumb. "There may come time when I ask you for favor, vampire king."

"I see." Dorian bit back a condescending smile at the demon's nerve. "And in exchange for this favor?"

"As I said, your father's secrets are now your secrets. I

kept his. Perhaps I will keep yours too." He glared at Dorian, letting his words sink in.

Worry spiked in Dorian's chest. Did Chernikov know about his father's illness? Or was there some other past indiscretion lying in wait for the perfect opportunity to leap out from the shadows and ruin his life?

Perhaps Chernikov was simply baiting him.

Poor strategy on his part.

"Rather than keeping my secrets," Dorian said coolly, "I'd much rather you keep your demons on a leash and out of my territory. And in return, I'll grant *you* the favor of overlooking the recent violations. Next time, I may not be so forgiving."

Tension simmered between them, but eventually, Chernikov broke into a raucous laugh. "You are... what is saying? Cheeky bastard. I like that in a bloodsucker."

Dorian didn't give a fuck *what* he liked. He finished his vodka, then rose. "If there's nothing else, Nikolai, I shall take my leave."

And be grateful I'm not leaving with your head in a bag...

"Only one more thing, Dorian Redthorne." The demon handed over an unopened bottle of vodka from his stash on the table. "A gift from home, in honor of mutual... friendship."

Reluctantly, Dorian took the bottle, knowing he was accepting a lot more than an innocent gift, but seeing no way around it without causing himself another fucking headache.

Whatever arrangement Chernikov had with Dorian's

father, it clearly went far deeper—and much farther back in time—than Dorian had realized. Something told him it was all connected to that mysterious sculpture—a piece which, not unlike the Chernikov demons he'd fed on, would probably come back to bite him in the ass.

"Thank you for the gift," Dorian said anyway, then turned to Marlys, signaling the end of the meeting. She rejoined them at the table to close out the spell, remove the rings, and pack up her belongings. Then, she and Dorian were off.

The moment he was outside, Dorian pitched the vodka into the closest trash bin and retrieved the cell from his pocket, pulling up Aiden's number.

"Aiden? We've got a problem."

CHAPTER TWENTY-THREE

An hour into the party, Dorian stood on the lower patio overlooking the Hudson River, contemplating drowning himself in that godforsaken infinity pool—an impossible feat for a vampire, but he'd do his damnedest to try.

No one had cancelled, no one was leaving early, and no one would give him a moment's peace in his own home. He'd answered enough inane questions about the house to fill an entire issue of Architectural Digest, smiled at dozens of terrible jokes, sympathized through lengthy debates about the homogenization of Manhattan restaurants, and warded off no less than three propositions, two of which from married women whose husbands were also in attendance.

This, Aiden Donovan, is why I don't host parties.

Worse, while the Armitage people, the museum's board of directors, and variously intolerable supernatural socialites *ooh*ed and *ahh*ed over his art collection, drank his champagne, fawned over his vintage cars, all but ignored the eight-piece string ensemble for which he'd paid handsomely, and ingratiated themselves in ways civilized beings should find utterly embarrassing, all Dorian could think about was Charlotte.

He hadn't seen her since the JHS run-in, but they'd talked on the phone every night this week, save for last night—he hadn't been able to reach her. It had become the best part of Dorian's evenings, making her laugh and making her come, sending her into the best kinds of dreams —and sending himself into a cold shower. Despite her many offers to repay the favor, he'd refused; when Dorian finally came for the woman haunting his every thought, it would be by *her* touch, not his own.

He hadn't mentioned the party again. In fact, there was a lot he hadn't mentioned. She'd wanted to keep things simple, no attachments, nothing too complicated. And as much as he wanted to know more about her, to see her, to feel the soft touch of her velvet skin beneath his lips, he didn't want to push her. Not like that.

So instead, he lingered in the familiar space between frustration and obsession, attempting to soothe the everpresent ache in his balls with copious amounts of alcohol.

"Dorian Redthorne, I've been looking for you," a voice called from behind, shattering his perfect visions of Charlotte and filling him with contempt so hot and sharp, it felt as if a swarm of hornets had invaded his lungs.

"Renault Duchanes." Turning to face the scoundrel, Dorian forced a hospitable smile, holding it in place even as he noticed the man's entourage. "Welcome to Ravenswood. I'm so glad you could join us."

There were four other vampires in the group—one female and three males. Duchanes introduced them as members of his house, though Dorian had never seen them before. Unsurprising, considering how quickly most of the other families sired new vampires to do their endless bidding. House Redthorne was unique in that Dorian's brothers were related by blood, but that was a rare occurrence that required an entire family be turned at the same time.

Outside his own unfortunate gene pool, Dorian didn't know any parents who'd subject their children to such torture. Still, while Dorian's family was full of enough dysfunction to keep a hundred therapists busy for a thousand years, he wouldn't trade them. There was something about blood and shared history that had made them loyal to one another in ways that sired vampires—despite their vows and the adoption of their sires' names—were not.

In addition to the vampires, Duchanes had also extended the invitation to their bonded witch, whom he now introduced.

"Jacinda Colburn," he said proudly, as if she were a prized steer.

The woman extended a hand glittering with rings, offering a mysterious smile.

Dorian shook her hand. It was cold to the touch. "Pleased to meet you, Ms. Colburn."

Glancing around to ensure they had at least a small

audience, Duchanes cleared his throat, and Dorian braced himself for the inevitable performance.

"As a gesture of goodwill and friendship between our two great houses," Duchanes announced, "for this evening, House Duchanes offers the services of our bonded witch to the brothers of House Redthorne."

For fuck's sake.

"Very generous of you, Renault, but that won't be necessary."

"Oh, but it's no trouble. Jacinda would be honored to assist you in any way."

Turning to the witch, Dorian put on his most dazzling smile, trying to recall what he knew of the Duchanes witch. "You're an earth witch, Ms. Colburn, are you not?"

She lit up at the question, her own smile broadening. "I am."

"It's not my area of expertise," he continued, "but I'm told the gardens at Ravenswood are home to over four dozen species of medicinal herbs and flowers. You're welcome to take clippings of anything you'd like for your practice."

"Really?" Her blue eyes sparkled, making her appear much younger than she probably was. "Thank you, Mr. Redthorne."

"Please. Call me Dorian."

"Dorian," she said with a smile. "Thank you."

Beside her, Duchanes seethed. Dorian's refusal of his offer was an insult, but everyone standing there knew Duchanes' kindness was artificial at best.

What are you after tonight, bloodsucker?

"Very well," Duchanes said. "We shall share a drink instead." He snapped his fingers, and two women stepped forward from his group.

Human women—a blonde and a redhead, both wearing short cocktail dresses entirely inappropriate for the autumn night. They couldn't have been more than twenty years of age, with pale skin, glossy eyes, and deep hollows beneath their cheek and collarbones.

Dorian's gut churned, his vision swimming with red. They were obviously unhealthy and not well cared for. But unless he had clear evidence of coercion or compulsion, there was nothing he could do; the women were of consenting age.

"Gentleman's choice." Duchanes gestured for Dorian to take his pick.

He took a swig of his scotch, letting it linger in his mouth a moment before smiling at the women. "I've no need to partake this evening, but I appreciate the offer."

"Your house is amazing, Mr. Redthorne," the redhead said. "Like something out of a magazine!"

"Thank you."

"That painting in the foyer, is that a Chantuille?" the blonde asked.

"Chanteaux," he said. *"Blackbirds in Flight."*

The blonde woman placed her hand on Dorian's forearm, slinking further away from Duchanes to give Dorian what she probably thought was a furtive look, but he couldn't help but notice the tremor in her hand. "Maybe you could show me around? I'd *love* to see the other pieces in your collection."

"Ah, another time, perhaps," Dorian said, grateful to see Aiden approaching. "Lovely to meet you all. The garden paths are extensive—feel free to explore."

"You're not coming with us?" she asked.

"I'm sorry. If you'll excuse me, it seems another matter requires my attention."

Pulling away from her touch as well as her disappointed gaze, Dorian walked past the whole group, making a beeline for his friend.

Without waiting for Aiden to speak, Dorian grabbed his arm and dragged him through a side door that led into the massive garage.

The scent of car wax, motor oil, and tires calmed his nerves, the stately presence of his cars a familiar comfort. Thankfully, he and Aiden were alone.

"How soon before these dreadful beasts leave my home?" he asked.

"Don't be daft. We haven't even served the second course of appetizers."

Dorian sighed into his drink, then tipped the glass, finishing it with a gulp.

"I see Duchanes took your invitation to heart," Aiden said. "Brought the whole bloody house."

"And his... donors." Dorian's fingers tightened on his glass, wishing he could slam it into Duchanes' smug face. The sight of those emaciated women made him want to do something violent. "And Malcolm wanted to ally with this reprobate. What the hell was he thinking?"

"I'm not sure he was."

Dorian shook his head, attempting to free himself of his thoughts, but it was an exercise in futility. The party and Duchanes both weighed on him, but so did last night's conversation with Chernikov. He and Aiden had spent the afternoon paging through his father's journals and walking the twisting, dark pathways of the crypts, but if there were ever any clues to where his father had hidden the Mother of Lost Souls sculpture—or to the details of his agreement with the demons—time had long ago destroyed them.

"No one's getting in there tonight, mate," Aiden said, as if he could read Dorian's thoughts. It certainly felt that way; even when they were children, Aiden had always seemed to know just what to say, just how to put Dorian's rattled mind at ease.

"If anything can ruin us, Aiden, I'm certain it's contained in those crypts."

"Where it shall remain until you and your brothers discover and eradicate it."

"Don't let anyone else in the garage tonight, either," Dorian said, bolting the door they'd come through. "I don't want them breathing on my cars. I already caught the old man trying to take the Rolls Royce for a joyride."

"Armitage still has a driver's license?"

"No, the old codger. Thankfully I got to him before he found the keys."

Aiden clapped him on the shoulder, his smile unwavering. "Sounds like you're having a splendid evening, just as I predicted. Have you had enough to drink?"

"Just so you know, I'm holding you responsible if any of these prats steal the family jewels."

"Didn't your father sell off the family jewels to book our passage to America?"

"It's a figure of speech, Aiden. Don't test my patience."

"You don't have any patience. But if it makes you feel better, I don't think your guests are thieves. After all, they've paid handsomely for the privilege of your company."

"That's fine, as long as you understand it's coming out of your pay if they are."

"You need another drink. Here, have mine." Aiden handed over his scotch. "I insist."

Dorian downed it quickly, then set the glass on a shelf behind them, taking a deep breath. "All the bloody yakking. The smiling. And now House Duchanes is here, bringing down the value of my property with their very presence. I don't like it."

"It's for a good cause."

"We should've just made a donation."

"I'm not talking about the children's museum. I'm talking about Isabelle and the company we're about to acquire. Despite your best efforts, and the fact that you wouldn't let the geezer drive your car, it seems Armitage and his board members are quite enamored of you."

"Is that so?" Dorian asked. He'd never admit it to

Aiden, but the news filled him with more than a modicum of relief.

"Word is, Mr. Redthorne, you're the dog's bollocks." Aiden pressed a hand to his heart, shooting Dorian a wistful smile. "If only they could figure out why you're still single."

"Any theories?"

"Oh, the usual. Deep emotional wounds, fear of commitment, only-child syndrome, take your pick."

Dorian laughed. "I've got a house full of siblings, you knob."

"I'm just the messenger." Aiden clapped him again on the shoulder, giving him an encouraging squeeze. "Come along now. If we don't get back inside, they're bound to come looking for you."

"I hate this, you know. Worst idea you've ever had."

"You say that about all my ideas. Especially the good ones."

"This time I mean it."

"Great! Now that we've got that sorted." Aiden opened the inner door that led into the massive kitchen, now bustling with caterers and bartenders. "Come on, then. In you go."

Dorian followed him inside, then punched in the alarm code, securing the garage behind them.

After fixing themselves another round of drinks, the men weaved through the crowded kitchen and into the great room, Dorian doing his best to avoid eye contact while Aiden deflected the talkative guests. By the time they reached the expansive open foyer, Dorian was feeling marginally better.

Aiden had been right; the guests were having a grand time, laughing and chatting amongst themselves, enjoying the hors d'oeuvres and drinks his caterers delivered on elegant silver trays. Now that they'd seen Dorian at home, behaving himself in a mostly civilized manner, perhaps the Armitage mages *would* feel more at ease about their relationship, softening them for both the acquisition as well as the Redthornes' eventual offer for Isabelle. And of course, the museum would be able to do some great work with the proceeds.

As much as Dorian hated to admit it, he was glad Aiden had suggested hosting the event. Despite his anxieties and general aversion to putting his private life on public display, Dorian couldn't imagine the evening being a more smashing success.

But then the greeters ushered in a late arrival, and Dorian's heart nearly leaped out of his chest. All around him, dozens of dark, depraved gazes slid to the entryway, every one of his guests as captivated as Dorian himself.

There, standing in the foyer, dressed in a black satin dress that exposed her delicious curves and elegant gloves that reached her elbows, was one very devious, sexy-as-sin, copper-eyed woman.

His woman.

CHAPTER TWENTY-FOUR

Charley gave herself thirty seconds to cut the pity party and get her head in the game.

Never mind Dorian's sexy voice, or the fact that she'd missed out on it last night, too nervous about the impending job to answer his calls or texts.

Never mind Travis' filthy hands, how she'd fought him off the entire drive up from the city.

Never mind that she'd hardly gotten any sleep, jolting out of bed at every creak and groan, convinced Travis had found a way into her adjacent hotel room.

Never mind that she'd lied to Sasha, telling her that Rudy was sending her on an overnighter for an important conference.

Charley took a steadying breath, willing herself to forget it all. None of it mattered. Tonight, right now, standing in this gorgeous Elizabethan mansion in the shadow of the Catskill Mountains, Charley had *one* job.

Get in. Get the intel. Get out.

And above all, don't get noticed.

After checking to confirm no one had followed her up the ornate hardwood staircase, Charley slipped into one of the mansion's dozen bedrooms and shut the door behind her, confirming what her quick observations of the first floor had already implied.

This guy is fucking loaded.

She hadn't even done a thorough sweep yet, but she'd already determined it was exactly the kind of exclusive, eclectic cache Rudy had predicted: paintings from the Italian Renaissance, Russian avant-garde, and contemporary works the owner had likely commissioned directly from the artists; exquisite New Kingdom jars and statues made of Egyptian alabaster and faience; silk scrolls and wall panels from thirteenth-century Japan. The entire home was a museum in and of itself—and that wasn't even counting the classic cars Travis had mentioned. Charley knew a lot more about fine art and architecture than she did about automobiles, but by the way he'd gone on about them, those beauties had to be worth millions.

Millions that someone else worked for. Someone we're going to hurt...

Shaking off the ever-present guilt, she sent Rudy a coded text to hint at her initial findings, hoping it was enough to keep his incessant check-ins at bay. *Having a lovely evening,* she wrote. *Even better than expected. I think a family trip to the region sounds like a great idea! The more, the merrier. LOTS to do here.*

With heavy tapestries drawn over the windows, the bedroom was too dark to explore unaided. Charley flipped on the phone flashlight, quickly scanning her surroundings. It wasn't the master suite, but even this secondary bedroom was flush with paintings and beautiful antique furniture.

She made her way to a large walk-in closet full of women's clothing and shoes, everything protected by clear plastic garment bags.

Interesting.

Rudy's surveillance had indicated the homeowner lived alone—not with a woman. Then again, with everything bagged up and put away, it was likely the woman who'd once occupied this room hadn't been here in a while.

A low shelf along one wall held an assortment of jewelry boxes, and inside the largest, Charley found a piece that took her breath away.

With gloved hands, she fingered the ruby-and-diamond bracelet, admiring the way the gemstones sparkled in the flashlight beam.

It'd been more than a decade since she'd earned a place on her father's crew with that minor jewel heist in Sleepy Hollow. But for a fleeting moment, warmth spread in her belly, a familiar rush that made her feel both excited and dirty.

Excited, because she'd never forget the look of pride on her father's face when she'd shown him her score.

And dirty, because rifling through a stranger's personal heirlooms and possessions was one of the most despicable things a person could do. More than just a crime, it was a violation, pure and simple.

With a deep sigh, Charley put the bracelet back, grateful the only thing she'd be taking tonight was information.

Through an open archway at the back of the closet, Charley entered a small dressing room, just large enough for a chair, a full-length mirror, and a chest of drawers.

On the wall above the chest was a painting of a dour woman gazing into a mirror. The reflection staring back at her was that of a young girl. Though Charley couldn't make out the true vibrancy of the colors in the dim light, she knew the woman's hair was dark, the child's light, their eyes the same haunting shade of pale blue.

She knew the painting by heart.

Memory's Memories, by Viola LaPorte.

It was one of her father's. From the missing cache.

Tentatively Charley reached for the painting, tracing the frame with a trembling finger. Tears blurred her vision as she realized with shocking clarity that she'd been searching for something like this for the last five years, ever since Rudy had shown up at her father's penthouse with his head down, unable to meet her eyes.

He's dead, Charlotte. I'm so, so sorry…

All the auctions, the high-society events, the fundraisers… It wasn't just because she was afraid of Rudy, afraid of ending up on the street, afraid of losing her sister. It was because she'd hoped, on some deep, impossible level, she'd find the missing cache, piece together the clues, and follow the trail to her father's murderer.

And here, tonight, was her first clue.

It shouldn't have surprised her. With a $70 million street value, a cache like that didn't just vanish. It might go underground awhile, but it always resurfaced, usually in pieces. A painting here. A vase there. Even one piece could lead them to the rest.

This was it. Her one piece.

Charley blinked away her tears and looked again at the painting. If this one had shown up, others would follow. Maybe they already had. Maybe they'd even be in this very house.

She tried to text Rudy, but her brain kept tripping up, her hands shaking, the gloves making it all the more difficult. She needed to get out of there, get some air, and get her head on straight.

Because after tonight, everything was going to change.

Out beyond the Hudson, the rolling hills of the Catskills turned lavender beneath a curtain of mist and moonlight, an ethereal sight that only made Charley feel more alone, more confused. She'd wandered out to the gardens, trying to decide how to tell Rudy about the painting, but now that the cool night air had cleared her head, she was rethinking it.

Rudy had always believed Charley's father had double-crossed them. He and the others had agreed they couldn't waste precious resources seeking vengeance for a man who'd betrayed his crew, no matter that the man was their own flesh and blood. As far as Rudy was concerned, it was a business decision, plain and simple. She didn't have to like it, but she had to live with it.

Now, Charley leaned against a maple tree at the edge of the garden, its leaves shivering in the breeze, and closed her eyes.

What the hell should I do?

Rudy was hell-bent on stealing the artwork in this house. It was worth a fortune—probably the biggest score the crew had ever attempted. If he discovered the painting and anything else from the missing cache, he'd likely fence it, no love lost. Charley could try to reason with him, but in the end, he'd just tell her to let it go. To move on.

And after five agonizing years, the only piece of evidence in her father's murder would vanish again.

No. She couldn't let that happen. If Charley was going to trace that painting back to her father—to whoever killed him—she needed to do it alone.

And that meant going back inside, finishing the job Rudy had sent her here to do, and coming up with a solid plan before he and Travis made their next move.

She'd just decided to head back to the event when she was unexpectedly corralled against the tree, strong arms encircling her from behind, a dark command whispered hotly in her ear.

"Come with me. Don't make a sound."

CHAPTER TWENTY-FIVE

The New York art scene was small and incestuous, Dorian reminded himself. It wasn't out of the realm of possibility for Charlotte to be here. A coincidence, yes—but not impossible. She seemed intimately familiar with the inner workings of the art world; perhaps she'd heard about the fundraiser and decided to attend. Perhaps she was a companion to one of his guests. Or maybe she was employed by the museum—she *did* tell him she had a work event tonight.

You're a fool, Redthorne. A bloody fool.

No matter his justifications—his hopes—Dorian could no longer deny the fact that she was dodgy. He'd followed her out to the gardens with every intention of confronting her about it too. But by the time he'd gotten her into the guesthouse, his priorities had changed.

Outside the nonstop fantasy streaming through his

mind, he hadn't seen her in days, and his memory was a poor substitute for the real thing. Her black dress clung to her curves, long hair hanging in loose waves over her shoulders, dark red lips damn near hypnotizing him.

And the gloves? Devastating.

An awkward silence crept in.

"You look stunning," he finally said.

"You're not so bad yourself, Mr. Redthorne." Her gaze trailed down to his feet, then back up, her smile devious. "The tux suits you."

"Really? I bloody hate it." He loosened his bowtie, unbuttoning the top two buttons on his shirt.

Charlotte smiled again but didn't say anything else. He hadn't yet turned on the interior lights, and in the dim, moonlit entryway he couldn't quite read her expression, though she'd come with him willingly after the garden ambush—almost eagerly. Still, her heartbeat was erratic now, and she hadn't uttered more than a surprised greeting in the gardens, offering no explanation for her presence at his fundraiser, or—more importantly—for why she'd been sneaking around upstairs.

He hadn't asked about that yet. Part of him was afraid of the answer—afraid he'd have no choice but to send her away for good.

Or worse.

Who *was* this woman?

Was she somehow connected to Duchanes? They'd both been at the Salvatore auction as well, but... no. Charlotte had seemed genuinely afraid of the vampire when Dorian had found them in the bedroom that night.

Had Armitage sent her to spy? To unearth secrets more desperate and depraved than the truths that had left the Redthornes unallied and witch-less?

Dorian took a breath, steadying his nerves. Ravenswood held only one dark secret, and right now, that secret was secured in the crypts, undeciphered from the mountains of journals his father had left behind.

Besides, the idea of a spy seemed preposterous, even for Armitage. The old mage was becoming a huge pain in Dorian's ass, but he was a by-the-book pain in the ass.

No. Whatever Charlotte was up to, it was her own brand of trouble.

Trouble Dorian couldn't get enough of.

"So, this was your work event?" he asked, reaching up to brush a lock of hair over her shoulder, his hand lingering on her soft skin.

She sucked in a breath and glanced up into his eyes, the sparks between them as undeniable as ever, burning Dorian's resolve to ash.

"And your boring party?" she asked.

Dorian ran his hand down her arm, fingers encircling her gloved wrist. "What are the chances?"

"I was wondering the same thing."

"Do you work for the museum?"

"No, I'm a… consultant." Her pulse picked up, thrumming against the gentle press of his thumb. "But my company is a major supporter of their work. When we heard about the event, we couldn't pass it up."

Dorian relaxed, but only slightly. Even if her story were true, which he doubted, it didn't explain why she'd been snooping upstairs, like she'd been snooping at the Salvatore auction.

"Have you been inside the manor yet?" he asked—a small test.

Please don't lie to me, woman…

"Oh, yes. It's incredible, but it's… it's so overwhelming in there." She wrinkled her nose—the most adorable look of distaste Dorian had ever seen. "I kind of hate parties, to be honest."

"That makes two of us."

"We're practically fugitives."

"The opposite of party crashers."

"Party dodgers." Charlotte laughed, the music of it stirring something deep within him. "My dad used to say I was the easiest teenager ever. He never had to worry about me sneaking off to parties. I spent my weekends flipping through art history books and—"

Dorian's mouth was on hers in a blink, silencing her as he took her into his arms. Even as he'd followed her upstairs, watching from the shadows as she snuck into the first bedroom, he'd wanted to kiss her.

She sighed in his embrace, nipples erect beneath the dress, and when she finally parted her lips and allowed him to deepen their kiss, all the awkwardness evaporated, bringing them right back to those precious, stolen moments in the Salvatore closet.

By the time they broke for air, her eyes were large and glassy, lipstick smeared across her mouth like blood. The sight sent a dark thrill through Dorian's heart.

He ran his thumb along her lower lip, and Charlotte opened her mouth. Her teeth scraped his skin as he slid into the soft, wet heat, his cock straining against his pants.

The remembered scent of fresh blood rose anew.

He wanted to bite her.

He wanted to feed.

Slowly, he drew his thumb from her mouth and dragged it down her chin, down her throat, wrapping a hand around her delicate neck.

He could compel her to remain absolutely still. To tilt her head and offer the vein, welcoming the bite as readily as she'd welcomed his mouth against her flesh in that closet...

Forty-nine years, one month, and sixteen days.

That was the last time Dorian had fed on a live human. Since that fateful meal, he'd spent his days and nights burying his innate desires so deeply, he'd sworn nothing could unearth them again.

And yet...

Dorian closed his eyes, fangs burning through the gums, desperate for a taste of her sweet, seductive blood. More than the velvet touch of her tongue, more than her soft, breathy moans, the very thought of feeding on her broke through nearly every wall he'd erected over those dangerous desires.

He was holding on by a gossamer thread. One wrong move, and it would snap.

"What are you thinking about?" she whispered, breath warm on his lips, pulse strong and steady beneath his grip.

Taste me, it whispered in time with her heartbeat. *Taste me, I'm yours.*

Taste me…

Taste me…

"All the filthy, beautiful things I want to do to you," he said, his voice thick as he sank deeper into his own depravity. He still hadn't opened his eyes, and now, all he could see behind them was blood.

Blood, glittering against her neck like fresh berries in a bowl of cream.

Blood, running along the edges of her collarbone, pooling in the hollow of her throat.

Blood, coating his lips and tongue as he licked it from her flesh, savoring every drop…

Don't do this, Redthorne. Fight it, or she'll die…

The thought sobered him just enough to allow him to speak again.

"And you?" he asked, his words no more than a whisper in the darkness. "What are you thinking about, love? Tell me. *Please* tell me."

Distract me from the thought of sinking my fangs into your flesh and bleeding you dry…

"I'd much rather show you, Mr. Redthorne. If you're into watching."

Dorian opened his eyes just in time to catch her wicked grin, and then his crazy, mysterious, reckless as hell woman dropped to her knees.

In a single, fluid motion she unfastened his pants and freed his stiff cock, grasping it in her firm hands, warm beneath the satin gloves.

Her touch was fucking incredible.

And just the distraction he needed.

"I'm *definitely* into watching." He slid his hands into her thick, silky hair. "Show me."

She released him and tried to remove the gloves, but Dorian stopped her.

"Leave them," he ordered.

"If you insist, Mr. Redthorne." Fisting the base of his cock again, Charlotte glanced up at him and brought her mouth closer, tongue darting out to tease the tip with a slow, maddening circle.

Every time Dorian thought he had the upper hand, she shattered him. Her laugh, her touch, her devious eyes, her mouth...

Screw his power games, screw his control. He'd given most of it up the moment she'd stepped inside Ravenswood Manor. She wasn't here for the fundraiser—that much was certain—and Dorian didn't know how much longer either of them could continue this game of make-believe. But for now, Charlotte was his again, gift-wrapped in satin and secrets, just like before.

Her eyelids fluttered closed as she took him in deeper, moaning against his flesh.

"Fucking *hell*, Charlotte," he breathed. "You're out to ruin me."

She pulled back, dragging her tongue along his shaft, breath hot on his skin. With another smoldering gaze, she looked up and said, "I don't want to ruin you. I want to *taste* you."

He almost came right there.

"Turnabout *is* fair play," she teased, then closed her lips again, sucking him into a state of sheer euphoria.

Desperate to regain even a fraction of control, he knotted his fingers into her hair and guided her into a perfect rhythm, fucking her hot mouth, thrusting as deep as he dared. But Charlotte wasn't ready to give up so easily. She reached behind him and cupped his ass, driving him in even deeper.

Harder.

Faster.

She glanced up again, her eyes alight with some new challenge, those blood-red lips wrapped around his cock, her tongue swirling against his flesh.

In that moment, Dorian utterly lost it. All of it. His control. His composure. His mind.

He tried to pull back, but she only sucked harder, determined to do it her way.

His hands tightened in her hair, and she moaned again, the sound vibrating straight to his balls.

That was all it took.

His orgasm exploded, spilling in a hot torrent down her throat, his legs shaking, his growl as feral as the wolves that roamed the woods beyond.

Charlotte slid his cock out of her mouth and swallowed, a mischievous grin lighting up her face.

Dorian finally released her hair, and she got to her feet, smoothing out the wrinkles in her dress. Her cheeks were dark, her lips swollen, her hair wild, and she'd never looked more beautiful. More alive.

Glancing at the door, she said, "We should probably clean up and get back to the party before anyone notices we're missing."

"Nice try. Did you honestly think I'd let you escape?" Sliding his arms around her waist, he found the zipper at the back of her dress and tugged it down, tracing the path of her freshly bared skin. "Before I've had a chance to show you all the hot, dirty things I've been dreaming about?"

The dress slid off her shoulders, pooling around her hips like black water. Dorian lowered his mouth to her breast, tonguing her nipple through the red lace of her bra while his fingers slipped down the front of her panties.

She was wet with desire, smooth and slippery beneath his touch.

"What if someone comes?" she asked, gripping his arms.

"Oh, someone *will* come. *You*."

"But this house—"

"Is mine," he said, realizing in that moment she didn't know. She'd come to the fundraiser with no clue about its host—another red flag Dorian tucked away for later examination.

Right now, he had better things to do.

"No one will enter unless I command it," he said, nipping at her earlobe. "No one will come to your aid." Then, in a low, dark whisper, "You aren't leaving here until I've got you dripping wet, trembling, and *screaming* for mercy. Understood?"

CHAPTER TWENTY-SIX

In that moment, here's what Charley understood.

One? The real Charley, behind all the art-world glamour, was wild and reckless.

Two? The real Charley was borderline stupid.

Three? She was already more than halfway to fulfilling Dorian's dirty promises. Wet and trembling? Check and check.

Four? Alone in the guest house, away from the crush of the party, she couldn't *wait* to scream for him.

But... five... Despite the fact that she was still coming down from the high of that blow job—the smooth perfection of his cock, the sheer power that had coursed through her veins as she brought him to ecstasy—a new alarm sounded in her head.

It was faint and fuzzy, struggling to find its way through the electric buzz, but it was real.

Heat pooled in her stomach with a twist of fear that had

nothing to do with Dorian's punishing hands.

What did he say about the house?

Charley shut her eyes, but she couldn't focus, thoughts slipping away as he teased her with deft strokes, tongue hot on her nipple.

"God, you're... so good," she breathed, her nerves singing for more.

Still, the warning in her head continued to gnaw.

To gnaw and gnaw and fucking *gnaw*, until it finally made a crack big enough for the truth to slip in.

The house... is mine...

"Relax, love," Dorian murmured, flattening his palm against her clit as he dipped a finger inside, another one fluttering behind it, teasing her backdoor until she was panting for so much more.

No one will enter unless I command it...

Wait. Had he meant...

No. She must've misheard.

Swatting away her thoughts like gnats, Charley let out a breath, sinking into the decadence of his touch.

Dorian slid a hand up her spine, then cupped the back of her neck, his fingers moving faster inside her, the pressure of his palm so perfect, her core was already tightening in anticipation of the inevitable release.

"You are always so wet for me. So..." He slid in deeper and curled his finger, making her gasp. "...ready."

But God, those annoying thoughts would *not* leave her alone.

"Dorian... The house... It's..."

Her words fell away as he captured her mouth in another deep kiss, his low moan bringing her closer to the edge even as her adrenaline spiked.

What are you doing, Charley? Danger! Danger! Retreat!

Instead of retreating, her body arched into his touch, urging him deeper, breath ragged as he thrust inside, faster and faster.

The fear coursing through her veins mingled with the sheer pleasure Dorian was unlocking. She was out of her mind, completely at his mercy.

The house, she thought, wrapping her hands around his shoulders. *It can't be his. Not Dorian's...*

"That's it," he said, his voice like liquid silk as he moved in for the kill, slow, then fast. "Focus on my touch."

"Dorian, I... *God.*" Her thighs tightened, the now-familiar heat cresting between them.

"Come for me, Charlotte."

"Fuck, yes!" The wave crashed, but Dorian didn't stop there. He plunged deeper, harder, pushing the first pulse of her release into a second one, bigger and more intense, unleashing a scream that refused to be contained, refused to be tamed.

Just like he'd promised.

And then, as she spasmed through the very end of it, Dorian's earlier words crashed through all the ecstasy, all the layers of denial with a sharp clarity she could no longer ignore.

The house... is mine...

Dorian Redthorne, the man who'd brought her to the

edge with every blissful stroke, who'd awakened her long-buried fantasies, who'd made her feel wanted in ways she never thought possible… was the host of tonight's thousand-dollars-a-head fundraiser.

Otherwise known as her mark.

"This is your home?" she finally managed, opening her eyes. "You live here?"

God, she hated the desperation in her voice, but her blood was turning cold, her body going rigid with panic.

"Mmm." He nuzzled her neck, inhaling her scent. "Welcome to Ravenswood, love. Now tell me…" He kissed his way north, moving to her ear with a long, hot sigh. "What's got you so frightened all of a sudden?"

The whisper passed softly through his lips, caressing Charley's skin with a gentleness that belied his intensity. With every second that passed, Charley was falling deeper into the web she'd spun around herself.

Soon, she'd have no escape.

She'd known it was coming. Ever since Rudy had seen them together at the Salvatore auction and learned about the Whitfield, Dorian was in his sights.

She just didn't think it would happen so quickly.

Her brain was flatlining, unable to process it all. But despite the disastrous turn of events, that treacherous little body of hers was still drowning in pleasurable spasms.

"I'm… I'm okay." Charley let out a long, slow breath, dizzy with lust, even as the crushing reality chipped away at her denial.

"Good. Because *that* was just an appetizer."

Charley's heart skipped, her mouth watering for more.

Dorian Redthorne was pulling apart that sticky web, kiss by kiss, breath by breath, one strand at a time.

With his honey-brown eyes boring into hers, his hand still resting between her aching thighs, Charley was powerless. And that, more than his identity or high-dollar art collection, made him the most dangerous man in her world.

The realization left her more than bare, more than exposed. She felt like she'd turned herself inside out, and it filled her with a sudden restlessness that bordered on mania.

Forcing herself to take a step back, she broke away from his touch and attempted to pull her dress back up.

But Dorian was right there again, sliding his hands around the back of her neck, smothering her with a kiss full of white-hot fire Charley felt deep in her belly, a demanding intensity she couldn't resist.

When he finally pulled away, his gaze was unrelenting. "Stay the night with me, Charlotte."

Now, even more than the night of the auction, she wanted to accept. To forget—for one final night—who she really was.

Why she was really here.

Charley burned with guilt. Even at his most commanding, Dorian had shown her nothing but pleasure and kindness.

Looking at her now, awaiting her answer, his eyes held a glimpse of vulnerability—there and gone in a blink.

There has *to be another way. We can't rob this man…*

Charley sighed, resting her palm against his perfectly-stubbled cheek. "Dorian, I don't—"

A loud rap on the front door saved her from answering.

"Redthorne?" a man called. "You in there, you bloody traitor?"

Dorian cursed under his breath.

"I'm busy," he snapped, but he was already heading for the door.

"Armitage is looking for you," the man said. His accent was English, like Dorian's, but less formal. "He thinks you've ditched him."

"I have. Now, if you don't mind—"

"Actually, I do."

Charley pulled the dress up and grabbed her purse, heading off in search of a bathroom.

Dorian was clearly annoyed at the interruption, but to Charley, the man's timing couldn't have been better.

Now, staring at her stained lips in the bathroom mirror, Charley was truly afraid.

Not of Dorian, but of herself.

How could I be so careless?

She touched her fingers to her lips, the ghost of his kiss making her ache.

That's how, girl. That is exactly *how.*

It reminded Charley of a paper Sasha had written for her psychology class. *Check this out*, Sasha had said, thumbing through her source material over breakfast one morning. *Doctors say the line between passion and madness is so thin, the chemical profile of the brain of a person experiencing the early euphoric stages of love is nearly identical to that of a person going insane.*

The girls had joked about it at the time, vowing to stay single and sane for life. But now, thanks to Dorian Redthorne, Charley was beginning to understand exactly what the doctors meant.

She closed her eyes as a sharp pain split her skull, feeling like her brain was fracturing into different people. One wanted nothing more than to finish the job and make a clean break, becoming no more than a distant memory for Dorian. The other wanted to call the police and turn herself in, saving Dorian a whole lot of trouble and heartache in the process.

But there, somewhere in the middle, lived a woman who wanted something different. Something better.

Freedom.

Charley sighed. Right now, that woman needed to stay locked away.

As the men continued their bickering, she cleaned herself up, wove her hopelessly tangled hair into a loose braid, and reapplied her makeup. Finally satisfied, she slid open the bathroom window and stuck her head out, drinking in the cool, misty air. For a hot minute, she considered crawling out like a grounded teenager, but the idea was fleeting. This side of the guest house faced the woods, and beyond the light from the bathroom, there was nothing but blackness.

Any sane, self-preserving person would've bolted the minute she'd connected the dots about Dorian. But even if she'd had a ready excuse, Charley couldn't bail; things were way too volatile with Rudy. Reporting back with no more than a few meager details about the upstairs bedroom would be disastrous—for her *and* for Sasha.

Charley shuddered at the thought.

Before taking over the operation, Rudy used to be the muscle. Her father had tried to shield her from that side of the business, but he couldn't protect her forever, and it wasn't long before Charley started witnessing more violence. At first, she'd told herself it was all part of the territory. That Rudy only hurt the people who screwed them over. That he wouldn't do it otherwise.

But cruelty quickly became his life's work, and Rudy was damn good at his job.

Now, the old memories resurfaced.

Rudy, pummeling a man into a permanent coma for lowballing them.

Rudy, slicing up a woman's face to send a message to her husband.

Rudy, brutally killing the dog of a freelance associate who'd threatened to rat them out after a failed heist.

The cries of that animal still haunted her nightmares, nearly a decade later.

Other than an occasional shove or a too-firm grip around the arm, Rudy had never been overly physical with Charley. But lately she sensed his patience thinning. And while these days Rudy preferred to manage rather than muscle, Charley knew his old tendencies weren't gone. They were just dormant, waiting for the right opportunity to unleash hell—an opportunity Charley didn't want to give him by blowing this assignment.

With her body cooling off from Dorian's touch, Charley's survival instinct was finally kicking in. Her emotions, her libido, even her guilt had to take a backseat to the more pressing matter of personal safety—hers *and* Sasha's.

That old "someday" vision flickered through her mind, but right now, she needed to do her job. That meant getting the intel for Rudy, and getting the lowdown on the LaPorte painting.

Figuring out how to sabotage the robbery? That would have to come later—if it could come at all.

Charley shut the window, turning to face herself again in the mirror. She needed a solid plan.

Travis wouldn't be picking her up for at least two more hours, giving her plenty of time. The first floor would be easy. She'd blend in with the crowd, work her way through each room, and catalogue everything important: artwork, entrances, doors and windows, locks, alarm systems. As long as Dorian was distracted by his obligations as host, Charley could then move on to the second floor, picking up where she left off.

With any luck, she'd be out of there and on her way back to the city before Dorian suspected a thing.

Feeling slightly more sure of herself, Charley applied a final coat of lipstick, then dropped the makeup into her purse, ready to execute her plan. Despite the turn of events, she had no reason to believe it wouldn't work.

She was Charlotte D'Amico, after all. Trained by the best in the business.

All she had to do was set aside her personal feelings, her *severely* malfunctioning moral compass, and—oh, right—her last shred of human decency.

No problem! I'm sure my father is already saving me a seat in hell...

A soft knock interrupted her morbid thoughts.

"Charlotte," Dorian said, "are you dressed? I'm afraid duty calls."

"Just a minute." Charley closed her eyes, committing to memory the sound of her name on Dorian's lips. It might be the last time she heard it.

Steeling herself, she grabbed her purse and opened the door, arranging her features into a mask of polish and poise.

Dorian stood before her, his bowtie back in place, eyes sparkling as he held out an arm to escort her back into the home her associates would soon liquidate. "Shall we face the music?"

With a casual familiarity she didn't quite feel, Charley looped her arm through his and smiled. "Lead the way, hot stuff."

CHAPTER TWENTY-SEVEN

A firing squad had assembled outside the guest house, each man more handsome and intimidating than the last.

All four of them stared openly at Charley—some curious, others hostile, all of them devastating.

"I see my brothers are here to roll out the red carpet." Dorian sighed, then gestured at the men before them. "Malcolm, Colin, Gabriel, and Aiden. Meet my companion, Charlotte…"

There was an awkward pause as Dorian undoubtedly tried to recall her last name.

"D'Amico," she blurted out, too quickly to think through the consequences. She'd never intended to share it, but considering she'd already shared her phone number and a good deal of her body with Dorian, one more detail hardly mattered.

Besides, she was a phantom, right? Nothing would be traced back to her.

"You must be a VIP, Ms. D'Amico," the one called Gabriel said. "Our brother *never* allows guests in the guest house." He forced a laugh, but his eyes held nothing but venom.

Charley fought off a shudder. She knew a mask when she saw one, and Gabriel—despite the good looks and finery—was six-and-a-half feet of pure, icy darkness.

"These overbearing savages are my brothers," Dorian said. "Though you'd be hard-pressed to see the resemblance—clearly, I got the looks of the family."

"If only your maker had been more generous when handing out brains," the dimpled one—Colin—said. Unlike Gabriel, he seemed kind. Warmth radiated from his smile.

"Five Redthornes? Brothers?" Charley looked them over, doing her best to smile through the heat gathering in her cheeks. "Wow. That's... wow."

"Four, technically," Aiden said. "I'm not a Redthorne, though I *am* Dorian's favorite. Best mate and business partner too."

"Oh? What sort of business?" She tried to remember what her uncle had said about Dorian's company on their drive home from the auction. Fierce... something?

"Dorian and I run a company called FierceConnect," he said. "We're essentially a social network and platform for online gamers." He shared a bit more about the business, his twinkling eyes putting her at ease.

But despite his friendly demeanor, she sensed a discomfort in him—in all of them.

After Aiden's brief overview, it was a long beat before

anyone spoke again, the brothers still staring at her, undoubtedly piecing together what she and Dorian had been up to before the interruption.

"Well," she said, "this is even more awkward than the time I lost my virginity to Stanley Kopoweicz in the back of his parents' camper while his mother was mowing the lawn, so…"

Dorian stiffened beside her, but Aiden cracked up.

Charley pressed a palm to her forehead and blew out a breath. "I did *not* say that out loud."

"I didn't hear a thing," Aiden said somberly. "But for the *oddest* reason, I'm suddenly in the mood for a campout."

She couldn't help but laugh. Even Dorian cracked a smile.

"What brings you to Ravenswood, Ms. D'Amico?" The last one—Malcolm—asked. His tone was casual, but the question was anything but, and behind those eyes Charley spied a deep wariness.

"I'm an art consultant," she replied. "My company supports the museum's charitable endeavors."

"Really? Which firm do you represent? Our father just passed—I'm sure Dorian told you—and we may need someone to valuate the—"

"Thank you, Malcolm," Dorian said, "for putting your usual damper on the moment. Now, if you don't mind, I'd like to escort my guest back to the manor."

Their arms were still linked, and Charley looked up at him, momentarily dumbfounded.

His father just passed?

240

"I... I'm so sorry for your loss," she stammered. "I didn't know."

"Wonder what *else* he's left out of the family history," Gabriel grumbled.

"We weren't close," Dorian said sharply, more to Gabriel than to her. Then, turning back to Charley with a smile clearly meant to appease her, "And no, we don't need a consultant. We need drinks. Shall we?"

He tried to steer her away from his brothers, but Gabriel stepped in front of them.

"Don't forget your obligations, *brother*. The guests of honor are asking for you. Unless you'd rather I tell them you're..." His gaze roved over Charley, lip curling. "...entertaining."

Dorian's muscles tensed beneath Charley's grip, a low rumble vibrating in his chest.

Jesus, she did *not* need to cause a fight between the Redthorne brothers, no matter how badly Gabriel needed a beat-down.

"It's fine," Charley said, unlinking herself from Dorian's arm. "Go find your guests. There are a few people I should say hello to, anyway."

Dorian glared at his brother another beat, then finally sighed and turned back to Charley, his eyes sparkling once again. "If you'll excuse me, Ms. D'Amico. I'm afraid we'll have to continue our conversation later."

"Count on it, Mr. Redthorne. Oh, and for the record?" She flashed a devilish grin, stretching up to bring her mouth to his ear. "You're *definitely* the hottest brother."

CHAPTER TWENTY-EIGHT

"Ravenswood was built in 1815," Dorian said, "modeled after our family home in England, which was built in the late sixteenth century by my great, great... well, someone a great deal older than me."

Isabelle and her father laughed as Dorian led them through the tour, pointing out the architectural marvels and artwork that gave his home its unique character. In the shadow of all the terrible things his father had done, Ravenswood was a shining achievement—one Dorian would always cherish. He loved the rich oak wainscoting, the molded plaster ceilings, the Renaissance paintings adorning the long gallery on the second floor. The deep crimson of the interior walls reminded him not of blood, but of passion—a fire that still smoldered inside him.

"It's gorgeous, Mr. Redthorne," Isabelle said, running her hand along the intricate strapwork of the mantle in the first-floor hall. "If this were my home, I'm not sure I'd ever leave."

Perhaps it will be, Dorian thought.

At thirty-nine, Isabelle was older than most witches who entered into a bonded partnership, but her experience, discretion, and professionalism were legendary. Dorian often wondered why she'd never been placed before, but according to Lucien, Isabelle was extremely discerning and hadn't found a vampire house that suited her.

Tonight, she seemed relaxed and happy—almost at home. Dorian hoped that was a good sign.

That hope was enough to temper his irritation at losing precious time with Charlotte, and it carried him through the rest of the tour, culminating at his study, where he'd planned to offer Isabelle and Lucien a drink from his prized collection of rare scotch before slipping away to find his woman.

"The study is one of my favorite rooms in the manor." Dorian opened the heavy oak door and stepped over the threshold, but what he found on the other side turned his hopeful mood to dust.

The twin, unmistakable scents of blood and sex assaulted him, followed immediately by the sound of a soft, sloppy moan.

Across the room, Gabriel sat in a chair before a roaring fire, hands buried in the hair of a woman kneeling before him, cock buried in her mouth.

He glanced up and caught Dorian's gaze, his irises as red as the blood slicking his mouth, both evidence of a fresh feed. In the raging firelight, he glowed like the devil himself.

The scent of her warm blood brought Dorian's hunger into sharp relief, his own fangs slicing through his gums, the ache inside him sending a tremor through his very bones.

He gripped the edge of the door to steady himself and held his breath, willing the craving—along with his murderous fury—to pass.

Gabriel knew damn well what the scent and sight of fresh human blood would do to his brother, but he offered neither an apology nor an attempt to hide his actions. Instead, he flashed a cocky smirk and a show of fang, then closed his eyes and tipped his head back, losing himself in the pleasure of his plaything.

Duchanes' plaything, Dorian realized, noticing the woman's red hair and sparkly dress.

So many indiscretions, so many blatant risks, Dorian didn't know where to begin. Rage tore through his chest, and he took a step toward his brother, wondering if he had the strength to kill him.

But he wouldn't get the chance to find out. Not tonight, anyway. Isabelle's firm, no-nonsense touch on his arm drew him back.

"I'd love to see the kitchen, Mr. Redthorne. My father tells me the marble flooring was imported from Italy?"

She held Dorian's gaze, her eyes urgent and imploring despite the lightness in her tone.

Dorian sighed. Isabelle was an empathic witch; clearly, she'd sensed his barbaric intentions.

Doing his best to calm himself, he put on a smile and pulled the door shut, cutting off the sights and smells of his reckless brother, swallowing the bitter realization that Gabriel—no matter how many decades passed, no matter how desperately Dorian had tried to make amends—would never forgive him.

"My apologies. It seems my study is… otherwise occupied." Spotting Aiden at the end of the hall, he gestured for him to join them. "Isabelle, allow me to introduce my friend and business partner, Aiden Donovan."

Aiden brought her outstretched hand to his lips in greeting, peppering her with the usual pleasantries.

"Aiden," Dorian said with another forced smile, "Isabelle and Lucien would like to see the marblework in the kitchen. Perhaps you could show them?"

"I would be delighted." He held out his arm for Isabelle's hand, and without another word, led her and Lucien away, giving Dorian some much-needed space.

It wasn't enough, though. Not with the tang of blood so heavy on the air.

Dorian gripped the handle on the study door, overwhelmed by the sudden urge to storm back inside, rip out his brother's bloody fucking heart, and toss it into the fire. It was only Isabelle that kept his violence at bay; the memory of her imploring gaze reminded him just how much was at stake.

Tearing out still-beating hearts? That was the old Dorian

Redthorne. The monster he was supposed to convince Armitage he'd left in the past.

Old ghosts nipped at his heels.

Dorian needed to get as far away from Gabriel as he could.

Grabbing a drink from a passing butler, he retreated to the basement. From there, he made his way to the elevator at the back, punched in the security code, pressed his thumb to the blood scanner, and slipped inside, descending into the one place he knew no guest, no matter how curious, could follow.

CHAPTER TWENTY-NINE

Three brothers? A best friend? A dead father?

The situation at Ravenswood just got a lot more complicated. Rudy was *not* going to be happy.

Still, Charley had work to do.

Starting in the sitting room, she glided through the crowd, drifting from one conversation to the next, laughing at the right jokes, asking unmemorable questions, never saying anything suspicious or extraordinary, all the while taking copious notes with her eyes.

In less than an hour, she'd canvassed the first floor, discovering a small gallery's worth of beautiful artwork, resplendent but never ostentatious.

Her dad would've appreciated it. He would've *stolen* it, but he would've appreciated it first.

Maybe it shouldn't have mattered, but in Charley's eyes, it made her father human. Faulty and corrupt, like his daughter—but human. And that humanity? It was the thing that separated the father she loved from the uncle who all but owned her.

Charley thought of them both as she disappeared down a set of stairs into an exquisitely furnished basement. She wondered what her dad would think of her now—taking orders from Rudy, barely dodging Travis' threats, desperate to find a way out of the game.

He'd be horribly disappointed. And I wouldn't blame him.

With practiced but weary eyes, Charley cased the basement, identifying the artwork she knew Rudy would want. There was also a high-end media room, complete with the most sophisticated video and sound system Charley had ever seen, but they'd probably leave that alone. Luxury electronics were valuable, but they weren't unique. Rudy's clientele preferred the exclusives: one-of-a-kind art, rare artifacts, things they couldn't order online with a flash of their Amex Black cards.

At the back of the basement, Charley spotted two sleek black doors. The first was just a utility room, but the other looked promising.

A safe room?

No, not a room. An elevator.

She drew a quick mental map, orienting herself with the level above. She hadn't seen any elevator doors up there. Maybe this one only went down.

A sub-basement?

Charley looked for the button to call it up, but found

only a keypad and some kind of fancy fingerprint scanner with a digital screen below it, blinking back at her now.

ALARMED... ALARMED... ALARMED...

Excitement flooded her chest, the rush so familiar it was hard not to bask in the momentary high. Whatever the Redthornes had stashed down below, it had to be more valuable than the millions of dollars in artwork displayed upstairs under significantly less security.

More valuable—or more secret.

Charley's skin tingled. She knelt down on the floor and peered underneath the gap, confirming her suspicions; in addition to the keypad and scanner, the elevator was alarmed with a laser security system.

There was no way she could crack it—not without more time.

For now, the chamber below would remain a secret.

Unless I can convince him to give me a tour...

No. It was bad enough she was facilitating the robbery of Dorian's art estate. Whatever lay hidden below could *stay* hidden. She'd just have to tell Rudy the basement was a bust. Hopefully, he'd buy it; time was of the essence during a heist, and they'd have their hands full on the main floors, especially if Travis wanted the cars...

Charley's insides burned.

It's not going to happen. I'll figure something out before it gets that far. I won't let Dorian suffer.

Rising from the floor, she smoothed out her dress and took a deep breath, eager to move on. But when she returned to the staircase that led out of the basement, her eyes landed on a narrow library table with a protective glass top. The table itself was unimpressive, but the marble statue under the glass was anything but.

Charley gasped.

It can't be...

But it most definitely was. The missing dick was a dead giveaway.

Heart in her throat, Charley approached the table for a closer look at the sculpture—a first-century Roman statue of Hermes, carved in marble after a style favored in Greece hundreds of years prior.

The dick was filed away in antiquity, a mystery the art world had never solved. The statue was absolutely authentic—the mismatched wings on the sandals, the ornately carved hair and musculature, the missing member. It was exactly as Charley remembered from her art books.

It was the real deal.

It was priceless.

And—mindfuck of all mindfucks—it was another piece from her father's missing cache.

Charley's heart hammered, her palms sweating inside the satin gloves. Why did Dorian Redthorne—*her* Dorian Redthorne—have two pieces of art from the heist that had basically killed her dad?

Had Rudy known about these pieces?

Was he home sipping his martini, laughing his ass off as he sent her out to chase after her father's ghost?

Was this all a fucking game to him?

Questions rushed at her from the deepest, most fearful parts of her heart. Charley was so lost in thought and worry, she didn't even hear the man behind her until it was too late.

"Is something wrong, Ms. D'Amico?" he asked. "You seem a bit… confused."

Charley jumped and spun around, coming face-to-face with Malcolm, his mistrustful gaze boring straight through her.

"No, I…" She took a step back, bumping against the glass-topped table, her mind whirling as she tried to recalibrate.

She should've apologized. She should've acted drunk. She should've turned the charm on full blast, forced out a nervous giggle, and invented another excuse about getting lost on the way to the powder room.

But with Malcolm towering over her, all she said was, "I need to speak with Dorian."

"And you thought you'd find him down here?" He glanced over her shoulder at the table behind her. "Under the glass, perhaps?"

"Please, Malcolm. If you could let your brother know I'm looking for him—"

"Well, well," he said suddenly, his gaze shifting to the elevator. "It seems the devil's ears are ringing."

The door slid open, and Dorian walked out alone, his tie undone again, eyes red, jaw tight. His hair was a hot, sexy mess.

"Dorian," she whispered, fingers curling at the thought of running her hands through it.

And though he shouldn't have been able to hear her all the way across the room, he glanced up immediately, his eyes and mouth softening at the sight of her.

"Ms. D'Amico," he said, approaching them so gracefully, he practically glided. "Is my brother harassing you?"

"Hardly," Malcolm said. "I found her here, looking as if—"

Dorian cut him off with a raised hand, the two brothers glaring at each other over the top of Charley's head.

Were they always at odds, or was it just her? She was starting to get a complex.

After another few seconds of silent dick-measuring, Malcolm finally retreated, heading back upstairs and leaving them blissfully alone.

"What's wrong, love?" Dorian asked. "He didn't frighten you, did he?"

Charley had a million questions now—*where were you? What's down there? What's up with your crazy family? Why didn't you tell me about your father?*—but she couldn't hold his gaze.

Instead, she turned toward the table and pointed at the statue beneath the glass. "Where did you get this?"

"Hermes?" Dorian slipped his arms around her from behind, resting his chin on her shoulder. Then, sliding his hands across the front of her thighs, "Care to make a bid? I'm willing to part with it for the right offer."

This can't be happening…

Charley wanted nothing more than to sink into the warm comfort of Dorian's strong embrace, to lean back against him and feel every muscled ridge of his body molding to hers. She wanted him to reach up and cup her breasts, to growl into her ear with that deliciously deep, commanding voice. Maybe then she could forget about what she'd found. About where she'd come from. Who she was.

But when she turned around in his arms and met his eyes, Charley knew she couldn't forget. She was casing her almost-lover's house, and she'd just discovered another piece of art connected to her father's murder.

She couldn't pretend it wasn't happening, no matter how badly she wanted to surrender. "*Where*, Dorian? Tell me where it came from. I need to know."

Dorian backed Charley right up to the glass, pressing his hands against the case and trapping her inside his arms, his gaze narrowing suspiciously. "Why?"

Charley's heart rattled in her chest, the voice in her head screaming for her to forget about Hermes, forget about the LaPorte, and seduce her way out of yet another sticky situation with Dorian.

But she couldn't let this go.

"Tell me," she pressed.

"I don't know what your interest is, Charlotte, but obviously you're upset."

She didn't need to confirm it—every muscle in her body was vibrating.

"Clearly we've got some things to discuss," he said.

"You think?"

"It's settled then." A hint of his rakish smile broke through. "You'll stay the weekend."

"I'll... *what*?"

Disarmed. That's how Charley felt. Despite her racing heart and the mistrust swirling between them, Dorian's smile drained the fear and tension from her body, replacing it with that mind-erasing desire he was so damn good at igniting.

"Something tells me this isn't about what we need to discuss." She pressed her hand against his firm chest. "You've got ulterior motives, Mr. Redthorne."

Dorian leaned in close, dragging his lips down the long column of her neck, pressing a hot kiss into the hollow of her throat. "And you've been dodging me, Ms. D'Amico."

Damn. Her list of regrets was growing exponentially by the minute, but telling Dorian her last name was no longer one of them. She'd *never* get sick of hearing it on his lips.

"I wouldn't dream of it," she breathed.

"It would be futile, I assure you." Dorian fisted her dress, slowly lifting it to reveal her bare legs. The cool basement air teased her skin, casting her flesh in goosebumps even as Dorian's touch flooded her core with molten heat. "I can be *very* persuasive."

Charley sighed, eyelids fluttering closed as Dorian slipped his fingers inside her underwear for the second time that night. He was totally distracting her, leading her dangerously away from her purpose, but all she could do was follow him right off the path, straight into oblivion.

She craved his touch. Needed it.

"Always ready for more," he whispered, nipping at her earlobe. "I love that about you."

Before she could respond, Dorian claimed her mouth in a violent kiss. He slid his other hand behind her head, bringing her closer, teasing and biting until she was certain he'd draw blood...

The sudden pinch of sharp, eager teeth on her fleshy lip made her gasp, but she didn't pull back, not even as the warm, salty blood leaked into her mouth. Dorian moaned into the kiss, his fingers thrusting deeper between her thighs as he sucked and licked and devoured and *claimed*.

Tingling heat gathered in her core, but suddenly, Charley couldn't breathe. He was destroying her with his kiss, marking her flesh, and she couldn't fucking breathe.

She tried to speak but managed only a muffled plea.

Dorian ignored her.

Panic flooded her limbs, and she shoved against his chest, desperate for air. But they were too close, her resistance easily mistaken for play, and Dorian persisted, his grip tightening in her hair as he plundered her with his tongue and fingers.

Stars danced before her eyes, her legs weakening, the slide of his fingers relentless as he licked and sucked and stole the very last breath from her lungs.

The edges of her vision turned gray.

She couldn't hold herself up. Couldn't scream. Couldn't even see.

She collapsed in his arms, and Dorian crushed her

against his chest, moaning into her mouth as he thumbed her clit and fucked her with those mad, unabating fingers.

What is happening to me? I can't... This is... I'm going to... holy shit...

The orgasm tore through her in a blinding rush, her body clenching around his fingers, heat spreading down her thighs and up through her chest, the intense pleasure mixing with the fear of certain death—a cocktail that sent a surge of raw adrenaline shooting through her veins.

With her last bit of strength, Charley shoved hard against his chest, finally breaking the kiss.

She gasped and sucked in air, her heart ready to explode.

Dorian pulled his hands away and stumbled backward, staring at her like he had no idea what the fuck had just happened. He glared at her mouth, his own streaked with her blood, his gaze drunk and delirious.

He was so far gone she wasn't sure he even recognized her.

Crazed laughter bubbled up through her lips, and Charley pressed a hand to her chest, panting.

"Wow. Gave me quite the scare, Mr. Redthorne." *Not to mention the hottest five minutes of my life.* "Okay, then. Still breathing. Good sign."

"I'm... sorry." He shook his head, muttering to himself. When he looked at her again, the haze had cleared from his eyes, replaced with something that looked a lot like guilt. "I didn't mean to get so carried away. It... It won't happen again."

He turned on his heel, about to walk away.

Charley was more than ready to let him go, desperate for a literal and figurative breather from his unwavering intensity, but then she remembered the statue.

"Dorian, wait! Aren't you going to tell me about Hermes?"

He stopped and let out a deep sigh. "*That's* what's on your mind?"

Heat burned in her cheeks, but she couldn't stop now. "I need to know. It's important."

"Fine. I've got another deal for you, then." Dorian glanced toward the upper floor, where the din of revelry still floated above them—laughter and clinking glasses, classical violins, footsteps echoing on marble. "As soon as I clear these *wretched* people from my home, I'll fix us a night-cap, and I'll tell you anything you want to know about Hermes, as well as anything else in my collection."

Charley did some quick calculations, hoping she had enough time before Travis came sniffing around. With a little more of that luck she'd been banking on all night, she could get the scoop on Hermes, finagle a tour of the upstairs, and sneak in some questions about the LaPorte painting too.

"You've got yourself a deal, Mr. Redthorne."

"You haven't heard the rest of the terms, Ms. D'Amico." He finally turned to face her, running his thumb across his mouth and wiping her blood from his lips. His eyes held a dangerous spark.

Suddenly, Charley felt like a rabbit caught in the jaws of a predator. "Terms?"

"Think of it as a confessional. I'll tell you about the art. And you, my little prowler..." He gripped her chin and lowered his gaze to her own still-bloodied mouth, the deep tenor of his voice buzzing across her skin. "You'll tell me why you're casing my home like a common thief."

CHAPTER THIRTY

What. The fuck. Was that?

Charley could barely get her legs to work as she stumbled out of the manor, sucking in the cool night air like her life depended on it.

They hadn't even had sex. Yet somehow, every encounter with Dorian Redthorne made her feel like she was drowning.

And Charley was really, *really* developing a taste for drowning.

"You're out of your damn mind, girl."

Taking another steadying breath, she walked along the cobblestone path behind the manor, past the spot where Dorian had ambushed her earlier, past the guest house, past the brambles and bushes and trees until the imposing Elizabethan giant was no more than a blur of stone and warm yellow light behind her.

With every step, her mind cleared a bit more, refocusing

on the stolen artwork she'd discovered, unleashing a dozen new impossible scenarios in her mind.

She was so wrapped up in her art-world conspiracy theories, she didn't even see the man on the path until she'd crashed right into him.

"Whoa, easy." He reached out to steady her just before she fell and twisted an ankle, cold hands gripping her elbows.

"I'm so sorry!" Charley plastered on a smile, slipping the socialite mask back in place as she found her footing.

But when she glanced up and met his gaze, all bets were off.

Her blood went cold. Even a fine tux couldn't hide the asshole inside.

What the hell is he *doing here?*

"Mr. Duchanes," she ground out, taking a step backward and shoving a hand into her purse. Beyoncé 2 awaited her command, and this time, Charley wouldn't drop her.

Duchanes bowed slightly, clasping his hands behind his back and giving her wide berth, as if he wanted to appear as meek and non-threatening as possible. "Enjoy the rest of your evening. And watch your step."

Without another word, he scooted past her and disappeared up the path toward the house, clear out of sight.

Charley released her grip on the stun gun and blew out a breath.

Two events in a row with that creep. God, sometimes she really hated the art crowd. At least he hadn't tried anything this time; Dorian's implicit warnings at the auction must've really gotten to him.

Rattled but undeterred, she continued along the path in search of a quiet place to rest her bones and figure out what she was going to tell Dorian about her "prowling" tonight. Clearly, he'd spotted her snooping around upstairs, and despite the intense moments they shared in the basement, he had to be wondering why she'd gone down there in the first place. She didn't want to complicate things with more lies, but it wasn't like she could spill her guts and beg for mercy, either.

God, what a fucking mess.

A soft snick caught her attention, and she glanced up to see another man leaning against a sycamore tree several paces off the path, half hidden in shadow.

Gabriel.

Perfect. There was no way she could pass by the tree without him noticing, and she didn't want yet another Redthorne brother to accuse her of sneaking around.

Locking her smile back in place, she said, "Looks like I'm not the only one trying to escape the crowd tonight."

He turned to her slowly, his movements as liquid and graceful as his older brother's. When he met her gaze, his eyes held the same coldness she'd spotted earlier.

But it wasn't his cruel gaze that pinned her in place.

The sudden, unexpected flash of the blade in his hands paralyzed her, unlocking a flood of memories Charley had dammed up years ago.

Where you off to, little girl?

Not so tough when Daddy's not around, are ya?

Don't struggle, D'Amico bitch...

Instinctively she pressed a hand to her abdomen, just above her left hipbone, where the ropey, silver scar burned fresh.

"Yet here you are," Gabriel said with a sneer, "*crowding.*" His tone dripped with impatience, but he didn't move toward her—just pressed the knife to a round, red object in his hands.

An apple. Just a damn apple.

Charley let out a breath as a long curl of apple peel fell to the ground. Gabriel carved off a slice and brought it to his mouth, eating it right off the blade.

"I'm sorry," she said. "I don't mean to intrude."

"Then don't." Glaring at her with that unnervingly cold gaze, he carved off another slice, then turned back toward the view of the rolling hills and the Hudson River beyond, dismissing her.

She didn't need to be told twice.

Leaving Gabriel to his brooding, Charley ambled further down the path, finally finding an unoccupied stone bench with a perfect view of the river. There, slipping out of her uncomfortable high heels, she sat down and gazed out across the expansive landscape, trying to catch her breath.

Rudy.

Travis.

Ravenswood.

Dorian.

His brothers.

Duchanes.

Hermes.

LaPorte.

Her web was getting stickier by the minute. Charley didn't know how many more twists and turns she could handle tonight, but she couldn't bail now. Not with so much on the line.

Charley took out her phone, laughing when she saw the latest artistic endeavor from Sasha—a picture of two perfectly round grapefruits topped with cherries, a huge zucchini sliding between them. *Thinking of you!* she'd texted.

A+, Charley replied now. *Sadly, the conference is bereft of photo-worthy fruit. I'll have to up my game later.*

Up your game all you want, Sasha texted back. *I'm still the reigning fruit-smut champion. ;-)*

I'm soooo not worthy.

Keep practicing! I have faith in your dirty mind! Hey, chat later, k? Heading out for a late dinner with Darcy.

Have fun! Love you.

Love you too, Chuck.

Charley smiled. Sasha sounded so happy, and that made Charley happy, bolstering her for the work ahead. Sasha might be the reigning champion of fruit smut, but Charley was a champion too—of disguises, of lies, of sleuthing, of playing each and every role assigned to her like a god damned queen.

For her sister, Charley could endure anything.

In that moment, she made her decision. She'd take

Dorian up on his offer and stay the weekend. Maybe her acceptance would disarm him a bit—distract him from the fact that he'd caught her sticking her nose where it didn't belong.

Besides, spending the weekend with Dorian Redthorne was a much better option than sitting in traffic, fending off Travis' bad breath and questing hands.

Confidence sufficiently boosted, Charley sent a quick text to Sasha that she wouldn't be home until Sunday night, then shot off another text to Rudy, who'd miraculously given her some breathing room tonight.

Still having a great time, she said. *Can't wait to tell you about all the sightseeing I've been doing!*

Thank you for the update, he replied. *Looking forward to catching up later.*

She bit her lip, knowing this next part wouldn't go over well, but hoping to spin it in her favor anyway.

Actually, she replied, *I've decided to stay the weekend. Still so much to explore! Why don't we touch base Sunday night?*

The telltale dots flickered across her screen, and Charley's insides bubbled. She really hoped he wouldn't make a big deal out of this, but Rudy didn't like it when she went off-script, even if it led to better intel. He liked thinking everything was his idea.

"Come on," she grumbled. "Cut me a break."

His text finally popped up, but before she could read it, a shadow fell over her face, and she shoved the phone back into her purse, quickly getting to her feet.

Two men she'd never seen loomed on the path before

her, drinks in hand, tuxedos impeccable, their smiles perfectly pleasant.

But every nerve in her body went on high alert.

Gabriel may have glared at her with annoyance that bordered on contempt. But these guys?

They looked at her like they wanted to eat her. And she was far enough from the main house that if they tried, no one would hear her scream.

"Lovely evening, isn't it?" one of them—a man with gray hair and a trim, matching beard—said.

"Sure is." Charley smiled, gripping Beyoncé 2 inside her purse. "I was just leaving, if you'd like the bench. Great view out here."

"The scenery *is* rather enchanting," the younger of the two said, his beady eyes roaming her curves.

"I wouldn't go *that* far." Graybeard frowned at Charley, sniffing at the air between them like a dog. "Redthorne royals cavorting with trash. What has the world come to?"

Redthorne royals? What?

"Sometimes trash has a certain… appeal." The junior guy reached forward and touched Charley's hair, his eyes dark with malice.

Oh, hell no.

All pretense of politeness shattered. Charley removed the weapon from her purse and took a step backward, aiming Beyoncé 2 at the douchebag who'd touched her. "Careful, boys. This trash bites."

"She said *bites*," Junior said. "That's so cute."

"Woman, you don't know the meaning of the word,"

Graybeard said. "But you will." He flashed a cruel smile, his teeth sharp and long, almost like... *fangs*?

What the fuck?

Her mind flashed back to the bedroom at the Salvatore. Hadn't she thought the same thing about Duchanes?

Junior reached for her again, but this time Charley was ready for it. She squeezed the trigger, plugging him square in the chest.

Her mouth quirked into a triumphant grin, but it didn't last.

The asshole should've dropped to the ground, muscles jiggling like a Jell-o mold. Yet there he stood, unmoving, unaffected, still grinning at her like she was the main course.

Charley was sure of it now. The men had actual, real-life, terrifying fangs.

"Was that supposed to hurt?" he asked, plucking the probes from his chest.

"Maybe it's a kink?" Graybeard said. "Young people are into pain these days."

Junior laughed. "Then I suppose it's your lucky night, gorgeous."

In a blur, they dropped their drinks and surrounded her, Graybeard hauling her backward against his chest, Junior crushing her from the front, snatching at her breasts.

"Help!" Charley screamed, knowing her cries would likely go unheard. "Fire!" she tried again, recalling all the self-defense stuff she'd picked up over the years. Weren't people supposed to be more likely to help if you yelled *fire*?

Graybeard fisted her hair, jerking her head sideways and exposing her neck. Junior leaned in and licked her flesh, groaning with sick pleasure.

Charley choked back bile. She didn't care how strong they were, how determined. She would *not* let this happen.

She struggled against their hold, using her elbows, her knees, the back of her head, anything to get in a hit. But it was no use. The men were impossibly strong, like two stone walls closing in from all sides, determined to turn her into a pancake.

But not before they had their fun.

"Fire!" she screamed again, then slammed her head backward, finally connecting with Graybeard's face. She heard the crunch of bone and hoped she'd taken out a few teeth, but the man behind her only laughed.

"I love it when they fight." He released his hold and shoved her away. "Run along, little plaything. Fast as you can."

She took off at a run down the hill, doing her best to stay upright in bare feet on the dew-slick grass. Her heart slammed against her ribs, lungs burning, feet stinging as rocks and sticks sliced through her skin, but she didn't dare stop. Not until she was certain she'd left them far behind.

For a fleeting instant, she actually thought she'd escaped. But when she took a chance and glanced back over her shoulder to check, her forward momentum came to a crashing halt.

She'd run smack into them. Even though they'd given

her a clear head start, somehow, they'd gotten out in front of her.

How the fuck...?

"You're fast, gorgeous," Junior said. "I'll give you that."

"Not fast enough." Graybeard laughed, resting his arm on the younger man's shoulder. They leered at her again, their eyes even hungrier than before.

The reality of the situation sank into Charley's gut like a sharp-edged rock. Now, she was even further from civilization, trapped at the bottom of a hill in the darkness with two raving psychopaths, no weapons, no phone, nothing but crickets and moonlight.

She dropped into a crouch and fisted a nearby rock. If she was going down, she was going down fighting.

The men laughed again and took another step toward her, their smiles twisting into grimaces, those awful fangs flashing like blades.

But then, just before they descended and shredded her flesh, they fell to their knees, strangled gasps leaking from their mouths.

Dark blood spread across the front of Graybeard's shirt like spilled ink.

Beside him, Junior was covered in even more blood— more than Charley had ever seen in her life.

His head, she realized, was gone.

And there, like something out of the worst B-movie horror flick ever made, two of the so-called Royal Redthornes towered behind them, fangs bared.

Gabriel clutched his knife, his arms and chest covered in

blood, eyes wild with rage. Now, instead of an apple, he held a severed head.

Dorian's expression mirrored his brother's. A hunk of raw, red meat glistened in his hand, blood leaking out between his fingers.

Charley blinked.

Not meat. A heart. Graybeard's fucking heart.

Charley blinked again, and the bodies of the men who'd ambushed her turned to ash before her eyes, scattering across the hillside.

And Charley—master thief, champion of champions, fighter to the death—dropped to her knees, puked in the grass, and promptly passed out.

CHAPTER THIRTY-ONE

"Breathe, Charlotte. Just breathe."

Dorian pressed the damp cloth to her forehead, wishing she'd say something. After she'd passed out, he'd carried her inside and cleaned her up, changing out of his own bloody garments and slowly bringing her back to consciousness, only to have her spiral into a screaming panic.

He'd had no other recourse but to compel her, and while the compulsion had silenced her shrieks of terror, the shock was still working its way through her system.

She'd been sitting in the study for well over an hour now, her eyes glassy in the firelight, her breathing shallow and erratic as Dorian knelt before her, willing her to return from the darkness.

He'd never seen anything like it before. Compelling someone to forget a traumatic event—*any* event—didn't merely calm their fears or silence their reactions. It literally coerced the mind to write over those memories with new ones, as swiftly and completely as a novelist edits a scene in her story.

"You wandered out behind the property and slipped on the hillside," Dorian said now, repeating the scenario he'd crafted for her earlier. "Gabriel and I heard you calling for help."

What they'd actually heard were her screams; the sheer terror in her voice sent twin bolts of fear and rage through Dorian's heart. He was already outside looking for her when it happened; Gabriel had arrived at the same moment. The brothers didn't even speak. They simply acted, instantly eliminating the threat.

When news of the attack reached the manor, Aiden made quick work of clearing out the guests and staff under the pretense of a burst pipe. Gabriel and Malcolm had gone off to search the grounds for Duchanes, while Colin manned the crypts, just in case the vile bastard attempted to break in.

Duchanes. The name burned a fresh path through his chest, igniting something darker than hatred, more vile than loathing. The vampires who'd attacked his woman belonged to that deplorable house. They'd defied all customs and rules, entering his home under false pretenses, using his generosity against him, attacking a guest on his property. And not just any guest, but a woman he'd claimed as his own.

It meant war.

In some ways, Dorian was relieved. Politics was complicated. But war? War simplified things.

Duchanes would suffer. His bloodline would burn. And then, when the last of his house was forgotten and scattered to the winds, Dorian would personally send his enemy into the jaws of hell.

But first, he needed to take care of Charlotte.

"Dorian?" a weak voice called, pulling him back to the moment.

Dropping the cloth, he took her hands and pressed them to his mouth, breathing in her scent. "Thank the gods and the devil both. How are you feeling?"

She blinked down at him from the chair, her eyes still unfocused, her brow furrowed. "I think… I need a drink."

"Of course." He got to his feet and headed for the small bar he kept stocked in the study, pouring her a hefty dose of his favorite scotch. "I don't have gin on hand, but—"

"It's fine. Anything is fine." She reached for the glass, then downed it in a few gulps, wincing at the burn.

"Better?" he asked.

She held out the glass for more.

He poured a little less this time. "Careful, love. You've only just regained consciousness."

Heeding his advice, she took a measured sip, fighting off a shiver. "What happened?"

Dorian pulled a blanket from another chair and draped it over her shoulders. "You had a fall. Nothing to worry about—just a slip and a good scare." He told her the story he'd invented, sending gentle waves of compulsion through her mind.

"It's weird," she said. "I remember walking along the path, and seeing Gabriel by the tree, and sitting on the bench by myself. I texted my sister, and then... I don't know. It's all a big blank."

"You may have a concussion," he said, knowing damn well she didn't. "I'll keep an eye on you tonight."

She offered a watery smile, the first he'd seen since their encounter in the basement hours earlier. "Thank you, Dorian. I... I'm sorry for the trouble."

"It's no trouble at all."

"Where is everyone else?"

"I sent them home."

Charlotte squeezed her forehead and groaned. "Oh, God. I ruined the whole party."

"Nonsense." Dorian knelt before her again, sliding his hands up her thighs. "It was the perfect excuse to cut short an otherwise dreadful evening."

She laughed, but it rang hollow, her eyes still glazed with confusion.

Dorian lowered his gaze, his mind racing. Other than a few cuts on her feet, which he'd already healed with his blood, Charlotte didn't have any physical injuries—he would've sensed them. So why wasn't she accepting the compulsion? Even if the ordeal had left her drained, her mind should've been clear by now.

"What's wrong, love?" he asked.

"It bothers me that I don't remember falling. I don't

remember you guys finding me, either. You said Gabriel was with you?"

"Yes. I was already looking for you—I ran into him on the path. That's when we heard you calling for help."

She nodded, but Dorian sensed her mind was still spinning, working over the details and searching for the holes in his story. He was about to try another round of compulsion when Aiden entered the study, Gabriel and Malcolm right behind him.

Their grim faces said it all.

"Nothing?" Dorian asked anyway, rising and crossing the room to meet them. He didn't want Charlotte to overhear.

"Not a trace," Gabriel said. The blood on his shirt had dried to a muddy black, and Dorian curled his hands into fists, another wave of fury rippling through him as he thought of the Duchanes traitors.

"How is Charlotte?" Aiden asked.

Dorian glanced over his shoulder and found her holding the drink in her lap, staring into the fire as if the flames held all the answers. "Hard to say. She doesn't remember much."

"That's a good thing, isn't it?" Aiden asked.

Dorian sighed and shook his head.

"Didn't you compel her?" Malcolm asked, unable to keep the superior tone from his voice.

Dorian glared at him. "Didn't you seek an alliance with a murderer?"

"We don't know that Renault gave the order for the attack," he said.

"Where is he, then? If he's innocent, he should be just as eager to uncover the traitors of House Duchanes as we are. Instead, he's fled the scene like a—"

"Dorian." Aiden gripped his arm, forcing his attention back to the matter at hand. "The compulsion. It didn't take?"

Dorian shook his head. "Doesn't seem so. Not fully, anyway."

"Dorian?" Charlotte called out now, her tone more curious than anything else. "Am I going to turn?"

"Turn?" Dorian exchanged a shocked glance with Aiden, then returned to his woman, kneeling before her once again. "What ever do you mean, love?"

"You bit me." She touched her lip, still swollen from their encounter in the basement.

"That was an accident," he said gently, reaching up to stroke her face. "You're all right."

"I've read all the books. Seen all the movies. My sister is kind of obsessed, so we've got a whole library full."

"I'm still not sure what you mean." Dorian forced a gentle smile, but inside, cold fear gripped his heart.

Charlotte finally met his eyes. "If a vampire bites someone, they turn. Everyone knows *that*."

"And the good times keep on coming," Gabriel muttered from the doorway.

Ignoring his brother, Dorian rose from the floor and held out his hands, helping Charlotte out of the chair. "Why don't I take you to bed. Everything will make a lot more sense in the morning."

Nodding, she got to her feet and yawned, and for a brief moment, Dorian thought they'd sufficiently dodged the bullet.

But then she placed her hand against his chest and looked up into his eyes, her heartbeat suddenly kicking into high gear.

The change came over her in an instant, her gaze turning from vacant and confused to sharp and discerning. Adrenaline flooded her bloodstream and she gasped, some dark, terrible realization taking root in her mind.

"Stay away from me!" She jerked out of Dorian's hold, her glass clattering to the floor.

Dorian raised his hands and took a step back, giving her space. "Charlotte, I'm not going to hurt you. You're safe here."

"You're a... you're a vampire!" Her eyes darted around the room, her face as pale as the moon. "You're *all* vampires. Those men outside... Fangs and... So fast and... Oh my *God*." She squeezed her eyes shut and pressed her hands to the sides of her head, as if her mind was ready to explode.

Dorian could only imagine what she was going through.

"This is fucking insane!" she shouted.

"Charlotte, listen to me." Dorian took a step toward her, his voice low. "Please let me explain."

She finally opened her eyes, her gaze alight with confusion and anger and so much raw, unchecked fear it made his heart ache.

Dorian would never forget that look in her eyes. And he'd never forgive himself for putting it there.

"Just breathe," he said again, his tone deep and even as he willed a fresh wave of compulsion to take hold. "You had an accident behind the gardens. You fell, and—"

"Are you trying to manipulate me?" she demanded, the anger in her eyes starting to edge out the fear.

"She's got your number, brother," Gabriel quipped, clearly enjoying the disastrous turn of events.

"Of course not," Dorian said to Charlotte. "I'm trying to explain what happened. You've had a rough night, and—"

"Compulsion, right?" she asked. "That's what it's called. You're trying to use your vampire mojo on me to convince me I'm imagining the complete and utter shit-show I've witnessed. Those men who attacked me were vampires. You and your brothers are vampires. And rather than admit it, you want me to think I'm going crazy. Do you have any idea how messed up that is?"

"Charlotte, it's not that simple. I'm—"

"Don't. Don't come another step closer." She grabbed the iron poker from the set beside the fireplace, brandishing it like a weapon. It wouldn't do her any good, but Dorian admired her guts.

"I remember now," she said. "I remember *exactly* what happened tonight. I remember... God, I remember what happened in Central Park too!"

"What happened in Central Park?" Aiden asked.

"Not now, Aiden." Dorian turned back to Charlotte. "If you'll let me explain, I'll—"

"You'll *what*? Spoon-feed me more lies? Erase my memories?"

"Charlotte—"

"Get back, or I'll shove this thing through your heart!" She tightened her grip on the fire poker, tears spilling down her cheeks. "How long have you been messing with my mind? From the very start? Did you... Oh, fuck *me*. Of *course*."

Her eyes filled with a pain so sharp and all-encompassing, Dorian felt it echo through his own heart.

In that moment, he knew exactly where her mind had gone.

"Trouble in paradise, brother?" Gabriel taunted.

Dorian whirled around to face him. "Leave us. Now."

"As you wish, *highness*." Gabriel swiped a bottle from the bar. Then, pointing at Charlotte as if she were a pest in need of exterminating, "Take care of that, or I will."

He left without another word, Malcolm trailing after him, shaking his head as if he were judge and jury in all things Redthorne. Aiden offered a sympathetic smile, then followed them out, leaving Dorian and Charlotte to work through their monumental differences alone.

"Tell me one thing, Dorian," she said. Some of her anger had faded, but she still gripped the fire poker. "And don't lie to me."

"You have my word." Maybe his word didn't mean much to her in that moment, but Dorian felt the need to offer it anyway.

She turned away from him, as if she couldn't bear to

look at him another second—couldn't bear to see his face when she finally asked the question on her mind. "The times we were... together. Did you compel me to be with you?"

"I think you know the answer to that," he said gently.

More than anything he wanted to go to her, to take her in his arms, to show her with his touch and his kiss when every last word had utterly failed. But he couldn't—not now. She was too upset. Too angry.

"Really?" she snapped. "Because an hour ago, I thought I knew a *lot* of things. Primarily, that vampires were a myth. Yet here you are, tearing out people's hearts, turning them into—"

"Not *people*, Charlotte. *Vampires*." His composure crumpled, the reminder of how close she'd come to death unleashing a new fury inside him. "*Duchanes* vampires who would've done *unspeakable* things to you, bled you dry, and tossed your corpse in the river without so much as a backward glance had Gabriel and I not intervened."

"Duchanes? As in, the same asshole from the auction? I saw him earlier."

Dorian nodded solemnly. "The vampires that attacked you were members of House Duchanes."

"*House* Duchanes? What does that even mean?"

"Essentially, a house is a vampire coven or family— usually one of considerable means."

She took in the information, her brow furrowing. "That means you and Malcolm and everyone... You're House Redthorne?"

"Precisely."

"One of the vampires who attacked me… He said something about the Royal Redthornes. Are you guys…" She swallowed hard, shaking her head as if the word had gotten stuck inside. "Are you royalty?"

Dorian folded his arms over his chest, impatience flaring. "Yes, the Redthornes are the ruling vampire royal family. But that's hardly the crucial—"

"You're a prince, then?"

Silently he held her gaze, the muscles in his jaw ticking as he waited for her to figure it out.

"King?" Charlotte pressed a hand to her throat, her voice notching up a few octaves. "You're a fucking *vampire* king?"

Dorian closed his eyes, the reality of the situation descending upon him like a storm.

Charlotte had somehow broken his compulsion, shattering even his previously successful attempts. It was a nearly impossible feat for a human—one that had even eluded hunters trained to resist vampire magic.

Yet here she was, a woman who'd entered his life like a tempest, unravelling every spell, reclaiming every memory he'd stolen, turning his entire world upside down.

And now, she'd be immune to all future attempts at compulsion—from Dorian or any other vampire. Within the walls of Ravenswood and without, anything she heard, anything she witnessed would remain lodged in her memories until the day she died.

To say she was a risk was a gross understatement. She

had the power to expose him, to destroy his family and their kind. To destroy everything his father—for good and for ill—had built and protected.

Now, it was Dorian's responsibility to keep this family safe. To keep their secrets buried, no matter how much his brothers despised him.

By all means, he should end her life. Take care of it, just like Gabriel had demanded.

But for Dorian, it was too late. His heart would not allow it, no matter how great a risk she posed.

Charlotte was nearly murdered by the beasts of House Duchanes—a near miss that had filled him with a terror darker than any he'd ever known, even in his bleakest hours.

Tonight, as Dorian carried her unconscious body up the hill, he'd made a solemn vow to protect her.

And he intended to keep it… or die trying.

But he wasn't about to share that with Charlotte.

"Not *a* vampire king, Ms. D'Amico." He blurred into her space and wrenched the fire poker from her hands, hurling it into the wall with a force that splintered the oak wainscoting. "*The* vampire king. So unless you're eager to find out just how much power a two-and-a-half-centuries-old royal vampire whose already developed a taste for your blood possesses, *never* threaten me again."

CHAPTER THIRTY-TWO

A fresh string of profanities gathered on Charley's tongue, but before she could let 'em rip, Dorian folded her into his arms, lifted her off the ground, and tipped the whole world sideways.

Charley's stomach dropped right down to her feet, and she dug her fingers into his shoulders, squeezing her eyes shut to stem the tide of nausea. When she finally opened them again, she and her captor were no longer in the study.

"What the hell did you do?" she breathed.

"It's called a blur."

"Yeah? I'm pretty sure you left my internal organs behind."

Dorian kicked a door closed behind them, then set her on her feet.

"Just breathe," he said again—refrain of the hour. "The feeling will pass."

She did as he asked, and the new room slowly sharpened into focus.

The master bedroom.

It was massive and imposing, with deep red walls, dark wood paneling, and gorgeous hardwood floors covered in Turkish rugs. Ornate tapestries hung over the windows, and every piece of furniture looked as if it belonged in some ancient British castle rather than in a mansion in Upstate New York.

A colossal four-poster bed dominated the back wall, each intricately carved column the size of a small tree. The whole thing was topped by a huge oak tester, with black-and-gold damask curtains hung from each corner.

The room was truly fit for a king.

A creepy one.

"I take it this is *your* bedroom, highness?" she asked, forcing a little more sass into her voice. As it was, her skin was covered in goosebumps, her heartbeat thrumming at a fevered pitch.

Vampires.

They were all vampires.

Her brain was still railing against the idea, even though she knew—deep down—it was true.

Malcolm, with his holier-than-thou attitude and mistrustful eyes. Gabriel, the brother with the biggest stick up his ass. Colin, with his kind dimples and shiny hair. Aiden, with his cute jokes and sparkling eyes. The men that had attacked her.

Even Dorian, a man she'd been inexplicably drawn to from the start—the proverbial moth to the flame.

"It is," he finally replied.

"You blurred me up to your bedroom?" Charlotte let out a nervous laugh. "I think you were confusing my screams of protest with my screams of passion."

"Not likely. I can assure you, the difference is *quite* distinct."

"Then let me make something even *more* distinct. This?" She gestured between the two of them. "Is *not* happening. And don't you *dare* try any of that compulsion bullshit again. There's a word for that, Dorian. Forcing a woman to—"

"I've already told you—I did *not* compel your desire. Even if it were possible, it's a line I would never cross."

"Why?" She folded her arms across her chest and leaned back against one of the bed's oak columns. "Because you're such a nice chap?"

His eyes blazed again, two embers in a face of stone. "Because even the most evil among us have their limits."

A shiver rolled through her body, but she stood her ground. "Then how does it work? You just… erase people's memories whenever you feel like it?"

Dorian shoved a hand through his hair, clearly flustered.

But Charlotte wasn't going to let this drop.

"A skilled vampire can compel humans to forget recent events or conversations," he said. "He can manipulate memories to make you believe you saw something other than the truth. He can order you to perform certain acts, or say certain words, or even take your own life. But he *cannot* compel a woman to want him." He stepped closer, trapping her against the column, glaring down at her with those intense eyes. Then, brushing his fingertips across her collarbone and taking a deep draw of breath, "He cannot compel her body to respond to his touch, nor to create the *unmistakable* scent of her darkest desires."

Charlotte closed her eyes, the shiver finally breaking through, rattling her from head to toe.

It would've been so easy to give in. To push aside everything she'd seen tonight—to bury it with her guilt and shame and all the other dark things she kept locked in a box —and fall into his eager embrace.

But she wouldn't. Not this time.

She looked up at him again and shook her head. "I'm *not* sleeping with you tonight, Dorian. Forget it."

Dorian sighed and took a step back, breaking their connection. "I didn't bring you here for sex, Charlotte."

"So we're gonna sit around and play Scrabble, then?" She shoved against the column behind her, but it was as immovable as solid stone. "God, this thing was probably made in the middle ages."

"Renaissance, actually." He glared at her, broody as ever.

"Seriously? Fine. I've got a better game. Twenty questions. Me first." She popped her hands on her hips and glared right back at him. "Why the fuck didn't you tell me you're a... a bloodsucking vampire king?"

"And when, pray tell, would I have done that?"

"Oh, I don't know, maybe before you—"

He rushed at her again, wrapping her in another impossible embrace, pinning her arms at her sides. His mouth was so close, she thought he might bite.

Images of their insane kiss in the basement flashed through her mind, the coppery tang of blood lingering in her mouth.

"Before I *what*?" his whispered. New fire raged in his eyes, a hot mix of lust and anger, and beneath his firm hold, Charlotte felt the unmistakable power coursing through his veins. It wasn't just his superstrength, his speed, his commanding tone. It was something that ran much deeper, pulsing from the very core of his being.

A two-and-a-half-centuries-old vampire king…

Charley swallowed the knot of fear in her throat, trying to remain absolutely still. She didn't think there was a right answer to his question, and even if there was, she didn't trust herself to keep her voice steady.

But rather than press her for a response, Dorian simply released her, turned his back, and headed for the door. "Make yourself comfortable. I'll return as soon as I can."

"Wait. That's it?" She followed after him, mind reeling from the whiplash he'd caused. "You dropped the biggest bomb in history on me, and now you're leaving?"

"You've made it quite clear you're not looking for company tonight."

"Company, no. Answers, yes."

Keeping his back turned, he lowered his head and said,

"I'll answer your questions, but first I need to discuss some things with my brothers."

"Brothers, right. You mean your vampire coven? House? Whatever?"

"In this case, I mean both."

The words felt heavy and cold, and they hung in the air between them, setting Charley's mind spinning again.

The men he'd introduced as his brothers were also his vampire house. So that meant... They were also *literally* his brothers?

How was that possible, unless...

Oh, God. Dorian, Malcolm, Gabriel, Colin... they'd been turned into vampires at the same time. Maybe even Aiden too.

A tiny arrow of sympathy pinged her heart, cracking the hard wall she'd tried so hard to plaster over it.

She drew a breath to ask another question—a *million* other questions—but Dorian was already shutting down, his shoulders bunching with tension, the air thickening between them.

"As I said, I'll return as soon as I can," he said. "In the meantime—"

"Wait! My driver!" Charley blurted out, suddenly realizing she'd lost her purse in the mayhem. She hadn't texted Travis about her plans to stay. "I must've dropped my phone in the gardens. If he doesn't hear from me, he'll come looking—"

"He already has." Dorian turned and glared at her, a flash of triumph shining in his eyes. "I told him you wouldn't be requiring his services, as you're staying the weekend."

Charley folded her arms across her chest again, biting back a smile. She really wanted to be pissed right now, but the idea of Travis slithering his way out of an argument with Dorian made her damn near giddy. "And he accepted that?"

"Not... at first."

Her eyes widened, but Dorian shook his head.

"I compelled him to accept it. And then I compelled him to hand over your belongings and return to the dank hole from which he slithered forth."

At that, a small laugh escaped. "Sometimes, I call him the snake."

Dorian offered a thin smile in return, but the momentary levity wasn't enough to erase everything that'd happened.

Charley let out a heavy sigh. Her own guilt and deceptions collided in her mind with Dorian's, all the secrets and lies exploding into an epic headache. But right now, she couldn't give in to the pain, couldn't share any more laughs with Dorian Redthorne.

She needed to hold onto her righteous anger.

Yeah, she was a thief and a con and a *total* fucking fraud, and she was most likely going to hell.

But he was an immortal monster. And from the looks of things, she was about ten seconds from becoming that monster's captive.

"You can't keep me here," she said anyway, as if the words alone would make it true.

"I can, and I will."

"So I'm your prisoner?"

"You're my responsibility." Dorian sighed, his shoulders sagging under some new weight. "What those vampires did to you tonight was an act of war, and my brother and I responded in kind. By killing members of another greater vampire house on our property, House Redthorne has drawn a line in the sand that cannot be undrawn. You are as much a target as we are now, and there's no telling how and when House Duchanes will attack again—only that they will. So when I tell you to stay put, Charlotte, trust that I have my reasons."

"But I—"

"And trust that it's *not* a request."

"Dorian, wait—"

He left in another one of those annoying blurs, no more than a smudge in her periphery, slamming and bolting the door behind him.

Charley ran to it and yanked on the ornate handle, but it was no use.

He'd locked her in.

Trapped.

Caged.

Imprisoned.

Adrenaline flooded her insides.

"Fuck this bullshit right now." She darted over to a window, shoving aside the massive tapestries and pushing up the sash. Cool night air slid over her skin, bringing with it some of the calm rationality she'd abandoned the moment she'd seen Dorian in a tux tonight.

How can a man who looks that good be so damn bad?

She didn't have the answers. All Charley knew was she *hated* that he'd locked her in here, that he'd given her orders, that he'd used his considerable power against her. She hated that she'd become a target in some vampire war that was probably going on long before she came into the picture and would continue long after she left.

Most of all, she hated herself for the truth, shining bright no matter how desperately she kept trying to paint over it.

She craved that immortal monster's touch. Now, more than ever.

"I need to get the *hell* out of here."

Glancing out the window, she tried to calculate how far the drop was. It was too dark to tell, but pretty damn obvious that an escape attempt from here would only end one way: with Charley splattering on the cobblestones below.

She fisted her hair, growling in frustration.

The door was bolted. The windows too dangerous. She had no phone. There was no way out.

Not until Dorian *fucking* Redthorne decided to set her free.

Dorian fucking *vampire* Redthorne, she amended.

In a flash, all of Sasha's vampire books and movies rushed through Charley's mind. Vampires had weaknesses, didn't they? Garlic, holy water, stakes…

Stakes. That was it.

She scanned the bedroom, her eyes landing on a spindled table beside the bed. She removed the antique lamp that sat on top, gripped the table with both hands, and smashed it against the floor.

From the splintered pieces that remained, Charley selected the largest, sharpest spindle. Then, deeply channeling her inner Jersey Girl, she gripped her new stake, took a fighting stance a few feet in front of the door, and waited for that motherfucker to come back through it.

"Say hello to my pointy little friend, your *highness*."

CHAPTER THIRTY-THREE

Sipping his scotch in the chair before the roaring fire, Dorian made every attempt to leash the fury snapping and growling inside him.

Tonight had been a grievous disaster.

Duchanes had vanished.

The woman whose blood had damn near sent him into a spiral of madness and desire was presently locked in his bedroom, probably devising an escape plot—or one to murder him.

Armitage had left with the other guests, but the truth about the party's abrupt end would certainly reach his ears soon, if it hadn't already. Now, even if the old mage was still keen on the merger of their companies, Dorian doubted anyone in the Armitage line would so easily accept a bound partnership for Isabelle—including Isabelle herself.

Dorian couldn't blame them. After all, how could he

protect a bound witch if he couldn't even protect one of his most vulnerable guests?

His fingers tightened on the glass, mind churning.

He had no clear idea what had prompted tonight's attack against Charlotte. Though he suspected his refusal of Duchanes' many ridiculous offers—an alliance, blood slaves, Jacinda's services—had put House Redthorne on the coven's shit list, Dorian never would've predicted such a strong retaliation. It was an extreme response guaranteed to unleash hell on the offending party, and as little as he thought of Renault Duchanes, he'd never considered him a blatant, suicidal fool.

Which meant one of two things:

Either Duchanes truly *hadn't* known about the attack, and his men had mutinied, or Duchanes was willing to take such an insane risk because someone even more powerful than the royal vampire family was backing him.

Dorian recalled the altercation in Central Park. Duchanes had shown up at precisely the right moment to intervene with Chernikov's demons. His timing was almost too perfect; it couldn't have been a coincidence.

Bloody hell.

Webs of lies and deceit, power games, shifting alliances, innocent people caught in the crossfire… Dorian didn't know how his father had managed it for so many years—or why he'd wanted *any* of this responsibility in the first place.

Dorian certainly hadn't. But with his father dead and his brothers awaiting his orders, what else could he do but shoulder it?

"We cannot afford a war, Dorian," Malcolm said now, pacing the study. "We're still unallied, and after tonight's disastrous turn, what are the chances Isabelle Armitage will join us?"

Malcolm gave voice to Dorian's exact thoughts, but that didn't mean Dorian would accept them.

"Renault Duchanes' sired dung beetles attacked my companion at my own manor," he said. "You expect me to let such an infraction go unpunished?"

"Unpunished, no. But a war? Over a woman whose last name you didn't even know until this very evening? We should at least wait until we hear Renault's version of events."

"I would love to, but... Oh, *that's* right. Your new mate has mysteriously fled the scene of the crime." Dorian shook his head, disgust souring his drink. "Why are you so eager to take his side?"

"You're bloody *mad*, Dorian." Malcolm folded his arms across his chest, looking down his nose at Dorian in a manner he'd spent centuries perfecting. "The only side I'm on is House Redthorne's. Forgive me if I don't wish to send my brothers to the slaughter because you couldn't keep your cock out of some human woman's hot little—"

Dorian was out of his chair in a flash, slamming Malcolm into the wall beside the fireplace with a fist around his throat and a hand against his heart. "Do *not* finish that sentence unless you wish to receive the same treatment as our Duchanes guests."

"Oh, for fuck's sake." Aiden rolled his eyes. "You lot

have been repressing your emotions since you were humans bickering at the dinner table. Why stop a good thing now?"

A log toppled from the fire, shooting a rain of sparks from the fireplace.

Malcolm continued to glare, but finally raised his hands in surrender, and Dorian backed off.

"That's better," Aiden said. "Now, allow me to offer a perspective from someone who *isn't* part of this house of complete dysfunction." He jerked the fire poker from the wall, where it'd remained like an arrow since Dorian had chucked it there, and pushed the fallen log back into place. "I don't believe the attack was about Ms. D'Amico specifically—she was just an easy target. My feeling is, whoever's behind this wanted to make House Redthorne look weak— to sow discontent about the royal family's ability to protect its own and lead the supernatural communities into a peaceful future."

The brothers considered Aiden's theory. With the recent demise of their father, there was bound to be some upheaval—minor skirmishes, like Dorian's encounter with the demons in Manhattan, or some grumbling among the greater vampire covens who saw themselves as better leaders. But an attack on the royal family's home turf?

"It makes sense that Duchanes would test us," Malcolm said, "considering the refusal of the alliance."

"You think House Duchanes is the only house that wants to see our heads on pikes?" This, from Gabriel, who was unapologetically working his way through Dorian's collection of scotch. "Sure, he's the most likely suspect, but he's also got a few bats in the belfry. Something tells me the order came from someone higher on the pay scale."

"I thought so as well," Dorian admitted, returning to his chair.

"And if that's true," Gabriel continued, "tonight is just the start of what awaits us."

"Agreed," Malcolm said. "We have no idea who else is coming for us, what dangers lurk around every corner. We're going to need security, as well as—"

"We're the fucking royal family!" Dorian hurled his drink into the fire. It exploded in a burst of glass and flame, but quickly petered out, just like his ire.

For all the fury, his words were empty.

Long ago, House Kendrick was the royal family. Then Augustus Redthorne slaughtered them in the night, stealing the crown and everything that came with it.

What was to stop another ambitious house or supernatural faction from doing the same to the Redthornes? Especially now, when they were at their most vulnerable? His father had been a formidable force—a vampire whose methods of torture and brutality put warmongering generals and lone serial killers alike to shame. But Dorian?

He was as wet behind the ears as a newborn. He'd spent the better part of his immortal life trying to stay ahead of his father's long shadow, only to wake up one day and realize he'd been chasing it all along.

And now, that shadow belonged to him; too dark and vast to wrangle, too cold to embrace, but his nevertheless.

Augustus Redthorne had only been dead a week, yet his house was nearly as powerless as if he'd never taken the crown at all.

Dorian knew it. His brothers knew it. And more importantly, so did their enemies.

"Father was... He was ill," Dorian finally admitted, his voice dark and low once again. "He spent the last few months of his life searching for a cure for a human sickness that had taken him—one he'd worried might be genetic. One *I* worry might be our downfall."

The admission felt like a death, a dark burden torn from his heart, scraping the soft parts inside until there was nothing left but blood and agony.

Tears of frustration blurred his vision. In all his long years, he'd never felt so helpless, so useless.

"And you're telling us *now*?" Gabriel demanded. "How long have you known?"

"I *don't* know," he replied. "Not with any degree of certainty. I didn't want to speak of it until I had more information."

"When might that have been? When we were all lying beside father in a pile of smoldering ash?"

"No, Dorian. You're wrong." Colin, who'd remained lost in thought since he'd returned from the crypts an hour earlier, suddenly spoke. "I've seen the journals. I haven't been able to piece everything together, but I don't think he was trying to cure a human illness."

Memories flickered through Dorian's mind.

His father, staring into his microscope, muttering about

curses and cures.

Boxes of needles and syringes and tourniquets, fresh medical supplies arriving at Ravenswood nearly every day.

Blood draws—his fathers and his own—every crimson drop examined and measured and catalogued.

"From a strictly medical perspective," Colin continued, "nothing I've seen in his notes points to any known human ailments—cancer, Alzheimer's, Parkinson's, HIV, any number of neurological diseases one might look for in these situations. His research protocols may be mysterious, but they don't support your theory."

"Are you certain?" Dorian asked.

"If I were a human doctor, I'd say yes. But my very existence is proof that science and medicine have a great many gaps." Colin gave a thoughtful shrug. "Clearly there's more to the journals than meets the eye. I need more time with them."

"Of course," Dorian said, not sure whether he should be relieved... or terrified. If his father wasn't suffering from a human ailment, then what had killed him?

And what had he meant when he'd said it was genetic?

"What of the woman?" Malcolm asked, glancing up at the ceiling as if he could hear Charlotte's very heartbeat. "She's a distraction we can't afford."

"She's more than that," Gabriel said, amber liquid sloshing over the sides of his glass. "Dorian told her about us. That makes her a liability."

"She broke the compulsion," Dorian said. "I didn't have a choice."

Gabriel unleashed a bitter laugh. "You never have a choice, do you, brother? Everything that's happened, all the darkness you've brought upon us, and it's *never* your fault."

Dorian seethed, but he didn't argue the point. How could he? Gabriel may have been the only one ballsy enough to speak it aloud, but all of them were thinking it. Even, Dorian guessed, his dearest friend Aiden.

"She knows about us now," he said calmly, "and she's clearly a target for Duchanes, regardless of who gave the order. Beyond that, I... I care for her."

It was another admission, another death, and Dorian didn't have the courage to meet their eyes.

"She's *your* responsibility," Malcolm said.

"One I gladly accept." Dorian rose from his chair and headed toward the door, done with his brothers, done stewing in his shame and guilt. Just before he made his final exit, he dropped a hand on Gabriel's shoulder, still not meeting his eyes, but needing to say the words anyway. "I appreciated your assistance out there tonight. She would've died without it."

"I didn't do it for her."

"That doesn't change my gratitude, nor the fact that I'm glad you're here."

"I'm not doing this for your gratitude, either." Gabriel jerked away from his touch. "When the dust settles and you've finally secured the bonded witch, I'm leaving. And I never, ever want to see you, hear you, or smell your traitorous blood again, *your highness*."

CHAPTER THIRTY-FOUR

"Don't take another step, dickhead." Charley stood in front of the bedroom door, stake at the ready.

"*Dickhead?*" Dorian glanced at her weapon, a smile quirking his lips. "I see we're feeling rather confident now."

"I swear on my father's grave, Dorian Redthorne. I *will* stake you."

"Oh, I've no doubts about your intentions, Buffy."

"So you have a death wish?"

He strode toward her, stopping only when the pointy end of her makeshift stake was pressed against his sternum. "That depends. Are you strong enough to break through the bone and pierce the beating heart behind it?"

"Test me and let's find out."

Dorian raised his hands in mock surrender. "By all means—have a go. But Charlotte?" He grinned again, fangs descending before her eyes, sharp and terrifying in the moonlight. "Don't miss."

Her whole body trembled, their gazes locked in a fierce battle of wills, her stomach flip-flopping. Never before had she felt such an acute mix of terror and exhilaration. It rendered her speechless and paralyzed, lost to the magnetic pull of a dangerous monster she should've run from.

Should've killed.

You are my ocean tide, Dorian Redthorne, come to steal my soul...

"Lesson one," he said, and the room spun into a smudge of indiscernible shapes and colors. Before Charley could suck in another breath, she was face-first against the wall on the other side of the room, his body pinning her in place, her pathetic stake clattering to the floor.

Dorian gripped the back of her neck in one impossibly strong hand, the other capturing her wrists behind her back. Then, mouth close to her ear, "If you're going to threaten an apex predator after he specifically warned you not to, best to follow through."

"Fuck... off." She jerked against his hold, but it was no use. He was a wall of solid muscle and supernatural strength, and he had her exactly where he wanted her.

Trapped. Helpless. Vulnerable.

"Quite the conundrum, isn't it?" He dragged his mouth along the curve of her neck to her shoulder, then back again, pausing behind her ear, his breath hot. "You've managed to trigger the predatory response in a beast that could kill you faster than you could draw your next breath."

"Do it, then, you fucking monster!" she cried, tired of

the power games, the secrets, the lies. She'd come all this way to spy, to help her crew rob him blind… Maybe she deserved to die at his hand. At his bite. "If you're so set on killing me, finish it!"

"Killing you? Now that doesn't sound like any fun at all." He spun her around, then pushed her back against the wall, wrists pinned above her head as he shoved a muscular thigh between her legs.

She squeezed her eyes shut, refusing to look into his eyes. Refusing to give him the satisfaction of seeing her fear.

Her desire.

"What am I to do with you, little prowler?" he asked, lips brushing her mouth, her jawline. His thigh pressed closer, teasing her. "Posing as a guest at my fundraiser. Snooping around my manor. Threatening to stake me in my own bedroom."

"I don't care *what* you do with me."

"Somehow I doubt that." He shifted his thigh, sending a zing of pleasure through her core.

Charley fought off a shiver. It took her a full beat to realize her hips were moving, rocking against the delicious pressure of his thigh, desperate for the heat, the friction.

She knew she should stop. Beg him to let her go. To forget they'd ever crossed paths.

But she couldn't.

Because deep down, beneath all the bravado and F-bombs, Charley *wanted* to be here. Wanted him.

"Look at me, Charlotte."

"Go fuck yourself, *highness*," she muttered, but there was no fire behind her words, and they both knew it.

Dorian released her wrists and hooked a finger under her chin, tilting her face up, his voice dropping to a whisper. "*Look* at me."

She finally opened her eyes, and Dorian stared at her with such intensity, she thought she might catch fire. His eyes were golden and fierce, his mouth an invitation she wanted to accept, again and again and again.

"Option one," he breathed, "or option two?"

The reminder of their stolen moments in the penthouse made her heart stutter. But tonight, he wasn't just asking for a forbidden rendezvous in the closet. He was asking her to forget everything she'd witnessed, everything he'd done, everything he was.

He was asking her to submit, completely and without reservation.

And in that moment, despite all the dangers, despite all the warnings clanging in her head, Charley knew that when it came to Dorian Redthorne, there was only one answer.

There would *always* be only one answer.

"Two," she whispered. "Fucking two."

His mouth descended in a hot rush, crushing her lips, owning her. He fisted her dress and tore it in half, pushing it down to her hips as his mouth continued to devour a hot path along her flesh—her neck, her breasts and... oh, *fuck*... her nipple...

She slid her hands into his hair and lost herself to the delicious pain of his teeth grazing the stiff peak, his tongue soothing the ache. Without breaking his kiss, he gripped her hips and spun her away from the wall, moving them toward the giant bed.

"What's... what's happening?" she breathed, every nerve sizzling with heat.

He pulled away from her nipple, then slid his hand between her thighs, dragging his fingers over her soaked underwear.

"Remind me again how you like to be fucked," he replied, his tone dark with desire. "Soft and slow was it? Wait, no. That's not right. I believe your exact words were... 'I like it rough. Don't you *dare* disappoint me.'"

Charley didn't have time to confirm. In another impossibly fast blur, he pushed her onto the bed, then flipped her onto her stomach, running a hand up her back and fisting her hair. Climbing on top, he licked the back of her neck, then pulled her hair just right.

"Put your arms above your head, Charlotte. Now."

She did as he asked, and he tore the remaining scraps of the dress from her body, binding her wrists to the bed with a piece of the black satin. She was powerless beneath him, her hands tied, her body pinned by his impossibly strong form, her breath coming in short, wild bursts.

The mattress shifted as Dorian rose from the bed and stripped off his clothes. Charley tried to turn over to watch, but before she could get a good look, he was on her again, one hand tangled in her hair, the other smacking her ass.

"I did *not* give you permission to move." He smacked her again, then brought his mouth to her flesh, soothing the white-hot sting with soft, luxurious kisses. Electric jolts of pleasure zipped across her skin, making her shiver.

Another slap, another kiss, and Dorian slowly worked the underwear down her hips, tossing them to the floor.

Sliding his fingers inside her, he shifted positions and brought his mouth back up to her ear, his voice so sexy it almost made her come.

"Whose pussy is this?" he demanded, thrusting in and out, deep and perfect.

"Yours. God, it's yours."

"Whose?"

"Yours, Dorian."

"You mean yours, *Mr. Redthorne.*"

She tried to turn over, but he pushed her back down again, hand wrapped around the back of her neck. "My bed, my rules. You'll call me Mr. Redthorne tonight. Is that clear?"

"Yes."

He squeezed her neck, making her gasp.

"Yes, Mr. Redthorne," she tried again, wanting nothing more than to please him.

"That's better." He slid his fingers out, then fluttered over her clit, sending another jolt throughout her body before plunging back inside.

Holy *shit,* did he know how to work her.

Charley was face down on a bed of black satin sheets, her gasps muffled by the pillow, still in her bra, ass in the air, every inch of her body craving his touch. Hard, then soft. Fierce, then soothing. The flood of sensations made her drunk and dizzy, desperate for more.

Nothing in her life had ever felt so good, so right.

So incredibly, mind-blowingly perfect.

A clear sign you're crazy...

"Tonight," he said, "in my bed, you'll neither speak nor move without permission. Is that clear?"

"Yes. I mean yes, Mr. Redthorne," she amended.

"Hmm." Dorian removed his fingers, and the mattress shifted again, indicating he'd gotten up. She waited for the return of his touch, but it never came.

She opened her mouth to call for him but thought better of it. No talking, no moving without his permission. It was all part of the game, and Charley loved every sinfully hot minute of it.

A lot of men thought they knew how to dominate a woman, but for them it was all about ego gratification. She'd been disappointed in the bedroom more times than she could count, most notably—and most often—by Travis, the snake.

But a man like Dorian knew how to be real. How to test her boundaries, push her to the edge without ever taking advantage. Submitting to him came easily. His demanding touch and firm commands were like a down payment—a promise that he'd always bring her to sheer bliss.

In return, she trusted him with her body.

With her life.

In so many ways, she was dancing on the razor's edge between life and death.

And it was sheer fucking ecstasy.

Hot, strong hands gripped her thighs, and Charley yelped. She hadn't heard him, hadn't felt his return to the bed. But suddenly he was there, spreading her wide, his mouth descending to her depths.

"You're beautiful, Charlotte," he said, and she felt the heat of his words between her thighs. "So fucking gorgeous."

Dorian licked a path from her clit to her taint, then back again, and everything melted away: her job, the LaPorte painting and Hermes sculpture, the lies she'd told, the risks she'd taken, the attack in the garden, the knowledge of Dorian's true nature.

All that mattered now was this sexy, dominating man, his tongue lighting a fire deep in her belly, his kiss a drug on which she'd happily overdose.

He brought her close with his mouth—so close she was certain she'd fall—but then he pulled back.

Another slap stung her skin, and Dorian moved up the length of her body, kissing the ridges of her spine, her neck, her ear.

His cock was smooth and stiff between her thighs. She couldn't help it—she *had* to move, even if it meant risking punishment. Her hips rocked against the silky sheets, arching toward him, begging him for more.

For all of it.

"Once a bad girl, always a bad girl," he murmured. "You *really* shouldn't disobey me."

With one hand clamped around her hip, the other around the back of her neck, Dorian thrust inside her.

Holy.

Fucking.

Hell.

Again and again he drove into her, then pulled out slowly, slamming back into her slick heat with a force that only made her want more.

She sighed into the pillow, arching up to bring him in deeper, her body so needy, so hot for him. Beneath her flesh, the sheets felt soft and cool, a delicious contrast to the heat from the muscled force of nature attacking her from behind.

After all Charley's fantasies, the memories of his touch in the closet, their dirty nighttime phone calls, their interrupted games in the guest house, the wild kiss in the basement... *nothing* could've prepared her for the intense feel of his punishing cock.

Sliding his hand into her hair, he tugged her head back, brushing his lips against the shell of her ear. "I've been wanting to do this ever since I saw you in that penthouse lobby. All I could think about was tying you up in my bed, fucking you so hard and deep you'd bloody well *taste* it."

She whimpered beneath him, the commanding, masculine sound of his voice mingling with the devilish words to push her close to the edge again, her entire body wound as tight as a drum.

Charley had never been fucked like this, so raw and primal and perfect. She was on fire, drenched with lust. She wanted to make it last, to remember it, but she was already slipping away, her muscles tensing for the release that was so, so close.

"You want to come," Dorian said, reaching around her hip to stroke a finger over her clit. "I can feel it."

"Yes," she replied, barely conscious. His touch, his words, everything he did turned her into jelly. She wouldn't be able to hold out another minute, even if he commanded it.

"Tell me what you want."

"I... I want to come, Mr. Redthorne."

A groan of pleasure erupted from his chest, and he increased the pressure on her clit, fucking her harder, faster, unrelenting.

"Come for me, Charlotte," he finally demanded. "Come for me *hard*." He slid into her deep, and with a final stinging slap against her ass, Charley came with a force like a hurricane, her cries nearly shattering the windows as Dorian pounded into her, driving himself right over the edge along with her, finally collapsing on top of her with a growl so guttural, so possessive, it would haunt her dreams for decades.

Maybe longer.

For a few minutes, neither of them moved, content in their sticky embrace, their bare flesh cooling, the crickets outside the open window singing them into a state of peace.

Perfection.

Charley's throat constricted with a knot of unshed tears. She swallowed them down, burying her face in the satin pillow, counting the strong, steady beats of Dorian's heart against her back.

She hadn't felt so fucking good—so *alive*—in years.

For the first time in her life—in the arms of a vampire who'd torn the heart from one of his own kind to protect her—Charley felt safe.

CHAPTER THIRTY-FIVE

Dorian removed her bra and unbound her wrists, caressing each one with kisses so gentle, they felt like butterflies fluttering against her skin. As she slowly turned over onto her back, he took her face between his hands and gazed into her eyes, his own swirling with hidden mysteries Charley had only just begun to explore.

"You're a goddess, Charlotte D'Amico," he whispered, brushing another gentle kiss to her mouth. "And you're *mine*."

She nipped at his lower lip, but before she could deepen the kiss, he swept her into his arms and rose from the bed, carrying her into the master bathroom.

His touch was a tender contrast to the fierce, carnal possessiveness that had overtaken him earlier, unlocking something in her heart that probably should've stayed buried.

The kind of man who could take her to the edge, test her

limits, talk dirty to her all night long, and wake her up with soft cuddles and kisses and breakfast in bed...

She forced away the memory of her earlier thoughts. *Nothing* about this could end with breakfast in bed. It was a one-time deal, and now that they'd gotten it out of their systems, they needed to move on.

Dorian set her on her feet beside the massive glass shower doors, then reached inside to turn on the dual shower heads, his arm brushing across her back. Between her legs, the evidence of their passion ran down her thighs, a hot slide that had Charley heating up all over again...

Until it dawned on her what that hot slide actually meant.

"Fuck." She gripped the edge of the vanity top behind her, her stomach twisting. In the crazy heat of the moment, they hadn't bothered with protection. "Fuck, fuck, *fuck!*"

"That's a lot of fucks." Dorian turned to her, eyes full of concern. "What's wrong, love?"

"We didn't use anything." She shook her head in frustration, warm liquid still dripping down her thighs. "I'm not on the pill, Dorian."

"Oh, I see." He ran his thumb across her cheek, a smile touching his lips. "Vampires cannot reproduce. Nor can we transmit the sort of ailments that might otherwise concern you in a situation like this. But if it puts your mind at ease, it's been quite some time since I've... been intimate."

Intimate. God, she loved the way he talked. She used to think he was just extremely proper, but now she realized it was also a function of his age. He'd come from another time, arriving here long before her own ancestors had even set foot on this soil.

The whole situation was a hundred-and-one kinds of crazy.

"I'm sorry to worry you," he said, still stroking her face. "I didn't think to explain before things... escalated."

Charley blew out a breath. "It's okay. I mean, it's good. About the... not having to worry about... It's really good."

Really good? What the hell was wrong with her? When had she turned into a nervous teenager?

Right about the time you started fucking a hot vampire and shut off half your brain...

She closed her eyes, forcing the spin of her mind to stop. She didn't want to think about the impossibility of it all right now.

But hell, how could she not?

She'd just had the most intense, amazing sex of her life... with an immortal fucking vampire.

She was standing in the luxurious marble bathroom... of an immortal fucking vampire.

A sinfully hot man had brought her to ecstasy like no man had ever come *close*... and he was an immortal fucking vampire.

"You're an immortal vampire," she blurted out, the reality smacking her in the face again. "Jesus Christ, Dorian. You're a fucking vampire! You have fangs and you're insanely fast and stronger than a freight train on steroids and you... you drink blood, for the love of God!"

313

"God has nothing to do with this, Charlotte. I assure you."

"But you're not human!" She pushed against his chest with her fists, suddenly desperate for space. For air. But the steam from the shower was quickly filling the room, and Dorian's presence was so imposing, so all-consuming, she felt like the walls were closing in.

"Call me a monster if it eases your conscience, love, but we both know the truth." He fisted the back of her hair and tugged, forcing her to look at him. "You sing a *very* different tune when the monster shoves his tongue between your thighs."

Her knees weakened at the memory of his demanding mouth, taking and taking and taking until she was a hot, trembling mess.

Charley's fists uncurled, her palms flattening against his chest, his skin warm and slick in the steamy bathroom. His cock was already hard again, nudging her belly, ready for more.

She was so close to giving in, so close to climbing into his arms, wrapping her legs around his hips, and letting him take her any way he wanted. On the bathroom sink, against the shower door, under the water... She could think of a million fantasies, each one more delicious than the last.

But her head was too heavy, her body spent from their battle between the sheets, and suddenly all she wanted to do was melt under the hot shower and evaporate into noth-ingness.

"I'm sorry, Dorian," she said softly, lowering her eyes

and taking a step back. "I need to think, and I can't do that with you here."

"What are you saying?"

"I'm asking you to leave."

"You're telling me I can't use my own shower?"

"Are there no other showers in this mansion?"

"A dozen, actually, but—"

"Then find a different one!"

"Charlotte—"

"I can't *breathe*, Dorian!" She turned her back on him and stepped into the shower, losing herself for a moment under the rush of hot water.

When she opened her eyes again, Dorian was gone.

The bedroom was too quiet.

With a towel wrapped around her head and Dorian's robe wrapped around her body, Charlotte crept out of the bathroom, scanning the bedroom for signs of her vampire.

The bed had been remade with clean sheets, the splintered night table and stakes cleared away. Her ruined dress and undergarments were gone, along with Dorian's clothing.

And the vampire himself was nowhere to be found.

Disappointment settled into her stomach.

"Careful what you wish for, girl," she muttered.

On an antique bench at the foot of the bed, she spotted the overnight bag she'd left in Travis' car and her purse, but her phone was missing. Just as she'd feared, she probably dropped it while she was careening down that hill, trying to avoid becoming a vampire snack.

Someone had also left a silver tray on the low dresser. It looked like a fancy room-service tray, with a teapot of hot water, a small basket containing at least ten different kinds of teas, and a porcelain sugar-and-creamer set that was probably older than Dorian. Beneath a silver dome, she found a bowl of fresh berries and grapes, and a selection of gourmet cheese and crackers that had her stomach grumbling.

She hadn't eaten since she'd left the hotel in town, too nervous about the job to keep anything down.

With a surge of gratitude, she plucked a strawberry from the pile and popped it into her mouth.

Behind the fruit bowl, tucked into a tiny pewter place card holder, was a note written in elegant script.

I thought you might like some refreshment.
Sweet dreams, Charlotte.
—Dorian

She pressed the note to her chest, shaking her head as if that alone could erase all the craziness from her brain.

Dorian fucking Redthorne.

How *dare* he be so kind, so thoughtful? He was supposed to be pissed at her for kicking him out of his own bedroom. He was supposed to be cold and distant. He was supposed to love her and leave her, just like the rest.

He was supposed to be a monster. One she could hate. One she could justify stealing from. One she could easily walk away from.

But instead, he'd taken care of her.

He'd given her space.

He'd cleaned up the mess.

He'd brought her a midnight snack.

And, she realized, he'd left the bedroom door ajar.

Charley didn't know if it was a test or a show of trust, but right now, she didn't care. She was too exhausted for an escape, too overwhelmed to snoop.

After indulging in a cup of lavender vanilla tea with cream and a big helping of everything else, Charley pushed the door closed, crawled between the cool, black sheets, pulled Dorian's robe around her body, and waited for the darkness to take her.

CHAPTER THIRTY-SIX

The scent of coffee pulled Charley from a decadent dream, the effects of which still lingered between her thighs. Reluctantly, she opened her eyes, the dream vision receding as she took in the sight of her unfamiliar surroundings.

Dorian Redthorne's bedroom. Annandale-on-Hudson.

She was alone in the king-sized bed, the sheets cold and smooth, the coffin-like decor no less imposing in the daylight.

Kings… Coffins… Vampires.

Everything came back in a rush.

It *hadn't* been a dream. More like a waking nightmare.

Liar, she thought, scolding herself. If last night was such a nightmare, why was her body still begging for his touch? Why was the burn in her thighs such a delicious reminder of what had transpired in this very bed?

"Because you're certifiable," she whispered. "That's why."

Slowly dragging herself to the windows, Charley slid open the tapestries. Outside, the lush grounds were velvety green carpets, mist rising from the river like steam from the bath.

Charley took a moment to bask in the early morning sunlight. Sometimes she forgot how different everything looked outside the imposing steel-and-glass metropolis she called home.

What a difference a day makes.

Twenty-four hours ago, she was sitting in a hotel room prepping for the job, Rudy's warnings playing on repeat in her head. *Believe me when I say there is no room for error on this one, Charlotte...*

She'd promised him—promised herself—she wouldn't screw up.

Last night, when she'd found the stolen goods from her father's cache, she'd made a second vow—that she'd follow the trail and expose her father's killer, no matter how long it took, no matter how great the risk.

But how could she keep *either* promise when the man at the center of it all was an immortal vampire king? One who'd rocked her world, rocked her body, and—with every passing minute—was coming dangerously close to rocking her heart?

Dressed in the leggings and button-down flannel she'd packed in her overnight bag, Charley grabbed her stuff and headed for the kitchen downstairs, ready to call an Uber and say a final goodbye to Dorian Redthorne.

She found him bent over the stove, sprinkling herbs into a pan of scrambled eggs with a concentration that had her biting back a smile and rethinking her plans.

"I hope you're hungry, love," he said without turning around, still focused on his culinary creation. Of course he'd known she was there—in addition to his other super-powers, Charley realized he probably had a superior sense of hearing and smell.

"I could eat," she admitted.

Just a little breakfast, some coffee for the road, and then I'm outta here...

"Have a seat." He nodded toward a sunny breakfast nook at the other end of the kitchen, the table already set for two.

"No brooding vampire princelings this morning?"

Dorian laughed, finally turning to face her. Gone was the formalwear, the suits she'd gotten so used to, replaced with a pair of dark gray sweatpants and a white T-shirt that clung to every muscle, his hair a beautiful mess, his eyes bright.

God, what a thing to wake up to...

"That's what Aiden calls them too," he said, still grin-ning. "They're up and about—we're just not the sort of family that crowds around the table for pancakes and Saturday morning cartoons."

"So I gathered."

He transferred the eggs to a serving platter, then

brought it over to the table, making a few more trips for the rest—Belgian waffles, fresh berries, bacon, roasted potatoes, cinnamon buns, fresh-squeezed orange juice, and coffee. The whole spread looked and smelled even better than her favorite Manhattan diner breakfasts, and when he finally sat down across from her and gestured for her to dig in, she was overwhelmed with the same deep sense of comfort and familiarity she'd felt sharing hot dogs in Central Park—the kind of familiarity typically reserved for couples who knew each other so intimately, words were no longer required.

Total fucking fantasy.

It wasn't self-pity—just par for the course in her line of work. Don't get too close, too attached, too hopeful.

It hadn't been a problem for her before. But now, Dorian Redthorne was giving Charley a taste of what she'd been missing out on... and she wanted more.

She didn't know whether to smile or cry. So instead, she poured herself a mug of coffee from a silver carafe and said, "I can't believe you made all this. It smells amazing."

"And here you thought I was just a pretty face with a huge—"

"Waffle iron, by the looks of things." Charley reached over and carved off a slice of waffle, then took a bit of everything else, quickly loading up. She eyed the strawberries, but there was no more room on her plate.

"Allow me." Seeing her predicament, Dorian plucked a strawberry from the bowl and leaned forward, slipping it between Charley's lips, watching intently as she bit into it. A trickle of sweet, red juice ran down her chin, and Dorian caught it with his thumb, then popped the rest of the berry into his own mouth. "Hmm. I could eat breakfast with you all day, love."

"Could you?" She glanced down at the plate as more questions bubbled up inside. "Seriously? Because I thought vampires drank blood for breakfast."

His smile faltered, and he leaned back in his chair, reaching for the coffee. "We drink blood to survive, but eating regular food is part of what allows us to hold onto our humanity."

"What happens if you skip the O-positive and *just* eat regular food?"

He met her gaze across the table, his eyes cold and severe. "It's not a pretty sight, Charlotte."

"Tell me," she demanded.

"We're eating breakfast."

"I want to know."

Dorian set down his coffee mug, impatience tightening his jaw. "Without regular ingestion of human blood, a vampire will lose all trace of his humanity, physical and otherwise. He'll revert to his natural monstrous state—a pale, mindless, physically-deformed *nightmare* who exists only to hunt, to fuck, and to feed on whatever helpless creatures cross his path. He retreats to caves and tunnels, as sunlight blisters his skin so horribly, it exposes the muscle and bone beneath. Eventually, over many years, he will decompose, alive and conscious till the bitter end."

The strawberry turned to lead in her stomach, and Charley lowered her eyes.

The awkwardness crept back in between them, a thousand new questions burning through her mind like wildfire. There was so much she wanted to know—about vampires, about his family, about Dorian himself—but every time she opened her mouth to ask another question, her words turned to ash.

It was crazy. All of it. And it wasn't her world. She shouldn't have gotten a single *glimpse*, let alone an up-close-and-personal tour.

But she had.

Charley took a few more bites, but despite her grumbling stomach, she couldn't eat.

Setting down her fork, she said, "I think it's probably best if I head out."

"You want to eat in the gardens? I can bring everything—"

"No, Dorian. I want to go home."

"Now? But you'd planned to stay the weekend. I haven't even told you about the art you asked after, and despite my best efforts to scare you off..." He offered a small smile, breaking through some of the tension. "It's clear you have questions about other things as well."

"You mean about mindless vampires and werewolves and bogeymen?" Charley rolled her eyes, waiting for him to tell her she'd seen too many movies.

But Dorian said nothing.

"*Are* there other supernatural beings?" she asked. "Not just vampires?"

He speared a bite of waffle with his fork and shrugged. "I thought you wanted to go home."

"I don't know *what* I want anymore. That's the problem." She rubbed her eyes, her resolve weakening. Curiosity was definitely winning out—not just about the stolen artwork, but about the whole new world Dorian had opened up. With a single glance, he'd smashed through the lid on Pandora's Box, and now that those demons had escaped, there was no putting them back inside.

"Wait... what about demons?" She looked up at him again, her heart sputtering.

"You've got questions, I've got answers." Dorian's mouth curved into a smug, sexy smile. "Perhaps I can tempt you with another deal."

Charley shook her head, but she was already smiling again too. "State your terms, Mr. Redthorne."

"I'll allow you to return to the city this afternoon, if you'll allow *me* to take you on a brief detour first."

"Where?"

"A place I think you'll love. It's not far."

"Hmm. So you can murder me and drink my blood?"

"Charlotte, I don't need to leave the comfort of my own home to drink your blood, nor do I need to murder you." His eyes glittered with mischief, despite the warning lurking beneath the surface.

Still, he *had* saved her life. Not just last night, but that night in Central Park too. Maybe he wanted to scare her, but Charley's gut told her he didn't want to hurt her.

Just the opposite, actually.

His eyes softened, and he let out a deep sigh. "You have questions only I can answer. I'm offering to do just that. But you need to show me a little trust too."

"I know. It's just... a lot to process. *You're* a lot to process."

He reached across the table and took her hand, stroking his thumb over her skin, sending ripples of heat up her arm. "Spend the day with me, love. Let me show you my favorite place in the world."

"Just talking, right?"

"If that's what you wish, then yes. Just talking."

Charley drained the last of her coffee, then set her mug down on the table, decision made.

"Fine. But I've got a pre-condition." She smirked and nodded toward the door beyond the breakfast nook—the one that led out to the garage, where Dorian's collection of priceless automobiles awaited. "*I'm* driving."

CHAPTER THIRTY-SEVEN

Sitting in the passenger seat of his red 1962 Ferrari 250 GTO, Dorian wiped his damp hands on his pants.

I can't believe I agreed to this.

"Don't worry," Charlotte said, downshifting smoothly to take the next curve. She reached over and patted his knee as she accelerated into the turn. "This isn't my first rodeo."

"But it's not a rodeo, is it? No." Dorian removed her hand and placed it firmly back on the wheel. "It's a priceless piece of machinery careening down a mountain road with a driver who may or may not be plotting my demise."

"*Careening*? Please. I'm in complete control." Charlotte laughed, her hair whipping around her face in the breeze. She took her hand off the wheel to brush away a few strands that had blown into her mouth. "I'm surprised you actually let me drive it."

"No more than I, believe me." When he'd led her into the garage, she'd headed straight for the classic red Ferrari, admiring it with such reverence that when she finally turned to ask for the keys, Dorian swore there were tears in her eyes.

There was no way he could've turned her down. Not about the car. Not about anything.

And that, frankly, scared the hell out of him.

Dorian opened his eyes as the engine whined, Charlotte waiting until the last possible second to shift into fifth gear.

"This car is unbelievable," she said. "So responsive. I feel like I could drive it with my eyes closed."

"I'd really prefer you didn't." Dorian's heart rate skyrocketed as they glided into another curve, the sun-dappled road cutting through a swath of eastern red cedars and paper birch trees. The power in the engine was unmistakable, and when Charlotte flashed him another smile, her whole face lit up.

He'd never seen anything so pure, so radiant.

They reached a long straightaway, and Charlotte gave it more gas. The car wasn't built with a speedometer, but from the blur of scenery along the road, Dorian guessed they'd hit eighty.

"Do I make you nervous, Mr. Redthorne?" she asked.

As nervous as Dorian was, Charlotte's enthusiasm was contagious. He couldn't help but appreciate her skill. She handled the car with such ease, such unrestrained joy, it was as if she'd been born driving it.

Not only that, but every time she wrapped her hand around the gearshift, a bolt of heat shot straight to his cock.

"No," Dorian said, forcing himself to relax. He curled

his hand around the back of her neck, stroking her earlobe with his thumb. "Apparently, I trust you."

"How much longer? I mean, until we get there, not until you stop trusting me."

"The turnoff is round the next bend." He trailed his fingers down her arm, then down along her thigh, wishing she'd worn a dress instead of the tight leggings. Still, there was something soft and sweet about her casual clothing, her messy hair, her makeup-free face. It was another facet of what he now understood was a deeply complex, contradictory woman—one he wanted to know. To care for. To keep safe, just like he'd vowed last night.

"Right here, love." He pointed at the nearly hidden turnoff up ahead. "Make the right at the tree trunk, then drive all the way to the end."

Charlotte downshifted, navigating them onto the rough road. A few moments later, they arrived at the end, no more than a small dirt clearing among the trees.

They were, as he knew they would be, alone.

"Dorian, this is incredible." Charlotte stepped out of the car and walked a few dozen yards to the edge, a rocky ridge that sloped down into the valley a hundred feet below. Beyond, the Catskill Mountain range stretched out before them, red and gold in the autumn morning light.

"Why do I recognize this place?" She turned, hitting him full on with that bright, copper-eyed gaze. "It's like a painting come to life."

"Precisely." He pointed at a rocky outcropping several feet away. "That's where Cole Diamante sat to paint—"

"*Fall of Secrets!* Of course! I've seen that painting a hundred times at the Met. It was Diamante's last landscape. After that, he moved on to portraiture, but he never achieved the same level of critical acclaim before his death. Too bad, really. His portraits are exquisite too."

Dorian laughed at her exuberance. "Is there anything about art you don't know?"

"I didn't know this place was here."

"Well, there *is* something else you don't know about Cole Diamante, but if I share this secret, you must promise not to tell a soul."

"I swear it." She made an X over her heart, her eyes sparkling.

"Cole hasn't passed on—he's only retreated from the public eye."

"What? Are you sure?"

"Quite. He owns this land, and he's a former associate of mine, though he doesn't venture out much anymore."

"But that would make him over a hundred and fifty years old!" She narrowed her eyes. "Vampire?"

"Wolf shifter, actually."

"Seriously? So wolf shifters *are* a thing?"

"Yes, though they're increasingly rare. They mostly travel in packs and stick to their own kind, generally preferring the forests to the city. Cole is a lone wolf—always has been."

"I can see why he likes it out here. It's beautiful."

The breeze picked up, blowing her hair into a wild frenzy around her head.

Charlotte didn't squeal, didn't try to smooth her hair back into place. She only laughed, throwing her arms out and twirling into the breeze, spinning until she was out of breath and the air finally stilled.

When she stopped and looked at him again, there was so much light in her eyes, it nearly blinded him.

"*You're* beautiful, Charlotte D'Amico." He grabbed her and pulled her close, pressing his lips to hers. She stiffened in his arms, but then relaxed, parting her lips for him as he drank her in, her mouth warm and soft, her gentle murmurs stirring him into a frenzy.

Entirely too soon, she broke their kiss and gave him a playful shove, glaring at him with a mix of amusement and annoyance. "Just talking, remember?"

"Forgive me." Dorian gave a slight bow. "I was... overcome."

"Don't let it happen again." She found a flat spot on the ridge and took a seat, patting the space next to her for Dorian to join her. When he did, she said, "Okay, enough about shifters. I need Vampire 101, lightning round. Ready?"

"What's a lightning—"

"Garlic. Myth or fact?"

He laughed, understanding her meaning. "Myth. Like any good gourmet, I adore garlic."

"Holy water?"

"Mostly myth, although witches can enchant water with certain spells that vampires find... uncomfortable."

"*Witches*? As in, broomstick riding, spell-casting, fortune-telling—"

"Wait, is this still the lightning round? Because witches are a topic all their own."

Charlotte blinked rapidly, then sighed. "Okay, we'll save witches for later. What about walking in daylight?"

"A feat made possible by… witches."

"Seriously?"

"Witches and vampires have a long, complicated, and mostly symbiotic history which I'll tell you more about after the lightning round."

"When you go to someone's apartment or house, do you have to be invited in?"

"We haven't for a good seventy or eighty years now."

She cocked her head and smirked. "Witches?"

"You're an excellent student," he said with a wink. "That spell was born of necessity in modern times. As cities became more crowded, with a high percentage of renters and property turnover, tracking down owners to ask for permission to enter became more challenging. So, for the vampire who can afford it, there's an easy fix."

"Sounds like witches do a lot of favors for you guys."

"For which they're *extremely* well-paid, I assure you." Dorian sighed, still bristling about Marlys' exploitative prices.

"What about stakes?"

"Deadly. But only when they're made of wood, and only if you manage to pierce the heart, like I told you last night. Otherwise, you'll just piss us off."

"Can vampires be killed by anything else?"

"Several things," he said with a wry laugh. "Forgive me if I don't readily disclose them."

She peppered him with a few of the other popular myths—sleeping in coffins, turning into bats, no reflection in the mirror—which Dorian quickly dispelled. But soon they reached the end of the lightning round, and in the heavy pause that followed, he knew whatever came next was going to alter her reality forever.

She knew it too. Her face had changed, the playfulness dimming from her eyes. More than anything, Dorian wanted to hit the proverbial pause button, take her into his arms again, and kiss her until she'd forgotten that he was a vampire, forgotten she'd ever wanted to know about the dark world that existed alongside hers.

But it was too late for that.

"Dorian," she said somberly, "how do you get your... blood supply?"

"Vampires are not required to feed from live humans," he said, hoping to put her at ease.

"But some do anyway, right?"

"Yes—usually through a consensual arrangement with a human donor. Of course, the system is imperfect, and the balance of power isn't exactly even, but we have laws that forbid the killing of humans. For the most part, they're honored."

"Do you? Drink from live humans, I mean?"

"Not in... many decades." Sensing this wouldn't be enough to satisfy her, he added, "Vampires only need to feed about once per week. I have an arrangement with a local hospital for blood bags, and short of that, I occasionally consume the blood of demons."

"*Demons*?"

"They're entities of hell, bound to human vessels but void of human souls. Since the vessel itself is human, their blood still contains the same basic nutrients, though it's not winning any points for taste."

"Holy shit." She shook her head, her voice dropping to a shocked whisper. "Everything you tell me is crazier than the last. All of it."

"It isn't a simple conversation, Charlotte. There is so much you don't know. You claim you want answers, but perhaps it's not—"

"Last night," she said suddenly. "You told me I wouldn't turn into a vampire, even though you bit me. How is that possible?"

"Vampires are made by vampire blood—it has nothing to do with being bitten. It just happens the two activities often go hand-in-hand."

"How so?" she asked. When he hesitated, she folded her arms across her chest and said, "A deal is a deal, Dorian. If you don't want to talk about this, then we're done here."

Dorian nodded, turning to look out across the vista. He didn't want to see the look of fear and disgust in her eyes when he shared the rest.

Last night, she'd called him a monster. She had no idea how right she actually was.

Bloody hell, it felt like he was opening up a vein. But she was right—a deal was a deal, and he owed her an explanation.

Even if the truth sent her running out of his life for good.

"In order to become a vampire," he began, "a human must be *very* close to death, and then they must ingest vampire blood—usually by drinking or injecting it. Some humans willingly turn, often through a mutually beneficial arrangement with their vampire sire."

"And the ones who *aren't* willing?"

From the corner of his eye, he caught Charlotte pulling her shirt collar close around her throat, an unconscious gesture she probably didn't even realize she'd done, but one Dorian couldn't unsee.

His chest burned, hating that he'd put her on guard, fearing for her life.

But he had to press on.

"What typically happens there," he continued, "is that a vampire bites the human, drains enough blood to stop the heart, then forces the victim to ingest his blood. Vampire blood has rapid regenerative properties and will almost immediately restart the human's heart and begin transforming his remaining blood into vampire blood, thus initiating the change." Dorian leaned back, bracing his hands against the cold rock slab. "On the plus side, our blood allows us to heal quickly, and can also heal human wounds, provided the human isn't already near his death."

"What if he *is* near death?"

"If a human has lost enough blood for his heart to stop,

vampire blood will take over his system and turn him, as I've described. But if the injury is less severe, it will simply aid in the regeneration process, allowing human blood to replace itself and fight off the transition before it happens."

"Sounds risky."

"It is. And many humans who *do* begin the transition don't survive it." An old, familiar chill gripped his heart, but he shook it off, continuing. "Many people believe vampires are soulless, but that's not true—we retain our human souls, even after transitioning. We're immortal, but that doesn't mean we can't be killed. Doesn't mean our souls aren't bound for hell, destined to an eternity of demonic enslavement right alongside the human sinners."

Next to him, Dorian sensed the skip of her pulse. Unsurprising, given the subject matter. It was a miracle she hadn't yet run for the hills.

"Tell me about the demons," she said instead, her tone dark but nevertheless eager for more.

"Demons are entities of hell, capable of possessing human hosts—either by force or through a demonic deal."

"How does the deal work?"

"In rare cases, a human willingly offers to share his body, allowing a demonic entity to hitch a ride, but still retaining his human life. The human is able to access the demon's powers, and the demon has a physical body in which to carry out his bidding. When the human dies, the demon takes over the vessel completely. In a more typical deal, however, a human signs over his body and soul for collection at the end of a set time period—five or ten years, usually—in exchange for a short-term gain, like fame, money, a political appointment, that sort of thing." Dorian thought of Jonathan Braynard, the NYU student whose soul he'd spared in the alley last week. "When it's time to collect, the demon takes residence in the body, and the soul is sent to hell."

Charlotte gasped. "I can't believe anyone would willingly sign up for that."

"They don't always read the fine print. But even when they do..." Dorian shook his head. "Desperation is its own form of insanity, Charlotte. It can drive people to do a great many things they might've once called irrational or even suicidal."

She shuddered beside him, rubbing her arms. "Demon deals... Hell slaves... Shit. They *really* didn't teach us this stuff in Catholic school."

"It's not in the interest of religious institutions to delve too deeply into the supernatural. They pick and choose from myriad myths and histories, twisting them just enough to brand us all as evil and keep you on the righteous path, stuffing their coffers in exchange for answers they don't actually have."

"That about sums it up." She let out a faint laugh. "How did they even get here?"

"The demons?"

"Yes. And the shifters. And the vampires. And the witches. All of you. You said the religious institutions pick and choose, but do *you* even know?"

"We have our histories and legends, just like you." He

finally turned to face her again, reaching up to tuck a lock of hair behind her ear. "Most of it, as you might imagine, can be traced back to witches."

"Tell me," she said, completely captivated.

"Witches are the world's oldest magicians, guardians of elemental magic and the liminal spaces between all realms. As such, they are tireless explorers and experimenters. It's said they created the first vampires through complex blood rites, all in service to deepening their practice of healing magic and immortality spells. Their deep connections with animal familiars allowed them to literally experience the lives and gifts of these creatures, and from there, create the first shifters."

"And the demons?"

"The demons are creatures of hell, but the witches— eager to access and experiment with their dark and immeasurable powers—opened the gates that allow demons to pass between realms."

Charlotte's eyes were full of wonder. "So all of these beings... they're here? Around us?"

"Constantly, though humans greatly outnumber us, and rarely learn of our existence. It's better for everyone that we remain a secret."

"But still! This is one town, in one state, in one country, and I've already encountered more vampires than I can count on one hand. How are you all not killing each other or trying to take over the world?"

"How do you know we aren't?" He flashed a dark smile, but then shook his head, the shadow of his responsibilities never far from his thoughts. "The supernatural races co-exist through a tenuous policy of mutually assured destruction. Conflicts lead to discovery, and widespread discovery would almost certainly lead to our extinction. For that reason, it's in everyone's best interest to avoid killing each other."

"And killing humans."

"Precisely."

"What about Duchanes? And the vampires who attacked us in the park?"

"The men in the park were demons. As for *Duchanes*..." Dorian seethed with fresh anger at the mention of his name, his vision clouding with red. "He will be dealt with accordingly."

Even now, Malcolm and Gabriel were on the hunt, sweeping the area around Ravenswood while Aiden had returned to Manhattan, seeing what rumors he might unearth from the other greater vampire families. Colin had spent the night in the crypts, where he was still undoubtedly poring over their father's journals.

"But what if—"

"I don't want you to worry about him. I don't want you to worry about *any* vampires, or demons, or bogeymen, or even a lowly paper cut." He took her face between his hands, brushing her cheeks with his thumbs, the very idea of anything hurting her sending him into a dark inner rage. "I meant what I said last night, Charlotte. You're *mine*."

Her eyes shone with unshed tears. "What does that even mean? You hardly know me."

"I've been alive for two hundred and fifty years, Charlotte. I hardly know *anyone*, and it's hardly a prerequisite for a promise."

"What promise?"

"That I won't let anything happen to you. *Ever*."

At this, a tear slipped down her cheek, and he brushed it away. Then, tracing a path over her eyebrow, he said, "I think I've already learned something about you. See, this one arches a certain way when you're having a good think."

Charlotte smiled, and it felt like the sun had just burst through the clouds. "Just that one?"

"It's one of your beautiful mysteries. So what is it, love? Tell me what else is on your mind."

She shifted closer to him, tucking herself into the spot beneath his shoulder. "This might be a personal question."

"Aren't they all?" Dorian put his arm around her, pulling her even closer, pressing a kiss to her head. Her hair smelled different today—she'd used his shampoo last night —but he could still sense the orange-and-vanilla beneath it, and he took a deep inhale.

"How... how did you become a vampire?" she asked.

He'd known it was coming, but still, the question slammed into his heart, rattling against the iron gates and knocking something loose.

"That's... not an easy story." And outside of those precious few who'd lived through it themselves, Dorian had never shared it with another soul. It lingered, as so many of his ghosts, in the deep recesses of a fractured mind, in the darkest parts of a shuttered heart. "Perhaps we'll save it for another day."

He closed his eyes and waited for her rebuttal, but she seemed to understand his pain, and graciously let the matter drop.

They enjoyed a few more moments of peaceful silence, and then she pulled out of his embrace, got to her feet, and walked back to the car alone, her shoulders heavy with the secrets he'd shared.

And the ones he hadn't.

As much as he'd wanted to be totally honest with her, Dorian had been alive long enough to learn the hard truth:

Some skeletons were best left undisturbed.

CHAPTER THIRTY-EIGHT

759462.

Now that she'd seen Dorian enter the alarm code at the front door, Charley couldn't get the sequence out of her mind, no matter how badly she wanted to obliterate it.

It was the kind of perfect intel most thieves would risk their lives for, and all Charley had done was glance up at the right moment. A mindless, two-second effort after she and Dorian had gotten back from their drive; it hadn't even occurred to Dorian she might be watching him.

That she might have a *reason* to watch him.

759462. It was everything Rudy needed to bleed Dorian's priceless art collection dry. Everything *she* needed to win back Rudy's elusive trust.

That's my girl, her father's voice echoed. *Resourceful as always.*

Shame burned through her heart, and for a moment she pictured herself in the mines of hell, shoveling coal into a furnace alongside all the vampires and terrible humans who'd ever existed.

"Are you still intent on leaving me today?" Dorian asked as they headed into the grand foyer.

Charley sighed. "I'm just anxious to get back to my sister. But if it helps, I'll be thinking of you the entire ride home."

"Not especially." Dorian cupped her face, his eyes glittering, despite his frown. "One last drink before you go?"

"Why not? I always love a good day-drink."

"Splendid. I've got just the thing."

They headed into the study, where the fire was crackling, the room cleaned of all evidence of last night's arguments and broken glass. Charley wondered if his brothers had taken care of it, or Aiden, or some mysterious housekeeping staff who'd remained totally invisible.

Settling into the same chair she'd occupied last night, Charley pulled the blanket over her shoulders and welcomed the fire's warmth, her head still spinning from all the things Dorian had shared with her. Vampires, shapeshifters, demons, witches... It was enough to send anyone to the nuthouse. Yet nothing he'd confessed had scared her off. Not from him.

There were still so many questions to ask, so many rabbit holes she wanted to go down. In a perfect world, she *would* stay the whole weekend. The whole month. A blissful, perfect vacation from all her regrets and bad choices, where she could wake up every morning to a gourmet brunch, spend the afternoon driving through the autumn mountains and learning all there was to know about the supernatural world. Then, at night, she'd slip between dark satin sheets with the vampire whose every demanding kiss set her skin aflame.

But now, after seeing that security code, her mind kept veering right back to the topic they *hadn't* covered.

The stolen art.

Dorian poured two drinks at the bar, then turned and handed her a glass full of amber liquid. "A rare vintage Cognac, about half as old as I am."

Charley grinned, bringing the glass to her nose for a deep whiff. "Mmm. An antique in a glass."

She sipped, letting the smooth taste linger on her tongue. It was—like everything connected to Dorian Redthorne—elegant, delicious, and a little overwhelming.

She couldn't even imagine what the bottle must've cost him.

When he finally settled into the chair next to her, she looked up at him and said, "Before we say our goodbyes, there's something else we need to discuss."

"Another deal? Perhaps a negotiation that ends with me tying you to my bed for a *proper* punishment?"

Her thighs clenched, butterflies twirling in her stomach at the thought.

But she had to stay focused. To get through this, or it would all be for nothing.

"You haven't told me about the art, Dorian."

Disappointment flashed in his eyes, but he recovered quickly. "Remind me which pieces you were interested in."

"Well, all of it, of course. But first, I need to know about the Hermes statue and the Viola LaPorte painting."

"Ah, yes. The pieces you were so diligently investigating last night."

Ignoring the burn of shame in her gut, she said, "How did you acquire them?"

"Quite legally, I assure you. I work with a highly discerning, highly reputable buyer. He knows my tastes, and contacts me when something that may be of interest crosses his path." He sipped his Cognac, relaxing deeper into his chair. "He acquired the LaPorte for me about three years ago, Hermes... maybe six or eight months later. They both came from separate estate auctions, I believe."

"You believe? Or you know?"

"Does it matter?"

Charley closed her eyes, returning the glass to her lips. She *really* didn't want to disclose anything else, but she sensed Dorian would make things a lot more difficult if she didn't at least give him a breadcrumb or two.

She just needed some liquid courage first.

After a few more sips, she said, "What I'm about to tell you can't leave this room. Do I have your word?"

Dorian's eyebrows lifted. "I can't imagine what could be so secretive about a perfectly legal transaction I made years ago, with a broker who's made dozens of similar transactions before and since."

"Your *word*, Dorian."

Concern warred with curiosity in his eyes, but eventually, he gave in. "Fine. It won't leave this room."

"At one time, both pieces belonged to a single collector in the West Village."

"Really? I didn't acquire them together. As I said, I'm fairly certain they came from different estates."

"Prior ownership isn't the only thing they have in common." Charley stared into her glass, firelight dancing in the amber liquid. She tried not to think about the fires of hell. "The LaPorte and the Hermes, along with the rest of the man's collection—approximately seventy million dollars in art and artifacts—were stolen from his apartment five years ago, never recovered. As far as I know, yours are the first pieces to surface."

"That's… impossible."

"I wish it were."

Dorian leaned forward in his chair, his eyes narrowing. "Charlotte. How on earth do you know about this?"

"It's my job."

"So you investigate art heists for a living? I thought you were a consultant."

"I *am* a consultant. And in my line of work, sometimes I come across stolen pieces. It's not as unusual as you might think."

"Why haven't I heard of this before? An art heist of that magnitude should've made the papers."

Charley's cheeks heated, and she took another sip of Cognac, unable to hold his gaze. "The theft was never reported. I suspect the collector wanted to keep his name out of the spotlight."

"Which brings me back to my question. How did *you* find out about it?"

"I—"

"Dorian," a voice from the doorway called. "Ms. D'amico."

Dorian sighed. "Good afternoon, Gabriel. Is there something we can assist you with?"

"Found this at the bottom of the hill. Thought you might want it back." He crossed the room and handed Charley her cell phone, scuffed up but still functional.

"Thank you," she said, not sure if she was more grateful for the recovery of her phone or the break from Dorian's scrutiny.

"Anything else?" Dorian asked his brother.

"Malcolm and I are heading back out now—I just wanted to return the phone."

Dorian nodded. "Keep me—"

"Informed," Gabriel said, already turning his back. "Of course, your *highness*."

He was almost to the doorway when Charley spoke up again. "Gabriel, wait."

He stilled, one hand on the doorframe, but didn't turn around.

"I wanted to thank you," she said.

"You've already done so."

"Not for the phone. For last night. You and Dorian... You saved my life. I know you took a big risk. So... thank you. Again."

He let out a sigh, then turned his head, glancing at her over his shoulder. It was the first time she'd seen even a *flicker* of warmth in his eyes. "You didn't deserve what they did to you."

And then he was gone, leaving a chill in his wake.

Charley pulled the blanket tighter over her shoulders.

"No one ever accused my brother of being a gracious host," Dorian said. "Be grateful you've only got a sister, love. Brothers are more trouble than they're worth."

Charley smiled, but beneath the irritation, Dorian's tone held a note of softness. Sadness too, but it was clear to her that whatever their shared resentments, the brothers cared deeply for one another.

She thought of what Dorian had said earlier, about how his brothers and his vampire house were one in the same. He hadn't wanted to talk about how he'd become a vampire, but Charley suspected whatever had happened that fateful day was at the root of their fractured relationships.

Tragedy cast long shadows. She could only imagine what that meant for immortals.

"Sasha's the best," she said, trying to inject some lightness into the conversation, hoping to avoid any more questions about her so-called career.

"Sasha, the erotic vegetable photographer?" Dorian finally smiled, his eyes regaining some of their sparkle. "Older or younger?"

"Younger. She's nineteen. We didn't grow up together, though—different dads. I've only known her about five years. My mother kept us apart until she just… didn't want her anymore."

"What?"

"Yeah, she basically loaded her onto a bus and shipped her off to New York with nothing but some old clothes and my address." Charley told him the story, the familiar disappointment and disgust churning inside. "It all worked out, though. Sasha's the best thing my mother ever gave me. The best person I know. I used to wish…" She trailed off, catching the look of pity on Dorian's face. "Oh, God. *Please* don't look at me like that."

"Like what, love?"

"Like *that*." She reached over and traced her fingers across his forehead, then down to his jaw. "You feel sorry for me."

"No." He grabbed her wrist, turning her hand over to press a kiss to her palm. "I just wish I could take away your pain. No one should have to endure—"

"But we do, right? Endure?" Charley pulled her hand back, unable to take the sweet, tender touch of his kiss. "Anyway, regrets are pretty useless. Everything that happened in my life… It all brought me to this point."

"What point is that?"

She flashed a grin. "Oh, you know. Sipping antique Cognac. Hanging out in a gorgeous Elizabethan manor. Hobnobbing with elite supernatural art collectors."

Dorian returned her smile, his eyes turning curious again. "You never told me how you got involved in the art world."

"My father," she said. It was instant and automatic, one of the few truths she could still admit. "He was in the business. He's gone now, but after my mom split, it was just the two of us. I used to go with him to auctions and parties, tagging along and... well, snooping, I guess."

"Ah." He shot her a wink. "Some things never change."

"I've always loved looking at other people's art collections. My father recognized that early on and taught me everything he could. Paintings, statues, sculptures, tapestries... I wanted to know absolutely everything, and he always indulged my curiosities."

"When did he pass?"

"Five years ago. I still think about him every day, though." She tipped back the last of her drink, then sighed. As screwed up as it was, this part was all true too. Messy and complicated, colored with more than a few shades of gray, but real. "I guess that's why I still love looking at people's collections. Sometimes I run across a piece he loved, or one he taught me about, and I just... I don't know. Maybe I'm looking for a connection. A sign that he's still with me."

"Adrift," Dorian said softly.

Charley's eyes widened.

"Last weekend," he continued. "At the auction. It was the painting in the study, where—"

"I remember. I'm just surprised *you* do."

"How could I not? It was in that room that..." Dorian shifted in the chair, trying unsuccessfully to hide the sudden bulge in his pants. "Suffice it to say, the painting made quite a lasting impression."

"No kidding. Thanks to you, I'll never be able to look at it again without..."

...recalling the time a stranger cornered you in the study at the Salvatore penthouse and forced you to come for him, again... and again... and again...

The memory of Dorian's words echoed, and Charley closed her eyes, slipping back under the spell of those stolen moments...

"Fathers," Dorian said suddenly, scattering her thoughts. "Whether we spent our lives loving them or loathing them, even in death, they never quite leave us."

"No, I guess not." She opened her eyes, a knot of emotion tightening her throat.

Her feelings about her dad were so thorny, and it'd been a long time since she'd really talked about him with anyone.

Yes, her father was responsible for recognizing and nurturing her love of art—a love that had quickly become a deep, inextricable part of her being. In that way, he'd always be with her.

But he was also responsible for turning her into a criminal with no foreseeable way out. In his image, she'd become a phantom, a woman who'd seduced a stranger to distract him from her crimes, and now found herself hopelessly tangled in an impossible, no-win situation that could only end in ruin.

Charley's *and* Dorian's.

Here's your opening, girl. Tell Dorian the truth. Tell him everything, then throw yourself at his feet and beg for his forgiveness.

Maybe there *was* a way to stop this before it went any further. A way to stop Rudy altogether—not just from robbing Dorian, but from all the other heists to come.

If anyone could help her figure things out, it was Dorian Redthorne, immortal vampire king.

"What is it, love?" he asked, reaching out to touch her cheek again, his brow tight with worry.

"Dorian, there's something… I need to…" She sucked in a deep breath, then opened her mouth again, ready to confess every last sin. But when the words finally broke free, all that came out was, "I need to get back to Sasha."

CHAPTER THIRTY-NINE

"Will you do me a favor?" Charlotte asked.

They were standing in the circular drive, Jameson holding the limo door for her, ready to ferry her back to the city. Dorian had wanted to accompany them, but of course Charlotte insisted on going alone. He was lucky he'd convinced her to accept Jameson's services at all.

His woman, he was quickly learning, was not big on compromise.

Under normal circumstances, neither was Dorian. But nothing about his interactions with Charlotte D'Amico had *ever* been normal, and now, after the way they'd shared their bodies last night—not to mention their secrets this afternoon—Dorian's world was completely upside down.

All he wanted to do was drag her back into the manor, tie her down, and push her right back to the edge—a dark, dangerous place they both craved. He'd heard it in her soft moans of pleasure, felt it in the way her body had responded to his punishing touch.

Yet here she was, leaving him again.

Asking for *favors*, no less.

"What is it?" he asked, doing his damnedest to keep the frustration from his tone.

Keeping her voice low, she said, "Can you get in touch with your art buyer, try to find out more about Hermes and the LaPorte?"

"Why is this so important to you?"

"I... I can't tell you. Not until I know more." She closed her eyes, the lines around her mouth deepening. "But Dorian? This has to stay quiet. Please don't involve anyone other than the buyer and his connections. I can't risk it."

Trouble.

The alarm clanged in his head again. As much as he'd tried to deny it, her actions at the Salvatore and inside his own home last night—not to mention her evasiveness about the stolen artwork—convinced him she was into something nefarious. But Dorian couldn't discern whether she'd *caused* the trouble, or she'd just been caught in the crossfire.

He still wasn't convinced she didn't have connections to Chernikov, either, or the other greater vampire families looking to make a power play, or any name on the increasingly long list of enemies eager to turn the Redthornes to ash.

But deep inside, he wanted to trust her. To help her, even if he was only helping her put the final stake through his heart.

"What aren't you telling me?" he asked.

Again, she didn't answer.

"You're hiding something," he said, frustration finally bubbling over. "You've been nothing but cagey since our first meeting, and now you're standing on *my* property, asking for favors to which you're not entitled, nor have you earned. I *demand* to know—"

"Don't. Please." With a gentle touch, she cupped his face, her eyes full of regret. "I realize how shady this sounds, but—"

"Darling, you have *no* bloody idea. I've met career politicians more honest and straightforward than you, even *before* I compelled them."

A wounded look flickered through her gaze, and she removed her hand, but Dorian stood by his words. She *was* shady. Shady, frustrating, witty, intelligent, adventurous, beautiful, *incredibly* sexy, and quickly infiltrating his very bones.

"I *know* I haven't earned the right to ask for this," she said, "but—"

"You don't trust me. After everything we've already shared."

"You shouldn't trust me, either, Dorian Redthorne. We're still strangers. And we're talking about stolen artwork here. The kind of information that can lead to some *really* unsavory places."

"Like my bed?" He'd meant it to sound angry, but it came out more like a taunt.

Charlotte couldn't help her smile, and for a moment

354

Dorian was so relieved to see the light return to her eyes, he almost stopped caring about the secrecy.

"I wouldn't call your bed an unsavory place." She took a step closer, sliding her hands over his shoulders, the sudden press of her body after so long without it quickly sending him into overdrive.

He slid his hands into her hair, drawing her even closer. "I have other unsavory beds, you know. A great many of them. Beds you haven't yet had the pleasure of being bound to and thoroughly ravished upon."

His cock twitched at the thought, and her eyes darkened with desire, blood racing hot through her veins.

But then she closed her eyes and pulled back, leaving him with nothing to embrace but the crisp autumn air and an armload of regrets.

"Goodbye, Dorian Redthorne," she said softly. "Thank you, as always, for a lovely time."

Dorian pressed a hand to his heart. "Ah, she bids me farewell, and yet my questions remain unanswered, the mystery of Charlotte D'Amico eternally unsolved."

"I need more information," she said, impatience snapping through her words. "Can you do me that favor? Talk to your guy?"

In response, Dorian grabbed her shoulders and hauled her close, claiming her in a kiss so fierce, so protective, so possessive, it left no doubt about his intentions. Then, finally breaking for air, he kissed a path to her ear and whispered, "I'll let you know what I find out."

Charlotte gave him a grateful smile, which Dorian reluctantly returned. He'd given in to her demands today, but she was going to have to start talking, sooner rather than later. Because after this weekend, whatever trouble Charlotte was heading for, whatever "unsavory places" awaited her, Dorian was going right down with her.

Whether she liked it or not.

She slid into the limo, and Jameson closed the door behind her.

"I shall take good care of her, sir," he said.

"I've no doubts, Jameson," Dorian replied. Then, in a low voice, "Keep the GPS activated. I'll be right behind you."

CHAPTER FORTY

Charley could not stop shaking.

She was so livid, so out of her damn mind with rage, she could barely think straight, let alone get her body to cooperate. It was all she could do to give Jameson the address change, and hope like hell he didn't rat her out to Dorian.

She was in enough trouble with the vampire as it was. The *last* thing she needed was Dorian finding out she didn't go home, after she'd insisted over and over she needed to get back to Sasha.

Leaving Ravenswood, she had every intention of doing just that. But halfway across the Tappan Zee Bridge, she'd gotten a call from a frantic, freaked-out Sasha that changed everything.

Rudy had shown up at Perk today during Sasha's shift, where he proceeded to order a cappuccino, plop his sketchy ass at the counter, and lurk.

For five fucking hours.

He'd peppered her with questions about her dating life, about Charley's, about whether Charley's so-called "new boyfriend" had ever been to their Park Avenue penthouse. He wanted to know if Sasha realized her sister was "whoring around" upstate this weekend, and if she'd heard from their "slut of a mother" lately. He told Sasha she was a stunning young woman—that their mother was a fool to toss a girl like her into the trash.

Sasha was so rattled, she didn't even leave when her shift ended—she picked up a double, just so she wouldn't have to exit the café until Rudy was long gone.

Now, hours later, Charley barreled out of the elevator that led to his apartment, damn near kicking down the door.

After a barrage of knocks and kicks, Rudy opened the door, his smile greasy and smug. "And the succubus returns. I wondered when I might hear from you."

Beyond the entryway, Travis sat on the couch with a beer, shaking his head. "Not cool going off the radar like that, Charley."

"I lost my phone," she said.

"In Redthorne's bed?"

Charley rolled her eyes. God, she wanted to throttle them both. After everything she'd witnessed this weekend, everything she'd learned from Dorian about the creatures that lurked in the shadows, Travis had been downgraded from a snake to a roach—an annoying pest who needed a good dose of Raid.

Rudy needed a dose too, but unfortunately, he was still the boss—one Charley had to appease.

"Come in, Charlotte." Rudy's smile fell away, his eyes dark and sinister. "I hope you have something worthwhile to share, for your sake and for Sasha's. Did she mention we spent some time together today?"

Looking at him now, his hair slicked back, his calculating eyes, Charley wanted to claw his skin off, hold a knife to his throat, and give him a glimpse of the fear he'd instilled in Sasha.

But as furious as she was, she no longer wanted to tear him a new one.

That's what *he* wanted—confirmation that his tactics worked. That he'd gotten to her.

Fuck that.

With a curious smile, she said, "Oh, really? I thought Sasha had to work today."

Rudy's jaw ticked. "I dropped by Perk to say hello."

"Huh. I spoke to her earlier, but she didn't mention it. She gets a lot of customers, though—hard to remember just one."

Even if that one is *a filthy, dickless scumbag who thinks preying on young girls makes him powerful…*

He grunted out something that might've been a laugh or a warning or even indigestion, glaring at Charley with another silent threat. For a moment, she said nothing—just glared right back, wondering how such a human stain could hold so much sway over her life.

Her father may not have been up for any model citizen

awards, but Charley was damn sure he'd never stand for his brother and former second-in-command treating his daughter and her sister this way.

But her dad was long gone, and unlike Dorian, Charley didn't have super strength and immortality on her side. If she wanted to take back the reins of her wildly out-of-control life, she was going to have to do it herself—one small victory at a time.

Starting with taking charge at this meeting.

Ignoring her uncle's menacing glare, she dropped her bag in the entryway and headed into the living room, taking the chair farthest from the cockroach. "Let's make this quick—I've got things to do."

Rudy joined them, settling in next to Travis. He wanted to lecture her. She could feel it simmering in the air, quickly moving to a boil. But right now, he wanted the intel more. *That* was her leverage. That would *always* be her leverage.

For now, she needed to play it smart. Let them think she was all in, as promised.

"It's like you figured." She glanced down at the papers spread across the coffee table—twice as many surveillance photos as they'd shown her last time. "The guy's loaded."

"Loaded and locked down," Travis said. "Right?"

"*Extremely* locked down. The place is a vault." Charley updated them on the security situation, leaving out certain details, embellishing others, giving them just enough to salivate over while still buying herself some wiggle room to figure out her next steps. "And right now, he's got a bunch of family in town."

She'd expected that bit of news to piss Rudy off, but he only sighed.

Weird.

"For how long?" he asked.

"I'm not sure. Apparently, there was a death in the family."

Nodding as if this was no big deal, Rudy tapped the floor plans on the table. "Walk me through the house, room by room. I need to know what's in there."

Charley patiently pointed out each room—master bedroom, additional bedrooms, sitting room, living room, formal dining room, on and on—listing off some of the high-end pieces that had decorated each. She omitted the elevator, and glossed over the basement quickly, trying to keep their attention on the main floors.

"You sure you searched the basement completely?" Travis asked. "No poker room, media room, other places he might stash some art?"

Charley shook her head.

"I don't buy it," he said. "Rich jackoff like that? I bet he's—"

"Look, guys," Charley said, determined to keep control of the situation. "Dorian Redthorne isn't some frat-boy stockbroker. He's not even much of an entertainer—the fundraiser was apparently a once-in-a-lifetime event. He's just a wealthy, somewhat reclusive businessman and collector—that's it."

And an immortal vampire who could tear your beating hearts out of your chests...

The image almost made her smile, but it wasn't a serious option. For all his faults, Dorian wasn't a murderer. He'd said it himself—vampires had laws against killing humans.

Besides, if Rudy died, where the hell would that leave Charley? She had no access to money, to the deed of her father's condo. Rudy wasn't just her uncle—he was her benefactor. Her sole source of income.

"What about the cars?" Travis asked. "Tell me he showed you the cars."

Charley sighed. Being around these men always felt like a test, and she had a sneaking suspicion they still had people watching the property, which meant they might've seen her driving the Ferrari.

Again, she shared as little of the truth as possible.

"We took one of the cars out earlier," she said. "Honestly, I don't even know what kind it was. Cars aren't my area of expertise, but yeah, there are a lot of them, and they look pretty."

Not to mention, incredibly fun to drive. Despite the seriousness of the situation, it was hard for Charley not to smile at the memory of driving that Ferrari, the wind in her hair as she sped along the open road. She still couldn't believe Dorian had let her drive it.

"Pretty, or expensive?" Travis asked.

"Both?" Charley shrugged. "I don't really know. That's your department."

Travis nodded, surprisingly non-confrontational. She

could almost see the wheels turning in his head. As far as Charley knew, Rudy had never fenced cars before, but Travis' involvement seemed to change things.

"So that about does it," Charley said, rising from the chair. "I'll get you the list of pieces once I've had a chance to think about everything again, but this should give you a pretty good idea of what's going on over there."

"Very informative," Rudy said, unable to keep the note of satisfaction from his voice.

Charley finally relaxed. All in all, her presentation had been pretty convincing—she could see it in the way Rudy smiled now, greedy and eager, eyes glittering with the promise of a hot score.

But like a flower kept in the closet, Charley was fading quickly. It wasn't just the double life, the lies, the scamming.

It was that she *missed* him.

Somehow, in their short time together, Dorian Redthorne had gone from random hot hookup, to phone sex fantasy man, to Rudy's mark, to a real person, to an immortal vampire, and right back to a real person again— one she desperately wanted to know. To be near. Now, she wasn't just fantasizing about him; she was *thinking* about him. *Remembering* him and their conversations, the breakfast spread, the drive. *Craving* Dorian's touch, the sharp sting on her bare flesh, the soothing kisses that followed.

"Nice work, Charley." Travis pounded on the table, startling her from her thoughts. "You're quite the resourceful little slut."

Charley flashed him a carefree smile, refusing to take the bait. "I know, right? While you were jerking off alone last night, I actually got some useful information. As a matter of fact, I got more intel in one night than you managed to cobble together in all your months of surveillance." Then, turning to Rudy, "So when are we making a move?"

"You're on a need-to-know basis," he said. "The moment you need to know, I promise you, you will."

But that was the thing—Charley *did* need to know. Right fucking now. If she had any chance of throwing a wrench into the works, she needed to know exactly how and when those works would play out.

Fuck.

There was only one thing left to do.

It was a risk—one she'd never before taken. Not once in the five years since she'd been working for Rudy. But now, it was her only shot. And when she thought again of Dorian, of how quickly he'd opened his home to her, his bed, hell—even his heart—Charley knew she couldn't back down.

Popping her hands on her hips, she looked her dickbag, asswipe, shithead of a boss straight in the eyes and said, "I'm sorry, Uncle Rudy, but that's bullshit."

His eyebrows lifted, his lip already curling into a sneer. He was T-minus five seconds from erupting, but Charley couldn't pull back now.

"Look," she said firmly. "You guys sent me in there almost entirely unprepared—no mention of the family members in town, no mention of the size and scope of the fundraiser, and worse—no mention that the host was a man I'd already met before—one who obviously recognized me." Charley shook her head, still steamed about that particular trick. "Despite all that, I *still* managed to do my job. Now, out of everyone in this room, I'm the closest one to Redthorne—the *only* one who might be able to wrangle some additional info out of him, or lure him out of the house at the right time. Even with all the surveillance in the world, you two don't stand a chance without me."

"Careful," Rudy warned. "You're getting dangerously close to insulting me."

Charley's chest tightened, but she wasn't done.

"Dorian Redthorne isn't some drugged-up celebrity or bratty kid spending Daddy's trust fund. He's a serious collector, and he's not going to be taken so easily. Face it, guys. You wanna get close to that cache? You're gonna need *me*, every step of the way."

"Fuck." Travis tried to shove a hand through his hair but gave up when he couldn't break the gel barrier. "We haven't mapped everything out yet. We're still waiting on more surveillance photos from my other guy."

"Just how many other guys are in on this?" she asked.

No response.

"Fine, figure out the logistics," she said. "But when it's time to go in, I'm going in with you."

Rudy remained silent, and inside, Charley cheered. It was as close to agreement as she was going to get out of him.

Today's small victory achieved, Charley picked up her bag and headed for the door, tossing one last barb over her shoulder. "Call me when you boys are ready to stop measuring your dicks and start making a real plan. Until then, have a fan-fucking-tastic weekend!"

CHAPTER FORTY-ONE

What a fucking nightmare.

By the following Wednesday, Dorian was little more than a caged animal on display, pacing his office while Aiden ushered out the corporate investigators they'd spent the morning trying to appease.

Lucien Armitage's sons had sent them. In the wake of the attack on Charlotte at the fundraiser, they had new concerns about Dorian's ability to, quote, "manage his competing priorities."

And—rubbing a bit more salt in the wound—Lucien was still considering Renault Duchanes' bid for Armitage Holdings. On the advice of his sons, the offer wouldn't be dismissed unless Duchanes was found guilty of ordering the attack.

So Dorian had endured the investigations—two in as many days, with more lined up tomorrow—wasting precious time discussing his corporate and personal financials, his plans for integrating Armitage Holdings into FierceConnect's existing structure, how he saw their technology fitting into his current product offerings. They'd asked about his beta testing procedures, how many employees had access to his proprietary development schematics, whether his home and office facilities were secure. Today, they'd gotten even more invasive, assaulting him with questions about everything from his employees' schedules to how much unsupervised access his housekeeping staff had at Ravenswood, where they might uncover sensitive company data.

If he didn't need the merger to help smooth the way to a partnership with Isabelle Armitage, he would've called the whole bloody thing off.

And worse, despite Aiden's insistence that he play the consummate professional during these inane investigations, Dorian could hardly concentrate. His mind was utterly incapable of veering away from Charlotte for more than thirty consecutive seconds.

After trailing her and Jameson on Saturday, he knew she hadn't gone home—Jameson had dropped her at an address on Water Street, nowhere near the Park Avenue address Dorian had spied on her driver's license the night he'd found her purse in the gardens. Sitting in his black BMW M8 like a bloody stalker, he'd watched through the tinted windows as she entered the building. Then, no more than half an hour later, she exited and hopped into a taxi.

Again, Dorian followed her—this time, straight to Park Avenue.

Satisfied she was safely home, he took off, hoping they might catch up on the phone later that night. But in the four days since, he'd barely spoken to her. She'd ignored all of his calls, offering no more than a handful of noncommittal texts in return—empty promises about wanting to see him again, followed soon after with excuses about why she couldn't.

Work meetings!

Homecoming BBQ at Sasha's school!

Hair appointment!

Devil's balls, that last one had really stung.

"I'm starting to understand why you don't like people," Aiden said, returning to Dorian's office looking uncharacteristically flustered. "Sodding hell, that was torture."

"With more fun to come tomorrow." Dorian continued his pacing, keeping his back to the expansive windows. The sun felt overly bright today; his eyes ached as if someone had plucked them out of his skull, stomped on them, and shoved them back in.

"When was the last time you fed?" Aiden asked, tracking Dorian's movements across the office. "You don't look so hot."

"I'm fine."

He wasn't fine. The sustaining effects of the demon blood he'd recently dined on hadn't lasted very long, and the hospital from which he typically procured blood bags was experiencing a shortage. Dorian had been forced to purchase synthetic blood from Marlys—a last resort composed of cold extracted demon blood, animal blood, and a magic tincture so foul it had Dorian nearly wishing for death.

Dorian rubbed his eyes, trying to ease the throbbing behind them. It was maddening, but if they didn't secure a bonded witch soon, the sunlight was going to be the least of his problems.

Day by day, Dorian was losing his ability to process the nutrients his body needed from blood. And though his brothers and Aiden hadn't started showing the symptoms yet, he knew, deep in his gut, they would all eventually succumb to the same affliction.

"Dorian, are you certain you're—"

"I said I'm fine, Aiden. Is there anything else?"

"Actually, yes, if you'll allow me to share it without biting off my head." He settled into his favorite spot in Dorian's chair, helping himself to a sip of Dorian's coffee, long gone cold. "I've received word from Kate—my contact at House Connelly. Two of her sisters reported seeing demons at Bloodbath this week."

Dorian stopped pacing, his eyes widening. Bloodbath was an underground nightclub on St. Marks Place, owned by Duchanes and his associates. The clientele was mostly vampires, but more and more lately, Dorian had been hearing rumors of human guests—most likely blood slaves. The presence of demons was disconcerting to say the least —the monsters weren't supposed to set foot in Manhattan at all.

"How certain was she?" Dorian asked.

"Positive. They spotted them on three different occasions."

"Chernikov's?"

"They didn't know."

Dorian dropped into the leather chair across from Aiden, his mind turning over the intel. If they *were* Chernikov demons, he'd have another problem on his hands. He thought he'd made himself clear at his meeting with the Russian about keeping his demons on a leash.

Dorian *really* hoped Chernikov wasn't baiting him.

"Any sightings of the elusive Renault Duchanes?" he asked.

"No, and according to Kate, no one's talking about him either. She tried to get cozy with one of his newer sirelings, but the man was a vault." Aiden shook his head. "This isn't just about an attack on Charlotte. There are larger forces at play."

Dorian agreed. The attack at Ravenswood, Renault's convenient appearance during the Central Park demon attack, the bid for Armitage Holdings, and now, unidentified demons hanging out at Bloodbath... something told Dorian it was all connected.

He just couldn't figure out how.

"I want him eliminated," he said.

"We have to locate him first. Have you thought of asking Marlys to reach out to Jacinda?"

The idea had crossed his mind, but he'd dismissed it. Jacinda was Renault's witch, so even if she *did* know something, she wouldn't be eager to share it. And Marlys was a free agent, working for the highest bidder and doing her best to stay out of vampire politics. Asking her to take sides in the brewing Duchanes-Redthorne war was neither fair nor prudent.

"We'll find another way," Dorian said. "In the meantime, I'm going to ask Gabriel to keep an eye on Charlotte."

Aiden's eyebrows lifted. "Gabriel?"

"He's got a reputation for… tracking people down."

"Yes, and making them disappear."

"I don't need her to disappear. I need her to be protected. Gabriel can keep a close watch, make sure she's not still a target."

Aiden lowered his eyes and sighed, swirling the cold coffee in the mug.

"Say it," Dorian said.

"I think I'll keep it to myself."

"For fuck's sake, Aiden. If you've got something to—"

"What is it about this woman? You hardly know her, and she's already got your balls in a jar."

"Last time I checked, my balls are still *very* much in my possession." Dorian reached for his belt buckle. "Would you like proof?"

"You spent half the meeting today with a hard-on the size of the Eiffel Tower. It wasn't difficult to tell where your mind had wandered."

"Piss off," he said, but there wasn't any ire behind it. Dorian blew out a breath and loosened his tie, knowing damn well Aiden could spot his lies a hundred miles away. "I can't stop thinking about her."

"That's precisely the problem." Aiden rose from the chair, crossing to the other side of the office and rifling through the file cabinet. He slammed one drawer, then opened another. "This is a critical time for us, and here you are, allowing yourself to be distracted by—"

"What in the bloody hell are you looking for?"

"The lemon biscuits, you daft, obsessed bastard."

"First of all—obsessed? Hardly a fair assessment. Secondly, you ate all the biscuits, and you left crumbs all over my desk. And lastly..." He closed his eyes and pinched the bridge of his nose. "She isn't returning my calls. How have I already managed to fuck this up?"

Aiden slammed the last drawer. "So you're bloody well in love with her, then?"

"What?" The L-word electrified his blood, his heart damn near seizing. "I never said—"

"If you won't listen to me as your *very* concerned friend, listen to me as your business partner. We need to focus on this merger. Never mind Lucien's concerns about our financials—if you don't get yourself sorted out, we'll lose the deal on account of your inability to pull your head out of her *very* beautiful, *very* firm—"

"I'm handling it."

"You're not. You were sitting at that meeting, daydreaming about your wedding when you should've been reassuring the investigators about our capabilities."

"For fuck's sake, I'm not going to propose to the woman. I just want to spend time with her."

"You were picking out china patterns." Aiden shook his

head. "Just so we're clear, I'm not wearing a colored cummerbund to your wedding. Classic black, or I'm staying home."

"Are you quite through?"

"You're obsessing, and it's clouding your judgment."

"I don't need judgment. I need a plan." Dorian hit the intercom for Veronica.

"Brilliant!" Aiden resumed his spot in Dorian's chair, leaning back and propping his feet on the desk. "I'll be over here, popping the popcorn, watching your life implode."

Veronica strolled into the office, her eyes bright and eager. "Ready for lunch? I was thinking we could try the new Thai place on—"

"Never mind lunch," Dorian said. "I need to ask you a question. If you were a woman—"

"Seriously?" She popped her hands on her hips, glaring at him.

"Off to a stellar start, mate," Aiden said. "You really know how to make a girl feel special."

Dorian shook his head, flustered. "What I mean to say is… If you were a woman who'd just started seeing someone new, and that someone wanted you to know he cared—not in an overwhelming way, but—"

"Big gesture," Veronica said with a confident nod. "That's the way to do it."

"Gesture. You mean, like a gift?"

"Yeah, something to let her know you're thinking of her. But not just *any* gift. It has to be meaningful—something you know she'll appreciate."

Dorian nodded, considering his options. "She *did* quite like the Ferrari. Maybe I should—"

"*Ferrari*?" Veronica laughed. "Bless your heart. You one-percenters are just *adorable*!"

"Too grand?"

"I was thinking *flowers*, not Ferraris. But hey, you do you. In the meantime, I'm ordering some Thai. And maybe a raise, since managing your love life is *definitely* not in my job description."

Dorian watched her leave, his mind already percolating.

"She's right, you know," Aiden said.

"Yes—have HR put in the paperwork. Twenty percent ought to do it." Then, with a new idea taking root, he grabbed his phone, grinned at Aiden, and said, "Wish me luck."

Aiden laughed. "How about I wish you celibate? It'll be much better for our bottom line."

CHAPTER FORTY-TWO

Charley wasn't sure if there was a patron saint of thieves and liars, but someone was definitely looking out for her.

It felt like a miracle. Ever since their meeting, Rudy and Travis had backed off, allowing her to work from home all week with no more than a few texts and check-in calls.

She suspected they were busy gathering more intel from Travis' surveillance people, but she wasn't going to ask. For now, she enjoyed the respite, spending quality time with Sasha—breakfast at Perk during Sasha's morning shifts, to make sure Rudy stayed away. Fancy lunches in the city, courtesy of the credit card Rudy provided. And last night, she'd finally caved in to Sasha's incessant begging for a vampire movie marathon, seeing the bloodsucking fiends in a whole new light.

It made her miss Dorian even more, and she felt horrible about dodging his calls and texts. She did want to see him again—as soon as possible—but she needed more time.

Time to get a better handle on Rudy's plans. Time to strategize. Time to decide what—and how—to confess.

Every time her phone lit up with his name, her insides went as fizzy as a glass of champagne, her body heating up as if he were there beside her, taking charge of her pleasure with every delicious kiss.

But for the time being, she had to keep playing her role, convincing Rudy she was still an asset.

Friday morning, she sat on her bed with her earbuds in, poring over the Ravenswood schematics. In her notebook, she'd made a list of some of the artwork she'd found, and now she marked off their locations on the floor plan with a red marker, deliberately leaving off the pieces from the stolen cache.

She'd just finished making the last few notations when Sasha burst into her room, a ball of sunshine and smiles.

Charley shoved her work under the bed and plucked out her earbuds, forcing a big grin. "It's nine in the morning on your day off. Why aren't you sleeping? Something *must* be up."

"How did you not hear all that racket?" Sasha asked. "They've been setting up for twenty minutes!"

"I had my music on. *Who's* been setting up?"

"Delivery guys." Sasha grabbed her hands and hauled her off the bed. "Come on. You've *got* to see this."

"What on earth are you talking about?"

"Pretty sure Mr. Already Forgotten is not so keen on being forgotten."

A spark of intrigue warmed Charley's insides, and the

minute she stepped out of her bedroom, the scent of roses enveloped her in a sweet, heady cloud.

"Holy roses," she gasped, the sight nearly taking her breath away.

Hundreds. Maybe even thousands. She'd never seen so many roses in one place before—not even at a wedding. Deep reds, sunny yellows, fiery oranges—vases full of lush, gorgeous blooms lined the living room walls, set up on pedestals of different heights. The effect was incredible, like a vista of autumn hills in miniature.

It reminded her of the Catskills—the lookout point on Cole Diamante's land where Dorian had bared his supernatural secrets.

Emotion tightened her throat, her eyes glazing with tears. It was crazy and over-the-top, but it was so damn beautiful it made her heart ache.

"Open the card!" Sasha bounced on her toes, handing Charley a cream-colored envelope. "The suspense is killing me!"

Grinning, Charley slid open the flap and removed the note.

Ms. D'Amico,

Now that I have your attention, I thought I might tempt you with another offer.

Option one: you refuse my gift, continue to ignore my calls, and thoroughly ruin my day.

Option two: you join me for dinner and a sleepover tomorrow night at my home in Tribeca. There's one room in particular I'm dying to show you—a dark, secret place that's perfect for my beautiful bad girl.

I promise it's like nothing you've ever experienced—not even in your wildest fantasies...

So... what will it be, love?

Option one, or option two?

"Well? What did he say?" Sasha tried to grab the note, but Charley quickly stuffed it in her bra, her cheeks already hot from the naughty promises laced in every word.

"That is none of your business." She swatted Sasha on the butt and laughed, then scooted back to her bedroom for a some much-needed privacy.

"I don't know who sent those flowers," Sasha called after her, "but if you don't call him right now, I will!"

"Don't even *think* about it!" Charley teased, but she didn't need further prompting. The roses were the last straw. There was no way she could go another day— another *minute*—without calling that crazy, ostentatious, ridiculously hot vampire.

He answered on the first ring.

"So you've received my invitation," he said, his voice low and sexy in her ear.

"Option two," she said. "Always option two."

"I'm glad we're in agreement, love. I'll send Jameson for

you at eight o'clock tomorrow evening. Wear something...
comfortable."

"Um. Should I be afraid?"

"No." Dorian laughed, so rough and gravelly it made
her wet. "You should be utterly terrified."

CHAPTER FORTY-THREE

"Three conditions," Dorian said, his firm tone leaving no room for discussion.

"Conditions?" Charley gulped as he led her down a corridor in the basement of his Tribeca penthouse—all part of the building he owned. She hadn't even seen his actual apartment yet; the moment she'd stepped out of Jameson's limo, Dorian whisked her away without so much as a kiss hello.

"Normally I require a signed agreement," he continued, "but I'll make an exception. Just don't mention it to Aiden."

"A signed agreement? Aiden?" Charley's mouth went dry, a mix of curiosity and anxiety roiling in her stomach. She had no idea Dorian could be so… *official* about things.

Rough sex, dirty talk, bondage? *Hell* yes, she could get into all that—even with a vampire. Especially *her* vampire.

But a secret room? That required signed forms? That his

best friend, business partner, and fellow vampire knew about?

Just how kinky is this man?

"Maybe this isn't such a good idea," Charley said, second-guessing her decision to meet him tonight. "Let's go out for dinner instead. Suddenly I'm craving dim sum."

"The conditions are simple, really," Dorian said, ignoring her protests. They'd reached a door at the end of the corridor, and he punched a lengthy alarm code into the keypad above the handle—a code she thankfully didn't see. It beeped and flashed green, and he cracked open the door.

"One," Dorian said, turning to face her. His muscled body blocked her view into the dark room, but she could still make out the faint glow of colored lights, the hum of electronics in the distance. "What I'm about to show you is *highly* confidential. You must never tell a soul what we do in here."

Charley's knees weakened, but she nodded, anticipation barely winning out over anxiety, both rushing hot and prickly through her bloodstream.

"Two, *I* make the rules. For your own safety, you must obey me."

"But… rules?" Charley's voice was creaky and thin, her lips dry. She cleared her throat and tried again. "What's the third condition?"

Dorian winked—definitely not a good sign—and reached inside the doorway to grab something. When he finally revealed it, Charley's heart dropped straight into her stomach.

"Three, protective gear must be worn at all times." With a wicked grin, Dorian handed her a helmet and a set of kneepads, then fastened a thick black bracelet to her wrist. "Heart rate monitor."

Charley trembled inside, her heart already pounding, sending the monitor into a frenzy. The kneepads were light and flexible, but the helmet wasn't. The thing had a face shield that felt like bulletproof glass.

Whatever lay beyond that doorway was serious business.

"Frightened, little mouse?" he teased, clearly enjoying her torment.

Still. After so much build-up, there was no way she could walk away now. She had to know what awaited her in the darkness.

"I don't scare off that easily, Mr. Redthorne." With a defiant smirk, she pulled the kneepads on and fastened the helmet, hoping he didn't notice the tremble in her hands.

Could she do this? Give herself over completely to whatever dark fantasies lived in Dorian's wicked mind?

How far would he take it?

How far would she *let* him take it?

Her brain was screaming at her to run, to call the whole game off. But she'd missed him too much, missed his kiss and his touch, and beneath her jeans, she throbbed with fresh desire.

"Are you ready, Ms. D'Amico?" Dorian lifted her face shield and took her hand. She couldn't read his expression; he'd gone neutral.

Charley closed her eyes and took a deep breath. She'd had plenty of practice shutting off her brain, but she'd never ignored her instincts. Her physical being. Her desire. And right now, despite her trepidations, that desire was on red alert.

Whatever he's got in store, you fucking want *it, girl.*

Opening her eyes, she flashed another smirk. "Show me to my demise, Mr. Redthorne."

"With pleasure." Dorian led her inside and turned on the lights, bathing the room in a soft red glow that gave off an upscale club vibe. "But first, a drink."

Charley shivered, her nerves firing off in rapid succession as Dorian led her to the bar, gesturing for her to take a seat as he stepped behind it to play bartender.

A bar. Seriously. His freaky, secret sex dungeon had a bar.

It *was* like a club, just as she'd thought. A kinky, sexy-as-hell club that Charley—now that she was here—couldn't wait to explore.

But the moment she looked around—*really* looked around—her nervous anticipation turned into a giggle, and within ten seconds, that giggle exploded into unabashed, belly-aching laughter.

"Oh my *God*," she said. "This is a game room. As in... *video* games."

With a shameless grin, Dorian sliced a lime and dropped it into her drink. "What else would it be?"

Charley couldn't get her laughter under control. "But...

the helmet? And the whole 'the first rule of the secret room is don't talk about the secret room' thing?"

Dorian handed her a Sapphire and tonic. Pouring himself a scotch, he said, "Nothing I'm about to show you —including the gear you're wearing—is on the market. The game I have in mind for us is called Midnight Marauder, and it's still in beta. If the FierceConnect board knew I'd let you see it without signing the non-disclosure, they'd probably fire me from my own company. Cheers, love."

Charley clinked her glass to his, her laughter finally subsiding. After a long pull of her drink, she set down the glass and met Dorian's eyes. "I have a confession, but you're not allowed to laugh."

"Hmm." He leaned across the bar, trailing a finger along her collarbone. "I hope it's about your *naughtiest* fantasies."

A shiver overtook her, her body responding immediately to his touch, igniting a firestorm across her skin. God, she'd missed him. What had she been thinking, blowing him off all week?

Feeling the blush in her cheeks, she said, "I thought you had some kind of… room."

"Room?"

"A secret, kinky, sex-dungeon room."

Dorian's eyes glittered, his mouth wet from the scotch. "My, my, Ms. D'Amico. You have *quite* the imagination."

"It's your fault, Mr. Redthorne."

"I'd hate to disappoint you. Perhaps we can make a compromise."

Charley narrowed her eyes.

"You have to wear protective gear," he said, his voice dark and low. "But you *don't* have to wear clothing."

"You are a scoundrel and a reprobate," she teased, hopping off the barstool. "Now that you got me here under false pretenses, the least you could do is give me the tour."

"My pleasure. Follow me."

Unlike Dorian's sprawling manor, the game room boasted no fine art, no priceless ancient statues, no hand-woven tapestries from dynasties long past. Instead, it was sleek and modern, with black padded walls and surround-sound speakers. The bar took up one side of the room, complete with cocktail tables and chairs. A massive curved screen dominated the front of the room, and at the back, Charley spotted a half-dozen old stand-up arcade games—Ms. Pac-Man, Donkey Kong, Space Invaders, and a few she didn't recognize.

"This is incredible," Charley said. "Is this where you do your product testing?"

"One of the places, yes. I've got an entire floor of virtual gaming rooms in our office. We do beta testing for developers looking to launch new games and gaming technology on the FierceConnect platform."

"So you don't make the actual games?"

"No, we make the distribution and social platform for them. Gamers in every country can sign up, friend each other, buy games through our network, set up tournaments, design and test new games and modules, and play together in real time. Partnering with developers allows us to offer our users a huge selection of games, and it gives the developers access to our millions of users, which makes everyone happy all around."

Charley was beyond impressed. "I had no idea you were such a nerd, Mr. Redthorne."

"Believe it or not, video games are one of the few things I actually love about this era. Besides..." Dorian grinned, eyes sparkling with new mischief. "Didn't anyone ever tell you gamers make the best lovers? Excellent manual dexterity and control, not to mention our dogged persistence in the face of a worthy opponent."

He ran a hand over the curve of her ass, but Charley sidestepped him. She'd been wet since she'd stepped out of the limo; at this rate, she'd never get to see the actual games.

"Less flirting, more gaming," she scolded.

Dorian hit a button on the wall, and two round platforms rose up from the floor in front of the screen, each about eight feet in diameter, with waist-high control panels that looked like something out of Star Trek.

Before she could make another nerd joke, the screen lit up with a logo written in bloody, obnoxious lettering, brightening the entire room.

MIDNIGHT MARAUDER... TIME TO GET HOUSED!

"It's a virtual reality, supernatural street fight," Dorian explained. "Each creature has different powers—for example, vampires can blur, demons can conjure fire, shifters can alternate between human and animal form—so choose your avatar wisely. Anything you do with your body here will translate onto the screen, activating your avatar's different abilities. The more brutal you fight, the more entertaining it will be."

Charley laughed. "I see we're playing in full testosterone mode."

"It's the only way to play, love." Dorian helped her up onto one of the platforms, then stepped onto the other one. "Care to place a wager?"

"Hard pass." Charley touched the control panel in front of her, and a series of white lights illuminated the dashboard. "I've never played. And you basically invented this stuff."

"I've only played a few times." Dorian took a pair of fingerless gloves from his center console, nodding for Charley to do the same. They were covered in electrodes and sensors, and the moment Charley put them on, her heart rate monitor lit up in tandem.

The game finished loading on the screen, and a voice boomed through the speakers, rattling through her bones. "Welcome back, Bone Crusher. Are you ready to brawl?"

"Bone Crusher? Are you serious?" Charley scanned Dorian's stats. His avatar was a wolf-like creature with massive jaws and clawed fists the size of wrecking balls. "Twelve hundred forty-three hours of game play. You call that a few times?"

"It's a demanding job," he teased, securing his helmet and flipping the face shield down.

Charley did the same. The game sharpened before her eyes, so crystal clear it looked real. "These graphics are incredible. I can't even imagine the time and talent that goes into something like this."

"A whole team and then some."

She waved her hands at the screen, watching as her temporary avatar's hands mimicked the movement in real time.

"What do you think?" he asked.

"I think I'm about to get my ass kicked."

"Don't worry," Dorian said, his maddening laugh doing nothing to alleviate her concerns. "I'm an *excellent* coach."

After Charley set up her avatar—a horned demon princess she named Miss Demeanor—Dorian gave her a crash course, showing her how to work all the controls on her gloves. The game was incredibly detailed and accurate; every time she punched, kicked, or dropped to a crouch, her onscreen likeness followed suit, flashing her heart rate and game points as she did.

After a few practice rounds, "Miss Demeanor" finally started to get the hang of it, incorporating some of her special powers, like conjuring balls of hellfire and "smoking out" of her body when she was in danger of dying.

Charley had never been in a man's sexual playroom, but she had a feeling this was even better. Fifteen minutes into the game, she was hooked, and she loved seeing this unexpectedly playful side of her stern, commanding vampire.

"Okay," she said after she'd landed her first surprise hit, knocking Bone Crusher on his ass with a fireball. "This is kind of awesome."

"I'm glad you think so." Dorian paused the game and flipped up his face shield. "Time to up the stakes."

Charley knew that look. It flooded her core with molten heat. "You're so transparent, Bone Crusher."

"Option one," he said. "We shut off the game, head upstairs, and have dinner like civilized people."

"And option two?"

"Winner takes all... of the loser's clothes. One piece for every knockout. And the loser must do the winner's bidding for the rest of the night, no questions asked, no talking back, no disobedience."

"Tough call, Bone Crusher," she teased, flipping down her face shield. "But I'm gonna have to go with option two."

They sparred back and forth, trading hit for hit, until a quick error in judgment left Bone Crusher wide open. Miss Demeanor dropped to her knees and lunged forward, catching her opponent around the legs. The unexpected move sent him skittering backward, tripping over the curb, and landing on the sidewalk, flat on his back.

The announcer's voice boomed through the speakers. "Oooh, Bone Crusher! You got *housed!*"

Charley laughed. "Lose the shirt, Bone Crusher.".

"I hardly think that's fair," he said, his avatar struggling back to his feet. "We're just warming up!"

Taking advantage of his lapse in attention, she launched another fireball, knocking him back on his ass.

"Housed again, Bone Crusher!" the speakers boomed. "Your game is off tonight."

"Your game isn't the only thing I want off tonight," Charley said. "Lose the pants."

"I don't think so, love." After all his tough, winner-take-all talk, Bone Crusher abruptly turned off the game, stripped off his equipment, and leaped onto Charley's platform, sweeping her into his arms and bringing his mouth to her ear. "Since you have a fondness for playing dirty, Miss Demeanor, I've got a *new* game in mind."

CHAPTER FORTY-FOUR

Charley had won the game fair and square, yet minutes later, she was naked and blindfolded, flat on her back on the polished oak bar.

Behind it, Dorian fussed with glasses and drinks, ice cubes clinking into a bucket, liquid sloshing from bottles. Without her sense of sight, every sound took on a mysterious, erotic subtext that filled her with red-hot anticipation.

She'd wanted to tease Dorian for being such a sore loser at Midnight Marauder, but now that she was under his command again, she didn't dare speak out. She knew the rules—no talking without permission—and she was happy to submit.

All. Night. Long.

She felt as free and giddy as a teenager whose parents had just gone out of town. Sasha was staying at Darcy's tonight, and for the first weekend in months, Charley had no scheduled events, no auctions, no roles to play but the ones *she* chose.

Now, she bit back a smile and forced herself to remain silent, giving herself over to whatever dark, delicious plans her dominating, sexy-as-fuck vampire had in store.

"Are you ready to play?" he asked, cool and commanding as he stood beside her. She couldn't see him through the blindfold, but she could feel his powerful presence.

"Yes, Mr. Redthorne."

"Good girl." He smothered her with a devastating kiss. Eagerly she parted her lips, coaxing his tongue with deep, soft strokes. He tasted like scotch and sin, his hungry moan making her ache with need.

Finally breaking the kiss, he pulled back and said, "The game is called Hot or Cold. I'll guess something about you, and you'll tell me if I'm hot..." He wrapped his warm lips around her nipple, tonguing her in an all-too-brief tease. Then, without warning, he pressed an ice cube to her other nipple. "Or cold."

Charley gasped, thighs clenching in a vain attempt to staunch her throbbing desire.

"That's... not a fair game, Mr. Redthorne," she panted. "You've got complete control."

"Yes, that's the idea. Let's begin." He skimmed his hand across her abdomen, his touch smooth and electric, bringing every nerve to rapt attention. "You're originally from New Jersey."

"How did you—"

"Hot or cold, love?"

"Hot."

He rewarded her with another deep kiss, his mouth warm and silky. But it didn't last.

"It's the accent," he admitted softly. "Despite your polished exterior, a bit of New Jersey slips in when you're under duress. I find it *very* intriguing. Now, let's see..." He traced his fingertips from one hipbone to the other, back and forth, his touch as hypnotic as his voice. "You went to Catholic school."

"I've already told you that. I—"

"Hot or cold, Ms. D'Amico?"

"Hot. Definitely hot."

Another kiss, another soft moan. This time, he dipped his fingers lower, teasing her clit before sliding them inside her with slow, deliberate strokes.

A sigh of pleasure escaped her lips as she melted beneath his touch.

Charley was *really* starting to like this game.

"You studied art history in college," he murmured.

"Cold. I never went to—holy *shit!*"

Dorian ran an ice cube between her breasts, down to her bellybutton. His other hand was still occupied between her thighs, fingers stroking, the twin sensations of hot and cold driving her wild.

"You *studied* art history, though," he said. "That much is certain."

"Yes! I mean, hot. So fucking hot."

Removing the ice cube, he lowered his mouth to her

flesh, following the trail of the cold water, lapping it up with his tongue.

With a soft sigh, she writhed on the bar, hips rocking, blood simmering. She reached for his hair, longing to touch him, but he pulled back, removing his mouth and fingers both.

"Don't stop," she begged, reaching for him again. "Please, Dorian."

"*Dorian*, is it?" He lowered his mouth to her ear and licked the edge, his breath hot. "Awfully familiar for a woman lying naked on my bar, subject to my every whim."

"Mr. Redthorne," she corrected. "Please don't stop touching me."

"You are *extremely* sexy when you talk back, Ms. D'Amico. But it's also highly distracting, and absolutely against my rules." He slipped a fresh ice cube between her lips, his tone dark and commanding. "*Suck*."

With a soft moan, she followed his orders, wrapping her lips around the ice, working it with her tongue. Slowly, he dragged the dripping cube from her mouth and trailed it down her chin, past the hollow of her throat, between her breasts, down to her belly, skating over to her inner thigh.

She parted her legs, and he skimmed the ice cube back toward her center, finally reaching her clit.

Holy. Fuck.

The feeling was electric, and Charley gasped and arched her back off the bar, cold water dripping down in slow, erotic rivers as he circled her sensitive flesh. Each time she feared she'd go numb, he pulled back, lowering his face between her thighs, teasing her with his hot breath before returning with the ice.

She'd never played like this before, never felt anything so intense. The orgasm was already building inside, her nipples stiff and aching, her body humming like an electrical wire after a storm.

She wanted to feel him sink inside her, owning her flesh.

"Please," she begged again. The ice cube had finally melted, and she couldn't take another minute of his incessant teasing. "I need you inside me. Now."

"What did I tell you about talking back?"

With no more than a whoosh of air as warning, he was on top of the bar, hands gripping her thighs, pinning them down as he blew another soft, hot breath over her clit.

"You've been a bad girl," he said, "and now I'm taking a taste before I fuck you the way a bad girl deserves."

He spread her legs wider, then licked her clit, swirling his tongue against her flesh.

She fisted his hair, arching closer, desperate for the friction, the heat, all of it. "God, I love the way you touch me," she breathed. "I'm so close. I can't wait, Dorian. I—"

"You can." He pulled back, slapping her on the outer thigh, then soothing the sting with a kiss. "And you *will*."

He landed another light flick against her clit, then kissed her, slowly moving his mouth up to her belly, up to her breasts. She felt the heat of his bare skin hovering over her, though she'd never even heard him strip. Between her thighs, his rock-hard cock throbbed, hot and ready.

God, he was a fucking marvel. Everything about him left her spinning and desperate.

He grazed her nipple with his teeth, then sucked it between his lips, his stubbled jaw scraping against her skin.

"Open your legs," he ordered.

Her knees relaxed and spread wide again, inviting him in.

Dorian didn't hesitate. He buried himself inside her, finally giving in to her pleas, remembering *exactly* how she liked it.

He fucked her hard and furious, driving into her again and again, the glassware rattling beneath them. After all the ice play, the friction between her thighs was so hot and intense, Charley thought she might burst into flames.

She didn't care.

Incinerate me, she thought. *Burn me to ash.*

"Charlotte," he growled, low and guttural in her ear, his control quickly unraveling.

She was losing control too, her muscles taut, aching for the release he'd so far denied her.

Still buried deep inside, he rocked forward against her clit, pounding her harder with every stroke.

The blindfold slipped from her eyes, and he grabbed her face, his gaze boring into her, right into her fucking *soul*.

In his eyes, Charlotte saw her whole life spinning out from this moment, exploding like a newborn galaxy, then collapsing again, bringing her right back here.

Right back to him.

He stilled between her thighs and gasped as if he'd

sensed it too—some vast, inexplicable thing passing between them. Binding them.

"*Mine*," he whispered.

That was all it took.

Her body clenched around him, and she screamed his name, the hot rush of pleasure shuddering through her, tremor after tremor, wave after wave, and suddenly Dorian was thrusting inside her again, groaning against her flesh as he came hard, both of them falling and spinning and exploding into an endless sea of stars, their souls flickering in the distance, illuminating the darkness.

CHAPTER FORTY-FIVE

It was true what they said about absence making the heart grow fonder.

It also made for hotter sex.

Being with Dorian felt so perfect, so right, Charley could hardly remember a time without him—a time when he *didn't* own her, body and soul.

She was playing a dangerous game, but whenever her brain fired off a warning, she dismissed it, distracting herself with another tantalizing kiss, another deep thrust of his smooth, satisfying cock.

With every hour they shared, teasing and kissing and fucking their way through every room in his gorgeous Tribeca penthouse, Charley was falling deeper into the fantasy that this really *was* her life—that it didn't have to end.

And for a little while, she succeeded in forgetting about

all the shadows, the secrets, the lies, the inevitable goodbyes.

But then, as they lay face-to-face in his bed beneath the skylights, naked and warm from the shower after another hour-long sex-a-thon, Dorian cupped her cheek and sighed into the darkness, and the heaviness descended upon her like rain.

Before he spoke another word, Charley knew *everything* was about to change.

"What's wrong?" she whispered, frantically searching his face in the moonlight.

"I followed up on the artwork, like you asked."

Her eyes widened, her heart jackhammering.

"I contacted my buyer," he said, "and from there, I followed a trail of contacts. There were several buyers in between, but you were right—the paths converged onto a single source for both the Hermes and the LaPorte painting. A man named Vincent Estas."

"Vincent Estas," Charley repeated. She knew a lot of art dealers, criminal and legitimate, but this one didn't sound familiar. "Did you contact him as well?"

"No." Dorian closed his eyes, his muscles tensing. "Charlotte, Vincent Estas is a demon."

"A *demon*?"

"And not just any demon, I'm afraid."

"What do you mean?"

"Most demons operate in bonded crews similar to human crime families. There are several large organizations headquartered in the region, typically working out of

Brooklyn and Queens, with a few scattered across Long Island."

"Seriously? A demon mafia?" She shook her head, trying to process it all. "How powerful *are* these guys?"

"Quite, and growing more so by the day. The most powerful organization is run by a demon called Nikolai Chernikov—he controls nearly fifty percent of all demon-held territory on the east coast."

"And this Estas guy? He's part of Chernikov's organization?"

"No. Estas is bonded to the *second* most powerful crew —Chernikov's main demonic rival, Alexei Rogozin."

Alexei Rogozin.

Charlotte swallowed a gasp, squeezing her eyes shut as a rush of hot, terrible memories assaulted her.

Where you off to, little girl?

Not so tough when Daddy's not around, are ya?

Don't struggle, D'Amico bitch…

She remembered it like a dream—hazy and nonsensical in parts, sharp and inescapable in others. It was her birthday, and her father had promised they'd spend the whole day together. But before they'd even ordered breakfast at their favorite diner, Uncle Rudy called. He'd forgotten it was her birthday—*so sorry!*—and had promised an important client on Long Island they'd make a special delivery.

There was no way around it, so Charley tagged along. When business was done, her dad said, they'd drive out to Montauk at the very tip of the island, comb the beach for sea glass, and eat their weight in saltwater taffy.

SARAH PIPER

When they got to the drop-off point—a dingy, second-floor apartment above an abandoned pizza place—her dad and Rudy parked around back and ordered her to stay in the car while they made the delivery. A rusty metal staircase led up to the second floor, and she watched as they hauled a few nondescript boxes up top.

Ten minutes, they'd said. Fifteen max.

Twenty minutes passed. Half an hour. One hour, and suddenly, two men emerged from the back of the abandoned restaurant, heading right for the car. Charley sunk down into the seat, but it was no use.

They knew she was there.

They were looking for her.

What happened next is part of the haze, mixed up in her mind after years of reliving it in every nightmare, of scrubbing herself raw in the shower, of trying to outrun the ghosts that always seemed to track her down, no matter how much time passed.

But what she remembered clearly, even now, was the smell of garlic and sweat and cheap booze as the men climbed into the backseat and surrounded her, slamming the car doors behind them.

She remembered trying to reach for the door handle, desperate to escape.

Where you off to, little girl?

She remembered crying and begging as one man pinned her down on her back, the other shoving a hand up her shirt, squeezing her tiny breast.

Not so tough when Daddy's not around, are ya?

She remembered screaming and kicking, remembered biting the meaty hand that clamped hard over her mouth.

She remembered the man yanking off her jean shorts, her underwear. When she wouldn't stop kicking, he pulled out a knife.

Don't struggle, D'Amico bitch. I will make you bleed in more ways than one...

She *did* struggle, though. Knew if she didn't, they'd kill her.

Or worse.

She kicked and fought and scratched and bit for all she was worth, landing a hard kick in the balls.

The man groaned and grabbed her thigh, then shoved the knife into her abdomen, the pain eating through her body like acid, like teeth, like claws.

Stars danced before her eyes, and she thought it was the end. Death was breathing on her neck, waiting to take her.

But seconds later, she felt the rush of air as the car doors flew open. She heard two pops, felt the warm spray of blood on her face. The bodies slumped on top of her, making her gag. Her father stood behind one of them, his face ashen, the gun trembling in his hand.

She'd never seen such fear in his eyes.

Such ice-cold rage.

Such shame.

The next thing she remembered, she was waking up in a hospital bed thirty miles away, her father filling out a fake police report about a random attack in a random town they'd never even visited. When they finally left the hospital, it was in a different car.

Charley was fifteen years old.

In all the years that passed, she never had the courage to ask her father or uncle about that day, and they never had the courage to bring it up.

It existed only in her memory, the story written above her hip in a silver scar.

She never found out what happened to the bodies.

She never found out what happened to the car.

She never found out why they'd taken so long with the delivery.

She never found out whether Rudy had killed the second guy, or whether he'd just opened the door before her father shot them both.

She never found out who the men were, or why they'd targeted her.

It was the worst day of her life—worse, even, then the day her father died. And all she had left of it now—aside from the ghosts and the scar—was the name of the client who'd asked for the special delivery.

Alexei Rogozin.

CHAPTER FORTY-SIX

CITY STREETS RUN RED WITH BLOOD; 'CRIMSON CITY DEVIL'
ELUDES AUTHORITIES

August 11, 1972 - The mutilated body of a thirty-nine-year-old Manhattan father of two was found in a service alley on Canal Street in the early morning hours of August 10th. Witnesses who made the grisly discovery claim the man was lying in a pool of blood, with severe lacerations on his neck and shoulder. Police have not made an official statement, but an NYPD officer who agreed to speak on the condition of anonymity confirmed that the death has been ruled a homicide and shares many of the same markers as the previous twenty-seven murders attributed to the so-called Crimson City Devil. Authorities are urging extreme caution and have asked anyone who has information about this or any of the previous crimes to contact them immediately...

Sitting at his desk in the den, Dorian tipped back his scotch and flipped to another article in the bound leather book, each headline carving a fresh wound in his heart.

SUMMER OF SLAUGHTER EARNS NEW YORK 'CRIMSON CITY' MONIKER; NO END IN SIGHT FOR GRISLY CRIME SPREE.

CRIMSON CITY DEVIL STRIKES AGAIN.

POLICE EXHAUSTED AFTER THREE-STATE, SIX-MONTH MANHUNT BRINGS NO CLOSURE ON UNSOLVED MURDERS.

Every article had been meticulously clipped and mounted—a gruesome scrapbook created first as a souvenir and saved, later, as a reckoning.

No matter how many times Dorian forced himself through this particular punishment, the gnawing, acidic burn of his endless guilt never receded.

Nor should it.

He opened the top drawer of the desk and removed a spiral notebook, scanning the list of names and related notes he'd been keeping for four decades. He found the one he was looking for on the third page.

Marshall Goldman. Curator, Jewish Historical Society. Son of Landon Goldman, DOD Aug. 10, 1972. Whitfield painting — possible interest?

With a red pen, he made a small check mark next to Marshall's name, then closed the notebook, slipping it back into the drawer.

One more name, he thought. *One more deed.*

He tossed the pen onto the desk and reached for his bottle of scotch, pouring himself another drink.

Charlotte D'Amico was a deep, dark well of secrets, but

how could Dorian pass judgment when his closet was full of more blood-soaked skeletons than a hundred cemeteries?

His chest tightened with shame. Why had he pushed her so hard tonight?

She'd clammed up after learning about Estas and the demons, refusing to answer his questions, even though it was obvious something about his news had affected her. She'd turned away from his touch, her shoulders trembling, but no matter how many times he asked—*demanded*—she wouldn't reveal a thing.

I can't, she'd said. *I'm sorry, Dorian. I just can't.*

Eventually, in the long, cold silence that followed, she'd fallen asleep, and he'd escaped to the den at the other side of the penthouse, determined to burn off his anger with a bottle of scotch and a reminder of his own terrible past.

But now, all he wanted to do was slip back between the sheets and draw her close, as if by kissing her and bringing her to ecstasy, he could transform himself from a monster into the man she deserved—a man who would *always* protect and cherish her, no matter how many secrets she kept.

He flipped to another page in the scrapbook.

CITY MARKS ONE YEAR SINCE LAST 'CRIMSON CITY DEVIL' MURDER; KILLER WHO TERRORIZED NEW YORKERS NEVER FOUND.

The buzz of his cell phone yanked him out of the past, and Dorian picked up on the first ring.

"Colin? Is everything all right?"

"I have news," Colin replied.

Dorian braced himself. Although Colin was the most

forgiving of his siblings, they hadn't spoken more than a handful of times since his arrival. After the fundraiser, Colin had all but sequestered himself in the crypts with their father's journals, and Dorian had scuttled off to his penthouse in the city, eager for a break. The combined, prolonged presence of his estranged family at Ravenswood had created an atmosphere more oppressive than he could bear.

"I've just spoken with Malcolm," Colin continued, "and it seems the established vampire families are becoming more outspoken."

"About?" Dorian could hear the awkward pause in his brother's voice, the silent tension gathering. "Don't stand on ceremony, Colin. What are they saying?"

"Some don't believe you're fit for the crown."

"That's nothing new."

"Perhaps not, but the vocal majority is growing louder by the day. There are rumors—spurned on by House Duchanes—that House Redthorne framed Renault for the attack, murdered two innocent vampires, and possibly even murdered Renault himself, all as retaliation for his interest in Armitage Holdings."

"That's ridiculous. Renault disappeared from Ravenswood the moment his bloodsucking sycophants attacked Charlotte."

"Which only lends credence to their theory. House Duchanes and their bonded witch are claiming Renault hasn't resurfaced. They fear he's dead, Dorian."

"I don't buy it. If they truly believed he'd died at my

hand, they'd be banging down my door with torches and pitchforks."

"Yes, well. At the very least, they're putting on a good show of it, and it's riling up the other families. Many of them remained loyal to our line only out of their abject fear of Father's retribution. With him gone…"

Colin didn't need to complete the sentence.

With their father dead, what cause did the others have to support House Redthorne? Nothing but memory and tradition, Dorian feared. And in a world that valued money and power above all else, memory and tradition were little more than the dusty relics of a time long past.

"They're reaching out to all the vampires and witches who attended the fundraiser," Colin said, "asking for anyone who witnessed the attack to step forward."

Dorian seethed. "The only witness to the attack was the victim herself, and I'm not going to put her in any more danger than she's already in, nor expose her to the cutthroat world of supernatural political maneuvering."

"Of course not," he said softly. "I just thought you should know. How *is* Charlotte, by the way?"

The kindness and authenticity in his question took Dorian by surprise, and he didn't know how to answer.

"She's… well. Sleeping in the bedroom." Despite his dour mood, Dorian's lips curved into a smile as he pictured her in his bed, her auburn hair fanned out across his pillow, her rosy lips parted. He reached for his drink, eager to finish it off and get back to his woman. "Thank you for the update, Colin. I should—"

"Dorian, wait. There's more. It's... it's about Father's work."

Dorian's hand stilled on the glass, his heart thudding. "Have you deciphered the mysterious illness?"

"That's just it. There *was* no illness."

"But he was searching for a cure. I'm certain of it."

"Yes, but not for any ailment." Colin sighed, his voice dropping so low, Dorian had to strain to hear him. "He was searching for a cure for vampirism. And I believe he found it."

"What are you saying?" Dorian's own words were a whisper now too, the pounding of his heart nearly drowning them out.

"Father cured himself of vampirism. He was in the process of turning human again. That's what killed him, Dorian. Without his immortal blood, his body began to rapidly age, his cells deteriorating much faster than they could heal or regenerate. Essentially, he aged two hundred and fifty years in the span of a few months."

Dorian's ears rang, his mouth turning to ash. After a long pause, he finally said, "But why? Why would he do such a thing, knowing it would kill him? Knowing it would kill us? Bloody hell, if word got out, it could be the end of *all* vampires."

"Not just vampires. It looks like he found cures for shifters and demon-occupied humans alike, though I haven't been able to locate the specifics." Colin's voice dropped again. "I don't know how long he spent on such work, but one thing is certain, Dorian: Father gave his life in an attempt to usher in the end of supernatural existence as we know it."

Dorian's head spun with this new information. As much as his rational mind railed against it, he knew—deep in his bones—that Colin was right.

And he knew, with equal certainty, that if word got out, it would unleash a war the likes of which their communities —despite a long, blood-drenched history—had never seen.

"Who else have you told?" Dorian asked.

"Only you."

"I'll be back at Ravenswood tomorrow afternoon. Do not speak to the others until I arrive—we'll do it together."

"You have my word. What should we do about the—"

"Hold on." Dorian cocked his ear, a strange sensation creeping along his skin. "Something's wrong. I thought I heard…"

"Dorian? What is it?"

Dorian closed his eyes, trying to pinpoint the source of his sudden unease. The hair on the back of his neck stood on end, a chill racing suddenly down his spine. When he took his next breath, he tasted brimstone.

And then, in the span of a single heartbeat, a shriek of raw terror pierced the night, and the scent of warm blood flooded his senses.

Dorian's heart shattered like a bomb.

The scream—as well as the blood—had come from his bedroom.

CHAPTER FORTY-SEVEN

The unmistakable scent of Charlotte's blood wrapped him in a haze of delirium, but Dorian fought through it, half-blurring, half-stumbling across the penthouse.

There was a demon in his home. He felt its dark presence. His lungs were already burning, the taste of hellfire a grim warning in the back of his throat, but there was no time to heed it.

Charlotte was all that mattered. He *had* to get to her.

When he finally reached the bedroom, he was so weak from the hellfire, he could barely stand.

"Charlotte," he choked out.

She was naked, tied to a chair in the corner of the room, bound and gagged. A bright red gash wept from her wrist, ruby liquid spilling down her fingers, dripping onto the carpet.

Her wide, frantic eyes implored him, and she shook her

head, shouting something he couldn't understand through the gag—another warning unheeded.

With a burst of new energy, Dorian shot forward.

But he didn't get far.

A force like a freight train slammed into him from the side, and a sharp pain bit into his neck. Seconds later, he felt his heartbeat slow, his muscles twisting as if they'd come loose from the bone.

He dropped to his knees, and the room spun before his eyes.

Charlotte screamed and rattled in her chair, but her cries were still muffled by the gag, the scent of her blood still flooding his senses.

"Good evening, your highness," came the cruel taunt. "I'm so pleased you've finally decided to join us."

Renault Duchanes crouched before him, flashing his signet ring. A blood-tipped spike rose from the center—clearly the source of the pain in Dorian's neck.

"What... have you... done?" Dorian panted. The breath was leaving his body, the hellfire smoldering inside him, which meant the demon was near. Dorian had no idea where—he couldn't see through the blinding agony in his guts. He felt as if he were being consumed from the inside out—not just by hellfire, but by some ungodly microscopic enemy chewing through to his bones.

Duchanes beamed at his ring, fluttering it before Dorian's eyes like a prized diamond. "Just a little something Jacinda whipped up. Quite ingenious, really. For so long, it was believed vampires couldn't be poisoned, but witches can be rather clever when sufficiently... *motivated.*"

Dorian blinked back tears of anguish, barely fighting off a full-bodied tremor.

"Your blood," Duchanes said, taking great pleasure in Dorian's torture, "is locked in a fierce battle with the poison, leaving your muscles and internal organs to fend for themselves. One by one, your systems are shutting down. Ironically, the poison was crafted from plants procured from your very own gardens. Funny how life works out, isn't it?"

Dorian's mind flashed back to the night of the fundraiser, his words to Jacinda echoing.

...the gardens at Ravenswood are home to over four dozen species of medicinal herbs and flowers. You're welcome to take clippings...

Duchanes got to his feet and crossed the room to stand behind Charlotte, dropping his meaty hands onto her bare shoulders. The sight was more than Dorian could bear.

With a monumental effort and not an insignificant amount of pain, he pushed himself to his feet, stumbling toward her. But before he'd taken more than a handful of awkward steps, his lungs caught fire, the sudden burst of pain forcing him back to his knees.

Smoke leaked from his mouth, his vision flickering at the edges.

Duchanes let out a sick chuckle. "Did you really think I'd enter hostile territory without proper backup?" He snapped his fingers, and the demon finally revealed himself, stepping out of the shadows from the darkened bathroom. He held Dorian's gaze, two obsidian-black eyes shining in a pale face, conjuring enough hellfire to keep Dorian immobilized—but not enough to kill him.

Which meant Duchanes had other plans. *Worse* plans.

"Let… her… go…" Dorian sputtered, still trying to drag himself to Charlotte's side despite his broken body and the searing pain in his lungs. His eyes watered as the smoke gathered behind them, the scent of burning flesh stinging his nostrils. "Kill me, Duchanes. Just… release her."

"I have every intention of killing you, Redthorne. But not yet. First, you're going to pay for your egregious acts against my house." His tone turned chilly, his eyes wild with madness and determination. "You're going to pay for *decades* of insults and dismissals. You're going to pay for your father's cruelty against my sires. You're going to pay for the sins of your past, for every life you stole, for every drop of innocent blood you spilled. And through it all, you're going to watch from a helpless, pitiful distance as I suck your filthy human whore dry, until there's nothing left of her but agony and bones."

Charlotte's eyes found Dorian's in the darkness again, tears slipping down her cheeks.

Dorian was frantic, his heart fighting through the sluggish haze of the poison, the hellfire consuming him, but he couldn't break free of death's grip. He couldn't save her.

Duchanes unbound her from the chair and hauled her to her feet, his arm a vise around her arms and chest. Fisting her hair, he yanked her head sideways, exposing her neck.

Free from the binds, Charlotte tried to shake him off, but the vampire was too strong. Too determined. Too insane.

"Mmm, I do love a good struggle," Duchanes said, fangs emerging behind his lips. "Makes the blood that much sweeter."

With a wicked gleam in his eye, he descended, his mouth clamping down on her delicate neck as she screamed and writhed and begged.

The sight, the sounds, the scent of her fear... All of it shrank to a single point of light, a lit match tossed into a kettle of gasoline, igniting a fury so clean, so pure, it burned away Dorian's pain in an instant.

In that moment, Dorian had no muscles to destroy, no organs to shut down, no blood to battle the terrible poison.

There was only the beautiful, triumphant fury gathering inside him, focusing all of his reserves into a single, deadly mission.

"*I will end you!*" The words tore through Dorian's burning chest, scorching his throat, pushing him to his feet. In a blur that should've been impossible in his condition, he collided with Duchanes and wrenched him from Charlotte's body, slamming him into the wall.

In his peripheral vision, he saw the demon bolting toward him, but Charlotte was faster. She dove for her purse on the dresser, and in that moment, Dorian knew exactly what she was thinking.

Still channeling his deadly fury, Dorian pummeled Duchanes with his fists, battering his face and chest, bloodying him beyond recognition. Duchanes blurred out of his grip, then shot forward again, catching Dorian around his mid-section. But Dorian was ready for it. He took the hit, spinning with the momentum and launching Duchanes right into the fucking window.

It shattered on impact, and Duchanes fell to the street in a shower of blood and glass.

Dorian turned around just in time to see Charlotte drop the demon with a perfect shot, the taser blasting him with fifty-thousand volts of utter badassery.

"That's my girl." Dorian's lips quirked into a proud grin.

And then, the last of his rage receding, the pain returned with a vengeance, crashing over him like a tsunami, knocking him flat on his back.

Charlotte dropped her weapon and ran to Dorian's side, falling to her knees and taking his head into her lap.

She pulled the gag from her mouth, and her long hair fell onto his face, tickling his skin. He blinked up at her and reached for a perfect, silky lock, inhaling the orange-and-vanilla scent he loved so much.

Dorian's life force was fading. The demon was no longer a threat, but the damage from the hellfire was extensive, and Duchanes' poison still pulsed through his bloodstream, consuming a bit more of him with every faint heartbeat.

He didn't have much time.

If this is where I meet my end, he thought, losing himself in her touch, her sweet scent, *I shall spend my eternal damnation in utter gratitude…*

"Charlotte," he whispered. "I'm so sorry. I—"

"Shh. Don't talk. Drink." She pressed her wounded wrist to his mouth.

Dorian clamped his lips shut.

"Jesus Christ," she snapped. "Don't fight me on this, Bone Crusher. You *will* lose."

Dorian tried to bat her away, but she grabbed his arm and slammed it to the ground, her grip impossibly strong in the face of his weakness.

"You're going to die, you dickhead!" she shouted. "And you still owe me a Midnight Marauder rematch! So fucking *drink!*"

Still, he resisted, even as the first drops reached his tongue, the taste bringing him back to that sinful, erotic moment in the Ravenswood basement when he'd first sampled her blood. The scent filled his nostrils, chasing away the last of the smoke.

The urge to suck was nearly overwhelming.

Above him, Charlotte's eyes softened in the moonlight, glassy with emotion.

"I trust you, Dorian Redthorne," she whispered, leaning down to kiss his forehead. "I *know* you won't hurt me. Please drink. Do it for me. *Please.*"

Shifting her wrist, she pressed down harder, the blood seeping through his lips, warm and decadent on his tongue, instantly soothing.

Instantly sweet.

Instantly addicting.

The last of his resistance shattered, and Dorian opened

his mouth, fangs burning through his gums. He latched onto her wrist with a quick, hard bite.

Charlotte gasped, but she held firm, stroking his hair with her free hand, quietly urging him back to life.

Dorian closed his eyes.

Her blood filled his mouth completely.

And then, he swallowed.

He drank.

And he *sucked*.

Charlotte's blood slid down his throat in a warm, wet rush, a pleasant buzz spreading from his stomach to his limbs. Cell by cell, his body knit itself back together, healing the burned tissue and damaged organs, chasing off the poison.

It was a magic elixir, and it brought him back from the precipice of death.

It made him whole again.

It sharpened his instincts, chased the cobwebs from his mind, strengthened his muscles, remade his bones and skin and teeth. He felt the light return to his soul, the full, undimmed power awakening inside him after a long, dark sleep.

The familiar sight of his bedroom faded away as the craving took over, blotting out his rational mind. He was dimly aware of Charlotte's soft whimpers, the tremble in her arm, the faint tug as she tried to pull back, but none of that mattered.

He couldn't stop now.

He didn't *want* to stop.

He was *alive*, his heartbeat strong and steady, his cock rising to full attention as every exquisite drop tempted him into a deeper state of euphoria.

"Dorian," she whispered, faint and fading fast. "That's enough. I think you're…"

She tried to pull away again, but she didn't have the strength. Her muscles finally relaxed, her heartbeat slowing, the numb acceptance settling over her.

Let her go, a voice warned in his head. *Release her, or you'll kill her…*

Dorian squeezed his eyes shut, desperate to drown out the voice, to focus on the craving, the hunger, the deep haze of desire buzzing through his nervous system…

"Dorian," Charlotte whispered again.

CITY STREETS RUN RED WITH BLOOD…

"Dorian, *please*."

CRIMSON CITY DEVIL STRIKES AGAIN…

"I can't fight you," she said. "I'm not… strong enough."

NO CLOSURE ON UNSOLVED MURDERS…

"Dorian, *stop!*"

Dorian opened his eyes.

The reality of his situation slammed into his chest, bringing everything into sharp, undiluted focus.

He yanked her wrist from his mouth and shot to his feet.

Charlotte collapsed.

"No. *No! Charlotte!*" He dropped to his knees and gathered her in his arms. He'd taken too much blood; her lips were nearly blue, her skin pale and clammy, her pulse thready.

He needed to heal her. Fast.

Fucking hell, he was ready to carve open his chest and give her every last drop of blood he'd taken from her, but he couldn't. Dorian knew death when he saw it, and she was hovering right on the doorstep. If her heart stopped while his blood was in her system, it wouldn't heal her.

It would turn her into a monster.

"What have I done?" he breathed.

"Dorian," she whispered, her body twitching in his arms. "It's... it's okay."

"No, it really isn't." His throat tightened, his heart cracking in half. How could he have been so foolish? So selfish? "I won't let you die. Do hear me, Charlotte D'Amico? I won't let you die."

She lifted a trembling hand, pressing it to his cheek. "You... you've made me feel more alive than—"

"Shh. Save your strength, love."

He scanned the bedroom, frantic. The demon she'd blasted was still unconscious, but that wouldn't last much longer. Dorian knew more demons were already on the way —the scent of brimstone grew stronger with every breath. And while the shove through Dorian's penthouse window may have temporarily stunned Duchanes, there was no way it'd killed him; vampires could jump great distances and still land on their feet.

Bloody hell, he didn't want to move her, but he had no choice. The demons were closing in. There was no telling if Duchanes would return. They couldn't stay here another minute.

"I'm sorry," she whispered, her eyes glazing with tears. "For… everything."

"You've nothing to apologize for."

"If you find… Forgive me… I didn't…" Her eyelids fluttered, then closed, her body going limp in his arms.

"Hold on, Charlotte. Just hold on." Dorian carried her to the bed and wrapped her in the sheet.

On the other side of the penthouse, the front door splintered, the demons rushing in like cockroaches.

Brushing the hair from her eyes, he pressed one last, desperate kiss to her mouth.

Then, lifting her into his arms and drawing her close, Dorian stepped to the window ledge, took a deep breath, and jumped.

CHAPTER FORTY-EIGHT

The taste of blood lingered in Dorian's throat, conspiring with the overwhelming scent of all those damn roses in Charlotte's Park Avenue penthouse to make him dizzy. He paced the living room, a wild, frenetic energy chewing through his veins while Marlys tended to Charlotte in the bedroom.

Dorian had no idea what was happening—whether she was conscious, whether she'd survive the transfusion of blood and magic Marlys had planned. The witch had answered his desperate call, but the moment she'd arrived, she took one look at Charlotte, shook her head, then promptly booted Dorian from the bedroom with a spell he couldn't break.

An hour later, when Dorian was about ready to set those roses on fire, his brothers arrived. Colin had known something was wrong when Dorian abruptly dropped their earlier call; he and the others had left Ravenswood that instant, bound for Manhattan.

Colin had been granted access to Charlotte's room, offering his medical assistance while Marlys worked her magic.

Now, Gabriel and Malcolm watched Dorian with alternating looks of judgment, scorn, and pity.

Dorian wasn't interested in *any* of it.

"I want this building monitored round the clock," he said, shoving a hand through his hair. At this rate, he'd tear it all out by daybreak. "Charlotte and her sister must be kept safe."

"I don't have time for this," Gabriel snapped.

Dorian stopped pacing long enough to glare at his brother. "Yes, you made that *abundantly* clear when you ignored my orders to keep an eye on her."

"Children," Malcolm warned. "Let's not start this again, shall we?" He grabbed a bottle of bourbon from the mini bar set up in the corner, helping himself to a glass. "Your incessant backbiting is driving me to drink."

Gabriel ignored him, determined to say his ridiculous piece.

"Let me remind you, *highness*, she was attacked on *your* watch. In *your* bedroom. And who's responsible for nearly exsanguinating her? Oh, right!" He jabbed a finger into Dorian's chest, an inferno blazing behind his typically cold eyes. "*You* did this, Dorian. So forgive me, brother, but my priority is protecting my family from our enemies, *not* babysitting your human pet."

"Your priority," Dorian warned, one insult away from giving his brother the same window treatment he'd given Duchanes, "is what I command it to be. I'm still your king. If that is too difficult a concept for you to grasp, remove yourself from my city."

A low rumble vibrated in the back of Gabriel's throat, but Malcolm stepped between them before the argument could escalate.

"Bloody hell, the two of you make me want to tear my *own* heart out." He tossed back his bourbon, shaking his head. "*Yes*, we need to find Duchanes. *Yes*, we need to figure out whose demons have gone rogue. *Yes*, we need to eliminate the threats to our family. But Ms. D'Amico—despite her wretched choice in lovers—is an innocent human. We can't stand by and let Duchanes use her as bait."

Dorian and Gabriel continued to glare daggers at each other, but eventually, Dorian nodded, and Gabriel backed off.

"Any word from Aiden?" Malcolm asked.

"He's still looking for Sasha," Dorian said, pouring himself a scotch from the bar. He'd sent Aiden to track her down with little information to go on but what Charlotte had mentioned earlier—she was staying with a friend called Darcy in the Williamsburg neighborhood of Brooklyn —prime Chernikov territory. Dorian had no idea how he'd convince the girl to return with him, but he trusted Aiden to see it through.

He'd likely have to compel her.

Charlotte would kill Dorian for it later, but he couldn't

worry about that now. Sasha needed to be here with her sister, where both of them could be kept safe. He'd deal with explanations and cover stories later.

"Dorian," Gabriel said, his tone losing some of its earlier bite, "are you certain you can't remember anything about the demon who attacked you?"

Dorian shook his head. "Dark hair, average build, average dress—nothing particularly memorable."

"And you didn't see his mark?"

"There was no time. But if we're placing bets, my money is on Chernikov." Dorian could barely get the man's name out before the rage ignited inside him again. "Just like the demons Kate Connelly saw at Bloodbath—no one has been able to identify them, but my gut says all roads lead back to the Russian."

"We can't start a war with the most powerful demon in the city based solely on your gut," Gabriel said.

"My war is with Duchanes. As for Chernikov…" Dorian sighed. "You're right. We need more information."

"Which we can't get sitting around here, waiting for—"

"Dorian." Colin emerged from the hallway, Marlys following behind.

All thoughts of Chernikov and Duchanes vanished.

"How is she?" Dorian abandoned his drink, his heart lodged in his throat.

"She's going to be okay," Colin said, and relief swept over Dorian in a rush. "She needs to rest for a few days, drink plenty of fluids, and avoid anything strenuous."

Dorian was already heading down the hallway toward the bedroom.

Marlys grabbed his arm. "Where are you going?"

"I need to see her, Marlys."

"She's still in and out of consciousness."

"I don't care."

Marlys tightened her grip, her eyes blazing with a darkness Dorian had never before seen from his freelance witch. "You've done enough, Dorian Redthorne. I suggest you let her regain her strength."

"Dorian," Colin warned, "Marlys is right. We just got her back. We can't risk you—"

"I'm *not* going to hurt her again," he said softly. "*That* is a promise."

Most of Dorian's promises might've been worthless in their eyes—hell, a good portion of them were worthless in his *own* eyes. But not hurting Charlotte? Not drinking from her again? *Those* were promises he could now make without hesitation.

He'd always known her blood would drive him over the edge. Tonight, he'd gotten a glimpse of just how terrifying that edge could be, and he never wanted to go anywhere near it again.

Not even if his life depended on it.

Colin and Marlys must've seen the determination in his eyes, because they finally nodded and stepped aside, letting him pass.

Charlotte's bedroom was luxuriously furnished but surprisingly plain, with no personal touches except for a few framed photos of a young blond woman Dorian assumed was Sasha and one of an older man that was probably Charlotte's father.

Now, he stood at the side of her bed, looking down upon her sleeping form, a potent mix of relief and shame flooding his heart.

Her soft, dark lashes brushed her cheeks, her hair hanging limp around her face. The color had returned to her skin, her lips rosy and full, her breathing deep and even.

Her strong, steady heartbeat was music to his ears.

Dorian fell to his knees, taking her hand and stroking her silky-soft skin. The sight of her bandaged wrist—a wrist Duchanes had wounded, a wrist Dorian had fed from—filled him with anguish.

They'd only known each other a short time, but in those precious weeks, she'd ignited something inside him that could never be put back in its cage.

Something he thought he'd never know, never feel again.

Holding her hand, gazing at her angelic face, Dorian couldn't imagine facing another tomorrow without her.

"Please come back to me, love," he said. Tears burned behind his eyes, but he refused to let them fall—refused to let himself believe he had any more reason to worry. Instead, he pressed his lips to her hand, drawing her scent into his lungs, whispering his deepest confession into the darkness.

"I've bloody well fallen in love with you, Charlotte D'Amico. Now come back to me so I can prove it to you."

Saying the words, even at a whisper, made them real in a way Dorian hadn't expected, breaking through the iron gates inside him and pushing his heart to damn near bursting.

Love had always done its damnedest to ruin him. First, as a mortal man, when love blinded him to the darkness unfolding in his very home. That blindness led to the worst night of his life—his very last as a mortal man.

Then, a century and a half later, love blinded him again—a costly mistake that haunted him still, the ghost of the Crimson City Devil forever howling in his mind.

For Dorian, love and betrayal went hand-in-hand, a devastating marriage that could only end in pain and death.

But this time was different. Charlotte wasn't some traitor from his past. She was his future. She was his right now. She was his everything.

Heeding Colin and Marlys' warnings, Dorian released her hand. She needed to rest. Everything would look better in the morning.

With a soft, grateful smile, he leaned forward and kissed her cheek, lingering for a moment.

"I'll be waiting for you," he said. "Perhaps I'll even cook breakfast."

He was about to rise from the floor when he's knees brushed against something under the bed. He glanced down, spotting a notebook and what looked like floor plans.

His floor plans, he realized with a start.

He grabbed the pile of paperwork for a closer look.

The documents were from Ravenswood, marked up with red Xs and notes about the artwork displayed in each room. The list was meticulous, matching a similar list in the notebook, with additional notes about the security systems in his home.

Then, scrawled across the top of the second page, underlined three times, was his alarm code.

759462.

Dorian's head spun, a searing pain slicing through his chest as the pieces clicked into place.

Charlotte wasn't an art consultant.

She was an art *thief*.

And she was planning to take Ravenswood for everything it was worth.

The breath rushed from his lungs, his heartbeat thudding in his ears, the damn walls closing in on him.

All of it had been a bloody lie. Her kiss, her touch, the fierce desire in her eyes… There hadn't been a single honest thing about her.

He closed his eyes, unable to look at her, unable to bare another moment of the sharp pain tearing through him. Instead, he forced it back into the darkness, letting the flames of his fury forge it into another cold, impenetrable gate.

He was a fool to let anyone in.

He wouldn't make that mistake again.

Not for the rest of his immortal life.

Without sparing Charlotte another glance, Dorian gathered up the evidence, rose from the floor, and marched out of her room.

"Dorian?" Colin asked, alarm filling his eyes. "Is everything all right?"

Malcolm rose from the couch. "Where are you going?"

Dorian didn't have an answer to either question. At the moment, he could only spare one word, his voice trembling with fury.

"*Away.*"

And then, he left. Down the penthouse elevator, past the doorman he'd compelled earlier, and out into the oily gray Manhattan night.

With a stone heart rattling in his chest and a taste for vengeance smoldering in his mouth, Dorian blurred into the rhythmic rush of Park Avenue, leaving his beautiful, devastating traitor behind.

Colin and Marlys may have saved her life tonight, but as far as Dorian was concerned?

Charlotte D'Amico was dead.

It's not over yet! Dorian and Charley's story continues in Dark Seduction!

A supernatural war is brewing in New York City. As dark secrets come to light and deadly enemies emerge from the shadows, can Charley and Dorian find their way back into each other's hearts? Find out what happens next in **Dark Seduction, book two of the Vampire Royals of New York series!**

Vampire lovers! If you loved reading this story as much as I loved writing it, please help a girl out and **leave a review on Amazon!** Even a quick sentence or two about your favorite part can help other readers discover the book, and that makes me super happy!

If you really, *really* loved it, come hang out at our Facebook group, Sarah Piper's Sassy Witches. I'd love to see you there.

XOXO
Sarah

Paranormal romance fans, I've got even more sexy books ready to heat up your bookshelf!

THE WITCH'S REBELS is a supernatural reverse harem series featuring five smoldering-hot guys and the kickass witch they'd kill to protect. If you like sexy forbidden romance, dark magic, and heart-pounding supernatural suspense, this witchy adventure will leave you spellbound!

TAROT ACADEMY is a paranormal, university-aged reverse harem academy romance starring four seriously hot mages and one badass witch. Dark prophecies, unique mythology, steamy romance, strong female friendships, and plenty of supernatural thrills make this series a must-read!

ABOUT SARAH PIPER

Sarah Piper is a Kindle All-Star winning urban fantasy and paranormal romance author. Through her signature brew of dark magic, heart-pounding suspense, and steamy romance, Sarah promises a sexy, supernatural escape into a world where the magic is real, the monsters are sinfully hot, and the witches always get their magically-ever-afters.

Her works include the newly released Vampire Royals of New York series, the Tarot Academy series, and The Witch's Rebels, a fan-favorite reverse harem urban fantasy series readers have dubbed "super sexy," "imaginative and original," "off-the-walls good," and "delightfully wicked in the best ways," a quote Sarah hopes will appear on her tombstone.

Originally from New York, Sarah now makes her home in northern Colorado with her husband (though that changes frequently) (the location, not the husband), where she spends her days sleeping like a vampire and her nights writing books, casting spells, gazing at the moon, playing with her ever-expanding collection of Tarot cards, binge-watching Supernatural (Team Dean!), and obsessing over the best way to brew a cup of tea.

You can find her online at SarahPiperBooks.com and in her Facebook readers group, Sarah Piper's Sassy Witches! If you're sassy, or if you need a little *more* sass in your life, or if you need more Dean Winchester gifs in your life (who doesn't?), come hang out!

Made in the USA
Monee, IL
08 December 2020

51716215R00256